STEALTH
RETRIBUTION

VIKKI KESTELL
NANOSTEALTH | BOOK 3

Faith-Filled Fiction™

www.faith-filledfiction.com | www.vikkikestell.com

STEALTH RETRIBUTION

Nanostealth | Book 3
Vikki Kestell
Also Available in eBook Format

BOOKS BY VIKKI KESTELL

NANOSTEALTH
Book 1: *Stealthy Steps*
Book 2: *Stealth Power*
Book 3: *Stealth Retribution*
Book 4: *Deep State Stealth*

A PRAIRIE HERITAGE
Book 1: *A Rose Blooms Twice* (free eBook, most online retailers)
Book 2: *Wild Heart on the Prairie*
Book 3: *Joy on This Mountain*
Book 4: *The Captive Within*
Book 5: *Stolen*
Book 6: *Lost Are Found*
Book 7: *All God's Promises*
Book 8: *The Heart of Joy—A Short Story* (eBook only)

GIRLS FROM THE MOUNTAIN
Book 1: *Tabitha*
Book 2: *Tory*
Book 3: *Sarah Redeemed*

The Christian and the Vampire: A Short Story
(free eBook, most online retailers)

STEALTH RETRIBUTION
Copyright © 2017 Vikki Kestell
All Rights Reserved.
ISBN-13: 978-0-9862615-6-5
ISBN-10: 0-9862615-6-4

STEALTH RETRIBUTION

Retribution. Also known as "payback" or a more dated word: "vengeance." Arnaldo Soto has taken Emilio and intends to use him as bait to trap Gemma. It's an effective strategy, because Gemma will do anything—*anything*—to save the young boy.

The woman known as Gemma Keyes is gone, her molecular structure destroyed and reassembled as . . . something else. In Gemma's stead emerges a fierce weapon: part woman, part nanotechnology, her cellular composition conjoined with the nanocloud, their union formidable and indissoluble. She and the nanomites are now more than a match for her enemies—but Gemma has promised God that she will not visit retribution on Arnaldo Soto for taking Emilio.

The nanomites have made no such promise.

The third installment in the Nanostealth series will blow your mind.

Dedication

To all those who have wandered far:
the LORD is calling you.
"I have swept away your offenses like a cloud,
your sins like the morning mist.
Return to me, for I have redeemed you."
Isaiah 44:22

Acknowledgements

I have acknowledged and thanked
my wonderful team many times,
but they deserve every kudo I can apply.
Thank you,
Cheryl Adkins and **Greg McCann**.
I am honored to work with such
dedicated and talented individuals.
I love and value both of you.
Our *gestalt* is powerful!

Special Thanks
to **James Rutske**
for his technical expertise.

Scripture Quotations

Cover Design

Vikki Kestell

PROLOGUE

I lifted my hands to examine them. As I did, the light fixtures banding the cavern flickered; current jetted from the wavering lamps and slammed into my chest. The drawn energy coursed through my muscles and reverberated in my bones. It swelled and spread down my arms until it reached my fingertips, ready to burst forth.

With a curious and almost detached air, I watched as my body attracted more energy from the light fixtures. Electricity crackled around me, infusing me with might. I flexed and curved my fingers; tongues of current sizzled in the palm of my hand and built into a ball of pulsing blue fire.

Not far across the cavern, Dr. Bickel, Zander, and Agent Gamble, their expressions grave, could only watch. The nanomites had prevented them from interfering while the mites had effected this last, this final metamorphosis. Unable to come closer, my friends waited for the outcome. They waited for me.

Me. The transformed me. At the first, the nanomites had "simply" invaded me and had refused to leave. Then had come "the merge" and its powerful effects upon me. Now I faced *this*, the latest iteration of Gemma Keyes—or should I say, the "new and improved nanocloud"? The revived and restored nanocloud . . . superior in every way, the composite of six tribes and, at last count, more than twenty trillion nanomites. The nanocloud that had annexed and incorporated all of whom I was and the person I'd been.

Mine is not an honorary tribal membership, nor is ours a partnership where the nanomites and I are "joined at the hip," so to speak. It is so much more, and I was testing . . . probing to determine what was what.

This I knew: The nanomites and I were melded. We were irrevocably bound to each other. We were an *amalgamation*. My cells and molecules added mobility and organic functionality to their nano-sized electro-mechanical devices.

At the same time, the nanomites' computational abilities and vast knowledge banks were fused to my brain's synapse trees, furnishing me with, well, with extraordinary knowledge and insights—and much more, if my assumptions were correct.

I drew another deep breath and felt my body respond, my strength rise. The electricity I attracted from the cavern's lights (without conscious intent) swelled and snapped; it bent toward me and flowed into me. I raised one hand toward the electrical source, and current jetted into my palm—arcing and building within the span of my fingertips. I rotated my wrist, and the energy sizzled. Intensified.

"Gemma?"

I brought my hands together and stared with fascination as the shimmering bolus strengthened. It swirled between my extended fingers. As I moved my splayed hands apart, tendrils of electricity climbed from my fingers onto the ball; they wrapped themselves about the sphere to hold and feed it. The orb grew larger; its vibrations thudded through my chest.

"Gemma?" From yards away, Zander's repeated question radiated concern.

I stared at the globe of electricity sparking and thrumming in my hand. What could I do with it? What would happen if I . . . tossed it?

I thought that I knew the answer.

Nodding to myself, I brought my palms together, enveloping and squeezing the ball of fire until it shrank, diminished, and disappeared. The current receded up my arms, into my body, throbbing and vibrating as it went, until I'd absorbed it, holding it in readiness—for what, exactly, I didn't yet know.

With eyes closed, I took inventory, examining what I found, tucking the revelations away until I had time to ponder them.

"I'm all right, Zander."

I turned and walked toward my friends. My heart was calm and settled, even though I'd crossed over into a place from which I could not return.

In actuality, that demarcation—the line of no return—had been crossed earlier, but I hadn't known it at the time. I hadn't known then that "the merge" from a few weeks past had wrought physical changes in my body so significant that my body could not survive apart from the nanomites. In my ignorance, I'd held on to the hope that, at Dr. Bickel's command, the nanomites would vacate my body, and my life would, to a considerable extent, return to normal.

I had clung to the prospect that when we saved Dr. Bickel, I would get my life back. Rescuing Dr. Bickel from Cushing's captivity was supposed to have rescued me from imprisonment with the nanomites!

But when the Taser had decimated the nanocloud? It had been my death warrant as well as theirs, Dr. Bickel had explained.

"I believe the nanomites have made, um, certain alterations to your anatomy, Gemma. As I said a while back. Changes at the cellular level."

"Are you s-saying they can't leave?"

"Well, no, not precisely. I'm saying that they could leave, Gemma," he paused a long time before he framed the second half of his response. *"I'm saying that they could leave, but if they did, I fear that you . . . would not survive."*

8

The truth at its simplest was that, should the nanomites withdraw from my body, I would die—which also meant that if *they died*, I would, too.

And as a result of the Taser's discharge, many of the nanomites had already perished. As the mites that survived struggled to regroup, I was left in a stroke-like condition, my body weak and growing weaker.

In an attempt to save me, Dr. Bickel had revealed the treasure he had hidden in a niche in the cavern wall—stacks and stacks of silicon wafer carriers or clamshells. Each clamshell contained a single wafer containing uncut, unprogrammed nanomites; each clamshell was marked for the nanomite tribe it contained.

"Before I fled my lab in the AMEMS department at Sandia, I printed as many wafers as I could in the time I had. My technicians, Rick and Tony, kept the printer running without pause, day and night, right up until the morning Cushing and Dr. Prochanski set the timer on the bomb," he'd explained. *"You can see that I have multiple stacks of wafers for each tribe—enough nanomites to rebuild the nanocloud many times over."*

Dr. Bickel had presented a sample of the printed wafers to the mites that had survived the Taser's burst of voltage. He had assumed the active mites would cut the unprogrammed nanomites from the wafers and power and program them, thus reconstituting the nanocloud's depleted ranks. However, he never imagined that the nanomites would free and power *all* the printed mites—but they had.

The resulting number of active nanomites exceeded twenty trillion.

Twenty trillion!

Twenty trillion new nanomites comprised the reconstructed "nanocloud." (Nanocloud: the combined tribes' powerful *gestalt*—the combination of their knowledge, abilities, and cooperation that exceeded the sum of the individual tribes.) When the nanocloud came online, my body *should have healed*. Should have regained its near-preternatural strength.

Instead, I had only inched away from encroaching death. The nanomites had pulled me millimeters from the brink upon which I'd been standing but no farther.

I knew then . . . something else was very wrong.

When the mites had called me apart for a confab at the far end of the cavern, my suspicions had grown and been confirmed. Near the cavern's ceiling, where the light fixtures ringed the cavern's walls, I'd found them: a haze, a misty fog filled with beautiful colors.

The reconstituted nanocloud.

"Nano. You . . . you aren't in me?" I'd asked.

Some of us remain in you, Gemma Keyes. We are six. However, we are larger now, and we face a dilemma, Gemma Keyes. For this reason, we have requested the confab.

A dilemma? What in this universe did the nanomites consider a "dilemma"?

Gemma Keyes, we are six. You are Gemma Tribe. You have carried us. We cannot bear being apart from you, but . . . you asked for a count of our ranks. You understand that we are larger, much larger. When we were smaller, we effected changes to your body that provided us with a hospitable environment. When you became Gemma Tribe, we effected other, more fundamental changes to your body.

"Yes, I know." Fearful of what was coming, I had started to shake.

We made those changes without adequate forethought and without your express permission. This was . . . shortsighted of us. We understand that now; we understand that we placed your body's continued well-being in jeopardy, because you cannot live without us, Gemma Keyes.

I'd swallowed. "Yeah. I know that, too."

We did not foresee the day this fact would threaten your existence.

"What . . . what does that mean?"

The dilemma, Gemma Keyes. Our present ranks are too many to inhabit your body—the nanocloud is too large: It would kill you. The alternative, Gemma Keyes, would require further changes to your body— deeply fundamental changes at the molecular level. These changes would be necessary for your body to accept and accommodate the new and improved nanocloud.

So, there had been no choice, really. Going back to who and what I'd been before the merge was not possible—and without the reconstituted nanocloud, my body would have died. Had nearly died.

The only option, besides death, had been to go forward.

But I'd been too scared and too heartbroken to give my immediate consent to the nanomites, so I'd stalled. And I'd grieved.

You see, before I'd left my friends on the other side of the cavern to meet with the nanomites, Zander had declared his love for me. He'd come up to me, cupped my face in his good hand, and said, "I'll be praying for you, Gemma. Whatever happens, you belong to Jesus now. He has you. And whatever happens, I'll be right here, waiting for you."

Then he'd kissed me. A real, honest-to-goodness kiss.

"I love you, Gemma. I've been wanting to say that for a while."

His beautiful gray eyes had sought mine, looking for an answering declaration.

"I know. Me, too. I love you back, Zander."

That was before the nanomites had given me the bad news: No coming back from this.

No regular, normal life.

No happily ever after for Zander and me.

Oh, Zander!

So, I'd grieved . . . and a full-on hot mess like that takes a little time.

Eventually, I had given the nanomites the permission they'd asked and for which they had patiently lingered.

Hours later, the changes were complete.

⌘⌘⌘⌘

PART 1:
STEALTH REVIVAL

CHAPTER 1

I stopped a few feet from my friends, and they, wordless and apprehensive, studied me until Gamble asked, "What has happened, Gemma? You look . . . different."

"Do I?" I heard Gamble from a distance. I was turned inward, listening to the mites as they spoke—and they had much to tell me. "Hearing" them felt simpler. Less "them and me," more "us."

While the nanomites spoke, I tried to take an internal inventory. My mind seemed much more attuned to my physical workings, and I glimpsed bodily functions that were, in many ways, abnormal. Accelerated. I didn't query the nanomites on what I suspected, because their answers would have been irrelevant.

What was done was done and could not be reversed.

I think my friends could tell how preoccupied I was. As I focused on what the mites were saying, my companions held whispered deliberations.

Dr. Bickel, his observations slow and thoughtful, said, "If the nanomites freed all their printed fellows, I calculate that the nanocloud is much larger than it was before—on the order of seven times the previous size."

He struggled to reach a conclusion and put it into words. "Hmmm. Yes. See here, if we rightly consider the increased size of the nanocloud and factor in the conjoined computing functionality of all its members, we would be mistaken to view the nanomites in terms of mere 'additive' strength."

"Additive strength? Explain, please," Zander demanded.

"Certainly. I'm saying that rather than supposing the cloud to be stronger than it was previously simply by the addition of seventeen trillion nanomites to its original three trillion for a total of twenty trillion or more, we should, instead, ascribe exponential wherewithal to the nanocloud."

"You said the cloud is 'seven times the previous size.' Does that make the nanomites 'seven times' more powerful than before?"

"That is multiplicative. I said, *exponentially* greater: that is, not seven times its original might, but seven to the seventh power. Approaching a million times more powerful."

"*What?* But, what does that mean for Gemma?"

"The sheer numbers are one matter; we must wait and see how those numbers affect Gemma. The more concerning issue is how the nanocloud—the *gestalt* of the whole—functions in that exponentially greater manner—and how their greater functions impact Gemma."

"But . . ." Zander didn't finish, and I felt his eyes on me.

This was the part I dreaded, the place where the ugly truth would be spoken.

"You know how bones grow?"

"Yeah, I think so. Some cells grow new bone; others break down the older bone to be replaced by the new."

I nodded. "The nanomites needed a means of fusing themselves to areas of my organic physiology. They broke down . . . and destroyed segments of my molecular structure and reassembled it. Added their nanotechnology to it."

Zander's fear became apparent. "So . . ."

"So, I can't have a regular, normal life, Zander. I can't have a husband, can't be a wife . . ." My voice dropped to a whisper he couldn't hear, "or a mother."

My words strengthened. "I am part of the nanocloud; I will never be alone, never be separate from them. We are six tribes, one nanocloud."

Zander was, as I had expected, appalled—and I understood his revulsion. If it hadn't been for the reassurances I'd heard via that small but powerful voice, if that *Someone* hadn't assured me that all would be well, I might have elected death instead.

I stared into his horrified face and added the kicker. The clincher.

"I'm not really human anymore, Zander."

Zander shook his head and refused to surrender. "'Not really human?' I can't accept that! And what does that mean, anyway?"

I bent cold, heartless eyes on him, ending all debate. "It means we can't be together, Zander. Ever."

⌘⌘⌘⌘

CHAPTER 2

The nanomites broke in, urging me to get moving. I frowned and swept Zander's questions and concerns to the side. "We need to go. We need to use what time we have to our advantage."

Gamble again spoke up. "Go where, Gemma?"

"Out of here. To the car, Agent Gamble. It's vital that we complete our plan: Convey Dr. Bickel to the FBI's Albuquerque field office where he can reveal himself to the public and force a federal investigation into Cushing's illegal actions. Getting Dr. Bickel's story out into the public arena is the only way to keep him safe. It is our primary goal."

"And you, Gemma," Zander added, frowning. "Keep you safe, too."

I flashed him a small, shrewd smile. "My safety is no longer a concern. I should be more than a match now for anything Cushing throws at me."

Zander and Gamble exchanged wary looks, and Gamble cleared his throat. Changed up the topic.

"I've been MIA for going on four days, and my bosses are probably scouring the state for my dead body. I doubt my absence has escaped Cushing's notice."

Dr. Bickel turned to Gamble and asked him, "Are you saying the FBI office won't be a safe haven for me now?"

"I'm saying that getting you there may present more of a challenge, perhaps an insurmountable one. If Cushing has confirmed my connection with Gemma to her own satisfaction, the routes to the field office will be watched and manned—and she will have whispered her lies and threats into the ears of my superiors."

"Don't worry; we can get you there."

The three men stared at me. Gamble chewed the inside of his cheek, recognizing I had more to say. Yeah, well, I had to tell them the truth.

"The nanomites and I are an amalgamation at every level. The best of both me and them. Enhanced and powerful."

"Enhanced? Powerful?"

"Yes. I'm about as fit as a person can be, physically and mentally, thanks to metabolic acceleration and the training they've put me through. I have direct access to the nanocloud's knowledge, and I have direct access to the nanomites' abilities."

"Er, right, but if Cushing is as politically connected as we believe her to be, we won't get off this base, let alone across town to the FBI office."

Dr. Bickel spoke. "I agree. I'm rather amazed that she hasn't had her people inspect this place for us. For all we know, the moment we leave the tunnels, her soldiers may be waiting for us."

"Don't be concerned. If we encounter a difficulty, we will handle it."

Gamble frowned. "We?"

"Yes. The nanocloud. We are stronger now. Quite able to deal with any obstacles Cushing puts in our path."

The three of them, mouths hanging open, stared at me, but I was growing impatient.

"The game has changed. We go on the offensive now."

I started toward the back entrance to the cavern, when Zander's voice stopped me.

"Gemma. Wait a sec?"

I looked over my shoulder. The three men had not moved, so I retraced my steps.

Zander studied me, and I wondered what he saw.

"Gemma, you said, 'The nanocloud,' and then you said, 'We are stronger now.'"

I walked up close to him, where I could watch his eyes as I spoke. Reached out my hand and touched his. His fingers closed around mine and felt so good. So right.

And what did Zander feel? His eyes widened a little.

A warmth, a tingling, living warmth spread from my hand to his.

"What . . . what is that?"

"It's me, Zander. It's, well, it's us. The nanomites and I."

Dr. Bickel, who had been edging closer as we talked, reached out a hand and touched me. The same warmth spread to him. "My, my. They must be quite formidable now."

"We are."

Without another word, I led the way through the tunnels, setting a quick pace, navigating the twists and turns from memory. We emerged from the door in the mountain under a late-morning sun shadowed by dark, scudding clouds.

The others climbed and scrabbled over the rocks and boulders of the outcropping while I scaled the obstacles easily. What a difference! I no longer needed Agent Gamble's strong back and arms; my body was again healthy and robust.

Instead of hauling me as he had on the way up, Gamble boosted Dr. Bickel and helped him over the more difficult parts until the four of us stood together on the flank of the mountain and faced the trek before us.

The hike to the base perimeter fence, while substantial, sloped downhill—and that was good. I wasn't concerned about us being out in the open as we descended. I could handle that. I was more concerned about the toll on Zander, Gamble, and Dr. Bickel. They had eaten little during our hiatus in the mountain and were, understandably, hungry and weak.

At the thought of food, my stomach rumbled, but I ignored it. I glanced up, studying the sky, taking readings as I did.

"I don't want you out in this weather for long. The temperature is 40 degrees with winds gusting at between fifteen and twenty miles per hour. That puts the wind chill at around freezing. Let's move as quickly as we safely can, given the rough terrain. Once we cross the PIDAS, we'll make better time if we walk on the patrol roads."

Gamble frowned. "Yeah, and what about those patrols? We kept to the gullies coming up. To avoid being seen."

"Don't worry. We'll hide you. Just stay close to me." I was already moving downhill.

They obediently trailed behind me, and I slowed my pace so they could keep up. No one spoke, but I imagined them talking to each other with their eyes, expressing their questions and worry.

When we reached the PIDAS, I went straight at the cut links and pushed the section of cut fencing away. "Go ahead. I'll clean up here."

They crawled through; I brushed away our tracks and followed. I kicked the fence section back into place. Stood. Pointed my fingers at the cut links. Blue fire shot from my hands and fused the severed links together.

I turned. Three pairs of eyes watched me.

"That's a nice trick," Gamble muttered.

"Thanks. I have others up my sleeve."

"I'll bet you do."

Zander and Dr. Bickel did not comment, but my old friend had that speculative look on his face again. And Zander? He wouldn't meet my gaze. He just looked . . . whipped.

I pushed ahead of them to the second fence line. Same process.

From around the curve of the mountain, a car approached.

"Bunch up with me."

My friends followed my instructions; in a blink, the mites sheltered us beneath an umbrella of reflecting panels. We stood still and watched the car roll by. The driver didn't even turn his head in our direction. A second car wasn't far behind the first, so we waited until it had passed.

"Other tricks, huh?" Gamble aimed that question at me.

All I said was, "Let's go."

We marched across the road, down the slope, under the barbed wire, away from the PIDAS and headed for the dirt patrol road that led toward the base perimeter fence. The road was rutted in places but was easier to navigate than the desert floor.

"Come on. We're on leveler ground now. Faster. Stay near me in case anyone else might be watching."

We reached the chain-link perimeter, dropped down into the arroyo, and belly-crawled under the fence. Once we were on the other side and found the hiking trail, I paused.

"From here on, we walk in a tight line. The mites will keep us covered until we hit the trailhead. If Gamble's car is still there and we don't get ambushed, we'll take it."

Gamble had abandoned his car at the trailhead, and three nights and almost four days had passed. It was more than likely that the city had hauled Gamble's car away; it was also possible that Cushing had found it and was waiting for us to show up.

"If we spot any problems, stay behind me, okay?"

They nodded, and we set off. Like ducklings headed for the lake, we marched in a line, stepping off the trail once to let two unwary hikers pass us by. Fifteen minutes later when we reached Gamble's car, I paused again.

"Agent Gamble, I'm going to drive. The mites will disguise me and hide the three of you."

"If you say so."

We pulled away from the curb and, to any and all observers, the driver of the car was one middle-aged, baggy-eyed Kathy Sawyer. Witnesses would have testified under oath that I was alone in the vehicle.

I glanced once in the rearview mirror and took in Zander and Dr. Bickel's incredulity. From the passenger seat, Gamble first gawked, then laughed under his breath.

Kathy Sawyer grinned back. "Oh, yeah. Lots of tricks, Agent Gamble. Lots of tricks."

It felt good to be behind the wheel, to be moving and so close to achieving our objective. But, as I navigated through the neighborhood toward I-40, my empty stomach complained.

Loudly.

"Say, is anyone else hungry? Because I sure am—and I know a Blake's right down Central from here."

"Oh, what I wouldn't give," Dr. Bickel moaned. "It's been months!"

"Gamble, pool our money, would you? I'm gonna place a big order!"

***

Our drive across town was uneventful, even leisurely, while we devoured burgers, fries, and drinks. The clock on Gamble's dash read half past noon when I pulled into the parking garage where I kept my Escape. I borrowed Zander's credit card and fed it into the machine, paid for two days of parking for Gamble's vehicle, and pulled it into an empty slot.

Then I led them up the garage ramp to my car, and we climbed in.

"Whose car is this?" Those were the first words Zander had addressed to me since we left the cavern.

"It's mine. Or, actually, it belongs to my alter-ego, the woman you see me as."

"The mites are doing a stellar job of disguising you, Gemma," Dr. Bickel observed. He seemed quite proud.

"It was a little difficult for them to maintain this look . . . before, when there were fewer of them."

"And now?"

I shrugged. "We don't even break a sweat."

Gamble fidgeted. "So, what's the plan, Gemma? What do you have in mind?"

I turned in my seat so the four of us could talk. My features resolved themselves into Gemma's likeness again and, as the mites returned to me, my friends became visible, too.

Dr. Bickel nodded. "Whew. That's better. Very disconcerting, being invisible."

"Tell me about it."

Zander shuddered. "Yeah. And that other woman kind of creeps me out."

I was getting really miffed with him. "Well, she kinda creeps me out, too," I retorted, "but she's better than a driverless car."

"I only meant that it's a hard adjustment."

"Right. Hard on *you*? And how hard do you think it's been on—"

Gamble cut in. "Okay, okay. Now that we've had our group therapy moment and expressed our feelings, can we get back to the matter at hand?"

He faced me. "What is your plan?"

I took a deep breath and got myself under control. "We'll drive I-25 past the FBI field office. Check to see if anything seems out of the ordinary. You're the best person to make that determination, Gamble."

"And if things look clear from the outside?"

"You and I go in together—stealth mode. I'll keep you hidden until we reach your office. Then we look for an opportunity for you to get your boss alone and tell him about Dr. Bickel—leaving me out of the equation altogether. You ask your boss if he'll take Dr. Bickel in and grant him sanctuary and the opportunity to reveal himself to the world. Show everyone he isn't dead. Tell his story."

"My boss can't make that decision, Gemma. He's the ASAC—the Assistant Special Agent in Charge here in Albuquerque, not the SAC.

"Terry Wallace is the SAC. Besides, my boss is away, teaching a course for the National Executive Institute back at Quantico."

"Then, I suggest that you skip your boss and go straight to the top."

Gamble looked out the window, thinking. "I have my cell phone. I'd almost rather call Wallace first than go inside unprepared for what we might find."

"We won't know what is really going on from a phone call—and if you call, we'll lose the element of surprise, our ability to choose when and how we make our move."

Alarm had crossed Dr. Bickel's face. "You have a phone, Agent Gamble? Has it been on all this time?"

"Yes, but don't worry about Cushing using it to track us. I've got a little app that spoofs my location, sending it a hundred miles off course."

"Ah, I see. Quite interesting."

"Yeah. I had no signal in the mountain, and I have the ringer set on vibrate. As soon as we left the mountain, all the texts and voice mails I didn't receive while in the cavern started piling in. Felt like my pocket was alive."

"Maybe you should check them now," I said. "See how much trouble you're in."

"Yeah. All right."

We waited while Gamble scrolled through his texts and listened to his messages. I watched his face, but he gave little away. When he finished, he shook his head.

"Well, they don't know which to think—whether I'm intentionally AWOL or I'm in some sort of trouble. In either event, I've been told fifteen times to check in."

"What about Cushing's search for me?"

"No mention of that—which is curious in its absence, since the manhunt covered the entire state and included FBI resources."

We gazed at each other, thinking the same thing.

"You think Cushing has set a trap for you?"

"Not out of the question."

"Any mention of Zander?"

"No, but then I didn't report that he was riding with me when we left Albuquerque. The only people who saw him were the State bulls manning the checkpoints on I-25."

"So, he could be in the clear?"

"Possibly."

"Good. Let's do our drive-by as I suggested and see what we see, shall we? If nothing looks out of the norm as we pass by, we'll get off the Interstate and park a few blocks from the office, somewhere Zander and Dr. Bickel can wait. Then you and I will go in and check things out."

"You mean without being seen?"

"Yeah."

The prospect of running into Cushing or her agents had me reaching for my sticks. It was the first I'd thought of them since we'd left White Sands, but I suddenly felt semi-naked without their comforting weight nestled against my back.

"Um, by any chance, did my escrima sticks make it back with us?"

Zander arched his brows. "Your what?"

"Um, my fighting sticks. Kali-style Filipino fighting sticks."

The expression on Gamble's face was as astonished as the one on Zander's. Dr. Bickel, though, was quick to school them.

"Oh, my, yes. I witnessed Gemma in action with them—or should I say, since she was invisible at the time, that I saw what she did. She took out Colonel Greaves' guard while he was holding his sidearm on us—and she did it quite handily, I might say."

Gamble was familiar with the style. "Stick fighting is a demanding discipline, Gemma. How did you learn it? Did you receive training?"

"In a manner of speaking. The nanomites provided a virtual coach and a VR training environment." I laughed. "I was pretty uncoordinated growing up. Never played sports, no good in PE. Couldn't dance worth beans. But after the merge, I picked up the skills they taught me pretty fast. And I had incredible stamina. We practiced mostly at night, at least five hours at a time. Sometimes longer."

Zander stared at me. "Maybe that explains why you look so different."

Dr. Bickel agreed. "You have the lean, toned body of an athlete, Gemma. All muscle, not an extra ounce of fat. I think the term is 'cut.'"

I cleared my throat. "Okay, enough about me. I was hoping the sticks had made it out with us. Did you bring them, Dr. Bickel? I seem to recall you picking them up."

Dr. Bickel colored; a flush of embarrassment began at his collar and raced up his neck into his hairline. He opened his mouth to speak and shut it again.

Zander looked baffled, but Gamble laughed. "Out with it, Doc. It's obvious you did *something* with the sticks."

"Well, I admit that I did pick one up, but it wasn't to bring it along. It was to, um, actually, I used it to deliver a message to Colonel Greaves."

I remembered then: Greaves sending twin bolts of devastation my way, and Dr. Bickel scrabbling to retrieve one of my sticks as it fell from my twitching grasp. He'd delivered a message all right, and Colonel Greaves had received it loud and clear.

"You beat Colonel Greaves with it after he shot me with the Taser."

"Yes, I confess that I allowed my pent-up anger to vent itself." His embarrassment lessened. "Not my finest moment, I assure you; however, it was paramount that we, uh, *disable* the colonel so we could make good our escape."

"Oh, I'm convinced you 'disabled' him." I was thinking of the weight of the sticks and the sounds they'd made as they shattered Greaves' arms and hands.

Dr. Bickel shrugged. "I may not have needed to be so enthusiastic in my application, but it had to be done. Afterward, I helped you up, and we hurried to retrace your steps to the truck and get on the highway."

He returned to my question. "I left your sticks in the house where they were keeping me."

"All right. No biggie. It's just that I had gotten used to having defensive weapons."

Zander spoke up. "Before we go any further, I'd like us to stop and have a word of prayer."

"Very good idea," Dr. Bickel said.

Despite my tiff with Zander only moments before, I was glad for his suggestion. "Yeah. I agree."

Gamble's glance of surprise annoyed me, and I growled, "What?"

"Sorry. Just took you to be, I don't know, something of a skeptic. Hostile to the whole religious concept."

I shrugged. "I was raised as a Christian but got soured on God along the way. I've undergone several attitude changes in the last few days . . . including a return to my roots."

"Interesting. Well, I have no objection. I'm game if you guys are."

We joined hands and Zander prayed.

"Lord God, we are in dangerous waters, far from shore. I'm asking that you lead and guide us. Please help us, Lord, to listen for your still, small voice. As your word says, let us be attentive: *Whether you turn to the right or to the left, your ears will hear a voice behind you, saying, 'This is the way; walk in it.'* Please protect us, Lord, as we work to get Dr. Bickel to a safe place. We ask these things in the name of your Son, Jesus. Amen."

I whispered my amen after Zander's. I assumed my Kathy Sawyer persona and the mites hid the others again. We drove out of the parking garage toward the freeway.

Gemma Keyes.

"Yes, Nano?"

No closing of the eyes; no warehouse required. I heard them and answered inside, within my mind, as naturally, as unconsciously as breathing.

You no longer require the escrima sticks, Gemma Keyes. We are quite sufficient for any situation.

"Oh?"

You retain the training you received, and it will serve us well, but now we have weapons more effective than your sticks. We have only to use them.

By merely recalling the ball of pulsing current that had formed and grown in my palm back in the cavern, my skin warmed. When the lights on my car's dash began to dim, I pulled my thoughts back into line.

"Um, okay, Nano."

A few minutes later we were in the far-right lane of I-25, cruising by the FBI office at the leisurely speed of 50 mph. Gamble kept his eyes glued on the facility until it was in the rearview mirror.

"What did you see?"

"Nothing conclusive."

"Are you up for the next step?"

"If you can get us inside and keep me hidden, then, yes."

I took the Montgomery exit off the freeway and backtracked toward the FBI office. When I was within a few blocks of the office, I pulled into an apartment complex and parked. I reached under the driver's seat, retrieved the Escape's key fob from where it hung, and handed it to Zander.

"I don't use keys, Zander; don't need them. So, take these and, if we're not back in an hour and a half, drive to the parking garage. Wait there until late—say, after midnight. If we haven't caught up to you by then, take Dr. Bickel to the safe house."

I offered a small smile to Dr. Bickel. "You can give Zander directions, right? I hid the back-door key under a brick by the hose bib. As far as the neighbors know, the house is still vacant. Don't give them reason to think otherwise."

My smile grew a little. "Oh. And I left your bolt-hole tidy."

His brows shot up. "You found it? How?"

"The nanomites showed me."

"Gemma? I don't like this. I feel . . ." Zander's voice trailed off, but his expression showed the pain he hadn't voiced.

"You feel sidelined?"

"Useless is a better word. I want to help you, Gemma, protect you, but . . ."

His sweetness touched my heart. "I know, and I thank you, Zander; however, I'm not the one who needs protection."

I pointed to Dr. Bickel. "He is. Keeping him safe is your job at present."

I got out and Gamble followed me. He and I jogged down the walk side by side. I could outrun him with little effort, but I matched my pace to his and the nanomites kept us both covered.

We rounded a few corners before we came to Luecking Park, turned right, and neared the buildings of the FBI field office.

Gamble asked, "You planning to take us in the front door?"

"Yes. We wait for someone to enter and follow them through."

He huffed a loud breath.

"Does that make you nervous?"

"I've been in many a nerve-racking undercover operation, but this? Going in under *your* cover?" He sighed again.

"Gamble?"

"Yeah."

"Those tricks I have up my sleeve?"

"Yeah?"

"I can handle whatever Cushing might have waiting for us. Trust me, okay? Just be quiet as I get us in the door and up the elevator. If things get dicey? Stay behind me."

"If you say so."

⌘⌘⌘⌘

CHAPTER 3

Gamble and I stepped into the lobby of the FBI field office on the heels of a woman toting a briefcase. I grabbed Gamble by the arm and hustled him through behind her. It wasn't a very coordinated or smooth move, so we scuffed the floor a bit. The woman stopped, turned around, and blinked in confusion.

I kept my hand on Gamble's arm while the mites maintained their umbrella of reflective mirrors over and around us. We remained still and quiet until the woman, with a last mystified glance over her shoulder, marched up to the security checkpoint.

Other than her and the guard, the lobby was empty.

I whispered in Gamble's ear. "You recognize the guard?"

"Yes. He's a good man. A regular on this station."

"Okay. We'll get on the elevator as soon as that lady has gone up."

"I don't know if my badge will work on the elevator. They may have suspended my access."

"Not a problem, remember?"

We got inside the empty car and rode it to Gamble's floor. Got out. Went to his office.

The door hung open a crack.

"That's not a good sign," he muttered. "I keep it locked."

I said nothing as Gamble pushed open the door and we gazed at the mess: Someone had tossed Gamble's office. Drawers and files had been emptied onto his desk, then rummaged through. Discarded file folders and papers littered the floor.

"Okay. We know Cushing's been here. Where's the SAC's office?"

"Next floor."

I didn't want to take the elevator, preferring a more surreptitious approach; Gamble didn't want us to take the stairs. "The stairwell door on the executive floor is locked and alarmed."

"Not to me."

We crept up the stairs, and the door opened under my hand. We were at the end of a hallway not far from a sizable printer/copier machine.

That's when we saw the two agents, one a woman I knew on sight, the other a man I thought I'd seen before. Both wore street clothes, but they stood post outside a closed door down the hall.

I tugged Gamble's sleeve.

"Yeah. I see them. Definitely not FBI."

"They're Cushing's people. What's on the other side of that door?"

"Conference room."

"Ah. Okay, good."

"Good?"

"Yeah. Listen; hold my belt and stick close. Don't freak out when those two agents fall, okay?"

"When they—*what*? We're only reconnoitering, remember?"

I moved toward the agents, half-dragging Gamble, since he had a tight grip on my belt and was trying—in vain—to hold me back. When I was a few feet from the male agent, the guy straightened, alert but confounded. I flicked my fingers toward him and he spasmed, passed out, slid down the wall.

The woman saw him drop. She jerked and retreated a step.

Down she went. I caught her as she fell.

While I dragged her beyond the copier, I tried to recall her name.

Oh, yeah. Trujillo, I think. Of the REI backpack debacle. The tiny scrap of information that had led Cushing to me.

I went back, grabbed the guy, dragged him to join Agent Trujillo, and deposited him in the corner. Gamble followed behind, fussing as the guard's heels dug little telltale trails in the carpet.

"How long will they be out?"

"Maybe ten minutes or so."

"Don't know how I'm gonna explain this."

"Do you *need* to explain this?"

I was ready to start calling my partner "Grumble" instead of Gamble for all the low, growled complaints emerging from his mouth.

"Shut the whining, Gamble. We've got work to do."

"Yeah, but this is supposed to be a *look*, Gemma. Reconnaissance. That's all."

"Well, I need to 'look' in that conference room. Look and listen."

"But they'll know you've been here."

"You mean Cushing will? So? Just who's she gonna tell? The neat thing about being invisible is that nobody believes it."

I grabbed Gamble and started down the hallway again. When I reached the conference room I placed a palm on the door. The mites amplified the conversation and funneled it into my ears.

Gamble hissed, "Can you hear anything?"

"Well, not with you yapping at me! Nano. Let Gamble listen in, too."

Gamble settled as soon as the voices reached him.

Voices. Only two: Cushing and a man.

"Is that the SAC?" I whispered.

"Yeah."

We got quiet again and focused on the conversation behind the door.

"Ma'am, in the spirit of interagency cooperation, I have allowed your people access to my agent's desk, his files, even his emails and cell phone records. You have found nothing."

"Nothing except that phone call last Monday to a cell number *I* am familiar with but your agent should *not* be."

"In order to understand, I've asked whose cell that is, yet you refuse to tell me. Thanks for the interagency reciprocity, by the way."

"You are not cleared, Mr. Wallace."

"Oh, right. That's convenient, isn't it? Well, frankly, I don't know what else you expect me to do, General. Our man is missing. We've pinged his phone repeatedly and caught nothing from it until today—and the signal is about a hundred miles east of here. That doesn't bode well for him, and we are quite concerned for his safety.

"For all we know, Special Agent Gamble was carjacked or otherwise ambushed and left for dead by the side of the road. The signal could be coming from whomever stole his phone and has just this afternoon turned it on. I have people tracking the phone now—and I've told you repeatedly that we'll let you know when we find it."

"And *I* insist, Mr. Wallace, that your Agent Gamble has not been carjacked, as you suggest, nor any other such nonsense. He is aiding and abetting the terrorist, Gemma Keyes. As such, he must also be named as a person of interest and placed on a watch list."

There was a brief silence from beyond the door, and I wondered if Gamble's boss' boss was caving or counting to ten.

When he finally answered, his words were civil and controlled. Barely. "You know, General Cushing, we have been nothing but cooperative with your manhunt. We've spared no resource nor amount of manpower, but I will not put out an APB on a decorated veteran agent simply on your say-so. If you can suggest an alternative action, I'd be happy to entertain it."

Cushing started to answer when Gamble put his mouth by my ear. "The SAC is not happy with Cushing."

"I think I figured that out on my own, thanks."

"What I mean is that I know this man, and he's about a hairsbreadth from giving her the boot—with all political and bureaucratic politeness, of course, but the boot, nonetheless."

"And?"

"And I think the timing is great."

"You have an idea?"

"Yes. I think I should join their meeting."

I turned around, swept my hands across the space between us, clearing the nanomites' veil. Gamble's eyes were bright, his expression somewhat gleeful.

Maybe devious?

"I'd like to stoke the fire, Miss Keyes. Nothing like dumping fuel on an imminent combustion."

I snorted and grinned. "I like your enthusiasm. What's your story?"

"A version of the truth. That I got caught up in the recovery of one Dr. Daniel Bickel, renowned nanophysicist, a man the world believes is dead—courtesy of General Cushing's public assertions, by the way. Said Dr. Bickel tells us he has escaped the evil clutches of one General Imogene Cushing. Bickel claims he has been unlawfully imprisoned for the past three months. Oh, and Dr. Bickel is prepared to give evidence against her."

"But Cushing—"

"But Cushing, what? Like you said, what can she do? Think Special Agent in Charge Wallace will allow her to haul one of his agents away in cuffs never to be seen again? This is the very confrontation we need: It takes the focus off you and puts it where it belongs—on Cushing's illegal detainment of an American citizen.

"Think of the shock factor, Gemma: Cushing will have no response to my accusations, and we'll have Wallace as a witness to the confrontation. And, oh, yeah. Kidnapping and abductions are the FBI's purview."

I snickered and clapped my fingers over my mouth. I whispered back, "What I wouldn't give to be a fly on the wall."

"You're welcome to come with me."

"Don't mind if I do."

Gamble rapped on the door and the escalating "discussion" within ceased. A second later, a male voice rasped, "Come in."

Gamble opened the door and took a step inside. I followed behind him. "Sorry to disturb, sir. I heard you were looking for me?"

Cushing scowled at Gamble. The man whom Gamble had identified as the Special Agent in Charge of the Albuquerque field office raised his sandy-gray brows.

"Special Agent Gamble. You've been missing since Sunday evening."

"Yes, sir. Since General Cushing is with you and my absence pertains to her, I'd like to brief you on my actions, if I may?"

"The short version, please."

"Yes, sir. For the past four days, I have been assisting Dr. Daniel Bickel. Keeping him safe and secure from General Cushing, here."

The shock on Cushing's face was priceless.

"Who?" Wallace seemed confused. "I thought the manhunt was for a woman."

"I don't know about the woman in question, sir, but Dr. Bickel supposedly died in a fire at Sandia National Labs last March. Do you recall the incident?"

"Fire in a DOE laboratory? Two dead?"

Cushing sprang to her feet, emitting a strangled noise before she managed to bellow, "Mr. Wallace, arrest this man!"

"I beg your pardon? General, you can't be serious."

"I misspoke. I will take this man into custody, myself." She shouted toward the open door. "Trujillo! Black! Get in here!"

Gamble's mouth twitched, and Wallace's incredulity grew.

"General Cushing, you will do no such thing. You and your agents are without authority in this facility."

Cushing craned her neck, looking for her people to push through the door. When they didn't, she huffed and moved toward the doorway, but Gamble closed the door and positioned himself between it and her.

She glared a death-ray look at Gamble, then rounded on the SAC. "Mr. Wallace, the fire at Sandia was also a terrorist action tied to our present manhunt. This man," she pointed at Gamble, "has lied to you. He is, as I suspected, colluding with the terrorist, Gemma Keyes."

Now, this is what I love about Special Agent Gamble. In a crunch? When it's 'go time'? He doesn't flinch or pull back, as would be the natural tendency. No, he doubles down.

Gamble stepped within inches of Cushing and towered over her. He leaned into her personal space. He'd done that before, remember?

"General Cushing, you are a liar. You lied to the American people regarding Daniel Bickel. You attempted to kill him with the explosion in that laboratory, but he escaped and fled from you. You wanted to hunt him down with impunity, so you announced to the world that he died in that fire. You even staged his funeral and burial.

"That was last March. In September, you finally tracked him down, and you have been keeping him imprisoned without due process for the past three months. General, it is you who will be taken into custody."

Wallace frowned. "Agent Gamble, these are serious charges. Can you prove them?"

"Sir, I have Daniel Bickel. As he is *not* deceased, he can speak for himself."

During Gamble's indictment, Cushing's face had gone six shades of blotchy red, but the tops of her cheekbones paled to white, bloodless points.

"Agent Gamble, you have no idea what you have interfered in. This investigation has authorization at the highest levels. The. Highest. Levels."

I had been enjoying the show up until now. All along I'd known that Cushing had top cover, probably someone connected near the summit of the political heap, but when she emphasized "the highest levels," a shiver ran along my spine. I had to wonder, just how powerful *were* her masters?

I could see that Gamble was conjecturing the same—as was Special Agent in Charge Wallace.

"Gamble?"

"Sir, my suggestion would be to allow General Cushing to, er, depart. Then I'll bring in Dr. Bickel and we'll debrief him and see where his accusations go."

Wallace studied Cushing as she straightened, tugged her uniform into place, and regained her equilibrium.

"Very well, Agent Gamble. Please escort General Cushing and her people from the building. Then I want to see you."

"Yes, sir."

A thump sounded on the door. Gamble opened it; Agent Trujillo hung on the doorjamb; Black leaned against the opposite wall, and his head lolled precariously toward his shoulder.

Gamble grabbed and steadied Agent Trujillo. "Whoa. Hold it right there. What in the world—what's going on with you two?"

Gamble has *the* best game face I've ever seen. He put forward the exact right mix of concern and leery authority.

"General . . . Cushing," Trujillo rasped.

Cushing pushed past Gamble. "What is wrong with you? Why didn't you come when I called?"

Trujillo, usually in command of her senses and responses, stuttered, "W-we a-attacked. Knocked . . . out."

"You were attacked?" Cushing sputtered, backed up, and jabbed a menacing finger in Gamble's face. She spun toward Wallace while keeping her finger near Gamble's nose. "This man attacked my agents? He attacked my people?"

Wallace looked to Gamble. "Well?"

"Sir, I never laid a hand on them."

Well, that's true. He never touched them. *I* did all the heavy lifting. Literally.

"Agent Gamble, General Cushing left her people standing outside the door. Were they there when you arrived?"

Gamble shook his head. "Sir, I assure you that neither of these two individuals were present when I knocked at the conference room door. In fact, I saw no one in the hallway."

I shook with silent laughter. Yup. By the time Gamble had knocked, Agents Trujillo and Black were snoozing in the far corner of the hall, hidden from view by the copy machine.

Trujillo wagged her head as if to clear it. "General. She. Her."

"Her what?" Cushing demanded.

"Um," Trujillo's voice dropped to a soft hiss. "I think it was *her*. You know."

Huh.

I was surprised. Did Trujillo actually know about my invisibility or did she only suspect? I wasn't convinced even Cushing knew with certainty.

Cushing's mouth went slack. "Here?"

When Trujillo nodded, Cushing's eyes jetted around the room.

Looking for me.

I sniffed. Well, *let her*.

"Close the door," she barked. "Close it, I said!" She pushed Trujillo out and slammed the door, leaning her back against it. Panting. "Are you with us, Miss Keyes?"

A guffaw stuck in my throat. Cushing sounded like the medium of a cheap séance: *Are you with us, Miss Keyes? O Spirit of Christmas Past, are you here?*

Wallace slipped a nervous glance in Gamble's direction, who, adding to his other notable performances, managed to convey "cuckoo" and "nuts" with one tiny lift of a shoulder.

Wallace cleared his throat. "Uh, General Cushing. Ma'am. Special Agent Gamble will escort you and your people from the building now."

"No! She may be in here! She—" With the abrupt comprehension of how crazed she sounded, Cushing sucked up her protest. Squared her shoulders. Reestablished her composure.

She canted her head toward Gamble, her shiny sharky teeth bared. "We aren't finished, you and I, Agent Gamble."

"No, ma'am, we are not." If there were a means of making Gamble's short response more of a threat, I don't know what that might be. His face was stone, his eyes glittering pebbles—his manners flawless.

He gestured. "This way, ma'am."

Cushing gathered her things and marched on stiff legs through the conference room door. Her agents fell in behind her and Gamble took up the rear, herding them to the elevator.

I jetted down the staircase to arrive in the lobby before them. I was waiting when the elevator dinged its arrival.

Gamble was the portrait of chilly civility. "Goodbye, General Cushing. Have a good day."

Cushing barked a two-word response I won't repeat.

Black hurried to get the door for Cushing. Trujillo stood aside to let her pass. I followed behind.

Cushing's shoes clipped fast and hard toward the concrete steps leading down from the door. I hurled a hair-thin phalanx of mites toward her. The mites shot from my arm, dodged around Trujillo and past Black, and impaled themselves in the high, rounded part of Cushing's skirt, right where I'd aimed them.

In other words, they stung Shark Face right on the butt.

(Sorry; that's *General* Shark Face, ma'am.)

Cushing yelped and tripped on the top step. Black and Trujillo caught her, took her arms, and hustled her toward the parking structure.

The last I saw of the three of them, Cushing had shaken off her agents' help and was stalking ahead of them, rubbing her backside with one hand as she went.

When I glanced at Gamble, he was grinning every bit as much as I was.

"Nice touch, Gemma."

"Thanks. Liked it myself."

⌘⌘⌘⌘

CHAPTER 4

"I have to meet with Wallace now. Coming?"

"Wouldn't miss it."

We rode the elevator to the SAC's floor, got off, and went to his office.

"Close the door, Agent Gamble."

Gamble did as he was told.

"Take a seat, please, and help me understand what just happened."

"I can try, sir. Not sure I can explain the General's bizarre behavior, though."

"Let's start with where you've been the past four days."

"Yes, sir. As you know, we were called out to assist in the hunt for the suspect, one Gemma Keyes. I took my vehicle and went down I-25 toward the center of the search grid."

The moment we'd entered Wallace's office, the mites and I had jumped into the FBI's classified server, looking for any reference to Zander. When we came up empty, I put my mouth near Gamble's ear and whispered.

"No mention of Zander in the FBI files."

Without turning, he replied with an incremental nod.

"Around Socorro, I received a phone call from Dr. Bickel. He said General Cushing had abducted him and held him against his will in an isolated facility on the White Sands Missile Range and that he had just escaped from said facility. He requested that the FBI escort him to the Albuquerque FBI field office and render him aid and sanctuary."

"Why you? How did he have your number?"

Gamble shrugged. "Not sure, sir. I'd never spoken to the man prior to his call. All I can report is that I met up with him, listened to his story, and transported him back to Albuquerque."

"And it took you four days to get from there to here?"

"No, sir, but this is where the situation gets a bit involved. However, since his tale is so peculiar, I would prefer for us to debrief him here and get it all on the record, in detail, rather than piecemeal."

"Where is Bickel right now?"

"I have him safely stashed, sir, but will bring him in as soon as I have your permission and assurances that you will not hand him over to Cushing."

"I wouldn't hand my worst enemy's dog over to that woman."

"I'm glad we're in agreement, sir."

"Not entirely, Agent Gamble. While I don't trust Cushing any further than I'd trust a snake, I'm concerned that her threats of high-level authorization are real and that said authority may supersede ours. At that point, I'd be forced to comply with her demands."

Not gonna happen, I told Wallace in my head.

"I understand, sir; however, Dr. Bickel's first request is that he be allowed to broadcast the fact that he is alive. Once the public knows he is alive, much of Cushing's hold over him will be broken. She's only been able to keep him incarcerated because no one is looking for him."

Wallace cupped his chin and thought. "Any outstanding warrants or charges against Bickel?"

Gamble snorted. "Not for a dead man, sir—nor were there any at the time of his reported demise. Before the explosion and fire in his laboratory, Dr. Bickel held a DOE Q clearance—with Special Access—and his record was without blemish."

"Very well. We'll offer Dr. Bickel temporary asylum and the opportunity to give testimony on the record. If he wishes to hold a press conference, that is his right."

Having made his decision, Wallace stood. "Bring him in."

"Thank you, sir."

Wallace seemed to hesitate. "Do you anticipate any interference from Cushing on that point?"

"Nothing we can't handle, sir."

"We?"

"Us, sir. The agency."

I shook my head. *Right. The agency.*

***

Gamble and I left the FBI building via the doors leading to staff parking. As soon as we were out of sight of the field office, I added the mites' umbrella to him, and we began to jog.

"We should take Zander home before we bring Dr. Bickel in," I said.

"Agreed. No sense putting him on Cushing's radar. Then, as soon as we have Bickel safely inside our offices, I'll have our media liaison set the ball rolling on a press conference."

I said, "Okay," but I thought, *Leave that to me.*

We found Zander and Dr. Bickel where we'd left them, and they were relieved to see us. The hour and a half had flown by; it was after 3:30 now. We climbed into the Escape, and I, as Kathy Sawyer, drove off.

Gamble talked first. "Dr. Bickel, there's good news and bad news. The good news is that we have the SAC's permission to escort you to the FBI field office where we will debrief you and get your account on record. We'll do that this evening. The next order of business will be to hold a press conference. Probably first thing in the morning. The bad news is that Cushing knows I have you."

"Not so bad," I chimed in. "She won't see us when we take you in. We'll go in through the employee entrance under the nanomites' cloak of invisibility."

Gamble nodded. "Uh, right. And, Pastor Cruz, we've hit a patch of good news for you, too. Apparently, no one is aware that you accompanied me south on the search for Gemma, so we're going to drop you within a few blocks of your place."

"That's a relief. I told Pastor McFee I'd be on an LEO ride-along last Sunday night and the church office is closed Mondays anyway. My only hurdle will be how I explain to him why I've been out of the office this week—and why I didn't take my cell."

"Uh. Well, I don't know what to tell you about that."

"Don't worry. I'll figure out something."

We pulled up to a curb to drop Zander. He got out and squatted by my window, so I rolled it down and waited for him to speak. Must have been hard for him to address Kathy Sawyer and act like it was me, but he managed.

"Listen, Gemma. Things are crazy right now. I get that," he said. "But when Dr. Bickel is safe, and things calm down, you and I are going to talk."

I turned my face away, but Zander wasn't done. "Just talk, Gemma. So I can understand."

Sighing, I faced him again. "All right."

When Zander stepped away, I pointed the car toward the parking garage. I slipped the Escape into my slot, then Gamble, Dr. Bickel, and I walked down three levels to Gamble's vehicle. He climbed into the driver's seat, which was fine with me. The mites made sure Gamble was the car's only visible occupant.

As we pulled out of the garage, I asked, "Hey, Agent Gamble, may I use your phone for a few minutes while we're on the way?"

"Sure."

We headed back toward the FBI office. On the way, the nanomites and I used Gamble's cell phone's Internet service to hack into local news organizations' servers and plant the information I wanted them to see. By the time we arrived at the field office, we'd completed our tasks.

Managing or manipulating data online was nearly effortless for us now. All we needed was a connection to the Internet.

Gamble parked two blocks from the facility.

"Ready?" I asked Dr. Bickel.

"More than you can imagine."

I wondered how many times Dr. Bickel had pictured this day, how many times he had envisioned himself testifying against Cushing.

41

With the mites covering the three of us, we walked to the field office and through the employee entrance in the rear.

"I'd like to check the front lobby before we go up."

"What for?"

"See who the early responders are."

"Early responders for what?"

"For Dr. Bickel's 5:30 press conference."

Gamble actually got flustered. "His . . . You? You scheduled . . . you . . . how . . ."

That was before he barked at me. "I said *I* would schedule it, Gemma! Shouldn't you have let me make the arrangements as to time and date with the knowledge and approval of the SAC and the office's PR rep?"

"Oh, they've coordinated the event."

"What? How?"

"Via emails."

"What emails?"

"The ones I sent."

Gamble ground his fingers into his eyes, but I kept us moving toward the front lobby. A frazzled woman was directing the FBI's facility workers where to place a lectern, portable sound system, and rows of chairs—and through the glass panes that formed the front wall of the lobby, I spotted two vans pulling into the distant front lot.

Big, bold lettering and satellite dishes mounted on the vehicle roofs identified the vans as belonging to two Albuquerque television stations. Crew members piled out of the vehicles and began unloading cameras and light booms.

"Good. Things are moving right along."

"No, *not* good! Oh, man. Wallace is gonna have my skin."

"Nah, don't fret, Gamble. Everything's on the up-and-up. Special Agent in Charge Wallace himself gave the orders for this event."

"Somehow I doubt that."

"Well, according to the email your media liaison received, he did. And that same email is sitting in Mr. Wallace's 'Sent' folder, so it looks legit to me."

"You're killin' me, Keyes."

We huddled off to the side, the business of setting up swirling around us.

After a long pause, Dr. Bickel murmured, "I'm not exactly my most photogenic at the moment, Gemma. When did you say this circus commences?"

I glanced at a wall clock. "About twenty minutes. Need to spruce up a bit?"

"If you don't want video of a homeless old man going out on the ten o'clock news, then yes."

"Gamble?"

He sighed. "I have a shaving kit upstairs—if Cushing's goons didn't trash it with the rest of my office." He eyed Dr. Bickel's hair, thin but straggling past his collar. "Maybe take a little off the sides and back?"

"Haven't had a trim since the last one Gemma gave me, maybe late August."

We went up to Gamble's floor. Apparently, most of the staff had already left for the day; the offices we passed, bar one or two, were empty. I left Gamble and Dr. Bickel alone in Gamble's office to make Dr. Bickel presentable.

It was okay for them to be out from under my "cover," but it felt wrong. Dangerous, in fact. I would have to get used to it, though. Dr. Bickel was about to fly solo and, if I could trust this God I had just become reacquainted with and stop worrying, Dr. Bickel's reemergence into the public eye would be a terrific load off my mind.

I wandered back downstairs, gratified to see a bustling crowd of about twenty reporters, photographers, and videographers setting up in the lobby. Arms folded, stance rigid, the young guard at the security desk kept his watchful eyes roving about the lobby.

I was just as watchful, and I had to remind myself that the nanomites were "only" tiny electromechanical devices. Not omniscient; not omnipotent. Not able to read minds or discern what Cushing might do next. The nanocloud was powerful and the mites had tremendous abilities—but they had their limits, too.

"Nano, stay in the FBI's security system and keep tabs on the perimeter of this facility."

Just in case.

We will, Gemma Keyes.

A news anchor posed off to the side for some stand-up background tape. When I hovered nearby, I heard him say to the camera, "Our station was astounded to hear that Dr. Daniel Bickel, world-renowned scientist and former employee of Sandia National Laboratories, has been found alive. We say the news is astounding because Bickel was reported to have died in the explosion and resulting fire that burned his laboratory on Kirtland Air Force Base last March.

"This is what we know: Just prior to 4 p.m. this afternoon, our newsroom received word that Dr. Bickel would be giving a statement today at the FBI Albuquerque field office. I am standing in the FBI's lobby now, waiting for the press conference to begin.

"Aside from the obvious questions, such as, how did Dr. Bickel survive the explosion, and where has he been the past nine months, our reporting staff asks, why *here*. Why the offices of the FBI? Stand by as we deliver live coverage of this event, scheduled to begin in the next few minutes."

By the time the anchor wrapped up his background tape, I was grinning. The coverage would be perfect.

I had no idea how Dr. Bickel planned to address the press, but I wasn't too concerned: The main goal had been achieved. The world had been told—and would soon see for themselves—that Dr. Bickel was alive.

I waited at the top of the lobby where the lectern sat and where I could watch the press and be close enough to support Dr. Bickel should he need me. I didn't wait long. Wallace, Gamble, and Dr. Bickel emerged from the elevator.

Gamble had done wonders with Dr. Bickel's appearance in the little time he'd had. My friend was fresh-shaven, wore a reasonable haircut, and sported a shirt, tie, and jacket over his baggy jeans. I wondered which agent or staff member Gamble had coerced into lending his clothes to Dr. Bickel.

The woman who had been supervising the lobby setup approached the lectern. "Ladies and gentlemen, please take your seats." When the group settled, she gestured Wallace forward and introduced him. "Special Agent in Charge of the FBI's Albuquerque field office, Terry Wallace."

Wallace, also spiffed up for his appearance before cameras, stood in front of the microphones. I thought he held his mouth in a tight, pinched line—like maybe he wasn't entirely pleased or something. Okay, possibly a little irate? Well, I *had* sprung the news conference on him, but the man was a pro, and he was ready.

Like I'd counted on him being.

Cushing, on the other hand, I couldn't trust not to make her move before tomorrow, which is why I had made sure the news would break today.

"Ladies and gentlemen of the press, thank you for coming. This afternoon, Dr. Daniel Bickel entered our facility and requested sanctuary. As you are probably aware, it was widely reported last March that Dr. Bickel, at that time a Sandia National Laboratories employee, perished when an explosion occurred in his laboratory in the," Wallace looked at his notes, "in the Advanced Microelectromechanical Systems department.

44

"Dr. Bickel will speak for himself in a moment and provide an explanation as to how he survived the event that destroyed his laboratory, and he will detail where he has been the last nine months. Afterward, he will entertain a few questions. Dr. Bickel?"

My dear friend, looking a little worn for his ordeal despite Gamble's efforts, took the lectern. "Thank you all for coming. My name is Daniel Jerome Bickel. I hold dual doctoral degrees in physics and material sciences. My area of expertise is nanotechnology; ergo, I have often been referred to as a nanophysicist.

"Last year I achieved a breakthrough of historic proportions in my research and development. I cannot, at this time, provide details nor answer questions on the exact nature and scope of that breakthrough. What I can tell you is that my contract with SNL stipulated that no part or portion of my work would ever be weaponized by the U.S. Military or employed for surveillance on the American people—even in a legal capacity.

"Unfortunately, certain parties within the government determined that they would appropriate my work for military and 'national security' purposes. Despite my protests and unequivocal rejection of this attempt, a military liaison appeared at Sandia and was given executive oversight of my program."

I already knew the sordid details, but Dr. Bickel's clear, concise recitation of the events sucked me right back into the department where I had worked—and took me back to the perilous moments when I had overheard Cushing and Dr. Prochanski determine to kill Dr. Bickel.

"When this breach of contract occurred, I took steps to ensure that my research would be removed from the reach of those who would misuse it. I had, however, logged enough data on the Sandia servers to ensure that my immediate . . . supervisor, Petrel Prochanski, would believe himself to be in possession of my entire body of work."

Knowing the disdain with which Dr. Bickel had held Dr. Prochanski, it wasn't lost on me that he had first hesitated and then refused to use the term "immediate *superior*" when speaking of Dr. P.—nor had Dr. Bickel conferred upon him the honorific of "doctor."

I silently begged Dr. Bickel not to go off on a tangent. My sigh of relief was heartfelt when he cleared his throat and continued in the same reasonable tone with which he had begun—although he went straight to the knockout punch with this next sentence.

"I was well acquainted with the officer placed in charge of my work: Air Force Brigadier General Imogene Cushing. She and I had attended university together during our undergrad years and had, for a brief period, engaged in a romantic relationship."

I knew about that, too, but figured spitting details of his personal life into the public eye had to sting Dr. Bickel's ego—particularly when it was a mistake that had come back to haunt him.

"Even those many years ago, while earning my undergrad degree, I was theorizing my life's work, and Imogene Cushing was privy to my earliest research. It was during this period that I became aware of and concerned with the nature of her character. I learned that Cushing possessed uninhibited ambition and a ruthless determination to fulfill her goals.

"Fast forward to March of this year. Since I showed myself unwilling to deliver my nanotechnology to Cushing and Prochanski and as they believed themselves to be in possession of my complete data, the two of them decided to remove me from the equation."

Dr. Bickel looked up from his statement straight into the eyes of the cameras. "Yes, I am saying that Cushing and Prochanski formed a plan to kill me. That plan was an explosive device set to detonate when I and the two technicians most familiar with my work would be the only personnel within the laboratory. However, I discovered the explosive device and removed myself and my technicians from the laboratory."

The hush within the lobby was palpable. No one whispered or shuffled.

"Therefore, when the explosion occurred, only one individual was present and perished: Petrel Prochanski."

What Dr. Bickel left out was essential to his tale but possibly self-incriminating: When he had discovered the explosive device, he had changed the timer on the detonator, moving it up an hour. Dr. Prochanski, unaware of the time change, had lingered in the lab, thinking himself safe. Because Dr. Bickel had reset the timer on the bomb, he could, in point of fact, be accused of causing Dr. P's death.

Dr. Bickel was prudent not to provide too many details.

He continued. "I will reveal where I went when I left the lab prior to the explosion, but I first wish to put forth one means of verifying this portion of my statement: General Cushing took charge of the investigation into the explosion. Her results have been well-documented. She asserted that two individuals perished in the explosion, myself and Prochanski.

"With the world's most accurate forensic science support available to her, General Cushing announced and publicized my death—and yet here I stand. Subsequently, two funerals and burials were conducted—*and yet here I stand*. Exhumation of my 'body' from the plot where my remains were supposedly interred should yield either an empty casket or the remains of someone other than myself. More importantly, either result will prove, categorically, that General Cushing lied to cover up my escape."

Now members of the press pool were moving, some surreptitiously sending text messages, others whispering instructions to lackeys who ran for the front doors. I envisioned the excited phone calls and rushed instructions to hold air and print time for Dr. Bickel's story.

I was convinced of one fact: Tonight's headlines would set hair on fire across the nation.

Despite the restless fever of his audience, Dr. Bickel continued, "I must make it clear that General Cushing could not have acted alone in this cover-up or on her own authority. She could not have pulled off such an egregious deception of the public's trust without the political power of individuals high above her."

A voice shouted a question. "Where have you been the past nine months, Dr. Bickel?"

He nodded. "Very well; I'll advance my narrative to the day of the explosion. I left the lab an hour before the lab exploded, but I did not go far. I entered the old Manzano Weapons Storage Facility on Kirtland Air Force Base. I had previously located an abandoned devolution cavern within the mountain, one that had been sealed at the time it was abandoned and had not been entered since the 1960s."

He went on to describe how he had prepared the cavern as a hiding place, a facility where he could conduct his work in safety and without interference.

The evening had darkened, and the barrier at the top of the parking lot was far from the front entrance, so I didn't notice the military-like vehicles when they pulled up. My first clue that something was amiss was when the nanomites chimed a furious alarm.

Gemma Keyes! Gemma Keyes! Armed men are approaching!

The nanomites sent the security system's video feed to me. I recognized the threat mere seconds before a half-dozen black-garbed troops, their M4s up, burst into the lobby.

⌘⌘⌘⌘

CHAPTER 5

The assault was surreal, so unexpected and blatantly *wrong*, that, for several heartbeats, no one reacted. Dr. Bickel froze at the lectern; the small crowd did not move. Two seconds later, as though all of our reflexes kicked in at the same instant, chaos ensued.

Amid screams, overturned chairs, and scattering reporters, the soldiers drove a path through the press: Their objective was Dr. Bickel. He stumbled toward Gamble. Gamble drew his sidearm. I ran to his side and pushed his arm down.

"Don't. They will kill you. Get Dr. Bickel away and let me handle it."

In response, Gamble shouted, "Wallace! Get Bickel out of here!"

Wallace had already acted. I pivoted and saw him dragging Dr. Bickel to the elevator.

"I'll send help!" he shouted to Gamble as the elevator doors opened and he shoved Dr. Bickel inside.

No, I didn't want that. I gestured toward the elevator and the door to the stairs.

"Seal the building, Nano," I whispered. "In particular, don't allow anyone already in the building to enter the lobby."

Gemma Keyes, shall we cut the media's live video feed?

"Yes. Do it!"

Gamble stood to my left, his sidearm drawn but pointed at an oblique angle toward the floor rather than at the soldiers. The young security guard joined him. He was trembling but, with weapon drawn, he stood with Gamble.

I raised my hands.

The lights in the lobby dimmed and sparked as the building's power jetted into my body. The pulsing electricity shot down my arms. I thrust my hands toward the soldiers and a wall of arcing current burst from my fingers.

As though they had rushed into powerful, oncoming breakers, the soldiers flew backwards, tossed and tumbled across the room. I advanced on them, bolts from my fingers flinging their weapons from their reach.

Two attackers had missed the full impact of the blast; they dropped into a crouch and leveled their guns, looking for a target. Looking for me. Finding Gamble instead.

I rotated my wrist; a fireball of electricity spun within the breadth of my palm. I hurled the ball of fire; a thick column of nanomites shot from my hand and propelled the pulsing sphere forward. The soldiers flew apart, one crashing into a wall, the other into a camera and tripod. Neither got up.

Two or three members of the media had fled the lobby before the nanomites sealed the building; the rest were prone, hands over their heads. One adventurous reporter had taken refuge behind the guard's station and was directing his shaking cameraman. I would deal with them later; my more urgent attention was focused on the soldiers—and their reinforcements.

Another six-person team burst through the front entrance. Gamble shouted, "Gemma! Look at their weapons!"

I did. I knew what they were—and what they had done to me. To the nanocloud. To *us*. A fury born out of Greave's Taser and the death and anguish it had produced boiled within me.

"Nano. We must act preemptively."

I charged toward the men; my hands flashed, impelling a wide surge of nanomites. They deployed a wall of mirrors as a barrier of both shields and deflectors—and ahead of that wall they pushed a great, crackling pulse of electricity as insulation.

A veritable storm struck the soldiers of the second team: Lightning sizzled; a concussion wave slammed them. The glass in the lobby windows exploded outward, sending shards of glass onto the pavement, flinging the men themselves through the broken window casings.

I raced forward and leapt through an empty window frame, ready to finish what I'd started. I needn't have worried: The six men who sprawled on the concrete were unconscious. Their Taser-like guns had burst into flames and lay charring nearby.

"Nano. Is anyone seriously injured?"

These men will require medical attention, but they will recover.

"Okay. Thank you."

Now I needed to do what I could to mitigate the damage my actions would create if word of them were to get out.

"Nano, please—"

I whipped my head around as a shout echoed out of the dark.

"We have her, General!"

Other disembodied voices shouted their agreement.

"Move in!"

A woman.

Cushing.

Two things flashed through my mind in that moment: One was that the attack on Dr. Bickel had been a ruse—a ploy—intended to draw *me* out. The second was the memory of that awful nightmare I'd had in which Cushing and her people stormed the safe house and snared me in nets. I could still feel the weight of those nets pinning me down.

The horror of that memory sent adrenaline gushing through my body; the rush of boots on the pavement drove me to action.

Thermal imaging, Gemma Keyes. Four individuals.

"Got it."

In the moment it had taken to convey messages between us, I acted. Rotating both hands, I formed balls of fire and threw them. Again. Twice more. The nanomites drove the missiles to their destinations.

When the first bolus of pure energy reached its target, a man's scream shredded the night. No scream is ever pleasant; still, there is something so very primal and disturbing in a grown man's unreserved shriek of pain.

Quadruple that horrific sound: My projectiles had reached their intended destinations—the soldiers wearing thermal imaging goggles. I moved ahead; I couldn't pause to consider how the fireballs' intense light had fried the soldiers' open retinas.

I had to end this.

I brought my hands together and grew a sphere of brilliant current between my splayed fingers. I tossed it above my head where, like a living disco ball, it illuminated the area around me.

Cushing.

There she was, shaking with rage, waving her hands in my direction. "Deploy the nets! Take her!"

Bodies littered the ground; only two of her people remained on their feet. One of them searched in vain for me and babbled, "But I can't see her! Where is she?" He carried an unfamiliar-looking tactical rifle—as did the other soldier.

That guy, with a last look at the bodies scattered around him, shook his head, and dropped his rifle on the pavement. "I'm unarmed! Don't," his voice dropped off. "Please, don't."

Guess he didn't have a word for what had decimated all but two of eighteen men in less than four minutes. I sent a stream of nanomites to harmlessly put him out.

Cushing pointed at the last of her soldiers. "Aim straight ahead and fire! Take her now!" Like a cartoon caricature, Cushing was hopping from foot to foot in frustration.

The solder aimed dead ahead, depressed the trigger, and deployed a net. The net expanded and flew twenty feet; weights fastened to each corner of the net expanded the net and brought it down—but I was well away from its reach.

A flick of my wrist sent the last soldier to his knees and onto his face.

Gamble rushed toward Cushing; the security guard, eyes wide, kept pace with Gamble. I stepped aside and let them pass.

"General Cushing, you are under arrest. Get on your knees."

Leaving Cushing to Gamble, I sprinted back to the building: Now came the tricky part. An untried, unpredictable move. But first, I needed a reset point.

"How much time, Nano? How much time has passed since we responded to Cushing's attack?"

Seven point five minutes, Gemma Keyes.

"Mark that time, Nano."

Seven and a half minutes? Was that all? It seemed like an hour and yet it felt like the blink of an eye. I'd heard of the fog of war; perhaps that is what I was experiencing.

"Gamble. Gather everyone into the lobby. Quickly.

With Cushing in tow, Gamble shouted, "Back into the lobby! Now!"

The reporters who had run from the scene raced back. Their excitement, in its uncompassionate, predatory frenzy, grated on me: All they wanted was the big story.

Sorry. Not gonna happen.

"Nano. Is everyone who witnessed this event, other than Cushing's soldiers, inside the building?"

Yes, Gemma Keyes.

I sent squadrons of mites into the soldiers who had fallen outside with orders for the nanomites to send them into a deeper sleep state and to repair what injuries they could.

Inside, I disbursed nanomites to the twenty or so reporters and their crews who milled about in the lobby and to the FBI media liaison and security guard. Within moments, they (and the FBI's courageous young security guard) sank to the floor, unconscious.

I had almost overlooked the lone reporter and the cameraman who had kept his camera "rolling" during the melee. The two of them crouched behind the security station reviewing their "take." I sent the nanomites. As quickly as the streams of mites reached them, they crumpled to the ground, sedated. Nanomites flooded the camera, deleting the video.

Last of all I pointed to Cushing. She sagged, and Gamble lowered her to the floor.

Soldiers and press lay like scattered cord wood on the lobby floor. Gamble and I were the only people in the lobby who were awake, and his eyes cut around the eerie scene, looking for me. With a wave of my hand, the mites uncovered me.

Gamble was breathing heavily. "What now, Gemma? Why did you do that, make them all unconscious?"

I picked my way over the prostrate bodies until I reached him. "Because I can't have them talking about or reporting on what they saw— or what I did. While they are unconscious, the nanomites will erase their memories—everything that happened from the moment Cushing stormed the building."

Gamble's expression screamed incredulity. "How can they do that?"

"Consider it nano brain surgery, the removal of any synapses created during the past ten or eleven minutes. At the same time, the nanomites will implant chemical suggestions in place of the removed memories. I expect these people to be confused when they wake up, a bit disoriented, and susceptible to suggestion. When they compare notes, they will begin to share and agree as to what happened—and with each agreement, the 'memory' will solidify."

I muttered, mostly to myself, "I just hope no one questions how they all remember the same details so exactly."

Streams of nanomites returned to me soon after, reporting the completion of their tasks. Gamble and I had, at best, seven or eight more minutes to tidy up the scene.

"Come on. We need to haul all the unconscious soldiers into the lobby and pile them in a group. When they come to, you and Deputy Dawg over there will have your hands full."

When Gamble just shook his head, I pushed him.

"Hurry. We only have a few minutes."

He and I dragged the outside soldiers (quite unceremoniously, I might add) through the lobby doors and sat them against a wall. A total of eighteen soldiers and one general sprawled against a wall when we finished.

"I wonder where agents Trujillo and Black are." Their absence bothered me. A lot.

We piled the soldiers' guns against the opposite wall. Gamble studied one of the "net guns" and grunted. "A Taurus *Sicherheitstechnik* NetGun."

"Snicker what?"

"*Sicherheitstechnik*. Safety technology. The German humane way of capture."

"Great. I'll thank Cushing for her humanity if she ever gets me with one of those."

The security guard struggled to sit up. He was the first I'd asked the nanomites to wake, but I expected him to be confused and somewhat upset to find himself on the floor.

"Listen, Gamble," I whispered. "That guard has a vague memory of helping you stand down this group of soldiers. You need to go give him a hand up and thank him for his support."

"What?"

"You and your little buddy there handled what could have been a bloody standoff. You talked Cushing down while Wallace got Dr. Bickel to safety. The guard helped you. Backed you up."

Gamble's brows shot toward the ceiling. "Is that what he will think? Really?"

"Yes, it will be, but like I said, it will be a *vague* memory, not fully formed. You talk it through with him, give him some details, and it will gel. Solidify. Same thing with the reporters and soldiers. Even Cushing will have a similar hazy remembrance. By the time everybody talks about it—no matter how implausible—they will swear on a stack of Bibles that what they 'remember' is exactly what happened."

"So, I just pretend that he remembers standing with me against Cushing, and he will agree with me?"

"I've seen you act. Insert a few particulars. Embellish the scene a little. Pretty soon, those will become his actual memories."

We heard banging on the doors leading from the stairwell.

I jutted my chin toward the noise. "That's probably Wallace and the reinforcements."

"Why are they pounding?"

"I locked them out. I didn't want them seeing us in action. By the way, how many staff do you think are in the building right now?"

Gamble ran a distracted hand through his close-cropped hair. "The administrative and support staff leave around 4:30. Maybe five agents?"

"Okay. Go talk to the guard. I'll give you two minutes more before I unlock the doors."

I approached the stairwell and sent a stream of nanomites through to knock out Wallace and the other agents and edit their memories.

"Keep them out for two minutes, Nano, but unseal the doors now."

While those mites were working, the other nanomites and I went off to edit (and significantly redact) the media's "take" from the press conference. Using the moment we acted against Cushing's soldiers as a timestamp, the nanomites deleted every scrap of video, recording, photo, or text created after that moment. They left no electronic device untouched.

I hate to wax repetitive, but the digital world is awesome.

***

I called Zander later in the evening and filled him in on Dr. Bickel's press conference, Cushing's attack, how we'd defeated her storm troopers, and how the nanomites had rearranged what happened in the memories of all present. After Zander had heard the uncensored version, he was disappointed that he hadn't been able to witness it in person.

"What I would have given to see Cushing handcuffed and led away! How did she react?"

"The nanomites half-drugged her, so she was docile, actually. Passive. Kept blinking like she wasn't quite awake or aware of what was happening." Smiling to myself, I wondered just how "passive" Cushing would be when the massive dose of neurotransmitters the nanomites had triggered wore off.

"Still, I would love to have been there."

"Well, just watch the late news. The video should be entertaining. And while you're watching the reporters, remember how the nanomites erased all remembrance of us taking out Cushing's men and replaced their memories with Gamble and that security guard standing Cushing down." I snickered and Zander joined me.

I watched the ten o'clock news that evening from the comfort and familiarity of the safe house's basement room—and I pondered how strange human nature is. Sure, the segments were exciting. The reporters covered Dr. Bickel's return from the dead (and, more importantly, Cushing's arrest) with great enthusiasm. I even watched the online video snippet of Cushing being hauled off in handcuffs six times (and visualized Zander doing the same) before I could stop grinning.

What I mean about human nature being strange is that I could only imagine the crazy aftermath in the television newsrooms as the reporters and their crews returned and relayed the "reconstituted" events of the press briefing. Sure, we'd wiped their memories, but we couldn't control for every variance or outlier in the timeline.

Perhaps some of the conversations went like this:

"The first time you called the newsroom, you said you were under attack."

"We were! Those soldiers who burst through the doors had guns at the ready, just like a terrorist attack. At first, we thought they were terrorists. Got it all on camera, too."

"Right. Good work, by the way. But I'm somewhat confused. The next time you called, you were outside, running around the parking lot, babbling like a crazy person about some electric light show—bolts of lightning knocking soldiers down, throwing them around. Flying balls of fire. Exploding windows."

"What are you talking about?"

"Whadda you mean, what am I talking about?"

"I never ran around the parking lot. We stayed in the lobby while the FBI SAC hustled Dr. Bickel upstairs and two FBI guys—an agent and security guard—faced down a dozen and a half soldiers all on their own. You're just upset that we somehow missed the FBI actually taking them down."

"Wait. *You never ran*—listen, you clown. You called. I *heard* you running over the phone. Sounded like you were gonna have a heart attack, you were breathing so hard. You told me you were in the parking lot, then you said you were crouching beside the news van. It was obvious that you were terrified."

"Are you nuts? We never left the lobby!"

"And I say you told me you were *outside*, running from the terrorists and from blasts of lightning. Bolts of electricity and orbs of fire flying through the air. That's what you said."

"Look, boss, I don't know what you've been smoking—and, hey, I'm not judging here—but everyone on the crew will tell you the same thing: We never left the FBI building. As for thunder and lightning? Check the weather report. Clear as a bell."

I laughed as I browsed the online news items. Detailed, descriptive, lively, vivid—and uniform. Certainly, *too* uniform, if uniformity was what you were looking for. As the nanomites had awakened the reporters, Agent Gamble had praised their calm behavior in the midst of bedlam and had repeated his off-the-cuff rendition of his and the security guard's heroic stand against Cushing. All without firing a shot. According to him, the shattered lobby windows and the extensive damage to the lobby itself had been caused by the second wave of attackers when they breached the building.

Gamble had done a truly amazing job of adding bits of random factoids and tossing out colorful imagery as he and the other FBI agents debriefed the reporters and processed the soldiers.

Of course, those same details ended up in most of the reports.

So far, no one had noticed or commented on the missing twenty-three minutes between the start of Cushing's attack and its resolution. Although the period of actual "action" had been much shorter, it had taken Gamble and me many feverish minutes of moving and staging bodies before I gave the nanomites orders to wake everyone up.

As for Gamble and the security guard? I'd be surprised if they didn't receive commendations. By the way, the nanomites made sure Wallace and the few agents in the building did not recall coming to our assistance only to find the elevator unresponsive and the doors to the stairwells locked.

Yup. Nice and tidy.

⌘⌘⌘⌘

CHAPTER 6

She strode from the passenger boarding bridge into the Albuquerque Sunport, her heels making quick, indignant clicks on the tile floor. Today marked her third flight into this hick airport in less than six weeks, and Genie Keyes was one ticked-off woman.

As she threaded her way through the crowd, she blinked against the strong sunlight that poured through the airport windows. The flight attendant had announced that Albuquerque weather was a sunny, sixty-two degrees with a mild breeze—a far cry from the near-whiteout conditions at Reagan National this morning.

Genie slowed, paused, and gazed out the windows toward the Sandia Mountains—in particular, Sandia Crest. Bernalillo County might be enjoying a spate of balmy weather, but the Crest, rising five thousand feet above Albuquerque to crown the city's eastern boundary, was rimed with fresh snow. Its frosty white ridgeline was blinding in its radiance.

It was, she admitted, actually quite a beautiful sight—as long as the snow was "up there" and not down in the Rio Grande Valley.

"At least I won't be freezing my tail off this winter like I was back east," she muttered—like that would in any way resolve or even lessen the dire straits she found herself in.

She located her flight's baggage carousel and waited for the airline to offload its cargo. When her suitcases rolled onto the conveyer belt, she collected them, rolled them outside to the curb, and waved down a cab.

Her first order of business was a place to stay. She preferred an upscale hotel until she had time to shop around and select a satisfactory apartment. Unfortunately, she'd maxed out the third of her four credit cards when she'd put her belongings in storage and bought her airline ticket. With a grudging shrug of her shoulders, Genie acknowledged that the minimum monthly payments on the three cards would total more than the rent on her last apartment.

Her fourth credit card? She'd held back on using the high-interest plastic, saving it for the direst of emergencies. Did her present circumstances constitute such an emergency? Should she charge upwards of $300 a day for hotel and meals, adding to the already untenable payments?

No.

She'd run the numbers multiple times over the past several days while packing up her belongings. Each time, regardless of the scenario she employed, she'd arrived at the same conclusion: She was as good as broke. One or two months without a paycheck and she would default on her bills.

Despite her usual inclination to indulge herself, Genie was a realist. Even if an Albuquerque or Santa Fe law firm extended her a job offer and she began working within the next two weeks, her first paychecks would not arrive fast enough to balance first and last month's rent on an apartment *and* payments on her credit card debt—and as an attorney seeking employment, she could not afford any black marks on her credit report.

Another realization hit her. *I will need a car.* She hadn't needed a car to commute to work in the D.C. Metro area. She blew out a frustrated breath and shook her head: Another unforeseen expense.

The cab driver interrupted Genie's thoughts. "Where to, miss?"

Genie lifted her chin and gave the driver Gemma's address. As the cab pulled away from the curb, Genie fingered her key ring and the single key hanging from it—the key to her sister's house. When Genie had visited Albuquerque in early November—in response to Mrs. Calderón's paranoid phone calls—Genie had retrieved Gemma's spare key from under a flower pot on the side of the house and used it to enter her sister's house to snoop around.

Then Gemma's nosy friend had confronted Genie and threatened to have her arrested for trespassing! Of all the nerve . . .

Genie's eyes narrowed. The young man's unyielding attitude had surprised and unnerved Genie—as had his immunity to Genie's flirtatious wiles. Instead of pressing the argument, Genie had stalked to her rental car and driven away—with the house key in her pocket.

Yes, the handsome man's intensity had momentarily stunned her. Something in his eyes. Or perhaps it was the shock of him saying he was Gemma's *pastor.*

Pastor? Genie mouthed the word and sneered. *Ah, Gemma. I always knew you were a weak, emotionally needy brat.*

Zander Cruz. *Pastor* Zander Cruz. His name reminded Genie of her latest visit to Albuquerque.

Was I really here less than two weeks ago? And now I'm jobless and stuck in this town?

Genie inhaled a long, deep breath to calm herself, but the resentful thoughts refused to be pacified. First Cushing had tried to recruit Genie to return to Albuquerque and assist Cushing in her search for Gemma; when Genie refused Cushing's "invitation," the woman had threatened and manipulated the senior partners of Genie's law firm—and the partners, to placate Cushing, had forced Genie to assist Cushing.

In turn, *that woman* had used Genie in an absurd scheme—an attempt to entrap some FBI agent. When Cushing's ridiculous plan had miscarried, she had tossed Genie away like so much trash.

Not content with dismissing Genie without ceremony, Cushing had arranged for Genie to lose her job. The senior partners of her law firm had added to her punishment by blacklisting her everywhere but in New Mexico.

Genie Keyes did not appreciate being made a scapegoat. She rarely suffered an insult without repayment in kind—or better.

Payback. Yes.

Genie itched to repay Cushing, which is why, before she'd left Albuquerque two weeks past, she'd lowered herself to visit *Pastor* Zander Cruz in his dingy church office. She'd gone to Cruz with the intention of picking his brain and had even suggested that they shared a common enemy and could be of help to each other.

The exchange had not gone well.

Genie was still smarting from Cruz's dressing down. Or were his so-called "spiritual insights" what bothered her so much?

She shook off the disquieting memory of their meeting.

As the cab neared the house where Gemma and Genie had grown up with their aunt, Genie's stomach roiled. She knew that the side doorway between the house and garage had been boarded up: The SWAT team that had raided the place looking for her sister had destroyed the two doors. Genie's plan rode on whether the front doors were intact, the locks unchanged.

"Pull into the driveway, please."

The cabbie eased into the driveway, and Genie studied the front entrance. The security door and wooden door behind the heavy metal mesh seemed undamaged, unchanged.

Genie took another deep breath. "Wait for me while I open the door." She squelched her nerves, got out, and walked up the porch steps. She slipped the key into the first deadbolt. The key turned with ease, and Genie's mouth tightened into a small smile.

She waved to the driver to bring her bags before she entered the house.

***

On the other side of the cul-de-sac, Abe Pickering bit off a groan as he eased himself down to the floor, onto his knees. He leaned his elbows on the bed and sighed. "Don't mind me, Lord. I'm fine once I get down here. The 'getting down here' part is a little rough, but I don't mind none. I just want to spend some time with you and bring you my heart. Again."

As had been his three- and often four-times-daily practice since the police had informed him of Emilio's kidnapping, Abe bowed his head. He sighed and rubbed his hand across his skull, his fingers massaging what had been a wide gash and, under the gash, a cracked skull. The hospital had shaved his head down to the scalp and stitched the split skin together. Now that the swelling had subsided some, the healing wound itched like the dickens. His hair was coming back in, too, a coarse, white stubble that pricked and tickled his scalp.

He yanked his attention back to Emilio, and his heart thudded.

"You know I didn't ask for that boy, Lord. Thought Gemma was crazy, askin' me to keep and foster him! Still, you saw fit to give that child to me. Like you did with the Good Samaritan, you put that boy right in my path for me to tend to.

"You don't make mistakes, so I guess you knew I needed Emilio as much as he needed me. Anyways, I learned to care about that boy, Lord. I care about him a lot!"

Abe licked his lips. The police had called earlier in the day with additional information—and it was not good news. Abe's natural, human tendency was to blurt out something along the lines of, "If you were gonna take that child from me, why did you give him to me in the first place?" but he knew better than to blame God for the actions of a depraved sinner.

"Lord God, you are greater than any heartless, drug-dealin' criminal like this Soto fellow. You are greater than any gang, greater than any devil or demon. I call on you, Almighty God, to rescue my Emilio from this evil man's grasp. I'm asking in the name of Jesus that you come to Emilio's rescue and deliver him back to me, safe and sound, so's I can raise him right, Lord.

"I've never raised a child before, Father, but I'm willin' to try, willin' to do my best with him. When you bring him home to me, I will love that boy and give you all the glory. Amen."

Getting up from his knees was harder than getting down. His arms, ribs, and chest were still tender from the beating Emilio's uncle and two of his crew had laid on Abe and DCC's young associate pastor, Zander Cruz.

Abe leaned his arms on the bed, got one foot under him, and levered himself up until he could drag his other foot onto the floor and push himself to standing. He was panting when he stood upright, a little wobbly, but relieved.

"Thank you, Jesus! You are my Strength, Lord, even when I'm as weak as a baby."

He steadied himself, shuffled out to the kitchen, and poured himself a mug of coffee. Before he picked up the mug, he slipped his snub-nosed revolver into the pocket of his sweater. It was a longstanding habit, one he would not give up any time soon. Then he unlocked the door and shuffled to the swing on his front porch.

Abe lowered himself into the seat and set the swing moving at a slow, sedate pace. While he took his first sip of coffee, he scanned the neighborhood around the cul-de-sac as he always did, starting with Emilio's uncle's house on his left. According to what Arnaldo Soto had told Gemma, Mateo wouldn't be coming back: Soto had confessed to burying Mateo's body somewhere on Albuquerque's west mesa. Gemma had passed the word on to Abe through Zander about a week ago.

Gemma. Just about the whole state was looking for her. Oh, the news hadn't specified who exactly was being hunted—or why—but since that General Cushing woman was running the show, Abe knew it had to be Gemma.

"Lord, I'm reminding you about my girl, too. Please keep her safe? Thank you."

On several levels, Abe was grateful for the news about Mateo. He whispered, mostly to himself, partly in prayer. "I'm too old to take a beatin' like that again. In fact, if Gemma's nano-thingies hadn't helped me out, I might, right now, be havin' closer communion with you, Lord, than I'd planned."

Abe nodded at Mateo's house, its windows dark as the afternoon wore on toward twilight. "Glad that boy doesn't need to worry none about his gang-banger uncle, either. Mateo can't hurt Emilio ever again."

He sipped from his mug, his thoughts returning to Emilio. "Now that I've been approved as a foster parent, Lord, I can give that boy the stability he's never had. I'm grateful for the opportunity—long as I don't up and die any time soon, Lord."

He gave the swing another push with his toe. "Not that you need a reminder, Father," he added.

Abe turned his watchful gaze from Mateo's house onto the next one over, noting with pleasure how the Flores' shrubs, trees, and eaves were twined with Christmas lights. As the twilight deepened, the lights shone like brilliant stars.

Abe blinked. "Well! Gonna have me a boy for Christmas? Never had a child at Christmas—just might be fun! Guess I'd better get a move on and get my lights and tree up soon, hey, Lord? Got to be ready when you bring that boy home to me."

Abe was pondering what Emilio might like to find under the Christmas tree as he gave the Flores' yard a last look and shifted his eyes toward Gemma's home. Like Mateo's house, Gemma's place would be abandoned, cold and dark, the side door boarded up, and—

Abe jerked upright. Gemma's place was lit up, every window glowing.

"God bless America!"

He dropped his mug on the porch railing and stumbled down the steps. On his way across the cul-de-sac, he touched his pocket several times to ensure that the revolver was within easy reach. By the time he reached Gemma's front door, he was breathless; his heart pounded against his tender, aching ribs.

He rang the bell and stood to the side of the door. Just in case. Abe didn't know what "just in case" might be, but after the events of the last few weeks, he was taking no chances.

"Who is it?"

The voice was similar to Gemma's but strident. Higher pitched.

"It's Abe Pickering, Genie."

She didn't answer, but after he had waited fifteen or twenty seconds, she opened the inside door.

"Yes?"

"Surprised to see you here, Miss Genie."

"I'm house sitting for Gemma. Until she comes home."

"Are you, now? House sitting? Hmm. And does Gemma know you're 'house sitting' for her?"

Genie was prepared for any objections her presence might produce. "Why do you ask, Mr. Pickering? I understand Homeland Security is looking for her. Have you seen her? Been in contact with her? Should I call General Cushing and let her know that you've heard from Gemma?"

Abe stared through the security door's metal mesh. Genie stared back, daring him to object to her presence in Gemma's house. She had him over a barrel and knew it.

"I was just surprised to see lights on, is all, and you bein' here just a couple weeks back."

"Oh. Well, as it turns out, I've, um, relocated to Albuquerque. I'll be house sitting for Gemma for the foreseeable future or until . . . she returns."

The way she said it, said "until she returns"—like she knew Gemma was never coming back—bristled the hair on the back of Abe's neck. Bristled his temper, too. He had to talk himself out of the few choice words that sprang to his lips.

Lord, you better help me here. I don't want to say something I'll regret.

After a moment, he swallowed and tried to smile, the effort akin to cracking a cement slab. "Well, I'm sure Gemma would be glad to hear you are taking care of the place, Miss Genie."

He paused, then added, "If you need anything, let me know. Been fixin' little things over here for nigh on thirty years now, first for Lucy, then for Gemma. The furnace . . ." he took a breath, "the furnace can be contrary now and again, so you let me know if it gives you any problems, hear?"

Genie, backlit by the lamp in the living room, studied him. "All right." She seemed ready to close the door but hesitated. "I may do that. Thank you."

The "I may do that" seemed forced to Abe's ears, but no more odd than Genie thanking him. "Well, then. Good night, Miss Genie."

He turned and hobbled down the steps, and Genie closed the door behind him without another word.

He whispered as he crossed the cul-de-sac, "Lord? Whatever that girl is doing, it can't be good. House sitting? My left foot!"

He was still puzzling over the unexpected turn of events when he reached his own porch. "And she almost accepted my offer of help. Not like our Genie, Lord. Not at all."

He slowly climbed his porch, retrieved his coffee mug, and headed inside, a bit worried, his mind in a muddle. "Gemma won't like that Genie is in her house, Lord, but don't know what she can do about it—'specially as she's in hiding. But why, *why* would Genie want to stay over there? Not nearly as highfalutin' as she likes her digs. Surprised she'd even want to sleep there."

As he closed the door, Abe stopped, an inkling of a possibility coming to him. "And why would she 'relocate' here, anyway? She dislikes New Mexico, so why move here? Unless. Unless she had to, unless she was forced to."

He frowned. "Did that girl lose her job? Is she in financial straits?" Nodding his head, he answered himself. "Yep. Dollars t' donuts, I've hit on it. Only thing that explains why she would show up and take over Gemma's house. If she's flat busted, she's gotta have a roof over her head, and Gemma's place bein' empty is mighty convenient."

Abe knew whom he needed to tell—and right away. He reached his phone and dialed Zander's number. Zander had a way to reach Gemma. He could tell her. Warn her.

The phone rang and rang and went to voice mail. Again. Abe hung up without leaving a message. He'd already left several.

"Been doin' that for days now. Where are you, Pastor?" Abe didn't want to admit it, but his concern was growing, and he felt a little faint. "Emilio's been gone since Monday and, far as I know, neither Zander nor Gemma know 'bout it."

Holding the wall for balance, Abe made his way back to his bedroom. He leaned on his bed, but conceded that if he made it down to his knees, he might not make it back up. Instead, he sat on the bed's edge, and the comfortable, well-worn mattress embraced him.

He settled into the cushioned seat and bowed his head. "Lord, you know everything. You know everything 'cause you made everything. You know all the stars, all the planets, all the moons—and you know all this earth. You know every sparrow and you count every hair on our heads. Mind you, I ain't got as many hairs as I used to and some are mighty short, but m' point being', *you know*, Lord. You see, you hear, you know.

"You know where my boy Emilio is. You know where Zander is. You know where Gemma is. I need t' talk to Zander, Lord, if for no other reason than to ease my mind. Please have him call me, Lord? And I thank you."

Abe's stomach growled. He glanced at a clock and was surprised to see that it was past seven o'clock. "Well, hey there, Lord. Guess I lost track of the time." He felt better for having prayed again, and hobbled toward the kitchen. He opened the refrigerator and viewed his options.

"Got everything here for that spaghetti dinner I promised Emilio. Said I'd fix it t' celebrate when he came home to me." He stared at the vegetables in the crisper and the hamburger thawing in the meat drawer. The vision of a plate of pasta covered in good, meaty sauce made his mouth water.

But he shook his head. "No. No, sir." He closed the fridge and opened a cupboard, taking down a tall can of clam chowder. He snagged the ring on the lid and pulled up. Dumped the contents into a bowl. A moment later he was watching the bowl revolve on the microwave's turntable. "I might be actin' foolish, Lord, but I refuse to make spaghetti again until my boy comes home."

⌘⌘⌘⌘

CHAPTER 7

Across town, hours later, Zander got up from his knees. He'd spent the afternoon and evening in prayer for Gemma, Gamble, and Dr. Bickel. After Gemma had called him from Dr. Bickel's safe house to report their success, Zander had gone right back to his knees, giving thanks for Dr. Bickel's safe harbor at the FBI offices and for Gemma and Gamble's victory over Cushing's bald-faced attempt to snatch Dr. Bickel out of the FBI's care. He also offered thanks for—God willing—a return to some semblance of normalcy soon.

He glanced at the burner phone resting on the arm of his chair and sighed. "Lord, will there ever be a 'normal' for Gemma? For us? She seems so convinced that there can't be, but I'm not ready to throw in the towel—not by a long shot."

Gemma had declared that the nanomites' changes to her body meant she was no longer (not technically) *human.* She'd said, "It means we can't be together, Zander."

"But that can't be true, Lord! Gemma has a *soul*. No matter what the nanomites have done to her, you love her, and you reached down and saved her. And she said that you told her not to be afraid of what the nanomites would do. You even told her that you had plans for her—so I refuse to give up on her or on us."

Zander bowed his head and prayed for Gemma and for himself. "Father God, as unfeasible as this situation may appear, your word tells us that you are the God of the Impossible: *Nothing is too difficult for you.* I believe you brought Gemma into my life, that you brought us together for your purposes. And, Lord, because I believe that you approve of our love, I will also trust you to make a way for us. So, I will wait—with hope and confidence—for you to reveal your will to both of us. Amen."

He touched—for what felt like the hundredth time—the phone Gemma had given him, his only link to the woman he loved. He knew he needed to power the phone off and return it to its hiding place, the underside of his chest of drawers. As Gemma had reminded him, simply delivering Cushing into FBI custody was not the end. No; someone higher than Cushing, an individual or individuals not yet known to them, was still out there, still seeking the nanomites—and that meant they were hunting Gemma.

Unceasing vigilance was necessary.

The sight of the burner phone made Zander remember his own cell phone. He'd intentionally left it behind when he'd driven south with Gamble the last hours of Sunday night. He'd left it someplace in his duplex and hadn't thought about it since he'd returned home this afternoon.

"Let's see . . . It's gotta be around here somewhere." He scanned the living room and pawed through some books. "Maybe the bedroom?"

He found it on his nightstand—where he'd left it after Gamble had called and awakened him late Sunday night. When the phone buzzed, Zander had grabbed it from the charger, engaged in a semi-frantic conversation with Gamble, and dropped it back on the nightstand—and he had forgotten to plug it back in before he tore from his house to meet Gamble.

Zander pressed the home button.

Nothing.

"Great. Dead battery." He inserted the cable, set the phone down to charge, and set about tidying up the bed he'd left in such a hurry after receiving Gamble's late-night call.

He finished and turned to leave the bedroom when a series of texts and voice mails pinged their arrival. He picked up the phone and scanned the list. Three texts from Izzie. Two voice mail messages from the church office—most likely Mrs. Coyne, the church secretary. Another three from his boss, Senior Pastor McFee.

Lord, I'm pretty sure that I'm in trouble at work. I ask you right now to help me. You know that what I was doing was important—but I can't tell Pastor McFee that I was out saving Gemma—oh, by the way, the subject of a massive manhunt—and helping Dr. Bickel escape from the government. (Yes, he's supposed to be dead.)

Father, please grant me a measure of grace and wisdom in this situation?

He skipped their messages to review the remaining texts and VMs.

Wait. Abe had called a bunch of times? Zander counted. Five voice mails from Abe. Since Tuesday morning.

He tapped the first message and listened to Abe's heavy, agitated breathing before the man managed to speak. "Pastor Zander? I need t' talk to you right now. The police came by this morning. They say somebody stopped Emilio on his way home from school yesterday and took him!"

Horrified, Zander listened to the end of the message.

"The police say it's kidnapping, for sure. Pastor Zander, call me soon as you get this. Somebody took my boy!" Abe's labored breathing hung on the line a few minutes, and Zander realized that Abe was weeping, holding the phone to his chest to muffle the sound.

Before Abe disconnected, he managed to add, "Please call me right away."

Emilio! Zander's blood ran cold.

65

With growing dismay, Zander listened to Abe's other messages, all similar. On the last call, Abe seemed calmer, more collected, and he added further detail.

"Zander, the police say that Emilio's little friend, Sean—the other boy who lives in the same foster home—was able to give them more information. Guess the boys were walking home from the bus stop and the man in the car lured Sean to the door and then grabbed him by the collar. Wouldn't let him go until Emilio changed places with him. *That man wanted Emilio, not Sean.* And now the police are saying they are certain the man was that gangster, Arnaldo Soto!"

The calm deserted Abe. "Where are you, Pastor Zander? No one in the church office knows where you are, either. I'm worried 'bout you, son, and they are plenty worried, too, but I'm more worried 'bout Emilio. Please call me!"

Were the police right? Had Soto taken Emilio? Gamble had given Gemma the bad news about Soto while they were in the cavern: The gangster had escaped from the FBI with the help of four officers in the APD gang unit who were believed to be on Soto's payroll. But how would Soto know of Gemma's attachment to Emilio?

Zander checked his call log and saw that Abe had called again earlier in the evening. He hadn't left a message.

It was now an hour till midnight, and Zander knew Abe would ordinarily be in bed asleep, but Abe deserved to know why Zander had been MIA and to know that Gemma was all right. He also deserved Zander's comfort and support.

Zander sat on the bed and dialed. The line on the other end rang four times before Abe picked up.

"H'llo?" Abe's voice was slow with sleep.

"Abe, it's Zander. I'm sorry to call so late and wake you up, but I wanted you to know that Gemma is all right. She's safe, and I'm okay, too."

"Pastor Zander!" Abe was alert now. "Where have you been? I've been calling and calling—"

"I know. I'm sorry. I just now got your messages."

"But where have you been? Even Pastor McFee didn't know where you were."

"It's a long story and one you need to hear, but I am more concerned at the moment about Emilio. Are the police certain that Soto took him?"

Abe sighed. "That little boy, Sean? Although the man who took Emilio wore a baseball hat and sunglasses, Sean described him as dark with a Hispanic accent. And he said that one of the man's arms was wrapped in bandages—and the police said Soto's hand was broken."

"Too much of a coincidence, then."

Abe's voice softened to a whisper. "Seems that way."

"Soto wants Gemma. He wants payback. That's why he took Emilio."

"'Spect so."

"I'll pass this on to Gemma first thing in the morning. And I'll come by, catch you up on everything. There's a lot to tell you."

"Got something more to tell you, too, Pastor."

"Yes?"

"Saw lights in Gemma's house t'night."

"What?"

"Went straight over to see who was in there." Abe cleared his throat. "Ain't no way to sugarcoat this, Pastor. Genie has moved into Gemma's house."

"*Genie?*" Zander felt himself growing angry. "Genie has no right to be in that house! Their aunt left it to Gemma."

"I've been thinking on it, but I don't know exactly what we could do about it. Genie says she's 'relocated' to Albuquerque and is gonna 'housesit' until Gemma comes back. Practically dared me to contradict her."

Abe huffed. "You know what I think? I think Genie mighta lost her high-paying job in D.C., Pastor. I think she's broke and didn't have anywhere else to go 'cept here. That's what I think."

Zander was quiet for a while, processing the strange turn of events. When he spoke, he'd gotten his anger under control. "I suppose Genie can't hurt Gemma just by staying in her house. There's nothing there that can point to what's happened to Gemma or where she is at present. It's more . . . it's more the affront of it, I guess. It's just *wrong*. Offensive."

"We gotta be careful there, Pastor; that's just what the enemy wants. Get us riled up at Genie and distracted from the real war. Offense is the devil's snare, for sure."

Zander chuckled. "It is, indeed. Thanks for the reminder. Say, tomorrow is going to be a difficult day. I have a lot to explain to Pastor McFee, and I don't know yet what I will tell him. How about I come over to your place first? I can be there early and catch you up on everything since Sunday night. At least I have some good news for you."

"I could use some good news. How about I fix us breakfast, Pastor?"

"I accept!" Zander laughed, then stopped mid-chuckle. "Don't know how I'm going to break this to Gemma. About Emilio."

"I've been praying already."

"Thank you. I'm sorry you've had to shoulder this burden alone since it happened."

"It's gonna be all right, now I know you and Gemma are safe. God will answer. I know he will."

"Amen to that. I'll see you tomorrow, then, Abe."

Zander hung up and fell to his knees. "Lord, I can't bear to grieve Gemma's heart with this news. And Abe is right. The enemy would like nothing better than to wound Gemma, anger her, and cause her to seek vengeance on Soto. I pray, Lord, that you prepare her heart and give me wisdom as I speak to her."

He remained where he was, praying for Gemma and Emilio, until he felt a measure of peace steal over him. Then he went out into the living room and used the burner phone to call Gemma.

They had, since establishing this secret means of communication, always texted a call time in advance. His calling her directly would signal the seriousness of his call.

The phone rang and rang before it went to voice mail. Zander hesitated, then spoke. "Call me ASAP." He hung up and waited.

***

After watching the ten o'clock news, I headed upstairs to the kitchen. Boy, was I hungry. Famished!

I quick-thawed two thick steaks in the microwave, seasoned them, and set them to broil in the oven. While they were sizzling away, I popped three potatoes into the microwave and put together a tossed salad from the last of my greens.

The fridge was looking a little bare; my stomach grumbled its empty state, too.

As I prepared my meal, my mind revisited the events from the afternoon and evening. The nanomites and I had analyzed the news coverage against what we had intended to be reported; we looked for any details in the accounts that might prove problematic or that in any way pointed to the experiences we'd deleted from the memories of those present during Cushing's takedown.

When I sat down to eat, the mites and I reviewed the short battle after Cushing attempted to take Dr. Bickel from the FBI's lobby. I had more than my personal memories to evaluate: In addition to what my own eyes had seen, I was privy to the nanomites' actions and perspectives. With every bite of steak, I closed my eyes and reenacted the skirmish from their various vantage points, the mites providing a running commentary.

Before I finished eating, their memories were as much mine as theirs, and I could visualize the battle from multiple angles concurrently.

"Another nice trick," I murmured.

I was washing up when the nanomites interrupted to tell me the phone in the basement room was ringing. I say "ringing," but in reality, the ringer was off. With the ringer turned off, the phone's light came on, indicating an incoming call, but the phone made no noise.

Zander Cruz is calling, they told me.

"Of course. He's the only one with this number."

Odd that he would call out of the blue. I wiped the table and headed downstairs.

Gemma Keyes.

"Yes, Nano?"

We have many questions.

"About?"

Questions regarding the Jesus tribe and questions about Zander Cruz.

"Okaaaaay." On my way down the ladder, I had a brainstorm. "Say, what if we ask Zander to help answer your questions about Jesus? Zander knows Jesus better than I do and is something of an authority on the Jesus, er, tribe."

I mentally patted myself on the back: You're brilliant, Gemma Keyes. Brilliant.

Since he will be present, shall we at that time also ask our questions concerning him?

"Huh. Well, what did you need to ask about him?"

He said things to you that puzzled us. Your response was also puzzling.

Two steaks, a plate full of salad, three loaded baked potatoes, and half a quart of ice cream—something in the neighborhood of five thousand calories—were warming my tummy nicely, and I was feeling a comforting little drowse coming on. It had been a long, stressful, and physically active day, and I was ready for a few hours of peaceful sleep.

So, I wasn't really firing on all cylinders when I answered, "Um, what things?"

Shortly before we altered your molecular structure so that you could accommodate the entirety of the nanocloud, Zander Cruz said, "I love you, Gemma. I've been wanting to say that for a while."

"Nano!" I was outraged. If it weren't disturbing enough for them to repeat what should have been a very private moment, the nanomites actually repeated Zander's words in Zander's voice!

Creepy much?

You said we could ask you questions, Gemma Keyes. We have not yet asked those questions; however, we felt it expedient to place our inquiry within a context you would recognize. In response to Zander Cruz, you answered, "I know. Me, too. I love you back, Zander."

Ack! *My voice* coming from the nanomites!

"That's enough. I've changed my mind; you may *not* ask me any questions about Zander—especially in Zander's presence."

Growling, I grabbed up the phone and stared at it. Punched the screen to call back the last call received. Although it was nearing midnight, Zander answered on the first ring.

"Hello?"

I started to get a bad feeling.

"Zander. Is everything all right?"

"Uh, I need to talk to you. It's important. Can we meet somewhere? Maybe you could do that nano-disguise thing, and we could meet for coffee?"

I blinked. It hadn't quite solidified in my head that, with the entirety of the restored nanocloud living in me, I was no longer stuck on invisible. I could be invisible whenever I chose to be and visible the rest of the time; I could also "be" whomever I asked the nanomites to make me.

"Wow. Sorry—just realized. I can go out in public? Like to coffee? Okay, yes. Let's meet."

We picked a 24-hour diner and agreed to meet in fifteen minutes.

Before we hung up, I blurted. "Zander, this isn't about . . . you know, *us*, is it?"

He sighed. "No, it's not about us—but I'm also not letting you off the hook, Gemma. We will talk the 'us' thing through, just not tonight. Tonight, we have bigger problems."

That was über reassuring.

Not.

"You're scaring me, Zander."

He muttered, "See you shortly," and hung up.

I stood there, all the good of the day washed away by an unspecified, unknown dread.

Gemma Keyes.

"Yeah?"

What is this "us thing" for which you and Zander Cruz must remain on a hook? Which hook are you on? And does the "us" include the nanocloud and our six tribes? And—

Argh!

"Later, Nano! I need to meet Zander right now."

⌘⌘⌘⌘

CHAPTER 8

Zander was waiting for me when I arrived. I felt strange entering the restaurant fully visible after being unseen for two months. I had asked the nanomites to make me look like Kathy Sawyer—but about twenty years younger—and they had. Zander's watchful gaze passed right over me as he scanned the entrance.

I nodded to the hostess. "I'm meeting someone." I walked over and slid into the booth opposite Zander. Picked up the menu.

He stared. "Uh . . ."

"Relax. It's me."

"Honest?" He gaped and turned his head to the side as though a slantways view might convince him.

Well, even my voice was different, so I asked the nanomites to let me speak in my own voice.

We understood that a covert identity was prudent, Gemma Keyes.

"It is, Nano, but no one here will recognize my voice except Zander."

I tried again. "Yes, it's me." I was gratified (and Zander seemed relieved) to hear myself.

The waitress brought water and menus.

"Just coffee for us," Zander told her.

She was pulling the menu from my hands when the cover's full-color spread hit me: Pies. About fifteen varieties. Like, banana cream, loganberry, lemon meringue, death-by-chocolate, coconut custard, Dutch apple, deep-dish strawberry-rhubarb, and key lime.

I couldn't let go of the menu, and I tried not to drool on the table. "Ah, actually, I think I'd like a slice of pie with my coffee."

No, what I wanted was to sample every pie in the place—to infinity and beyond.

I glanced at Zander. "Um, you want pie, too, right?"

He shrugged. "Not really. I—"

"Uh, yes, he does. Yup, I'm certain he does. How about you leave the menus for a sec?"

"Sure. No problem. You'll find the list of pies on the back."

The waitress had no sooner turned her back than I whispered, "I would die for a slice of blueberry sour cream pie—but I want to try their pecan with a big scoop of vanilla ice cream, too. Please order a slice? I promise I can eat both of them."

Despite all the good the day had brought, Zander wasn't in a playful mood. He just looked at me. I'd never seen Zander sad. It shook me.

I slid the menus away. "What is it? Tell me."

"It's Emilio, Gemma."

"What?"

"On the way home from school Monday . . . someone took him. The police called Abe the next day and asked him a lot of questions."

I couldn't breathe. My worst nightmare had come to life. "Someone . . ."

"Gemma, it was Soto. The police are sure of it. It's why I insisted we meet tonight. I wanted to tell you to your face, not over the phone."

In the cavern, while I'd wrestled with the decision facing me, I'd recalled Soto's rant, the threats he'd spat at me as the FBI arrested and hauled him away. The dark premonition had terrified me. And, as I'd considered the nanomites' offer to save my life, Emilio's safety had been the deciding factor.

I'd given the nanomites permission to change me so I could keep that boy safe from Soto.

And I was too late.

Gemma Keyes. Something has disturbed you.

I couldn't respond. Couldn't move. My mind filled with just one word: "Emilio."

The nanomites heard my wounded cry, and they had been listening to Zander.

Zander Cruz says that the police have determined that our enemy, Arnaldo Soto, has taken Emilio? Will this evil man harm the boy? Is this why you are distraught?

"Yes. Yes!"

Then we will find him, Gemma Keyes. We will prevent Soto from harming Emilio.

Zander shook me. "Gemma! Gemma, snap out of it!"

"I . . . I have to find him."

"I know you do, and I believe that you will. But think: Why would Soto take the boy? Why Emilio? It's because of *you*, Gemma. Wherever Soto has taken Emilio, he will have laid a trap. For you."

"Yes. I get that."

"Well, then, I suggest we pray about this . . . situation. You and the nanomites are powerful, but God is more powerful. The nanomites have access to loads of information and knowledge, but they don't know everything, especially the future. On the other hand, God already sees the entire picture—he even understands Soto's heart and plans. We should pray for the Lord's guidance and wisdom."

I nodded. "Yes, you're right. I . . . I don't want to go off half-cocked or do something stupid that would endanger Emilio further. It . . . it's my fault, you know."

"What's your fault?"

"It's my fault that Soto took Emilio. Soto knows I care for Emilio, that he is my vulnerability . . . that I love him."

I groaned, seeing my sense of self-righteous outrage toward Soto in a much different light. "You see, I went to Soto's house before the FBI's raid just so that I could . . . I don't know, confront him? Question him? I asked him why he ordered Mateo to hurt you and Abe. Turns out it was all about getting Mateo to mess up so Soto could get rid of him."

Swallowing on a hard lump that refused to go down, I went on. "Of course, I was angry . . . and I guess I wanted to taunt Soto, make sure he knew that *I* was responsible for bringing the FBI down on him. Maybe so I could feel superior to him?"

I was certain that when I confessed my faults, Zander would look at me with accusation, that he would blame me for putting Emilio in danger. But Zander's expression, while serious, didn't change; all he said was, "Okay . . . How does all this connect to Emilio?"

I exhaled, trying not to sob. "Soto said he used Abe's CYFD complaint about Mateo's neglect of 'the boy' to goad Mateo. And I . . . I said, 'Emilio?' and Soto got this look on his face, like he could tell how I felt about Emilio."

I hung my head. "When Gamble's people were taking Soto out of the house, Soto screamed at me. Threatened me. I remember his exact words. He said, 'You think because I can't *see* you that I can't *find* you? Oh, *I will find you*—but first I'll find those you love.' I knew he was talking about Emilio."

Feeling worse than ever, I added, "I thought with Soto in FBI custody, I didn't need to worry about his threats."

"But then Gamble told you . . ."

"Yeah, then Gamble told me Soto had escaped." On a whimper I couldn't hold in any longer, I added, "And I-I see my motives differently now."

Zander touched my hand. "You mustn't think I'm judging you, Gemma. You belong to the Lord now and are answerable to him, not me. Yes, he holds us accountable, but he doesn't condemn. Instead, he corrects us by revealing the dark, hidden things in our hearts. That's what is happening. The Lord is showing you those hidden things so that you can confess them and be forgiven."

The waitress returned with our coffee and her order pad. "Did you decide on which pie you'd like to order?"

I couldn't look at her, so Zander shook his head. "We'll skip the pie after all."

With a shrug, she collected our menus and left.

As soon as she turned her back, Zander took my hand in his. "Gemma, the way forward goes like this: You confess your failings to the Lord and ask for forgiveness—not because you deserve to be forgiven and not because you will 'atone' or make up for your mistakes, but because Jesus has already paid for your sin on the cross."

"That's it? I just ask for forgiveness?" It didn't seem right to me. Didn't seem like enough.

"Not quite. There's also what the Bible calls 'repentance.' Repentance has two parts: It means that you are truly sorry for what you've done; it also means that you make a sincere decision to turn away from it. That's why it's important to verbalize what the sin is. First, you allow the Lord to reveal your failing, then you express your sorrow and make a decision of the heart to turn from it. Then you ask for forgiveness."

"But, shouldn't I make things right? Shouldn't I fix the mess I've made?"

"To the extent that you can, yes, you should; however, repairing the damage we cause follows *after* repentance and forgiveness. If we don't repent and allow Jesus to wash us clean *before* we rush off to fix the mess we've made? Well, we'll just make the same mistake again.

"What you expressed to me about confronting Soto . . . that sounds like retribution. You wanted to pay Soto back for what he'd had Mateo do to Abe. To me."

"Well, what he did was wrong!"

"Yup. It was. But we don't get to deliver our own form of justice. That's what the law and its punishments are for. Sure, the law isn't perfect; sometimes the system gets it wrong—but, wherever the law fails, God doesn't. No one ever 'gets away with it,' Gemma, because God is just and, in the end, everyone gets the justice they deserve. When we try to exact our own brand of 'justice,' we do a lousy job. On top of that, our hearts get messed up—which is precisely what you are struggling with at the moment.

"Our God is the God of hearts, Gemma; we need him to correct what is wrong on the inside before we address the problem we've created on the outside. Part of what he wants to correct inside you is your 'need' for retribution. He would like you to give that need to him."

"I guess so."

I wasn't crazy about the idea of God "correcting" me, and maybe it showed on my face, because Zander cracked a tiny smile.

"Nobody likes correction, Gemma. No one likes being told when they are wrong. We all fear it. But God says in the Bible that he is our Father, and all good fathers correct their children—for their own benefit as well as for God's purposes in our lives."

He squeezed my hand. "So, shall we pray, now?"

Reluctantly, I nodded.

"Okay, this is your part: Just like you've confessed to me, you confess to God our Father. Whatever he's revealed about your heart, you admit it before him, tell him you are sorry and that you turn from it. Then ask for forgiveness and help."

My mouth wouldn't move; my tongue was cemented to the roof of my mouth. I couldn't get a word out.

Zander seemed to understand. "This is between you and the Lord, so pretend I'm not here. You might start like this: 'Lord, you've shown me some things in my heart that aren't right. I see them now, and they are . . .' then you fill in the blank. Try that, Gemma."

With a deep breath, I dove in. "Lord . . . I see . . . some things now that I didn't see before. I-I see that I wanted to punish Soto for hurting Abe and Zander. And I guess that's wrong because it caused this awful situation with Emilio and it messed me up, too. I see that I can't make Soto pay, that I have to let you do it. Um, I'm sorry I tried to do your job, and I'm going to try really hard not to do that again."

I was surprised. It wasn't hard, once I'd begun. It was liberating. I glanced up at Zander.

He whispered, "Repentance isn't the ugly, hard, mean thing the world has said it is. Repentance is a gift from God, the first step in his setting us free. Repentance pulls down the strongholds in our lives. When repentance has its full sway, Jesus is able to free us from fear and condemnation."

Tears—unexpected and bewildering—dribbled down my cheeks, and a weird sense of sorrow filled my heart. I actually *was* sorry! The smoldering rage I'd held against Soto lit up like a beacon; the wrong in my heart became clear. Evident.

"I'm sorry, Lord, I really am!" I sobbed. I turned away from my self-righteous need to make Soto suffer, from the gratification I'd felt when I broke his hand; I turned my back on those feelings.

As a shudder ran through me, a hard place within me broke.

"Now you can ask for forgiveness, Gemma."

"Jesus, please forgive me. Please." Like hot water dissolving salt-crusted ice, the tension and shame of my mistake eroded away.

Then Zander took both my hands and prayed for both of us. "Lord Jesus, we come to you with humble and grateful hearts, thanking you for your grace that covers all our sins. Thank you for dying to make that grace and mercy available not once, but every time we need it. Thank you for making our hearts free."

When he finished praying, I was crying, and the peace Jesus had poured over me when I surrendered to him had grown. Gotten . . . bigger. Wider. Deeper. More precious. Nearly tangible.

We looked at each other, and I knew Zander felt it, too, because his eyes sparkled with wet tears of joy. And I'd never felt so connected. To anyone.

"What is this? This . . . tie we have?" I looked away, not wanting to open the can of worms that was our "love" relationship but needing to understand—because this feeling was, well, *different*. "I don't mean, um, romancy-schmancy, but the other thing."

Zander smiled. "It's what the Bible calls 'fellowship,' Gemma. It happens when Christ's fellow believers worship together, pray together, grow together. Fight spiritual battles together." The corner of his mouth tipped up. "Pretty powerful stuff, huh?"

"You have no idea! When Aunt Lucy talked about fellowship, I didn't know she meant *this*."

In that moment, Aunt Lu's voice in my head, all the memories of her from my childhood, felt like a treasure trove of good things, a wealth of spiritual knowledge, encouragement, and support that I could draw on. Because of my fledgling faith, I was finding value in my recollections of her.

"I brought you something, Gemma. A little gift."

"Oh?"

He lifted it from the booth's seat where it had been waiting: a book bound in dark-blue leather.

A Bible.

I took it in my hands and, for the first time, felt the need for what this volume contained.

"This is God's word, Gemma. Read it every day, and it will feed your soul; it will speak to your heart, correct you when you are wrong, and challenge you to come up higher. Study it, and you will not only learn who God is, he will also transform you into his image."

Transformation.

When Zander had first spoken to me about his faith, he'd said, "*The Good News is about change. About transformation—a transformation of the heart and soul. It's about letting God peel off the old, ugly, scarred man and letting him give you a new life, a life Jesus died to give you.*"

And, when I'd scoffed at him amid my perceptions of church, he'd answered, "*I dislike religion, Gemma. Religion does a lot of damage to people. It takes what should be the simplest, purest expression of God's love, something even a child can understand, and replaces it with some kind of formula—a complex and impossible set of rules and behaviors— when it is really about God's gift of grace and his power to transform us.*"

Zander wasn't finished. "Study in God's word is important to your growth as a Christian, Gemma. It is so important that if you don't make a habit of delving into it every day, you'll find that the living, breathing relationship you have with him at this moment—this connection with him that gives you such joy—has become stale. With Jesus, it's all or nothing."

"Aunt Lucy started every morning with coffee and her Bible. She never varied. I-I didn't get it."

But I was beginning to get it now. Jesus was nothing like I'd made him out to be. I took the Bible, caressed it with my hand, and nodded.

"Thank you, Zander. Really. Thank you."

"You're welcome. Let's pray once more, and ask the Lord to lead and guide you."

We joined hands across the table, and Zander prayed, "And now, Lord, we ask that you help Gemma find Emilio. We know that with you all things are possible, so we are asking that you direct her steps. And, Father God, please keep Emilio safe from harm. We ask these things in Jesus' mighty name. Amen."

Deep inside, in the place where Jesus lived in me, I added, *I don't want to mess up again, Lord. I don't want to make another mistake because of my ego—I don't want to ever again endanger those I love. Please show me what to do—and what not to do.*

***

I didn't waste any time when I returned to Dr. Bickel's safe house: Sleep could wait. At the same time, the understanding that God could and would help me stayed in the forefront of my thoughts.

Lord, I'm still very new to all this. Please lead me—lead us, the nanomites and me. Like Zander said, with you all things are possible. Thank you.

I got to work, and tried not to think about how many days Emilio had been missing.

"Nano. Let's jump into APD's network and download the case file for Emilio's kidnapping. We need every detail they've confirmed: The date, time, and place where Soto took Emilio. The description of the vehicle."

We delved into the police files and downloaded the data. Specifics for the car were spotty. Five-year-old Sean had been unable to provide a description other than "a big car," "black," and "windows you couldn't see through."

The street where Soto had taken Emilio ran deep within a residential area, and the police had found no video footage of the abduction. Notes in the file indicated that APD technicians had set a half-mile radius around the point of abduction and searched video from the nearest traffic cameras hoping to discover a vehicle that fit Sean's broad description.

Unfortunately, the nearest cameras were blocks from where the crime had taken place. So far, the police had found nothing helpful. I figured Soto had taken a winding, circuitous route through as many residential areas and back roads as he could to prevent his vehicle from being video recorded and identified.

"We can do better than that, Nano."

Yes, Gemma Keyes. We can.

We got busy.

Did you know? The earth's atmosphere is heavy with satellites. More than 4,000 satellites are presently in orbit; however, two-thirds of that number are inoperative, nothing more than "space junk"—dead, useless debris hurtling about the planet.

The remaining 1,419 operational satellites belong to civil, commercial, governmental, and military users. Of that number, only 374 are "earth observation and science" satellites—meaning 374 satellites have cameras focused on the earth. *Terra firma* is a great, big place for only 374 satellites to cover!

With APD's details in hand, we bored into the feeds of the satellites that had been overhead when Emilio was taken.

We combed through the take from those satellites, sifting for usable photos or video, scanning for the right overhead view. With the nanocloud's tremendous computing strength, our search took less time and effort than you might expect it to. Although the images we zeroed in on provided a brief and distant snapshot of the event, the nanomites enhanced, sharpened, and combined those images to produce a single composite photo of Soto's vehicle.

The photo was clear enough for us to search for and find its match in the footage of Albuquerque traffic and commercial security cameras. Inside a few hours from the start of our search, we spotted the black SUV three miles from where Emilio was taken.

"Gotcha," I whispered. I could breathe again.

"Nano, keep tracking that car. Get a license plate number as soon as possible."

I hoped APD planned to transfer the responsibility of the case to the FBI's Albuquerque field office; if the FBI took point on the investigation, it might be possible for Gamble to get involved—and Gamble's involvement would make it easier for me to disclose whatever I discovered.

I truly *was* contrite that my own need to confront Soto had placed Emilio in danger. This time, I intended to share my findings with the FBI, wherever they led, with no ulterior motives involved.

"No going into this on my own," I vowed. "No personal agenda or vendetta."

The past forty-eight hours had been long and exhausting, even for me. With mere minutes before day broke, I threw myself onto the cot in the basement and pulled a blanket up and over my shoulders. And slept.

⌘⌘⌘⌘

CHAPTER 9

As dawn broke, an executive jet belonging to an unnamed branch of the federal government sped toward Albuquerque. It touched down at 7:23 a.m. on a little-used Kirtland Air Force Base runway. Seven plainclothesmen deplaned and entered the two black SUVs waiting for them on the tarmac; two passenger vans, empty except for their drivers, also waited.

A mere seventeen minutes later, the line of vehicles drew up in front of the Albuquerque FBI field office. The drivers did not park in the designated lot far back from the entrance; they pulled their respective vehicles alongside the barriers and braked, leaving their engines idling.

Two of the men from the plane emerged and stationed themselves outside the vehicles. The other five men strode up the walkway to the FBI's front entrance. The man leading the way carried a thick briefcase and walked with a brisk, authoritative step.

The formation of stone-faced men glanced at workers sweeping up broken glass outside the building. The lobby windows and doors had shattered and spewed bits of thick safety glass everywhere. Although a worker was carefully knocking the last glass shards from the front doors, the five visitors did not pause. One of them nudged the worker aside and opened the door for the leader of the group.

The inside of the lobby could have been the aftermath of a terrorist attack. No part of it was unscathed: Every window had been broken, every piece of furniture, potted plant, and wall hanging damaged. The security turnstile hung crooked and useless.

The five men cut a swath through the debris and the workers who were piling it to the side.

Even the security guard's station was out of commission, although he stood his post nearby. He eyed the newcomers and produced his prepared greeting.

"Good morning, gentlemen. As you can see, the Albuquerque field office is closed for repairs today. Please return next Monday when we expect to be open again or call our general number to make an appointment if your business is of an urgent nature."

The lead visitor spoke as if he had not heard the guard. "Inform the senior agent on premises that we are here to take a prisoner into custody."

The guard studied them in silence, nodded, and placed the call. When SAC Terry Wallace picked up, the guard repeated carefully, "Sir, I have a delegation in the lobby asking to see the senior agent on premises."

"I see. Tell them I will join them shortly. Thank you."

Wallace logged into the building's camera system and viewed the five waiting men. Then he buzzed Gamble. "I think we've got trouble waiting downstairs."

"This about Bickel?"

"I would think so. Cushing, too, I expect."

"Well, that didn't take long. Look, sir, you saw what happened yesterday. If we let Bickel out of our custody, the world will never hear from him again."

"Noted. Meet me at the elevator."

Minutes later, the five visitors, their expressions impassive, watched Wallace and Gamble approach.

"Gentlemen, I'm Special Agent in Charge Terry Wallace. This is Special Agent Gamble. What can I do for you?"

Their leader offered no card or introduction. He did produce a sheaf of official-looking paperwork.

"Agent Wallace, I have here an order from the United States District Court for the District of Columbia. It requires you to immediately transfer into our custody General Imogene Cushing, the eighteen men in her company last evening, and one Daniel Bickel."

"By 'eighteen men,' you are referring to the armed soldiers who attacked this facility last night? We have declared their assault to be an act of domestic terrorism."

"I am hardly in a position to adjudicate what occurred here yesterday, Mr. Wallace; I am simply the messenger." He offered Wallace the stack of papers.

Wallace took the stack, glanced at a few pages, handed the paperwork to Gamble, and smiled with tight lips. "This is most unusual. I will, of course, need to have our counsel review the request."

"It is not a request. It is an order for immediate transfer; it states that you are to comply without delay."

"So you said." Wallace added nothing for a long moment. When he did speak, his words were measured. Polite but firm. "I comprehend the urgency of the order. Nevertheless, it will take a few hours to process General Cushing and the, er, others. However, I can tell you now that Daniel Bickel is not our prisoner."

"The order includes him."

"*I can read.* As I said, I will call in our counsel to examine the court's directive. Now, in view of our lobby's state of disrepair—" Wallace swept his hand to indicate the disorder, "—I suggest that you find a comfortable place to wait. Elsewhere. I will contact you when we've processed the prisoners, most likely by close of business today."

"Pastor Cruz? This is Pastor McFee."

"Yes, sir."

"Son, we've been very concerned about you. Are you all right?"

"Yes, sir, I am. Thank you."

"Then, where in the dickens have you been, and why have you not returned our calls and messages?" Now that he was assured of Zander's well-being, Pastor McFee's relief shifted to indignation.

"I apologize, sir. As you know, I was called out on a chaplain's run late Sunday evening. When the call came in, I was sound asleep; I awoke in a fog. The call was urgent and, in my haste and muddled mental state, I sent you a text—then set my cell phone down and left it behind."

"But you've been missing for days!"

A second call clicked in Zander's ear. He ignored it and let it go to voice mail.

"Yes, sir, I have. Again, I apologize. The situation became quite serious, and the LEO I was riding with requested that I remain with him as long as the issue was critical. I only returned home late yesterday afternoon. As you may deduce, I was pretty wiped out, and did not check my messages right away."

"And you couldn't have used someone else's phone to at least call in?"

"In hindsight, sir, I should have. Again, I apologize. It was thoughtless."

"What it was, Pastor Cruz, was irresponsible. We'll talk about this further in person. I expect you to be in the office shortly."

"Uh, about that, sir?"

"Yes?"

"While I was gone, a . . . family emergency came up. It cannot wait, so I need to tend to it before I come in. I'm not certain how long it will take. Of course, I'll take personal time for it."

The man on the other end exhaled a longsuffering sigh. "Very well, but I expect you to be in the office no later than tomorrow morning."

"I'll do my best, sir."

When Zander hung up, Abe lifted a quizzical brow. "You in trouble, Pastor Cruz?"

Zander stared with longing at his half-eaten burrito. "I have a lot to tell you, Abe. Then I need to talk to Genie. Figure out why she's here."

"Well, take your time. I've got makings for another burrito, so eat up. What you have to say can wait."

When Zander was full, he took his dishes to the kitchen while Abe poured him another cup of coffee. They sat at Abe's table and Zander rehearsed all that had happened since Gamble called him Sunday night.

The tale took an hour and left Abe slowly moving his head back and forth.

"This is near unbelievable. You're saying Gemma can . . . shoot electricity from her hands?"

"And more, Abe. Much more."

***

It was midmorning, but Genie had just gotten up for the day. She had laundered Gemma's sheets and blankets late the night before, but she hadn't slept well in her sister's bed. The sense that her perfectly ordered life was spiraling out of her control had been difficult to discount, to suppress.

Dark, discomfiting questions had plagued her well into the night before she fell asleep—as had the rebuke of a brash, impudent Hispanic man—a *blanking* pastor of all things. Yes, she'd invaded his office and his personal space, thinking to use and manipulate him, but it hadn't gone the way she'd planned. Not at all.

"*Spiritually, you are defeated, Genie. You are subject to the master of this world—to Satan himself. He controls you and this fallen world. You are just his puppet. Whatever he tells you to do, you do it.*

"*I do what I like, what I choose!*"

"*No, you do what you are told.*"

Later, he'd added, "*The devil owns you, Genie. He owns you lock, stock, and barrel. You think you don't submit to anyone? You say you are free? You are not. You're driven and compelled . . . bound over to commit evil—as he directs, not as you choose.*"

His statements, delivered with flat-footed, frank conviction, had struck an ominous chord in Genie's gut, a terrifying trifecta of implications. What he'd said had ripped skin from her inner eyes and—*for just an instant*—she'd caught a glimpse of . . . truth?

Genie shook her head. She refused to entertain the possibility that she had ever been deceived as he suggested, let alone in an ongoing manner. But last night? The rest of their "conversation" had flooded back into her mind, repeating itself *over* and *over*, dispelling any possibility of sleep. She'd remembered—no; she hadn't been able to *stop reliving*—the moment when he'd gotten up from behind his desk and, with infuriating gall, had "seen" her to the door.

Genie snarled in the back of her throat. *He treated me like an errant child.* That didn't stop the scene from playing on a continuous loop—the worst bit hammering her again and again.

"When you leave my office, I want you to see God differently than you do now—in fact, I want you to see yourself differently. The first step in coming to terms with God is acknowledging who and what we are. That's good news for you, Genie, because he isn't asking for your 'feelings.' Rather, he is asking that you acknowledge your brokenness."

Genie paged through local news on her cellphone while she drank her morning coffee. She was unaccustomed to brewing coffee with a drip coffee maker, and the result was worse than disappointing.

It was disgusting. Unacceptable.

She swallowed, made a face, and recalled her Gaggia Classic with longing. *Why didn't I ship my espresso maker?* The expensive machine, along with her other belongings, languished in a storage unit back in Virginia.

Forcing herself to take another sip, Genie laughed at what the hick New Mexico media services considered newsworthy. She skimmed an article about a dead scientist having been found alive and read with interest another report, this one concerning a thwarted assault on the local FBI office during a press conference with the same "dead" scientist. The man's name nagged at her. It seemed to ring a bell, but the attack on the FBI office was too entertaining and distracted her.

Who would dare try something so absurd in D.C.? No one in their right mind would attack the J. Edgar Hoover Building, Genie scoffed. The fortress-like, raw-concrete "brutalist" architecture of D.C.'s FBI headquarters was intimidating in itself; additional fortifications and security measures made the FBI office building an uninviting and unrewarding target for terrorists.

Only in Albuquerque, she sneered. *Middle of Nowhere, U.S.A.*

She put the cup to her lips and drank.

"Ugh! This is utterly gross." Genie slammed her coffee mug onto the table and drummed her fingers in frustration. "I need a car. And the location of the nearest decent coffee shop."

Car.

Genie's eyes went wide. Didn't Gemma have a car? Was it parked in the garage?

She was at the side door in a flash; the wood door's frame was splintered, as was the doorpost where the deadbolt had been ripped out when Cushing's people had burst in. She managed to yank open the door—and came up against a sheet of plywood fastened to the outside of the house.

"What a *bleeping* mess."

She strode out the front door, around to the side, and stared at the ruin Cushing's soldiers had left. The outside security door hung open, but it was bent out of square, and it leaned like a crazed drunk against the house's stucco siding. Cushing's people had wrecked the metal door while breaching the house. It would never close correctly again, let alone latch and lock.

Genie's anger toward Cushing found another grievance. "Like I can afford to replace two doors right now!"

The piece of plywood nailed over the doorway was surprisingly easy to remove; the nails had gone into stucco rather than wood. She grabbed an edge and pulled. Nails screed and came free; the plywood sheet fell to the steps revealing the open doorway behind it.

Hands on her hips, Genie surveyed the damage. "Maybe I'll take the old man up on his offer after all." It would be easier sucking up to him than squeezing hundreds of dollars out of her checking account.

Genie turned to the garage. Its side doors, too, were locked. With her face tipped up and pressed against the tiny, dusty window, she could just make out Gemma's old Toyota.

If I can't find the keys to her car, maybe I can sweet-talk a locksmith into making me a new set, she schemed. *Gemma Keyes/Genie Keyes—no big difference. I could convince the right man to be "understanding" enough to help me out.*

"May I help you?"

Genie's head came down so fast, she struck her chin on the window's edge and bit her tongue. "Ow!"

"I'm sorry, Genie. I didn't mean to startle you." Zander shrugged. "Seems like this is how you and I met the first time."

"You!"

All his accusations ran in her head. Had her nightmare come to life?

Zander chuckled. "Yeah, me. Again. And, like that first time, I'm wondering what you're doing in Gemma's house?"

Genie's eyes blazed. "That old man called you, didn't he? Well, it's none of his business and, I might add, it's none of your business, either."

"Actually, I have friends in Albuquerque law enforcement. I could make it my business to report you for trespassing. Then you could explain it to *them.*"

Genie's mouth thinned into a tight smile. "Yes, you do that. The answer is simple: This is my sister's house, and she's away at present, so I'm housesitting for her. Want to prove me wrong? Just have Gemma call you. Better still, have *her* call the police—or is she too busy hiding from Cushing?"

Her cold stare challenged Zander, her words a dare they both knew he couldn't take on.

He lowered his voice. "You know, invisible-like."

"I'll call her, but you need to know that I have no idea if she is near the phone we use."

"Do your best. We don't have much time."

Zander raced home and pulled the burner phone from its hiding place under his dresser.

***

The nanomites woke me.

Gemma Keyes. Zander Cruz is calling you.

Gemma Keyes. Zander Cruz is calling you.

"Okay. I'm up."

I picked up the phone and yawned. "Hey."

He didn't mince words. "Gemma, we've got a situation. Gamble needs you to get Dr. Bickel out of the FBI office as soon as you can. Apparently, people showed up first thing this morning with a court order for him and for Cushing."

I wiped sleep from my face. "I'm on my way."

"I'll let Gamble know."

On my way toward the FBI's offices, it dawned on me that I had but one place to hide my friend, and that was in his safe house. With me.

The little basement hiding place was about to get crowded.

⌘⌘⌘⌘

CHAPTER 10

Gamble found Dr. Bickel in the small interrogation room he'd slept in. The plan had been to move him to an FBI safe house, possibly later in the day. Until then, Dr. Bickel had been confined to his assigned room with the door closed. An agent had been taking his statements for the last two hours, with the intention that the remainder of Dr. Bickel's debriefing would be conducted at the safe house over several days.

Gamble knocked and entered, "Pardon the interruption. May I have a word with Dr. Bickel?"

The agent, leaving her notes on the table, excused herself.

"Hello, Agent Gamble. Are you ready to move me now?"

"Yes, but not as we'd planned." He took a few minutes to explain.

Dr. Bickel appeared thoughtful rather than anxious. "Cushing's handlers must be more powerful than we'd imagined. I'd always thought them to be high-ranking military."

"And now?"

"If I had to guess, I'd say well-placed and formidable politicians."

That hypothesis put a different spin on Gamble's perceptions, too.

"Well, Gemma is on her way here. Wherever she intends to take you must remain between the two of you. I'm sorry our hand is being forced like this."

"Don't be sorry. You saved us, Gemma and me. Got us to the lab safely and then here. You arranged the press conference. My friends and colleagues know I'm alive now, which was our first, most important objective. However, I am concerned about two things, given the reach of Cushing's handler."

"Which two things?"

"The first concerns the place where I was held on the White Sands Missile Range. The facility was, when built, an officer's house, but that was quite some time ago. Cushing had the house refurbished to serve as my prison and the garage equipped as a laboratory—all, I believe, in an attempt to keep my illegal incarceration a secret. Well, my DNA and other trace evidence can certainly be lifted from the room I lived in and used as evidence against Cushing, but only if the FBI gets there first."

He bent a somber look on Gamble. "The scene needs to be protected."

Gamble frowned. "You think Cushing's people will attempt to clean it?"

Dr. Bickel snorted. "Yes, but more thoroughly than what you have in mind. I think they'll destroy it."

"I see." And Gamble did see. "I'll bring this up to Wallace and push to have a team dispatched immediately. The other issue?"

"My so-called grave. Gemma said 'I' was buried in my hometown. We need to have the grave exhumed quickly, or those people will arrange for something to be done with whatever or whomever is interred there."

"The FBI can make that happen, too. Let me get your permission on record first, since you'll be in the wind for the foreseeable future."

Gamble called the female agent back into the room. "Get paperwork drawn up for Dr. Bickel to sign giving us permission to disinter his 'grave.' I want his signature witnessed and notarized, and I'd like a video recording of him giving us permission as backup."

He thought for a moment. "Can you get that done in the next hour?"

"Yes, sir."

Gamble left and went to find Wallace. The man was sequestered with the FBI's legal counsel. Gamble knocked anyway.

"Come in."

"Sir, may I see you?"

Wallace noted the look on Gamble's face and spoke to the attorney. "Excuse me; I'll be right back."

He stepped into the hall and closed his office door. "What is it?"

"Dr. Bickel just raised some legitimate concerns. He's convinced that Cushing will get rid of the evidence of his incarceration as soon as she leaves our custody—or perhaps it is already happening. Rather than 'clean' it, he thinks she will destroy the place where she kept him prisoner. It is an old house on the White Sands Missile Range that Cushing fitted up to keep his imprisonment a clandestine affair."

Wallace thought. "Call the commandant of the range and let him know that we're sending a team to process the scene. Ask him to dispatch a squad to preserve the place. On our end, we'll stall Cushing's release as long as we can to give the White Sands' squad time to get there. What's the other issue?"

"Dr. Bickel's grave, sir. Cushing had his 'remains' interred in his home town back in Georgia. Bickel is right now giving written and videotaped permission for us to exhume that grave before Cushing can get to it."

"Good. You run point on both of these issues. Put your teams together; use whomever is available."

Gamble went back to his office and placed a call to the Atlanta FBI field office. He gave the Assistant Special Agent in Charge he spoke with the name and contact information of the agent interviewing Bickel. "She will have the necessary permissions to you within an hour or so. And I can't stress how critical it is to move quickly before another request to exhume this grave comes in and we miss our opportunity."

"Another request?"

"I can't comment further. I can only say that Dr. Bickel is alive and, in order to prove his abduction and prove intent to collude and deceive, we must exhume whomever is buried in the grave marked as his before the evidence is removed."

The ASAC made notes and promised to have the grave secured before dark.

When Gamble hung up, he started assembling the personnel he would send to White Sands. He'd just finished sending out emails when his office door shut. All by itself.

***

I snickered. He'd noticed the door closing and realized it was me.

He kept his voice low. "Gemma?"

"Yeah, I'm here. Dr. Bickel is in a room down the hall, but someone is with him."

"The agent is getting Bickel's permission to open his grave back in Georgia. Should be done shortly. Then you are free to hustle him out of the building. I suggest taking him down the back stairs to the staff parking lot."

"Okay; I'll just go wait."

"Before you do . . . have you uncovered any leads on Emilio and Soto?"

"We're making progress." Just not fast enough.

"That's welcome news, but I had a thought."

"Yeah?"

"We believe Soto took Emilio to entice you into a trap. If that's true, why haven't we heard from Soto? He has the bait; why hasn't he dangled it in front of you?"

It had only been one day since we left the tunnels; however, four days had passed since Soto took Emilio. Gamble's question was a valid, worrisome one.

Why hadn't Soto reached out to me? Why indeed? I could think of a number of troubling possibilities, the chief being Emilio's well-being. Soto had killed Mateo and buried him on the West Mesa—so what if Soto wasn't planning a trap? What if he wasn't interested in revenge? What if mortally wounding my heart was good enough for him? What if Emilio was already—

I shook myself before I went down that rabbit hole. "I-I hadn't thought of that."

"Well, perhaps there's a good explanation why you haven't heard from Soto. I mean, how *would* he contact you? He doesn't exactly have your phone number or email address. And, unless Emilio has told him, Soto doesn't even know your name."

Gemma Keyes, we suggest that this evil man might reach out to you via a public forum, possibly employing a veiled communiqué.

Public forum? Communiqué? The nanomites' vocabulary grew every day.

"Like a newspaper ad?"

We will search newspapers and online media for such a concealed message.

I sighed. "Gamble, the nanomites think Soto might use a newspaper ad or something similar to reach out to me. They are looking." And now I was preoccupied with the idea.

"Good point. I wish them happy hunting."

"Thanks. I'll talk to you later."

Gamble had a thought and called me back. "Gemma?"

"Yeah?"

"Gemma, speaking of 'talk to you later,' I need a way to reach you, and I mean a method that is faster and less convoluted than going through your boyfriend."

"He isn't my boyfriend," I said automatically.

"Oh, *please*. I've seen and heard you two kissing and making gaga eyes, remember?"

"Yeah, but—"

"I don't need a relationship status update; what I need is a fast, surefire method of getting ahold of you when I need to. You can send the wedding invitation later."

My face flamed with his teasing, but his last playful jab stung. More than he knew. I think he realized he'd hurt my feelings when I didn't answer right away.

"Uh, look, Gemma, I'm sorry; that last bit was uncalled for. I apologize."

Have I mentioned what a great guy Gamble can be when he isn't all Special-Agent-in-your-face?

I sighed. "Yeah, okay, I forgive you. But FYI? Zander is something of a sore subject."

"I get that. Now. Again, I'm sorry. However, we're on several tight timelines here if we're to thwart Cushing, so back to the pressing need?"

"Let me think a sec."

I talked to the nanomites, and we tossed a few things around before coming to consensus.

"Do this, Gamble: Put an ad on Craigslist, Albuquerque. Something obscure, like, 'Wanted: Uncut Gemstones,' but don't leave a phone number with the ad. That way if anyone else happens to respond to the ad, they are forced to email you through the Craigslist site, and you can just ignore them. Otherwise, you might be inundated with calls."

"Uncut gemstones, eh? Gemstones as in Gemma? Cute. So, then what? You'll be monitoring Craigslist day and night? That doesn't sound like the quick response I need."

"The nanomites will insert a line of code into the webpage. The words 'uncut gemstones' will trigger an alert that they will receive immediately and pass on to me."

"Sure you don't want a big ol' Bat Signal in the night sky?"

I giggled. "Not yet, but I'll keep it in mind."

I left Gamble and hung out in the hall until the female agent, holding an armload of papers, left the room where Dr. Bickel waited. When I slipped inside, he glanced up.

"It's me, Dr. Bickel. I'm here to save you again."

He grinned. "Sounds good to me. I was becoming quite bored answering the same questions six different ways. Let's go."

The nanomites extended their umbrella of invisibility over him, and we left the room together, tiptoed down the staircase, and out into the cool air of a December early afternoon.

We drove across town to the parking garage. I returned my car to its regular spot and, covered by the nanomites, Dr. Bickel and I walked the few blocks to the safe house in companionable silence. I led him down the alley and over the low wall.

"I only use the back door," I explained.

I performed my usual security reconnaissance, watching for nosy neighbors and checking for foot prints or any other disturbance around the back porch before opening the back door. Once we were inside, the nanomites uncovered us.

Dr. Bickel stared around the kitchen. "I haven't been here in a while."

"Not much has changed." Inserting a hint of sarcasm, I added, "I did, however, stock the bathroom with toilet paper."

Dr. Bickel laughed. "And I'm going to be quite appreciative, I assure you."

He turned around and, catching sight of the real Gemma, studied me. You 've really changed, Gemma, and I like it. You've matured into a lovely, strong, capable woman. And you're quite beautiful, you know."

I chewed on his compliment while we climbed down into the basement hidey hole. Genie had been the pretty twin; I'd been the plain, stupid, dull one. No one—and I mean no one—had ever called me beautiful.

Except Zander. *"You'd think you didn't own a mirror, Gemma. You are a lovely woman."*

I sighed; my heart ached for what might have been, but I couldn't dwell on it, couldn't give in to the sorrow.

When I arrived at the bottom of the ladder, Dr. Bickel was surveying the tiny room. He grimaced. "The space feels smaller than I remembered."

"It's okay for one person, but not for the both of us. I'll sleep upstairs again."

"Is that prudent, Gemma?"

"It wasn't before, but it is now. I'm more than a match for whatever they might throw at me should they find us out. If they come, I will defeat or delay them; you, on the other hand, must promise to leave through the escape hatch at the first sign of trouble. We will meet up later at a designated rendezvous point."

"I built a number of deterrents into the security system, Gemma. I can trigger them as I go, but you'll need to be out of the way, first."

I nodded. "I've memorized your system. The nanomites and I can control it from anywhere in the house. I think it would be better, should we be discovered, if you just go. The nanomites and I will monitor the situation and trigger the deterrents when they will be most advantageous."

"I see."

I saw that it was hard on Dr. Bickel to admit that I was better equipped to manage the defense-in-depth system he'd designed but, truth be told, our positions had changed places. He had protected me when Cushing stormed his lab in the mountain; now I would protect him should she invade our safe house.

I pressed on. "Where shall we meet should this happen?"

"The parking garage seems the most likely spot."

"Okay. But hide and wait for me on the lower level. Don't go to my car until I arrive and we are confident we haven't been followed. If they have found this house, they likely have my identity and that means they will have a bead on the Escape, too."

I started gathering my things to take them upstairs, and my gaze fell on my most recent "bug-out bag," the backpack containing Kathy Sawyer's driver's license, checks, and credit card.

"Dr. Bickel, when and if you have to leave, be sure to grab both of my burner phones and this backpack. That will remove all Kathy Sawyer's identifying information from the house. I can't have my identity falling into Cushing's hands if she doesn't already have it."

He sat on the edge of the cot, put his hands on his knees, and murmured, "All right, Gemma."

I knew what he meant, what he was really saying: "You're the boss now, Gemma. You're in charge. I accept that."

The responsibility weighed on me, but it belonged there. On the other hand, I didn't want my friend feeling like he'd left one prison for another.

I piled all my stuff into a pillowcase, grabbed my laptop, and paused before I started up the ladder. "You don't have to stay down here except at night, Dr. Bickel. Why don't we figure out what to have for dinner? The fridge may be bare, but I have lots of things in the freezer. Steaks. Chicken. Salmon. And, if you're up for it, we can go grocery shopping tonight. Stock up on greens and fruit."

I was careful how I threw out the line and hook. "You can buy whatever your heart desires to cook with."

He perked right up. "I can cook?"

"Yup. In fact, I'm salivating already at the thought of your home-baked breads slathered in butter."

"Yes, yes. I'd be delighted to bake some bread. I should . . . I should take inventory and make that shopping list, shouldn't I?"

"Will you be making dessert tonight, too?"

He was right behind me on the ladder. "Why, of course! Let me see what I have to work with . . ."

I didn't catch his mumbled words after that, but it didn't matter.

Dr. Bickel was enjoying his freedom, and I was happy for him.

⌘⌘⌘⌘

CHAPTER 11

Imogene Cushing was waiting, but she knew she wouldn't wait long: The powerful individual she reported to would already have things moving. It was late afternoon when her FBI jailer unlocked the holding room.

Cushing was ready.

"General Cushing? Please follow me."

With her chin high and back ramrod straight, Cushing followed the agent through the hallway, down the elevator, and into the lobby. Most of the lobby's furnishings had been cleared away, but the room was still a mess. The windows and doors were missing glass; telling points of impact dotted the walls.

Impact from what? I thought no shots were fired.

She scowled as she looked around. *I can't reconcile what happened here last night. I know the orders I gave, and yet my people allowed themselves to be "talked down"? By one FBI agent and the equivalent of a mall cop? Why did my people disobey my orders? And why did I surrender? Nothing adds up.*

More troubling was the cloudy uncertainty that swirled in her mind. *It's as though I can't remember what happened.*

She didn't recognize the man who came toward her, but he knew her by sight.

"General Cushing. We've been sent to collect you. This way, please."

"Where is Bickel?"

"We don't have him, ma'am."

Cushing stopped, mid-stride. "What! Why not? He is essential to our mission; we must *not* leave without him."

The man leaned toward her so what he said would be heard by her alone. "The FBI says they didn't hold him."

"He was here. Right in this lobby giving a press conference."

"I understand; however, the FBI had no reason to hold him."

Cushing set her jaw; her anger was palpable. "And my people?"

"They have been released and are waiting in the vans outside."

Cushing ground her teeth and allowed him to usher her to the door. As they exited the building, four other men surrounded and escorted her to a waiting vehicle. When the doors closed on the two of them, the man who'd arranged for her release spoke.

"Ma'am, my team and I are at your disposal. However, I've been instructed to have you call this number at your earliest convenience." He handed her a cell phone with a number ready to be dialed.

She said nothing but took the phone and pressed "Send." A moment later, the call connected, and the familiar voice of her superior came on the line.

"I trust you are no worse for wear following your night in custody, General?"

Although his words were solicitous, Cushing knew better. She'd failed. Again. *And I don't know why or how—but it has to be connected to the nanomites.*

The nanomites. They were the only possible explanation for her incomplete recall of the events of the previous night. For her failure to capture Bickel and Gemma Keyes.

When I had them right in front of me, in my sights!

"Sir, I believe the subject has somehow recovered from the damage Colonel Greaves insists the Taser produced. What is more, I am convinced that the subject somehow manipulated last evening's events."

"You make two assertions, General. First you say the subject has recovered from what Greaves described as calamitous damage to the nanomites. That is interesting, is it not? It suggests that the nanomites have recuperative powers beyond our best hopes. It certainly makes them even more desirable, don't you agree?"

"Yes, sir. I do agree." Cushing didn't ask about the second of her assertions. She knew her handler would get to it.

"And you seem convinced that the subject manipulated the situation last evening. Pray tell, in what way?"

"Sir, I have been giving last evening's events considerable thought and have arrived at two conclusions. First, the FBI insists that a single agent and one security guard 'talked down' my team. I watched the local news in the holding area last night, and the media reports echo the FBI's assertion—although such a scenario flies in the face of my objectives, my orders, and the number of armed men I commanded last night.

"Secondly, when your people arrived this morning, they learned that the FBI offices were closed today. Why were they closed if our armed strike was resolved without firing a shot? What, then, caused the damage to the lobby? Glass blasted from the windows and doors, holes punched in the walls, furnishings overturned?

"Even as we were leaving the FBI facility just now, workers were still scurrying about, clearing up the damage, but the media reports mentioned no damage. That's odd, don't you think? Because, when your people arrived to get me early this morning, they observed shattered windows and scorched and pockmarked walls—not pockmarked by a firefight, not by rounds, but by something else entirely.

"What might that have been if not some weapon wielded by Miss Keyes? What is most personally disconcerting, is that I cannot recall with any confidence what actually happened after we breached the building. Rather than clear, detailed memories, I have vague impressions that seem more like suggestions than actual recall."

"What are you getting at, General?"

"Sir, I think the subject ordered the nanomites to wipe our collective memories—mine, my men, the reporters, even FBI personnel. In short, I believe the subject had the nanomites remove the memories of anyone within the vicinity and replace them with the absurd suggestion that two men managed to convince my armed tactical team to surrender without a fight."

"You realize how fantastical—how fictional—this sounds."

"Yes, sir." Cushing knew when to shut up and let her handler draw his own conclusions.

His muttered reply was not long in coming. "But if any of what you suggest is true, the national security implications—the PSYOPS connotations—are staggering."

"Yes, and I intend to obtain the proof we need, sir. I will personally compare the accounts of my men and the reporters who were present at Dr. Bickel's press conference. If my hypothesis is correct, they will parrot the same suggestions I was fed—and express the same vague disquiet I experienced. In addition, I should uncover a time lapse, a small window of time unaccounted for that would further my theory."

Cushing added, "However, more than proof, sir, we need *that girl*."

Cushing typically referred to Gemma Keyes as "the subject," but as Cushing's frustration grew, so flourished her personal animus toward Gemma. Nothing short of Cushing's death or complete incapacitation would pull her off her mission at this stage.

You have thwarted me at every turn, my dear Gemma, but I have the experience and tenacity to win in the end.

Ever vigilant of the big picture, Cushing ended the phone call with, "We should sanitize the White Sands site, sir."

"I have taken care of it, General. I arranged for a message to be delivered from you to your Agent Trujillo late last night. She proceeded immediately and will brief you on the outcome. Quite a capable woman, I must say. I must keep my eye on talent of her caliber."

Not the individual I would have selected, Cushing thought. *I prefer to use more . . . specialized personnel for questionable tasks.* Cushing didn't voice her reservations; she only answered, "Thank you, sir."

***

Gamble made his team selections before noon and assembled the members in a briefing room. His first remarks put them on high alert.

"I cannot stress enough the importance of your assignments: It is imperative that both teams complete their missions with all possible speed and meticulous attention to detail.

"Agent Larken, I am dispatching your four-person team to Georgia. Your orders are to exhume Dr. Bickel's grave no later than tomorrow morning and escort the remains to the Atlanta forensics lab under heavy security. You are to provide eyes-on vigilance over the remains until the pathologists determine to whom they belong—or until the pathologists disprove that they are those of Dr. Bickel."

Gamble fixed Larken with an inscrutable look. "I repeat: The remains are not to be left unattended and unsupervised *by your team* at any time, even once they arrive at the lab."

Gamble handed two folders to the team leader. The first folder contained official correspondence from the Albuquerque SAC to the Atlanta SAC requesting the Atlanta field office's assistance; the second contained multiple permissions for the exhumation, all signed by Dr. Bickel.

Then he handed over a sealed package. "This package contains a sample of Dr. Bickel's DNA to be compared to the remains you exhume. The chain of custody is not to leave your team's direct oversight. Arrange shifts as needed until the examination is complete."

"Yes, sir."

"Thank you. Wheels up in twenty minutes."

After the Atlanta team departed, Gamble briefed the second team on Dr. Bickel's incarceration. He left out all mention of Gemma's participation in his escape.

"What you need to know is that the scene where Dr. Bickel was held is at risk. Your task is to gather and preserve evidence that he was held there—specifically, hair samples and other DNA from his toiletries and the room he was kept in. Furthermore, I want Colonel Greaves, his aide, and all guards secured and interviewed.

"Draw your evidence-gathering kits and hit the road in two vehicles; push the speed limit and stop for nothing. I'll call you with further instructions after I've spoken with the range's commanding officer."

When the team left the briefing room, Gamble returned to his office and called the commandant of the White Sands Missile Range. After thirty minutes of runaround, Gamble was connected, and he explained the situation and his request.

The commanding officer, a decorated Army Brigadier General, was incredulous of Gamble's assertion that anyone had been incarcerated on his base without his knowledge or authority. That notwithstanding, the officer gave the FBI team permission to gather evidence from the house, but only if they were accompanied by a member of his staff and a four-man security squad.

Gamble agreed to the commandant's conditions. He hung up, called Agent Rains, his White Sands team leader, and told her where to rendezvous with their White Sands' guide.

"I don't care how late or dark it is; I want the scene secured tonight, and I expect your report by noon tomorrow."

"I understand, Special Agent Gamble."

⌘⌘⌘⌘

PART 2:
STEALTH
RETRIBUTION

CHAPTER 12

Dr. Bickel and I had eaten and eaten well. We'd dined on broiled salmon and seasoned rice, followed by cherry pie. Dr. Bickel had found the fixings in either the pantry or the freezer.

He'd fussed because he didn't have the ingredients to make a lemon tarragon sauce for the salmon. *I* thought I'd died and gone to heaven. And I think he was skeptical when I advised him to make twice as much as two people should eat, but after he'd watched me pack away a third slice of pie, his eyes had widened, and he'd laughed.

It did my heart good to see my old friend laughing. The deep lines around his eyes that hadn't been there on that last September day in the cavern relaxed. I relaxed a little, too.

"Why don't you finish up that grocery list?" I suggested as we lingered over coffee. "We can go shopping after we clean up. If the nanomites are able to hide both of us at the same time, I would think they can also hide you while they are disguising me."

It would be a variation, but when I put the notion to them, they assured me they could handle the task.

We can accomplish what you ask, Gemma Keyes; however, please do not sneeze while we are disguising you.

Face Palm

Oh, man! I snickered and grinned to myself, but I was a little uncertain if the nanomites had made a joke or if it was only funny on my side—and it was. It was *very* funny.

While Dr. Bickel explored the kitchen cupboards and jotted a list, I turned further inward.

"Hey, Nano. What about Emilio? What have you uncovered?"

Gemma Keyes, we have made several important discoveries.

"All right." But I thought it odd that I hadn't spontaneously known their "discoveries" since we now shared information without conscious effort.

The mites flipped images in front of my inner eyes, including close-ups of the SUV and its license plate. *Gemma Keyes, we captured the vehicle's plate number and looked up the registered owner. We found that the owner reported the car stolen just hours before Emilio was taken.*

I blew out a breath. "Okay. How long did Soto keep the car after he took Emilio?"

We estimate thirty-three minutes. Once we had the plate number, we also had the VIN and were able to access the automobile's navigation system.

"Thirty-three minutes? He kept the car for only half an hour?"

Yes, Gemma Keyes. Via the navigation system, we located the automobile parked alongside a city park in yet another residential area.

"He switched vehicles."

We agree. The switch was pre-planned, coordinated with his associates.

"Yeah . . ." I remembered then that Gamble had said four APD gang unit officers had sprung Soto from FBI custody—a big black eye for APD and a loss of face for the FBI. With most of Soto's upper tier management swept up on the raid on his house, the four APD turncoats had likely received "battlefield" promotions.

I wondered, though, how badly the traitors wanted to leave New Mexico and flee to safer space south of the U.S./Mexico border. If it weren't for Soto's need for payback, I assumed all of them would have fled south days ago.

An overhead image of the park appeared before me. It was an older park, with a playground and lots of mature trees. A number of trees lined one of the streets bounding the park. The trees' branches overspread the curb and, even in December, the branches held leaves.

"Are they parked under the trees? I can't see a thing."

That was, undoubtedly, their intention; however, the navigation system indicates that the vehicle is parked alongside the curb under the trees—just there.

The nanomites illuminated a tiny spot on the image.

"Then we've lost them? We can't track them?"

Gemma Keyes, all these details are moot.

Moot? Undoubtedly? What was *with* the nanomites' growing vocabulary anyway?

"What do you mean?"

These details are unnecessary because we have found the public communiqué from Soto.

"You found—"

I'd had enough. Something was very "off" between the nanomites and me, and I needed to get to the bottom of it. Yes, I was glad to hear they'd found Soto's message, but I also wanted to know why they'd hidden it from me—because they had. I should have known what they knew as soon as they'd discovered it. The fact that I *hadn't* known told me they had kept it from me.

"Nano, I need to ask you something, first."

Yes, Gemma Keyes.

"Nano, why didn't you tell me you'd found a message from Soto as soon as you'd uncovered it? You've been keeping data from me. Why?"

Gemma Keyes, we observed that you and Dr. Bickel were having important time together. We realized that this important time would improve the emotional well-being of you both. We did not want to interrupt this important time.

"So, you made the decision to keep information from me?"

Yes, Gemma Keyes. For your good and Dr. Bickel's good.

"I see." I did see, but I didn't like it—because it was wrong. I tried to be tactful as I chose my next words.

"Nano, I understand that you wish only good for Dr. Bickel and for me. You care about our . . . emotional well-being."

Yes, Gemma Keyes. That is true.

"Well, I need to tell you something . . . something that is vital to every person's emotional well-being."

We are listening, Gemma Keyes.

"It is about choice, Nano. People need to be free. Free to choose. It's . . . it's the way God made them. Choice is something God gives us."

Past Sunday school lessons and the voices of Aunt Lucy and Zander converged and clarified this principle as I'd never before understood it. In a single moment, a host of my life's conundrums resolved themselves.

"Nano, even when you care about a person, it isn't right to take away their freedom to choose."

We have observed that people often make decisions that run counter to their welfare.

"I know. I've seen that, too. However, God allows us to live by our choices—for good or ill—so that we are free inside."

This supposition seems counterintuitive, Gemma Keyes. Perhaps God is wrong.

"According to Zander, God is never wrong, Nano. People must be free to choose—but they must also be responsible for the consequences of their choices. Zander says people won't be responsible for their actions unless they are also free to choose them."

Perhaps Zander is wrong about people. Perhaps he is wrong about God.

"Well, so far, he's been right—but we're getting off topic. You withheld information from me."

Yes, Gemma Keyes. Temporarily. For your emotional well-being.

"Well, even though you did it for my well-being, I don't like it."

You don't like your well-being?

"No—and you know that's not what I meant. What I meant is that I don't like how you diminished me."

There. I'd finally hit the nail on the head.

"Nano, we are six, are we not?"

Yes, Gemma Keyes.

"Then don't treat my tribe as if it were less than the other tribes. Don't withhold my full participation in the nanocloud because *you* decide if or when it is good for me. Don't treat me like a child. I am emotionally stronger than you give me credit for."

The nanomites went quiet on me at that point.

I hadn't gotten angry; I hadn't acted all bent out of shape with them. I truly was trying hard to be rational and calm. Still, the nanomites were silent for a long time, and I grew impatient with them: After all, they said they had found Soto's ransom demands—and I needed to see them.

When the nanomites remained aloof, I pressed them. "Nano, show me what you've found. Now, please."

I intuited their reluctance but stood my ground. A moment later, a newspaper article appeared in my mind. As I took it in, my heart clenched: The six-inch by four-inch block was posted in the Albuquerque Journal's Obituaries section. It featured a striking photo of Emilio and this headline: **A Life Over Too Soon**.

I gasped, and Emilio's face swam in front of my eyes. "No!"

Gemma Keyes, we do not believe Emilio to be dead; we deem this to be Soto's means of contacting you. Please read the short article accompanying the photograph.

I scrubbed at the blinding tears and tried to focus on the print. I couldn't, not right away. I couldn't get past the image of Emilio's sweet face. He was wearing what looked to be a new polo shirt, and the photo's composition was nicely done, the quality as good as a school portrait. His body was turned to the side, away from the camera, while he looked over his shoulder, his face in partial profile, and smiled into the camera.

Smiled? Maybe with his mouth he smiled, but certainly not with his eyes. No, I knew Emilio too well to be fooled. His dark eyes raged against the camera and against the man forcing him to pose for the picture. Soto had to have taken the photo himself.

Regardless, I'd never seen anything so wonderful. I wanted in the worst way to reach out and touch my boy, to hold him close with my arms wrapped around him, to keep him safe from this ugly world.

From Dead Eyes.

When I was able to, I scanned the print next to the photo.

A Life Over Too Soon
Sweet little Emilio
was only 10 years old
when he was snatched away.
Friends who love him
will send flowers here

The subtle word difference struck me. "Friends who *love* him," not "*loved* him." Present tense, not past.

"It's a threat."

Yes, Gemma Keyes.

I ran through the text again. The word "here" was a link.

"Take me to the link, Nano."

A web page appeared, a plain, unadorned screen with a blinking cursor preceded by these words: To enter the memorial site, type the first name of Emilio's beloved uncle.

"Mateo," I whispered.

Agreed, Gemma Keyes. Do you wish to proceed?

"Yes."

The nanomites didn't need to step through the security rigmarole, but Soto didn't know that, did he? I watched as the nanomites keyed in the letters M A T E O and pressed "enter." Watched as the page advanced and a video screen appeared. The nanomites pressed "play."

Emilio materialized. He was sitting in a chair, wearing the same polo shirt as in the obituary's photograph, but he was no longer concealing his anger behind a smile.

In fact, if looks could have killed, Emilio would have been the only one in the room still alive. Everyone else would have been reduced to a glowing heap of slag on the floor.

A harsh, disembodied voice spoke from behind the camera. "Read it."

Emilio lifted a sheet of paper and read aloud from it. It was obvious from how he spoke that he'd been coached, that he'd read the message many times in preparation. It was also obvious why his "memorial" picture had shown his face in partial profile: A large bruise covered his left cheek.

As I took in the discoloration, a familiar rage smoldered in my gut.

Lord, please help me!

I took a deep breath as Emilio sneered in the direction of the camera and then began reading. "Invisible lady—"

Right there he gave a short, derisive snort. "Invisible lady, if you don't want Emilio's obituary to be real, if you don't want to be responsible for the kid's death, you must come and get him. No police. No FBI. Just you. This is your one and only opportunity to save him. If you screw up, he dies. If you don't show up, he dies. If you diver—" Emilio stumbled over the adult word. "If you *diverge* from the plan, he dies."

Emilio swallowed, knit those dark brows of his together, sucked in air, and continued reading. "Remember: only you. I will be watching, and my men will have a gun to the kid's head. One wrong move, one act of disobedience, and his brains get splattered on the wall—and it will be your fault."

Emilio's bravado buckled, and his voice shook as he finished. "One more thing: no 'invisible' tricks. Show up as yourself; if you turn up but we can't see you, the brat's dead. Here's a date and time; return to this site on that date and at that time. You will receive updated instructions then."

Emilio dropped the sheet. As it fluttered to the floor, he lifted another piece of paper and held it up. The camera zoomed in on a date and a time.

I gaped at the paper; the date was five days from now. Five days? It seemed an eternity.

"Soto must have decided that I might not find the obituary right away."

Very likely, Gemma Keyes; however, he will know now that you have found it. The video's counter has registered a visitor. Do you wish us to roll back the counter?

I thought for a minute. "Yes, for the time being. Let Soto sweat over it while we figure this out."

We have removed our visit from the site's log, Gemma Keyes.

There was a pause before the nanomites added, *The obituary began running yesterday and is paid to run through next Tuesday, the date Soto has selected for the meeting. The video was recorded Tuesday, the same day the obituary was submitted, one day after Soto took Emilio.*

"Do you have a source for the website?"

Yes, Gemma Keyes. We have gathered all available data for this website. The source is a local hosting site. We have gained access to the hosting site and are running the customer's credit card data now.

"Can't you trace the IP address of whomever uploaded the video?"

We have the IP address of the computer from which the files were uploaded, Gemma Keyes, but Dead Eyes has taken the computer offline. However, we are monitoring the hosting site. On Tuesday, while Dead Eye's people are uploading the instructions, we will trace their location.

"Good. Between now and then, we'll decide how to handle Emilio's rescue."

I went on, speaking more to myself than to the mites. "Soto has no idea what he's dealing with." I was talking aloud to myself. "He doesn't know why and how I can be invisible. He doesn't know about the nanomites. He sure doesn't know what we can do."

Indeed, Gemma Keyes. He will be no match for us. We are six, and we are quite optimal.

Beneath the persistent presence of the nanomites, I heard another voice whisper, *You are strong and capable, Gemma, but do not be overconfident in yourself. Rather, place your trust in me. For it is not by might nor by power, but by my Spirit.*

"I hear you, Jesus, but please help me to deal with the anger I feel! I don't want to make another mistake; I don't want to cause more grief."

Lean on me; I will guide you through.

"Yes, Lord, I will."

Gemma Keyes, who are you talking to?

"I'm talking to Jesus, Nano."

Why can't we hear him? We sense him, but cannot hear him. What is he saying?

"He is telling me to trust him, Nano. Not to be overconfident in myself."

The nanomites went all "quiet" again. I wondered what they thought about Jesus' warning against "overconfidence," given their assertion, *We are six, and we are quite optimal.*

Shunting those concerns aside, I reached for the Bible Zander had given me. "Lord," I whispered, "Zander says your words are food for my soul, that you will transform me into the image of Jesus if I read your words daily and apply them to my life. Please show me where to start?"

***

Genie's first full day in New Mexico had exhausted her. Although she was waiting to hear from the law firm she'd called while still in D.C., she had no assurances that they would extend her an offer—and she couldn't afford to wait.

I need a job. I must have money coming in or this whole house of cards will come down around my head.

She went online and changed her address at the post office and spent the remainder of the day poring over Indeed.com, LawCrossing.com, and the State Bar of New Mexico's classifieds.

She applied for every halfway-decent position she found. She also researched and downloaded the forms to transfer her license to practice law to New Mexico.

Tomorrow would be just as challenging. The locksmith would arrive in the morning, and she could only guesstimate what he would charge to cut a new key for Gemma's car. It had to be done, though. Genie had no other transportation options if she hoped to schedule interviews and begin working. Then there was all the nonsense attached to establishing residence in a new state: obtaining a New Mexico driver's license, a local checking account, etc. She contemplated one incidental expenditure after another, measuring her dwindling bank account against the expenses ahead.

And while watching for and guarding against that *blank blank* cat.

When Genie had reentered the house after her encounter with Zander Cruz, the mangy animal was sitting on the arm of the sofa, watching her. Genie's eyes narrowed in disgust, and she could have sworn that the creature's green eyes narrowed, too. In fact, although he sat so still that he could have been dozing, Genie got the creepiest sensation that the cat was mocking her. Mirroring her facial movements. Taunting her.

She had swallowed, afraid to move for fear he would leap from the couch and pounce on her. Near abject terror jittered around in her stomach, keeping company with astonishment.

I'm afraid? Me? I have a cat phobia?

*No; it's just **this** cat. This horrible, ugly demon cat!*

As though toying with Genie bored him, the animal had tipped his scarred head and opened his mouth in a yawn, a wide—*a huge*—fang-and-tooth disclosing gape. Genie was mesmerized—the way a mouse is mesmerized by the sway of a snake and cannot flee.

The spell had broken only when the animal arched his back and jumped from the couch to the floor. He wandered around the side table and lamp—and disappeared.

Worse than holding a losing stare-off with that devil cat was not knowing where he was. And, oh! how Jake knew how to hide from Genie! She couldn't find him anywhere.

It's only a two-bedroom house! Where can he be?

He must have sensed that Genie would toss him outside if given the opportunity, but the truth was that she was afraid to touch the ugly, dirty thing. Her preference—her fervent longing—was to call an animal removal service.

Like I can afford that.

They played Jake's twisted version of "cat and mouse" (actually, "cat and human") through the afternoon and into the evening: Jake skulking away and reappearing when and where Genie least expected him—scaring the living daylights out of her. Jake staring daggers at her; Jake stalking from the kitchen into the living room, howling a feral accusation—as though demanding some action or response from her! Jake leaping onto the kitchen counter while she tried to heat a can of soup on the stove.

After he'd chased Genie from the kitchen, Jake rioted. He flipped over his metal dishes and slid them across the floor. The discordant clank as the bowls smacked against each other and the cabinets jangled Genie's nerves—nerves that were already shot. When he pitched one of the bowls into the front of the stove—a particularly loud clang—Genie crept to the dining room and peeked around the corner.

Jake stared at her, and Genie blinked.

Could he . . . Was he . . .

She eased into the kitchen doorway. "You-you're hungry?"

From Jake's throat arose a growl that was both harsh and savage. He kept growling and shooting her wide, wild glares until Genie would have sworn he was chewing her out. Telling her "what for" in unmistakable terms.

"Okay! Okay! I don't *know* where Gemma kept the food—"
Jake bounded forward and pawed at the low cupboard next to the refrigerator. He batted and clawed at it.

"All right! Get away and I'll look. Go on! Shoo! Scat!"

Jake sat back on his haunches—a scant foot and a half from the cupboard. His tail twitched, jerking back and forth, and his tongue shot out and licked his nose and all around his toothy maw. Genie inched into the kitchen and, with one eye on the cat, grabbed the cupboard handle and yanked it open.

There. Right there on the bottom shelf was a three-pound sack of Little Friskies, perhaps a third full.

She grabbed the sack from the cupboard and picked up one of the two metal bowls. She filled it to overflowing. Set it down and, with the toe of her shoe, nudged it toward Jake.

Without another sound or glance, Jake buried his face in the bowl. Genie could hear the crunching, cracking, and snapping of his teeth on the dry kibble, the way he scooped up the food and threw it around in his mouth to get it between his jaws.

All the saliva in her mouth dried up.

"Uh, maybe you need water, too?"

With slow caution, she retrieved the other bowl and filled it from the tap. Placed it on the floor. Dared to scoot it closer to the other bowl. Jake stopped chewing, lifted his head, and skewered her with green-orbed disdain. Genie jerked her hand away. She backed out of the kitchen. A moment later she heard the lap-lap-lapping of Jake's tongue flipping water into his mouth.

Genie couldn't take anymore. After two days of travel and stress, she was physically and mentally exhausted. She climbed into bed with her clothes on, pulled the covers over her head, and fell asleep instantly.

She awoke in the night to a Dark Presence in the room.

On her bed.

Near her feet.

Holding her down.

Jake's glowing, green eyes studied Genie. She shivered, but held as still as she could, not knowing what else to do. If the cat attacked her, she would be forced to retreat under the covers, hoping their thickness would protect her from the worst.

Genie felt like the standoff lasted for hours. In reality, Jake watched her no more than three minutes. Then he shook himself, scrabbled at the blankets with his claws, turned around and around, and curled into a ball against her hip.

And purred.

To Genie's ears, Jake's rumbling resounded like the blows of a jackhammer. After a bit, the sound eased, and she realized he'd fallen asleep. His weight pressed against her hip, warming her.

Unable to resist her body's need for rest any longer, Genie herself slept. When she woke in the morning, she found that she hadn't moved all night, but Jake was gone. In the mounded blankets against her hip where he'd laid all night, she saw the imprint of the cat's curled body. She reached a tentative finger toward the impression.

It was still warm.

***

Late that night, after Dr. Bickel and I had shopped, I drove to the dojo and worked out. While I was glad of Dr. Bickel's quiet presence in the safe house, I found myself in a familiar spot—too much time on my hands and not enough to do with it. My anxiety over Emilio and the obituary the nanomites had discovered added to my hyperactive, jittery state. I needed to move, use my body, work it hard, and expend the nervous energy bursting from me.

After an hour of running through the patterns and routines that were now as familiar as my own skin, I spent two hours sparring against Gus-Gus. Since I had lost my own fighting sticks, I had to borrow the dojo's.

I used them well, but I wanted my own—and I felt it prudent to "re-arm" myself. Even with the power of the nanocloud active within me, I felt the loss of my escrima sticks. I'd grown dependent upon their comforting weight in my hands or in the quiver along my spine.

"Nano. Reorder a pair of kamagong wood sticks. No; just in case I need them, order three pair. And another quiver. Use expedited shipping."

Done, Gemma Keyes.

"Cool. Thank you, Nano."

***

Emilio listened to the wind howl. It sounded far away, but that was because he was in a basement. Emilio hadn't been in many basements; Albuquerque didn't have lots of houses with basements—but this place had one. Maybe it wasn't a house. It didn't have the "feel" of a house. And he sensed that he was in a solitary place, far from people and traffic.

He had no idea where that might be, because his captors had put a big bag over him and had carried him from the car into the building. All he knew was that he was surrounded by rough concrete walls and that the walls had no windows. Except for the dim light coming from the crack under the door, his cell was very dark.

He shivered, turned over on the mattress, and snugged the sleeping bag around his shoulders. The bag was cold and funny-smelling, like something wet that never really dried out all the way. The mattress never really warmed up, either, because it lay on the cement floor and the floor was freezing cold. Emilio shivered again.

He heard Dead Eyes cursing down the hall. Someone answered him. Emilio couldn't make out what the guy said, but it wasn't what Soto wanted to hear. Emilio ducked his head down in the dank bag and covered his ears. He could still hear Dead Eyes screaming. Something about a doctor.

Emilio had heard lots of yelling since they brought him here. He'd figured out that Soto's arm or hand was messed up. Even though he kept his hand bandaged up, Soto needed a special kind of doctor to fix it—the kind of doctor who fixed badly broken bones—and his men weren't having much luck getting one for him.

A little smile twitched Emilio's mouth. *She got you good, didn't she? Serves you right.*

Dead Eyes was in a lot of pain from his busted hand, too—and that made him short-tempered. Twitchy. Upset all the time. And when Soto got upset, he got crazy—like how Mateo would get just before he punched a wall or hit Corazón. Dead Eyes was especially mad because he had taken a picture of Emilio and put it in the newspaper, and Gemma hadn't found it yet. With every day that went by without her finding it, Soto got angrier and crazier.

Emilio used his toes to snag and pull the chilly bottom of the sleeping bag up and bunch it around his feet. Eventually, the bag would get a little warmer, and he would sleep. But before he slept he would think about Gemma and what she would do to Dead Eyes when she came to get him.

Soto thought he could use Emilio to get Gemma and hurt her, but Emilio knew better. She was too smart for Dead Eyes. Well, Soto would find that out for himself, wouldn't he?

Then she will take me back to the old man and we will all have spaghetti together: Abe, Zander, Gemma, and me.

Emilio thought about the nice bed that would be his when he got to live with Abe all the time. Abe would take care of him, and Zander and Gemma would help.

Soon, he told himself. *Soon.*

⌘⌘⌘⌘

CHAPTER 13

Gamble was in the office early Saturday morning. He kept himself busy while he waited for his teams to report in, but he couldn't shake the premonition that something was wrong, that circumstances bigger than he could control or manage were at work.

He didn't like the feeling.

When his phone rang shortly after noon, he grabbed it up on its second ring. "Ross Gamble."

"Special Agent Gamble, this is Agent Rains. I'm calling from Las Cruces."

The caution in the woman's voice set Gamble's teeth on edge. "What is it, Rains?"

"Sir, we rendezvoused with our White Sands counterparts last night and they provided exterior lighting as we requested; however, when we arrived at the specified location to secure the scene? Sir, I'm sorry to tell you . . . there was nothing there."

Gamble could hardly speak through his clenched jaws. "Explain, please."

"Our team and the Army squad spent an hour walking the property, about an acre in size. We saw evidence of earth-moving equipment and a large excavation, as recently as earlier in the day or perhaps the day before. Based on the size and type of the equipment tread marks, we deduced that the house had been bulldozed. Leveled, sir. We're fairly certain that they—persons unknown—knocked down the house, dug a hole, pushed the demolished remains of the house into the excavated hole, and covered it over."

Gamble cursed under his breath. "What else? Outbuildings? Signs of recent activity?"

"It was apparent that the property recently had a perimeter fence, and we made out the footprint of a concrete driveway that led from the dirt road to where the house—presumably—sat. Every bit of the fence and concrete driveway was removed and, we presume, buried with the rubble from the house."

"And what do our White Sands connections have to say?"

"Our counterparts are as flummoxed as we are. The house was an old cinderblock officers' residence from back in the 1950s, unoccupied for decades. They had no idea anyone was using it."

She paused. "There's more, sir, and it's bad."

Gamble pulled himself together. "Give it to me."

"I sent two agents back to the site of the house first thing this morning to see if we missed any evidence in the dark. While they did that, Agent Crowder and I came into Las Cruces to interview Colonel Greaves."

"Yes?"

"Agent Gamble, Colonel Greaves passed away last night."

"He's dead?" The news stunned Gamble—and sent his thoughts down a terrible path.

"Yes, sir. He had been hospitalized after sustaining multiple broken bones in his hands, arms, and legs last Sunday night. But, and here's the curious bit: According to his medical record, no one knew how he'd been injured—and Colonel Greaves wasn't saying. He underwent extensive surgery to set and pin the worst of his breaks and was expected to make a full recovery."

"Right—but now he's dead."

"Yes, sir. His physician suggests that Greaves suffered either a blood clot from his injuries or the rupture of a previously undiagnosed aneurysm. We'll know more after the autopsy."

I doubt it, Gamble snarled to himself. "What of the guards? Dr. Bickel said the house had a staff of guards that rotated shifts—we estimate between fifteen and twenty."

"We've been on that since we left the hospital. The guards weren't military, we know that much. From what we can surmise, Cushing hired a contractor to supply the guards—and there we've hit a brick wall. We have the contracting company's name, but the organization has disappeared. Closed up shop—although whether the company ever *legally* existed is in question. We found no articles of incorporation, no bank accounts, no website, and no physical address. Furthermore, the IRS has no tax documents or records for a company of that name. Thus, we have no names or employment records for the guards and no means of tracking them down."

"Better and better." Gamble's brows drew down into a hard line. "And what of Colonel Greaves' aide? He accompanied Greaves when Dr. Bickel escaped."

The agent's detached tone wafting over the line portended more bad news. "Sir, the corporal was struck yesterday afternoon by a hit-and-run driver while he was crossing a street. In the crosswalk. Broad daylight. DOA."

Gamble sighed. "Mighty convenient, don't you think?"

"Yes, sir. Too convenient."

She paused, as if she had more to add, and Gamble goaded her on. "What are you thinking, Rains?"

"I'm thinking, sir, that Dr. Bickel escaped late Sunday night and surfaced in Albuquerque on Thursday. Today is Saturday, and yet all evidence of Dr. Bickel's incarceration has vanished—more accurately, has been expunged. Professionally 'cleaned' in less than forty-eight hours of Dr. Bickel's reemergence into the public eye.

Gamble said nothing, but he agreed in thought, *Oh, it was professional, all right.*

"Someone went to great lengths to discredit Dr. Bickel's testimony or, at the very least, leave him with no leg to stand on, no proof of what might be labeled a tall tale, a fantasy. Sir, whoever coordinated all this? Had to have been someone with clout and resources. Someone or ones at a very high level."

That disquieting premonition that the circumstances were bigger than he could control or manage stole over Gamble again. "I concur, Agent Rains."

As he returned the receiver to the phone, he wondered what surprises awaited his Georgia team.

***

Like Gamble, Janice Trujillo tried to ignore the unease keeping her up nights, but it refused to be disregarded. Too many details were adding up, and she didn't like what the sum pointed to.

"What are these, Miss Trujillo?" Cushing was looking over a small number of items Trujillo had retrieved from the facility on the missile range before she oversaw its demolition and burial.

"I've been told that these, General, are escrima sticks. They're used in martial arts fighting."

Cushing picked one up, hefted the weight, and frowned. "They are quite heavy."

"Yes, ma'am. Made from a Filipino hardwood tree, *Diospyros blancoi,* whose lumber is called kamagong or, alternatively, "iron wood." The sticks can be lethal when wielded by an expert."

"And they were found in the house?"

"We interviewed Colonel Greaves' aide yesterday morning." She referred to her notes. "He said, and I quote, 'A blow from an invisible force sent my sidearm into the air. Whatever it was, it hit me three more times. When I awoke, I was in the hospital with two cracked elbows and a mild concussion.'"

"An invisible force."

The way Cushing breathed those three words bothered Trujillo. Cushing's thousand-foot stare made her look as though she were trying to see something just out of her view, just out of reach.

And then the general whispered, "If I could only remember."

More alarms rang in Trujillo's head. "Ma'am?"

Cushing straightened; her gaze snapped back. "And Colonel Greaves? What did he tell you?"

"The Colonel refused to speak to us, General. He said he would only speak to you."

"Indeed? That is . . . regrettable."

Curious. Cushing didn't seem too upset about Greaves' reluctance to talk.

"General, I've received news that Colonel Greaves passed away last night."

Cushing didn't react. She continued to study the heavy wooden stick. "General?"

"I heard you, Miss Trujillo."

Trujillo's senses were jangling. "And Colonel Greaves' aide was hit by a car yesterday afternoon not long after we interviewed him."

Cushing cleared her throat. "I see."

Trujillo thought *she* saw, too, and a cold chill washed over her. She kept her mouth closed until Cushing spoke again.

"Miss Trujillo."

"Yes, General?"

"I want you to trace these sticks. What do you call them again?"

"Escrima sticks, ma'am."

"Trace them. The market share for this product would be specific and limited, yes? Not a large population, I should think. Even a smaller number buying a particular brand such as this one." Cushing pointed to a tiny trademark stamped on the stick's blunt end. "And even fewer of this brand sold to parties in New Mexico."

She straightened. "Find out *who* in New Mexico bought these sticks, Miss Trujillo—and make this your only priority. I want to know who bought these, and *I want to know now*."

***

Gemma Keyes, we have further researched Arnaldo Soto's family and have uncovered pertinent information.

"Oh? Tell me."

The nanomites showed me three email accounts. Traffic between the three accounts was frequent, lengthy, and often dealt with Dead Eyes. When the emails weren't about Arnaldo Soto, they were about business problems.

"What is the relationship between these people and Soto?"

Estevan Soto is Arnaldo Soto's older brother. Miguel Soto is Arnaldo Soto's uncle, his father's brother. Esperanza Duvall is Arnaldo Soto's married sister, also older than Arnaldo. Esperanza Duvall is married to an American.

I scanned the email exchanges, frowned, and read more thoroughly, committing them to memory. If the messages and what they led me to deduce were true, then the three aforementioned Sotos comprised the bulk of power within the family—a large clan whose "family business" was a significant segment of a major Mexican drug cartel.

And Arnaldo's family was *not* pleased with him.

"Nano, recap what else you've learned about this family. Break it down for me." I wanted them to confirm my assumptions and fill in any blanks I might have.

As the nanomites recited bits of the information they had gleaned via their forays across the Internet, they pulled up images of Soto's family members: his uncle, Miguel; Soto's brother, Estevan; and sister, Esperanza.

Gemma Keyes, Dead Eyes' uncle, Miguel Soto, has been running the majority of the family's criminal operations for the past seven years, since the death of his brother, Ignacio. His health has declined, however, so he has been grooming his niece and nephew to assume the leadership of the family and their segment of the cartel.

"How do you know Miguel Soto's health has declined?" This was the kind of information I figured I might be missing.

Miguel Soto's medical records appeared. I perused them and found what the nanomites had alluded to: kidney failure requiring dialysis three times weekly. I read on and learned that, for the past six months, the effectiveness of the dialysis treatments had diminished. Without a transplant, Miguel Soto's prognosis was one year—two at the most—with decreasing health and mobility as his death drew near.

In addition, Gemma Keyes, we mined email correspondence between Miguel and his physician. Because Miguel has a rare tissue type, procuring a viable kidney donor for him has proven difficult. Two years ago, they had located a reasonable match and had scheduled the transplant. Ten days prior to the surgery, the donor was found to have contracted HIV, a recent infection. For that reason, the surgery was canceled.

"What about family? Aren't family members presumed to be the best possible match for an organ transplant?" *And in what way is any of this pertinent to Dead Eyes?* I wondered.

Yes; a family member should have yielded the best match. But of all potential family donors, all but one were ruled out.

And there it was.

"All but one?"

Yes, Gemma Keyes. Arnaldo Soto was the only familial match.

Some of the animus toward Dead Eyes expressed in the email exchanges began to make sense.

"Why . . . why didn't the transplant take place?"

Arnaldo Soto demanded that he be given a prominent position in the family in exchange for a kidney.

"And?"

His family expressed misgivings regarding his fitness as a leader. Arnaldo has a long history of troubling behavior: schoolyard bullying and animal cruelty as a juvenile, the brutal treatment of prostitutes while at university, and increasing numbers of angry and violent tendencies.

I snorted. "Let me get this straight: The heads of an amoral criminal family were concerned about the mental and emotional stability of a family scion? Cute. So, I take it the uncle and siblings didn't give in to Arnaldo's demands?"

Not initially. By way of a trial foray, they gave Arnaldo a minor role under a seasoned lieutenant, a longtime, trusted family employee. Soto balked at taking orders from a paid family underling and subverted the man's authority. He gathered likeminded foot soldiers who were loyal to him and led an uprising against his superior, thinking to wrest his position from him and assume control. The rebellion was bloody but unsuccessful.

If Soto had been anyone else, his supervisor would have executed him on the spot—as he did every gang member who had followed Soto. Instead, the lieutenant felt compelled to send Soto home in disgrace and report him to Miguel in the strongest of negative terms.

Miguel confined Arnaldo to the family hacienda under guard. However, because the uncle was desperate for his nephew's kidney, he gave Dead Eyes one last opportunity: He sent him to Albuquerque to assess a gang-related incident. A local problem.

"Oh."

The "gang-related incident"? It was me: *I* had caused that "local problem." I was the one who'd seen Mateo beating his girlfriend and had clobbered him with a chair. I was the one who'd incited Corazón to take the drug money sitting on the table and leave. *I* told her to steal Mateo's car.

Soto was to assess the situation, make necessary adjustments, and return to Mexico for the transplant.

"Soto cleaned up Mateo's mess all right, but he didn't go back. He got rid of Mateo instead."

That is correct, Gemma Keyes. Dead Eyes has remained in Albuquerque and refused all commands to return to Mexico. Over the next weeks that followed, the email chains between uncle, brother, and sister outlined Arnaldo's other treasonous deeds—including Soto's hijacking of the cartel's drug supply and distribution operation in New Mexico in order to establish his own fiefdom. However, Dead Eyes' most egregious act of defiance was his refusal to return and donate his kidney to his uncle.

Arnaldo was beyond family forgiveness.

"Nano, why did you bring all this up?"

I was reasonably certain of the answer, but if I were right, their plan was scary in its audacity.

Gemma Keyes, Estevan Soto and his sister, Esperanza Duvall, have placed a bounty upon Arnaldo's head.

"As in 'Wanted, Dead or Alive'?"

No, Gemma Keyes. Arnaldo Soto is wanted, but he is very much wanted alive.

I chewed my lip. "Nano, if we sent email to those three email addresses, to Soto's family, would you be able to spoof the origination IP? Could you ensure that they couldn't trace our email to us, to this house?"

Yes.

Their next words floored me.

We already have, Gemma Keyes.

***

The call Gamble had been expecting came in shortly after noon. It was 2 p.m. in Georgia when he picked up the phone.

"Gamble."

"This is Agent Larken, sir. We located the cemetery and Dr. Bickel's remains."

"Did you exhume the grave?"

"No, sir."

Gamble steeled himself. "Give me the details."

"Sir, Dr. Bickel's body was not given a conventional burial as reported. He was cremated, sir, and his ashes were interred in an urn garden."

Gamble sputtered a protest. "But the memorial service held here in Albuquerque for Dr. Bickel and Dr. Prochanski said that their bodies would be laid to rest in their home towns. News coverage of their deaths and the memorial service said the same."

"As we've discovered, sir, those reports were in error."

Gamble hung up and stared at the wall.

"As we've discovered, sir, those reports were in error."

Well, of course they were—and intentionally so. Dr. Bickel's only family members were distant cousins who lived in Idaho. No one in Georgia had attended the burial service; no one had visited Dr. Bickel's final resting place.

Cushing had lied at the memorial service and had counted on no one ever fact-checking her. Even if they had, it would have been too late—as it was now.

Because you can't pull DNA from ashes.

If confronted with the lie, Cushing would likely assert that the two sets of remains recovered from the lab's fire were in such sad shape that, *of course*, they had assumed they belonged to Dr. Prochanski and Dr. Bickel. When she had presented a closed casket at the memorial service and said that Dr. Bickel would be buried, she was offering "a simple kindness to his friends." However, cremation of the body and interment of the ashes at a later date had been the best solution.

"She's stalemating us at every turn," Gamble breathed. "At this point, Dr. Bickel's charges against Cushing amount to his word against hers."

No, it's worse. It's the fantastical story of a crazed physicist against the word of a decorated, two-star general.

As he rubbed his tired eyes, new and darker thoughts rushed at him, including one very bad premonition: Would Cushing seek a way to turn the tables, to clear her name? To countercharge Dr. Bickel for slander? Would she charge *Dr. Bickel* with the bombing of the lab and the theft of valuable government R&D?

For the murder of Petrel Prochanski?

***

Zander pulled into Gemma's driveway and got out of the borrowed pickup. He bounded up the front steps and rang the doorbell.

A high-pitched voice answered. "Who is it?"

"It's Zander Cruz, Genie. I'm here to fix the side door like I said I would."

He glanced up. Gemma's nosy neighbor, Mrs. Calderón, peered through her living room curtains at him. He gave her a friendly wave.

Sheesh. No wonder Gemma felt like she was living in a fish bowl.

Genie unlocked and cracked the interior door. She left the security door closed and bolted so that she stared at Zander through the metal mesh. "What do you need me to do?"

"Nothing. Just wanted you to know I was here. Of course, I'll be pulling off the old door, so you'll have to put up with a bit of a breeze for a few hours. Oh. And I'll need you to unlock the deadbolt if it's latched."

"All right." She closed the door in his face without another word.

"You're welcome," Zander muttered.

He spent the next few minutes unloading the replacement doors and other materials from the truck. Then he shoved open the broken door and surveyed the damage to the frame's jack studs.

He talked to himself as he made his plan. "Stain the new door. While it's drying, take down the bent security door. Rebuild the doorframe."

He set up two sawhorses and wiped the new door with alcohol and steel wool. Then he began to apply a coat of stain to one side.

Jake bounded from the porch and landed near him.

"Hey, Jake. How ya doing?"

"I'm not abusing him," Genie spat. She leaned against the cracked doorframe, watching him.

Zander, wiping off excess stain, grinned to himself. "Well, just so you know, Jake will tell me if you are."

"*Right.*" With a sniff of disgust, Genie turned away.

Zander chuckled. *Bet she's miffed that she hasn't got a door to slam in my face.*

Whistling to himself, he grabbed a pry bar and started to tear out the ruined studs.

⌘⌘⌘⌘

CHAPTER 14

Dr. Bickel fixed us a lovely Sunday-morning breakfast—and I salivated as the aroma of fried sausages permeated the house. We sat down together and ate with companionable conversation. He had a single egg, a sausage, and an English muffin to my three eggs, three sausages, three English muffins, and three chopped and fried potatoes.

Dr. Bickel smiled his appreciation. "You are enjoyable to cook for, Gemma."

"Well, a girl has to keep her strength up."

We laughed together, cleaned up the kitchen, and then I did something I'd never done before: I readied myself for church—not to attend as a spectator, as I had a few weeks back, but as a participant.

"I wish I could go with you, Gemma," Dr. Bickel murmured. "I would like to hear Zander preach."

"Well, maybe he won't be speaking this morning. Usually the senior pastor gives the message."

"Still, I've been giving it some thought, and I'd like to, well, I don't know what to call it . . . I'd like to return. To God."

I grinned at him. "That is so cool! I just did, you know."

"I do know. I can see it in you, Gemma."

I was suddenly shy. "It's not me, not anything I've done. It's all Jesus. He . . . he's so much different than I thought he was."

Dr. Bickel nodded. "Maybe Zander can come and talk to me sometime?"

I shook my head. "He can't know where you are—not as long as you're in danger. I know it's hard, staying cooped up in here, but that's how it has to be. For a while longer."

"We went to the grocery store."

We had. The nanomites had covered him while I shopped as the younger Kathy Sawyer. It had been relatively simple for Dr. Bickel to avoid other shoppers; he'd stuck close by me, under the nanomites' umbrella, and we'd bought everything he'd jotted on his list.

Easy-peasy.

"I hadn't thought about taking you with me."

The nanomites could likely disguise both of us, but navigating the crush of five hundred people within the same building concerned me—what if Dr. Bickel and I were separated? What if we were forced apart by the crowd? How would the nanomites maintain our disguises then?

But perhaps we could arrange something else. Something safer.

"Well, what if . . . what if we watched from up in the choir loft?"

Apart from the crowd. Less chance of disaster.

"Yes, please, Gemma."

I tossed my original plan to attend as Kathy Sawyer out the window, but I was more than okay with our revised strategy. Dr. Bickel and I— under the nanomites' cover—left the house, walked to the parking garage, and drove to Downtown Community Church.

We waited until the crowds entering the church thinned before we, rendered invisible by the nanomites, approached the church's tall front door. This time, as I looked above the doors at the round, stained glass depiction of Jesus with the lamb over his shoulder, it touched a precious place in my heart. I not only knew what the image meant in its biblical context, I now knew what it meant to *me*.

Jesus, you came after me and rescued me. I was a lost lamb and you didn't give up on me! Thank you. I will never stop being grateful.

I lifted the cord strung across the narrow staircase and led Dr. Bickel upstairs into the empty choir and organ loft. We sat together in the same place I'd sat Thanksgiving weekend when Zander preached.

I wondered how Dr. Bickel would react to the loud and spirited worship service. I even giggled as his mouth fell open. But when the music shifted to a slower, more majestic song, we were both caught up in its beauty. The words were plastered on the huge screens, so I managed to follow along and join in on a few choruses.

After the singing, Pastor McFee was to give the message. But first, Zander walked out onto the platform to greet the congregation and welcome visitors.

"Good morning, DCC family! Isn't it wonderful to worship the Lord with all your heart?"

"Nano," I whispered, "uncover us just long enough for Zander to see us."

The mites did better than I asked. As Zander swept his eyes over the congregation, the nanomites spun a sparkling arch across the tops of Dr. Bickel's and my heads and down our sides. With an aura that shimmered from one side to the other, Zander couldn't miss us. I smiled and waggled my fingers at him; just as quickly, the nanomites "disappeared" us.

Zander's reaction was priceless; amid the lively responses to his question, his grin spread wide; he laughed aloud and gave a little wave of his hand. The congregation may not have known what tickled Zander so, but they laughed with him and waved back.

Then he bowed his head in prayer. "Lord, we can never be grateful enough for the gift you gave us in Jesus. Your mercy, your love, your grace. They overflow in our hearts. May we walk worthy of the high calling of Jesus Christ. Amen."

The amens filled the hall as the DCC congregation agreed. Up high in our perch, Dr. Bickel and I joined our affirmations with theirs.

***

"General Cushing, we've traced the escrima sticks to an online purchase in November. Three weeks ago."

Trujillo wasn't enthused about reporting the information to Cushing. The more she reflected on the work she did for the general, the less comfortable she felt with the position she found herself in.

She'd flinched at the news of Colonel Greaves' death and that of his aide: One death was curious, perhaps suspicious. But two? Trujillo was convinced that Cushing had given orders to "dispatch" Colonel Greaves and his aide.

To whom Cushing had given orders for their deaths, Trujillo didn't know, but the fact that Cushing hadn't asked Trujillo or her fellow agents to perform tasks that were illegal or questionable told Trujillo a lot: It told her that Cushing had other means . . . other *people* at her disposal, people who operated outside the scope of the law—people to whom murder posed no ethical impediment or scruple.

Cushing huffed with impatience. "Well? Give me the file."

"Yes, ma'am." Trujillo handed Cushing the short dossier she'd assembled.

"Kathy Sawyer. Age 52. Terrible photo. Address is a box in a UPS store. Checking account, credit card, vehicle." Cushing reread the file and then began to peruse the list of credit card purchases. Trujillo had contacted most of the online retailers and assembled a list of the items Sawyer had purchased.

"I see she used her credit card to buy these sticks as well as two sets of practice sticks and shoes."

"Yes."

When Cushing finished reading the list of purchases, she came back to the same bit of information Trujillo had homed in on.

"She used her credit card to activate three pay-as-you-go phones. Why does anyone need three phones?"

"Husband? Kids?"

"Not if this is merely a cover, a fabricated identity for our subject. No, she has allies. Collaborators."

Trujillo felt a twinge of sympathy for the elusive Gemma Keyes. Perhaps she even felt concern. She didn't know *specifically* what the young woman possessed to warrant Cushing's rabid pursuit, only that it was connected to Dr. Bickel's missing research.

The concerning bit was Cushing's ruthlessness. If the general had no qualms about eliminating *loyal operatives* because they possessed intimate knowledge of her illegal activities, what would she be willing to do to the woman who held a secret Cushing so desperately wanted? Or, for that matter, what would Cushing be willing to do to Trujillo and the rest of her teammates when they, too, became "inconvenient"?

Trujillo swallowed down a frisson of foreboding.

"This Kathy Sawyer is twenty or more years older than our subject," she suggested.

"Indeed—so why would a woman of her age need escrima sticks? The same sticks that were left in the facility when Dr. Bickel escaped and, I would judge, that were used on Colonel Greaves and his aide as well as the guards. Colonel Greaves' injuries, in particular, were consistent with blows from a hard, blunt object."

Cushing stared forward, thinking. "I don't know if this Sawyer person is a cover or an accomplice, but your task is clear: Find this Kathy Sawyer and apprehend her."

"Uh, I have one more piece of information, General."

"Well, out with it."

"The martial arts supplier said he received another order from Sawyer yesterday."

"For?"

"For three pairs of escrima sticks. Identical to the last pair."

"To replace the ones left behind. This is a stroke of luck! Who's the carrier?"

"UPS, ma'am."

"Intercept that order before it reaches Albuquerque, Trujillo. I want geolocators attached to the order. When Kathy Sawyer picks up her package, we'll follow it—and her—to her lair."

"Should we stake out the UPS store where she has her mailbox?"

"No."

Trujillo was taken aback, but she knew not to argue with Cushing. *Why wouldn't she want us to capture the Keyes woman when she picks up the package?*

Cushing chewed the end of her thumb as she held an internal debate. "I don't want to spook Keyes. It's more important to track her back to her hiding place than try to apprehend her when she picks up the order."

Coming to a decision, Cushing added, "In fact . . . I want those geolocators switched off until *after* the shipment is picked up. When you've been notified that the shipment was picked up, wait two hours, then remotely activate the geolocators."

Trujillo wondered what the woman was hiding from her team. "Yes, ma'am. I'll take care of it."

***

Late that evening, the nanomites spoke to me. *Gemma Keyes. We have received a reply from the family of Arnaldo Soto.*

I shivered. *Lord, if the nanomites' idea isn't your will, please tell me? Don't let me make a mistake.*

"Show it to me."

I scanned the email and shivered again. The message, although not signed, was from Miguel Soto's email account.

In your message, you assert that you have located my nephew Arnaldo, and you indicate that he has created a significant problem for you. I believe you are sincere in your request for our assistance in solving your problem.

I have dispatched trusted emissaries to Albuquerque. My associates will arrive Tuesday and will await your further direction at the number below.

If your information is valid and results in the safe return of my nephew, you will be entitled to the posted bounty.

The email ended with a phone number.

"Nano. Send this reply: 'We will call the number you provided on Tuesday after Arnaldo Soto has sent his instructions. We can then inform your associates how to proceed.'"

Yes, Gemma Keyes.

"And Nano? Trip the counter on Soto's website so that he knows we've seen his post."

Done, Gemma Keyes.

***

After reading Miguel Soto's email, I was too restless to sleep. I jogged over to the martial arts school so Gus-Gus and the nanomites could give me the workout I needed.

Perhaps they gave me too much of a workout? I was so tense and aggressive, that I actually broke one of the school's sticks across Gus-Gus' thigh.

I left an envelope with money in it for my use of the dojo. I put in extra for the escrima stick I'd broken, and added a note.

Hey Doug,
Sorry about the busted stick. I guess I got a little too enthusiastic. If this doesn't cover it, let me know?
—Emily

I grimaced. *Emily? Sheesh. Why did I pick Emily?* I stuffed the note into the envelope with the money and headed home, hoping I could sleep a few hours.

I itched for the comforting feeling of my own sticks again. I was glad that I'd ordered three pairs—especially if breaking them was going to be an ongoing "thing."

"Nano—"

Gemma Keyes, your new sticks will not arrive until Friday.

I was not pleased. "What? I thought you used expedited shipping."

We have checked the supplier's database, Gemma Keyes. The sticks were backordered; the new shipment will arrive at the supplier's warehouse Wednesday. The supplier will overnight your order on Thursday. It will arrive Friday.

I grumbled, but had to accept the fact that not everything in life was measured in nanoseconds.

Lord? Zander says you know the end of an issue from the beginning, that your timing is perfect. All right. I trust you. I trust that your timing in this is perfect, too.

I had no idea.

⌘⌘⌘⌘

CHAPTER 15

I woke Tuesday morning keyed up, itching to move, needing additional exercise to blow off my anxiety over the day ahead. I scanned the nanocloud, but Soto's website had shown no fresh activity. I started to lace up my shoes for a run and thought better of it.

I'd better read my Bible before I begin my day.

Since Thursday evening when Zander had given me my own Bible, I'd read from it every chance I got. I read so quickly and was so hungry that it didn't matter where I opened to: I devoured what was in front of me—large chunks, whole books, and simple psalms.

At times, I wanted to call Zander and ask him what a verse or a passage meant. I didn't, though. He didn't call me, either. It was probably for the best . . . because despite the sweet fellowship we'd shared over coffee Thursday night, it hurt to think about what we might have had together.

Ducking Zander was the best way to avoid aggravating that raw, painful place. I figured that he felt the same way.

Instead, I forged ahead in my Bible and, while I had lots of questions, it also seemed like everything I read filled in a piece, a gap, or hole in my faith. Better than the answers to important questions were the moments when God's character filled me with awe. Yes, I was learning a lot, but so much of it was learning to know *him*.

I began to experience great reverence toward him—and I started to grasp his deep love for me. Sometimes, in those intimate encounters, I wept and didn't fully comprehend why . . . except that who Jesus was to me was changing. Growing. Expanding. Enlarging. And when it was all too much to contain, the tears would come.

I was re-reading the part of the Bible I found most fascinating: the gospels. I loved reading the very words Jesus spoke! This morning I was deep in the Gospel of Matthew, studying about seeking and asking, true and false disciples, and wise and foolish builders.

After I finished my Bible study, Dr. Bickel and I ate breakfast, and then I went for that long, vital run. As I set my pace, I continued to mull over Jesus' words regarding wise and foolish builders. I had memorized the chapter and, as I ran, I mouthed the passage. The comparison between the two kinds of builders helped me to grasp the point Jesus was making, which was how *hearing* what he said differed from *doing* what he said.

It was evident that the difference in outcome was nothing short of catastrophic.

". . . Everyone who hears these words of mine
and puts them into practice
is like a wise man who built his house on the rock.
The rain came down, the streams rose,
and the winds blew and beat against that house;
yet it did not fall,
because it had its foundation on the rock.
But everyone who hears these words of mine
and does not put them into practice
is like a foolish man who built his house on sand.
The rain came down, the streams rose,
and the winds blew and beat against that house,
and it fell with a great crash."

"Lord, please help me to do what you tell me to do. Don't let me build my house on anything other than your firm foundation, the rock of your certainty. When the winds blow and beat against me, please help me to stand strong in you."

I was on my fifth mile when the nanomites broke in.

Gemma Keyes, someone has uploaded additional content to Soto's website. It is a message for you.

Air whooshed out of my lungs. "Show me the page?"

It appeared before me. The message was short. Terse.

If you want the kid to live past today, park alongside Netherwood Park on Princeton Dr. NE. Leave your vehicle and walk to the corner of Schell Ct. NE and Morrow Road. Be standing on the corner at 4 p.m. sharp.

We will be watching from a distance. If we don't SEE you, we make a call and the kid dies. If we see anyone else, the kid dies. Try any disappearing tricks, and the kid dies—and I guarantee you'll never find his body.

If you obey my instructions to the letter, a car will pick you up at 4:05. You have one chance to save the boy. Don't blow it.

Below the paragraph were these words: *I agree to your terms* followed by a check box and a Submit button.

"Send our response, Nano." I kept running, but turned toward the safe house. "Were you able to trace the upload?"

I held my breath. Web content is created offline; it would have taken mere seconds for the site's owner to publish it to the website—a task so quick that even the nanomites might not have been fast enough to backtrack the point of origination to its source.

Yes, Gemma Keyes. We have the IP address of the computer from where the page was uploaded and have pinpointed the computer's location.

"Show me."

Like a large topical map, a satellite image of Albuquerque appeared before me. The nanomites zoomed in on the image, and we traversed I-40 westbound, out beyond Unser, beyond 96th, to somewhere between Atrisco and Rio Puerco, which bordered the Cañoncito Navajo Reservation.

We turned north and traveled on unmarked roads far out onto the west mesa, making lots of turns. I estimated that Double Eagle Airport and the City of Albuquerque's shooting range were somewhere east of our "whereabouts," but beyond those vague markers in my mind, I didn't know where we were.

Didn't matter. As we floated over the satellite photo, I memorized the route.

Gemma Keyes, this is the origination point of the message uploaded to Soto's website.

I zoomed in closer, scanned the area, took in the large excavated hole and nearby mounds of crushed rock in varying sizes. An old conveyor belt led from the edge of the hole to a rock crusher. Both pieces of equipment were rusted. Dilapidated. I homed in on the squat concrete building a couple hundred yards from the hole.

"This building?"

Yes, Gemma Keyes.

"This place . . . looks like an old gravel quarry."

Yes, rock excavation to produce gravel was the initial purpose of this site, Gemma Keyes. The quarry was abandoned six years ago due to noncompliance with safety regulations.

"So, the owners just left their machines?"

These machines were old and unsafe when they were left here, costly to repair or dispose of.

I hovered over the boxy building. "Can you call up schematics for this structure?"

A minute later a diagram appeared. From it, the nanomites created a 3D model and superimposed it over the building. I saw two floors and a large basement level.

I rotated the model and examined it from every angle. The first floor appeared to be typical office space; the second floor could have been a caretaker's quarters. The basement was partitioned into five rooms. For what purposes, I couldn't tell.

A red outline appeared around an interior room below ground.

The upload came from this room, Gemma Keyes. The computer is located here.

"Do you think what is left of Soto's gang is operating out of the basement?"

This image is not recent; however, we have counted three houses within a quarter mile of the rock quarry. If Soto and his gang are using this facility, perhaps he feels they would attract less attention at night by keeping below ground. Unexpected lights from a deserted quarry would generate unwanted curiosity.

"Good point." I went back to the web content and the computer that uploaded it. "Soto's computer. Is it still on?"

Yes.

"Does it have a camera?"

You have asked an astute question, Gemma Keyes. We shall hack into the camera remotely.

A moment later the satellite image gave way to the sights and sounds of what I hoped was Dead Eyes' headquarters. I said "sights," but the laptop sat on a table that faced the interior of the room. No one was presently sitting *behind* the computer—which meant that, at the moment, the laptop's camera gave me a great view of an empty chair and a rough cement wall rather than a look into the room.

The camera's audio, however, was more productive.

Three men spoke from the other side of the desk. I recognized Soto's voice immediately, even though the men conversed in Spanish.

I should probably take the time to learn Spanish. I speculated how quickly I might master the language, given my present rate of reading and memorization. A couple of weeks, maybe?

"Nano, can you identify who, other than Soto, is speaking?

We can tell you that the accents of the other two men differ from Soto's. We believe them to be American Hispanic males.

"Can you tell me what they're saying?"

Yes, Gemma Keyes. Soto is complaining about the condition of his hand. The many broken bones are causing him ongoing pain and he is concerned that the bones will knit improperly. He has need of a bone specialist.

The more outspoken American male insists that Soto can get adequate medical care in Mexico and is pressing for immediate departure. Soto, however, says he will not be returning to Mexico—that Mexico is not safe for him.

The nanomites paused. *Gemma Keyes, Soto just called the other man "Benally." Benally is angry because Soto promised that he would pay Benally money and then he could escape to Mexico. Benally says it is too hot for them in New Mexico.*

Gemma Keyes, is New Mexico temperature significantly warmer than that of Mexico? This does not seem consistent with historic temperature records.

I snickered. "It's slang, Nano. Benally was one of the APD gang unit officers who helped Soto escape. The FBI wants them pretty badly and is putting a lot of effort into finding them. The increased effort is called 'heat.' That's what Benally means by saying it's 'too hot' in this state."

The tone of the conversation has become quite tense, Gemma Keyes. It appears that Soto has no intention of paying Benally until he has "taken care of certain business issues," and Benally is unhappy at the delay.

"What of the third man?"

We believe he is an older member of Soto's gang, as evidenced by his frequent and sycophantic affirmations of Soto's statements.

How the nanomites used fifty-dollar words but managed to stumble over common idiomatic expressions would never fail to amaze (and amuse) me. "Sycophantic affirmations," my left foot!

The nanomites broke off and then added, *Soto has asked his man to go into the other room and print out yesterday's accounts. Soto told Benally that he wished to recruit Benally and his men into joining his organization. The accounts are to demonstrate that his business is flourishing.*

"Soto is running his drug business from the quarry."

It would appear so, Gemma Keyes.

"That's enough, Nano. Please keep monitoring them, but I would like to see the satellite image again."

It appeared.

What are you looking for, Gemma Keyes?

"Those." I pointed to the trail of powerlines leading away from the concrete building. "Soto needs electricity and bandwidth to manage his business. I needed to see where it was coming from."

I wanted to confirm that we had plenty of juice available for our needs.

***

It was almost noon. I knew I was cutting it close, but I also knew Gamble wouldn't pass on this opportunity.

The phone rang on his end and his familiar voice greeted me. "Special Agent Gamble."

"Hey, Gamble."

"Hi there. Haven't heard from you in days."

"I haven't had a reason to call you, and you haven't posted the Bat Signal."

Gamble chuckled softly. "No; I haven't needed you just yet. But it's your dime, Gemma. What's up?"

For the next twenty minutes, I chose my words carefully.

When I hung up, I called the phone number Miguel Soto had emailed the nanomites. I knew I would have to be even more judicious with my interactions with Miguel Soto's associates and how I coordinated my plan. In some respects, I was playing the part of a square dance caller—only this dance, if I made a wrong call, could prove deadly.

The phone rang.

"*Sí?*"

"Señor Miguel Soto asked me to call this number."

The voice on the end, although heavily accented, switched to English. "You are the sender of the emails?"

"Yes."

"You know where is our mutual friend?"

"Yes."

"How we find him?"

"I will text instructions to you, and you must follow them carefully. Do not deviate from the timing or the details. Is that clear?"

"One moment, please."

He muted the call on his end. I figured he was conveying my message to his superior. When he came back on the line, he said, "Now I, too, have a message for you."

"I'm listening."

"I am instructed to tell you: Do not, as your American movies say, 'jerk us around.'"

"It is not my intention to do so, but I must first satisfy Soto's demands in order to get close to him. When the timing is right, I will deliver him to you as promised."

"*Bueno*. We will wait."

***

Genie stared at her inbox. With the exception of a few automated replies, she'd received not a single response from the twenty-three applications she'd submitted for positions from Albuquerque to Santa Fe to Las Cruces.

It's too early, she told herself. *It's only been a few days. Too soon to expect an answer.* She toggled to another screen and stared at her bank balance.

Tired beyond belief, Genie trudged to the bedroom, stripped off her clothes, and fell into bed. She was too exhausted and disheartened to bother brushing her teeth or slipping on a nightgown.

But, as tired as she was, she couldn't shut down. For more than an hour, she stared at the ceiling, unable to fall asleep.

Close your eyes, idiot, she berated herself. *You can't sleep with your eyes open.*

But when she did close her eyes, all she could see was that blasted man, Zander Cruz, whistling while he went about framing up a new back door. Or, worse yet, Zander Cruz, preaching her a sermon.

"When you leave my office, Genie, I want you to see God differently than you do now—in fact, I want you to see yourself differently. The first step in coming to terms with God is acknowledging who and what we are. That's good news for you, Genie, because he isn't asking for your 'feelings.' Rather, he is asking that you acknowledge your brokenness."

Genie peered into the shadows of the room and, for the first time in her life, wondered—

A weight landed on the bed. She felt it shift. Pick its way across the bedspread.

"You!"

Jake settled near her hip as he had the last few nights—because Genie was afraid to push him off the bed. Soon after, Jake began to purr.

"At least one of us can relax."

The thing was, Jake's presence at night wasn't as terrifying as it had been. Listening to his contented breathing lulled Genie into a better frame of mind.

Without realizing it, she slipped off to sleep herself.

⌘⌘⌘⌘

CHAPTER 16

A few minutes before 4 p.m. that afternoon, I parked my car on Princeton Drive alongside Netherwood Park. I walked to the other side of the grassy, odd-angled plot to the corner of Morrow and Schell Court. As I passed a cluster of scraggly bushes not far from the corner, I palmed my phone and tossed it deep into the shrubs.

Six steps later, I stood at the corner as ordered. I waited passively, the nanomites calling the time as the minutes ticked down.

It is 4:03, Gemma Keyes.

"Thank you. Please send the text."

A stream of nanomites flowed from me to the bushes where I'd ditched my phone. They sent instructions and directions in two succinct text messages then powered off the device and returned to me.

We have sent the information, Gemma Keyes. It is now precisely 4:05.

"It won't be long."

And it wasn't. A late-model, nondescript Chevy eased up to the curb. Two men stepped from the rear doors. One of them gestured to me, and I followed him to the backside of the same scraggly bushes where I'd tossed my phone. With the shrubs shielding us from the street, the man patted me down.

Satisfied, he pulled a cell phone and spoke into it. "She's clean."

To me, he muttered, "This way."

I followed him to the vehicle and, at the jutting gesture of his chin, I climbed into the back seat. The two men slid in, one on either side of me. It was a tight fit, like being sandwiched between two bodybuilders on an airplane, their muscled arms overlapping mine. Then we drove.

Gemma Keyes, these men are not respecting the socially acceptable norms of "personal space."

"No duh, Nano."

My nose wrinkled. *Gross.* The guy on my left needed a shower.

No one in the vehicle uttered a word and, since I already knew the route, I watched the scenery go by, along the Interstate and paved state roads, then dirt roads, and finally back roads, some no more than one-way tracks through the desert.

Thirty-five minutes later, I looked ahead and noted two armed gangbangers flanking a chain-link gate. They wheeled the gate open and waved us through. The car's tires crunched their way across an expansive lot. We'd arrived at the defunct gravel quarry.

I slanted a glance around. To my right, I counted six vehicles—guarded by a pair of gangers. The vehicles were lined up side by side under a lengthy canvas awning in a splotchy brown and tan camo pattern. Several hundred yards to my left, I spied the rim of the disused quarry pit. We drove straight ahead toward the squat concrete building.

Two stone-faced hoods flaunting short semi-auto rifles eyeballed us as the car pulled up to the old building. They were joined by two others, similarly armed. The door to the concrete building flew open and yet another gun-toting gangster emerged.

Goodness. This place is positively bristling with firepower.

The man who'd patted me down got out of the car and jerked me after him. His buddy zip-tied my hands in front of me. Then they pulled me into the building and down a dark stairwell to the basement.

Not too gently, either.

Soto and one of his lieutenants waited for me downstairs in a spacious, open room with ugly concrete walls. Soto's lieutenant had a fixed-stock AR 15 slung from his shoulder, but Soto held no weapon; however, his right hand, up to his elbow, was heavily bandaged.

Before I acknowledged my adversary, I gave the room a once-over—and observed a third occupant, leaning against the wall, smoking a cigarette. He seemed too detached and observant to be one of Soto's common soldiers. I compared his face to images of the APD gang unit's members.

Ah. Benally. The APD turncoat.

When I turned my attention to Soto, his countenance was a contradiction of manic jubilation and uncertainty. Maybe he expected Xena, Warrior Princess—and instead got Gemma, the Plain and Unremarkable?

Well, maybe not as unremarkable as all that, but still. . .*just a girl.* Had to be messing with his sense of machismo that *a girl* had trounced him so thoroughly.

As Soto approached me, I sent the nanomites out to find Emilio and complete their recon.

A frown twisted Soto's face. He lifted one languid shoulder, mocking me. "You? You are the one? You do not look like much to me."

He stepped closer. Too close. In my face.

"Say something. I must be sure."

"As you wish. Where's the boy? That was the deal."

His mouth widened into a smile. "So! It *is* you." With his free hand, he first caressed my cheek, then gripped my chin and jaws. Squeezed hard. Kept squeezing and laughed as his fingers dug into my skin. "You believed I would set the boy free? That was foolish of you, don't you agree? I think you will watch him die—and I will enjoy your pain."

I ignored his threat; I was waiting on the nanomites. "Where is Emilio, Arnaldo?"

Gemma Keyes, he is here, two rooms away. Second door on the left.

"Thank you, Nano."

That was the information I'd been waiting to hear; now it was time to tweak the tiger's nose and set things in motion.

I lifted one shoulder, a perfect mimicry of Soto's own cold, cruel mannerism. "Hey. So, Arnaldo, speaking of pain, how's the hand? I understand you haven't been able to get an orthopedic surgeon to tend it for you. I bet all those crunched up bones, all those painful nerve endings grinding and scraping together, really hurt. Am I right?"

Stung, Soto jerked and took a step back. Then fury sent blood boiling up his neck into his face. With an open palm, he slapped me and cursed in Spanish. He raged against me, alternating slaps and curses, going on for about thirty seconds.

My ears rang, my eyes watered. It was difficult to restrain the nanomites, to keep them from acting until I was ready.

Gemma Keyes, he said—

"Never mind the translation, Nano. I get the idea."

But, it was untrue as well as uncomplimentary, Gemma Keyes. We are certain your mother never—

"Drop it, Nano. Pay attention."

Ignoring my swelling, stinging face, I smiled a wicked taunt. I arched a brow in Soto's direction, but addressed his men. "Ooooh, looky here, boys! Arnaldo's still the spoiled little rich kid, isn't he?" Then I took slow, deliberate aim at Soto. "Like I said the last time we met, *Arny baby*, you know how to dish it out, but you can't take it—and everyone here knows you can't."

I glanced toward his men. "Right? Am I right?"

I sent a knowing smirk toward Soto's right-hand man—who caught himself before he grinned back. The man's gaze skittered away, but not before Soto noticed—and not before I laughed.

A vein throbbed in Soto's temple; he breathed with quick, heavy gasps. But as I continued to show no emotion other than bored indifference, he calmed.

"So. You wish to know if my hand hurts? If it pains me? You are very confident in yourself, my dear, but you will find out soon enough how 'crunched up bone' and 'grinding, scraping nerve endings' feel."

He held out his undamaged hand and received a thick stick of wood, a reasonable facsimile of an escrima stick—decent enough if you were unfamiliar with escrima sticks but had been on the receiving end of an invisible one.

He slammed the stick on the edge of a nearby table: The edge splintered under the blow.

"Cut the tie from her wrists, then hold her hand on this table. I wish her to see—as well as feel—each blow coming."

Soto was positively bubbling with gleeful anticipation as one of his thugs slipped a blade between my wrists. With a *snick*, the tie parted. The two men who'd sat beside me on the ride to the quarry grabbed my arms.

"Which hand, Señor Soto?"

"Oh, her right one. Yes. On the table, just so."

"I don't think so. Not today."

Soto leered at me. "What do you mean, 'not today'?"

"Let me show you."

The two men holding me yelped, convulsed, and fell away as the nanomites sent voltage through them.

My hands opened. The overhead lights flickered as I pulled electricity into me and began to emanate a throbbing, vibrating aura, the glow of fiery heat.

I thrust my palms in Soto's direction. Current shot from me into him; he screamed as he flew across the room, slammed into a wall, and crumpled to the floor.

Pandemonium erupted.

I waited with placid patience while Soto's thugs scattered and regrouped on one side of the room with me on the other. They reached for their weapons and, as men in panic tend to do, they gave no thought as to how .45 caliber handgun and 5.56 NATO rifle ammo might behave in close quarters.

No matter how good your aim, rounds fired in a concrete room *will* ricochet.

In the microsecond before the men opened fire, the nanomites drew a dome of pulsing power over me. I could hear shouts and gunfire—the muffled and distant-sounding thuds of rounds as they hit the dome and were repulsed—but I turned my back on their assault and moved with purpose down the hall.

I had but one task before me: Get to Emilio.

When I opened the door to the room where he was, he jumped up. "Gemma! I knew you'd come!"

"And here I am. Come inside with me where it's safe."

My arms reached for him and drew him into the protective dome. He grabbed me hard around the waist and hung on. I wanted to stay right there; I wanted to just hold him, but it wasn't the time.

We walked through the large room, toward the stairs that led upward.

"Close your eyes, Emilio. Don't look." He did as I told him, but I asked the nanomites to make sure he would not give in to the temptation to peek.

Of the five men who had been with Soto in the room when I left, two were dead—including the traitorous APD officer, Don Benally. The thug who'd yanked me from the car lay bleeding against a wall.

The casualties of their own ill-advised gunfire.

I heard staccato footsteps at the top of the stairs. Since Soto and his lieutenant were no longer in the room, it had to be them.

"Come on." I pulled Emilio toward the stairs, and I reminded the nanomites of their instructions while we climbed out of the basement.

The scene as we stood in the building's doorway was worse than downstairs. Every one of Soto's men sprawled in the blood-soaked gravel yard. My "reinforcements," the soldiers of Soto's Mexican family, had used their three vehicles as shields as they plowed through the gate and mowed down Arnaldo's men. It was a slaughter, and I tried not to fixate on it.

Arnaldo himself stood alone where the fight had raged, his lieutenant crumpled nearby.

He screamed at me, "You did this? You brought them here?"

Two soldiers left the cover of their vehicle and moved toward Soto. Realizing they were coming for him, Soto decided to run back into the building. Bullets spat gravel around his feet, and he skidded to a stop. The men reached Soto, and the taller of the two began to zip-tie his hands together. When Soto screamed in pain, they settled for binding his arms at the elbow.

That's when they noticed me. The tall guy waggled his tactical rifle, indicating I should move toward the middle car, the one farthest from the building. I started walking, keeping Emilio snugged to my side.

I was about ten yards from the vehicle when a tall, raven-haired woman stepped from the rear of the car in one graceful, fluid movement. Her stylish espadrilles crunched on the gravel as she walked toward me; her long legs made each step seem languorous. Unhurried.

I recognized her from the pictures the nanomites had shown me.

Esperanza Duvall appraised me, up one side and down the other. She was an elegant woman, perhaps on the far side of thirty-five. She wasn't beautiful, but she was striking, and she was accustomed to the accoutrements of wealth and power. Even in the middle of an abandoned gravel quarry, she radiated sophistication and confidence.

I wondered what she saw when she looked at me.

She spoke. "You are who sent the emails?"

I nodded.

"What is your name?"

"Of course, I would rather not say." I thought for a moment. "You may call me Jewel."

"We are grateful to you for returning Arnaldo to his family, Jewel."

Her soldiers, in the same unhurried fashion she had used when she walked toward me, began to fan out behind her. As the men on either end of the line edged farther into my peripheral vision, I nudged Emilio behind me.

"I think you have an odd way of expressing appreciation ... Esperanza. You have nothing to fear from me—I've played this straight and haven't 'jerked you around.'"

"As they say in the movies, it is not personal; it is business."

"I wish no trouble with you."

She shrugged and stared into the desert. "Life often does not give us what we wish."

"I only came for the child. I don't care about the bounty."

She seemed surprised. "Indeed? Is that so?"

"Yes. When you leave, I will take the child and go. That will be the end of it."

She seemed to think on my words.

I decided to change the subject. To stall.

Because I needed more. More incriminating information for the nanomites to record and upload to their library.

"Your brother. I call him Dead Eyes."

A glint of humor flared on her face. "*Verdadero*. Our doctors tell us he is quite without conscience. A sociopath. He was always different, even as a child."

"I understand. I have a sister afflicted with the same condition."

"You have my sympathies."

"Thank you." I pushed ahead. "Arnaldo has been busy since he arrived in New Mexico. I understand that he really upset your applecart."

"This applecart? I am not familiar with the idiom."

"It means that it bothered you when he hijacked your suppliers and trafficking routes. It means that his stealing your drug revenue in the Southwest created problems. Angered the family."

"Our anger was to be expected, no? Arnaldo is impetuous, but not unaware of the consequences of such an action."

I jumped back in. "I was surprised that the family sent you, personally, to fetch him home."

"Why? Cannot a woman do this job? I thought all American women were ambitious. Emancipated."

"Sorry. I just figured it would be your brother."

She smiled. "Ah, but Estevan is not married to an American as I am. My husband and I own a home in California, another in Washington State, and a third in Hawaii. I also hold permanent U.S. resident status. The 'green card.' I am often back and forth from *casa la familia* in Mexico and our homes in the States."

"That must make running the Pacific Coast portion of the family drug business much easier."

"It has its practical advantages."

"What will you do with him, with Arnaldo, when you take him home? Will you force him to give a kidney to his uncle?"

Her mouth hinted at a smile. "No, I think not. I believe my little *hermano* will donate *both* of his kidneys."

I flinched, and my face must have reflected my horror, because she laughed—and at that moment, the gleam sparkling in her eye looked too much like her brother's.

"You're as much a sociopath as he is."

"Ah, no, Jewel! You are merely too soft. Too compassionate. One cannot be tenderhearted in this business."

Her tone and demeanor abruptly changed. "I wish to see the boy, first. Show him to me."

"Boy?"

"Yes, the child."

"I don't have a boy. The child is a girl."

Behind me, Emilio squirmed but, as much as he wanted and tried to, he couldn't protest aloud. The nanomites had sealed his mouth. And down in the basement, while the firefight between Soto's thugs and his sister's men had taken place? At my command, the mites had altered Emilio's looks.

Considerably.

"What is this? I was told Arnaldo took a boy, the nephew of a previous *teniente*."

"I'm sorry to disappoint you."

I pulled Emilio forward. He was outraged that I'd labeled him a girl, and he was scared because the nanomites had sealed his mouth shut. He fought me until the nanomites did their thing, sent neurotransmitters flooding into his bloodstream to calm him down. When he stood passively by my side, I saw that they'd transformed him into a very pretty girl—even in jeans and a dirty polo shirt.

Frankly, it kind of freaked me out. *So* wrong!

"This is, um, Dahlia. My foster daughter."

Esperanza Soto pursed her lips and frowned. I gave her credit for her surprise and distress. I had hoped that the picture of a sweet, innocent little girl would make it harder for her to give the order to kill us. I preferred that Esperanza and her soldiers drive away, leaving us unscathed.

It wasn't that I was worried about our safety or how Esperanza Soto felt; I only cared that she *remembered*—in vivid detail—how the child I'd rescued from her demented brother was not the nephew of Mateo, former lieutenant to the Soto cartel, not Emilio, whose whereabouts—for enough money—could be traced through the New Mexico State CYFD system.

I wanted Esperanza to recollect the pretty, feminine girl I pulled from behind me. Esperanza could send her most trusted people and bribe anyone she chose, but she'd never find a trace of me or my "foster daughter."

Esperanza sighed, as though making up her mind. "I am quite beside myself, Jewel, but, alas, I must be true to my orders."

She lifted her chin to her men and stepped back as they racked their guns.

Before she'd decided, the nanomites had jetted from me. Now they formed a barrier—not of themselves but of pure energy, a wall of current to repel the deadly rounds. Through the hail of bullets, I flicked my fingers toward the closest soldier. His gun flew from his hands, and I sent it high into the air. He shouted as the gun arced far overhead, straightened, and soared like a missile into the deep gravel pit. Another gun followed, then two more, and another, then the last.

The soldiers shouted and babbled and pointed at the swirling, crackling dome surrounding me and Emilio. One of them pulled an amulet on a chain from his shirt and held it toward me. Another drew a handgun, tossed it aside, and held up his hands.

Arnaldo Soto screamed aloud, "It's her! It's her! She's the invisible woman! Kill her!"

Instead, the men backed away. Even Esperanza's face and body language reflected her disbelief. "What power is this? What magic?"

"Whatever it is, Esperanza, you are outmatched."

I lifted my arms again and held out my hands, palms facing up. Current jumped from my fingers into the air to coagulate into a jumble of crackling fire. The fire congealed into a blue orb that throbbed and vibrated and grew larger and larger.

The air around us charged; my hair lifted and stood out from my head, a glowing halo, a portent of danger, and I began to rise, to slowly lift from the ground. The aura around me intensified—as did the mighty weapon I held between my palms.

Esperanza's men gaped at the flashing, blazing sight—of my transfigured features and form elevating six feet above the parking lot. Then I threw the sphere! Nanomites shot from me to push the bolus of energy faster, to blast it toward my target.

The orb of power struck Soto's line of cars and detonated. Vehicles exploded and hurled their parts into the air only to crash to the earth as fiery debris. Flaming shrapnel and shards of shattered glass rained down over the burning piles.

Esperanza, her face a mask of terror, turned and ran. I had the nanomites shove her—just a little. She stumbled and recovered; they shoved her again, just for good measure. She fell to her knees.

She held out her hands in supplication. "Please!"

"Go, Esperanza," I ordered. "Take your men and your evil brother with you and go. Don't ever return."

She hesitated. "Our weapons."

"You won't need them—if you leave now."

She glanced at the heaps and mounds of burning scrap metal and nodded. She waved her men in. "*Ven!* Put my brother in the trunk of my car. *Ahora!*"

In thirty seconds, Emilio and I were staring at the dust of their departing vehicles. The nanomites returned Emilio's appearance to normal and released his mouth. In his glee over our defeat of the Sotos, he forgot that he was mad at me for calling him a girl.

"Are they gone? Can we go?"

"Yes, and yes. But first?" I wrapped my arms around him and held him close. He hugged me back with a ferocity that made my heart glad.

Then I took his face in my hand and turned his cheek into the light. "Are you all right? Are you hurt anywhere else?"

"Nope." Emilio lifted his chin. "Dead Eyes din't hurt me much, but I hurt him. Bit him hard."

I grinned. "Good job. You are so brave, Emilio."

He blushed, but I could tell he was pleased.

I put my hand on his shoulder and pointed him toward the gate. "Let's go, shall we?" I didn't want him to dwell on the carnage about us, on the bodies scattered throughout the yard where they'd fallen, the pools of blood staining the sand. The sooner I got him away from this place, the better.

"We gonna walk all the way home?"

"No, just for a little bit. Until the FBI sends a car for us."

His eyes bugged out of his head. "The FBI?"

"Yeah. I have a good friend in the FBI. Nice guy—you'll like him! Anyway, as soon as they arrest all those gangsters—" I waved in the direction Esperanza Duvall's caravan had gone "—he will send a car for us."

Emilio pulled me to a stop. "The FBI's gonna get 'em?"

I laughed a little. "Yup. My friend and his FBI team are waiting for them down the road a couple of miles. Don't know how much of a fight Esperanza's men can put up since most of their guns are at the bottom of the gravel pit, but we'll have to wait until the FBI puts them in handcuffs and stuff. We'll mosey along until my friend sends a car for us."

"Dead Eyes ain't going back to Mexico?"

"No, he's not. However, the nanomites recorded everything he said to me down in the basement—you know, bragging about kidnapping you and doing other bad stuff. The nanomites transmitted the live audio to my FBI friend, Special Agent Gamble. Plus, he has the other charges from before. I think Dead Eyes will go to prison for a long, long time."

Emilio went quiet. I could tell he was troubled. We reached the gate and marched past its twisted, bent remains.

After we'd walked for a few minutes, Emilio found a way to express himself, "Dunno, Gemma. Kinda liked what that lady said. You know, about Dead Eyes donating both his kidneys? I mean, you gotta have kidneys, dontcha?"

"Yes, you need at least one kidney to live."

"Well, them takin' both his kidneys sounded okay to me."

"You mean because then Soto would be dead and we'd never have to worry about him again?"

"Yeah, and 'cause he killed Mateo."

"You know about that, huh?"

"The big *blank* told me he did. Even bragged about it and all."

I nodded. "Yes, that sounds like him."

"An' he scared Sean, Gemma, and Sean's just a little kid. I don' want Dead Eyes scarin' Sean again. I'd rather Dead Eyes be plain ol' Dead, not just Dead Eyes."

It is so ugly and wrong when kids are traumatized, when they are scarred by the horrors of this life. I know. I remember Genie terrorizing my childhood; I remember how it felt to lose my mom and dad on top of Genie's mistreatment. I didn't want Emilio damaged by the wretched things he'd seen and experienced any more than he wanted Sean to be scared.

I put my arm around Emilio's shoulders. "I understand, Emilio. I used to feel that way about Dead Eyes, too. Well, maybe I still feel that way. But how about we let the FBI take care of him instead, huh? They are pretty good at their job."

Emilio shrugged. "All I gotta say is they better not lose him again."

I seriously agree with you, kid.

I saw a car in the distance, coming toward us.

"Ready to go home to Abe?"

Emilio brightened. "Yeah. That would be great."

"Well, here comes our ride."

⌘⌘⌘⌘

CHAPTER 17

Gamble let us out at the curb in front of Abe's house. I don't know who was more excited, Emilio or me. On the drive in, we'd stopped and retrieved my phone from the bushes, and I'd called both Abe and Zander with the good news.

They were waiting for us on Abe's porch.

While I thanked Gamble and said goodbye to him, Emilio ran from the car and raced up the steps into Abe's arms, then Zander's, then back to Abe.

"Cute kid," Gamble observed.

"Yeah, he is. He's had a rough start, but we'll try to help him. Steer him right."

"Group project?"

I laughed. "Something like that, yes."

As I reached for the door, he said, "Talk to you soon, Gemma."

"You know how to reach me if you need me, right?"

"Right. Craigslist. Uncut gemstones."

Emilio had already flown into the house to "see his room"—as though it might have changed in his absence. Abe and Zander followed him inside. With the nanomites covering me, I left the car and skipped up to the porch steps. Just within the doorway, the nanomites uncovered me and I walked into Abe's arms—and then Zander's.

"Hi, sweetheart," he whispered into my hair. "I've missed you."

Oh! Oh, how good, how wonderful his warm breath felt. It was hard to pull away from his embrace, but I made myself do it. Then Zander took my chin and turned my face this way and that. I could see how sad the bruises Soto had administered made him.

"They will fade quickly, practically overnight," I promised. "The nanomites will fix them."

Zander's hand dropped, and we stood there, so close to each other, but no longer touching.

Abe, noting the strain between us, tipped his head. "I promised that boy I'd make him spaghetti when he came home to me. I can make four servings as easily as two."

My belly lurched and growled. "Can you make six servings? 'Cause I'm starving."

Abe and Zander laughed, and it broke the tension.

"That I can, Gemma. That I can," Abe assured me. "I promise you won't go home hungry. Say, close the front door, will you?"

Before I did as he asked, I peeked across the cul-de-sac to check on my old home—and stared in stunned surprise: There, parked in the driveway, sat my aging Toyota.

"Who . . . Why is my car in the driveway?"

I saw Abe and Zander exchanging glances. "Who's at my house? Do you know?"

Zander nodded. "Close the door, and I'll tell you, Gemma."

I followed Zander into Abe's living room; Abe went directly to the kitchen—which was probably wise, because I was getting pretty hot under the collar.

I put both hands on my hips. "What's going on, Zander? Who's in my house?"

"It's Genie."

Two-by-four to the gut.

"What? Are you kidding?" I was too astounded to be angry—for a moment.

Zander rubbed his neck. "Apparently, Genie got on Cushing's bad side when she was here last, so Cushing got her fired from her job. We think Genie's broke, Gemma."

"You *knew* she was in my house? And you didn't tell me?" The volume of my voice rose with each word.

"Hold on a sec. I haven't exactly had a chance to talk to you in the past week, have I? Abe says Genie got here last Thursday—a little more than a week ago, the same day we left the mountain and took Dr. Bickel to the FBI's field office. The same day I found out Soto had taken Emilio. The last time you and I talked face to face was that night at the coffee shop, and I didn't know about Genie until the following morning. You and I haven't even spoken on the phone since then."

My next demands were close to shouting. "You couldn't have called? Texted? *Sent a carrier pigeon?*"

Zander's voice rose, too. "And for what, Gemma? You've been worried sick about Emilio and have been preoccupied with finding a way to save him. Why would I distract you from that? What if I'd told you about Genie, and it threw you off your game? What if it had caused you to bungle getting Emilio back safely? What if he'd been hurt? How would you have felt, then?"

"You should have told me anyway!"

Okay, it was official: our first fight.

"And what purpose would that have served?"

"Because it's *my* house, not Genie's! I—"

Gemma Keyes. Stop. Look.

I spun on my heel. Emilio watched us from the hallway, his face scrunched in agony, tears streaming down his face.

"Oh, no. Oh, my God. No."

O Lord, what have I done?

Emilio ran into his bedroom and slammed the door.

I fumbled for an excuse, but I knew in my heart I had none. To make matters worse, Abe hobbled into the living room and folded his arms across his chest.

I knew that face: He was about to deliver a strong rebuke—and I deserved it.

"Gemma, for shame! All Emilio has known his whole life is abuse. Anger. Shouting. Hitting. Abandonment. He's just started trusting us, just started believing we would never do those things to him. Girl, you know I love you, but the pain you just caused that boy undid a whole lot of the good you thought you did him."

He leveled his next censure at Zander. "And, Pastor? Don't care if you are a minister; the same goes for you."

Zander hung his head. "You're right, Abe. Gemma, I'm sorry. I shouldn't have yelled, shouldn't have lost my temper."

"I-I shouldn't have . . . I shouldn't have gotten so angry, either. I-I need to tell Emilio. Tell him I'm sorry."

Zander put a hand on my arm. "No, Gemma. *We* need to tell him."

I nodded. "Okay."

We knocked on the bedroom door. When Emilio didn't answer, Zander turned the handle. "Emilio? Gemma and I need to talk to you. Emilio?"

The huddled lump under the covers, clear down at the foot of the bed, had to be him. The "lump" quivered and shook as he sobbed his heart out.

I sat near him on the bed and placed both hands on him. "Emilio. I'm sorry. It was very wrong of me to yell at Zander like that. I need to tell you I'm sorry—and I need to ask your forgiveness."

Zander added his bit. "Me, too, buddy. I was wrong to yell at Gemma."

When Emilio didn't respond, I broke. "Emilio! Please forgive me! I love you. Zander and I are sorry we yelled. Please. Please forgive me."

My shoulders sagged and shook with regret and grief. I hardly noticed when Emilio crawled out from under the covers until he climbed into my lap. He patted me the way I usually patted him, and I hugged him to my chest.

"It's okay, Gemma. I forgive you."

Sweeter words I'd never heard.

***

Eventually, we ate spaghetti and garlic bread. Emilio gobbled down his share, but I had two large plates to his one. To top it off, we had vanilla ice cream with chocolate sauce drizzled over it.

When Emilio dropped his spoon into his empty bowl with a great contented sigh, Abe grinned at him. "Young man, it sure is good to have you home."

"Yeah." Emilio ducked his head. "I mean, yes, sir."

We three adults laughed, then Emilio laughed with us.

"Well, you've been gone a fair spell. Your clothes are worse for wear, and it looks like you haven't had a bath in a while."

Emilio shook his head. "Nope. I mean, no, sir. Dead Eyes din't have no shower."

"We're back to square one, then. I don't have any clean clothes for you 'cept one of my t-shirts. We'll get your clothes from your foster home tomorrow. In the meantime, I'll run a bath for you and throw what you're wearing in the washer."

"Yes, sir. Can I have some of that bubbly powder 'gain?"

"Comin' right up." Abe sent Zander and me the 'stink eye.' "You two can get after the dishes. And finish up your business in a kindly manner."

We answered, "Yes, sir," at the same time.

They left the table and Zander and I started clearing the table. While we worked, Zander talked about Genie.

"Last Friday, as soon as Abe told me Genie had moved into your house, I went over and confronted her. Said she was trespassing."

"And?"

"And, from what I could tell, she has no place else to go. She said she was 'housesitting' while you were gone. Said if you objected to her being there, you could call the police."

He scratched his head. "Kinda had me over a barrel there, you know? In the end, I figured it was better for her to be taking care of the place than it was leaving it open to thieves or vandals."

I nodded, just to let him know I understood—not that I approved.

"Speaking of taking care of the place . . ."

"What?"

"Cushing's jackboots trashed your side doors when they stormed in, so I replaced them."

I nodded again. "Thank you. I appreciate that."

"What will you do, Gemma?"

"It's not my problem that she lost her job."

"No, but you'd better have God's heart on this before you go over there half-cocked."

I hung the dish towel to dry. Sighed. "You know, it seems like the thing I feel justified in doing—that I have a right to do—always end up being the opposite of what Jesus wants me to do. It's confusing."

"Confusing? Yeah, sometimes it is—giving mercy to an enemy when they don't deserve it? Sowing kindness when we've received harshness? In many instances, we have to stick to our principles and say 'no,' but there are times when I've discovered that God needs to do a work in my heart before I can take a 'principled stand' against wrong.

"His objectives are always the redemption of lost souls, the wholeness of our walk with him, and the restoration of splintered relationships. Ugliness in us or from us can't accomplish any of those goals. When I'm more intent on being right than I am in the salvation of those who are lost, I have probably missed the whispers of the Holy Spirit."

I scowled, unwilling to admit that he made sense.

"Yeah. I get it, Gemma. Genie doesn't deserve your mercy."

I glanced at him sideways. He was holding back. Baiting me. "What?"

He shrugged. "Just that I didn't deserve God's mercy, either."

I expelled a ragged, frustrated breath. "Oh, bother."

"Why don't we pray, Gemma? Once we invite the Lord into the situation, you'll be fine. You'll know how to handle Genie, and it will be right."

We sat at Abe's table and held hands.

Zander prayed, "Lord, you know how painful this is for Gemma. Please give her your heart. Show her what to say to Genie and how to say it."

He waited for me to pray, too. Finally, I murmured, "Lord, I second what Zander said. Please show me what to say to Genie. I . . . I don't want to blow it. I don't want to be a jerk, Lord. Please help me."

Zander added, "Amen."

"Amen, Lord."

Abe came wandering back into his little dining nook. "You two take care of your business?"

"Yes. We've prayed. Now I need to go talk to my sister."

All Abe said was, "You watch your heart, Gemma. Pay attention, you hear?"

"Yeah. Okay."

Calling the nanomites to cover me, I left Abe's.

It was the weirdest sensation in the world, walking across the cul-de-sac from Abe's to my house—as I had done countless times while growing up and after Aunt Lucy died—but this time knowing that Genie had taken over my house. Through our childhood and beyond, she'd taken and taken from me. Now, she'd stolen my house.

My home.

I felt the anger churning again and stopped mid-stride.

"You watch your heart, Gemma. Pay attention, you hear?"

"Lord, please help me. I thought I'd let go of my old life. Guess it took someone squatting in my house to prove that I haven't let it go, that I'm still clinging to what is dead and gone."

I reached the curb and sat down on it. "Jesus? Is this a piece of the 'laying down my life' thing we talked about in the cavern?"

Greater love has no one than this:
to lay down one's life for one's friends.

"And she's not exactly a friend, Lord. In fact, if-if it were anyone but *Genie . . .*"

Anyone but Genie.

I shook my head. Those three words underscored a different problem.

"I know you expect me to forgive her, but she doesn't deserve my forgiveness, God. She's, well, she's evil."

The passage from Matthew that had spoken a crucial truth into my heart, came rushing into my deliberations.

". . . Everyone who hears these words of mine
and puts them into practice
is like a wise man who built his house on the rock.

My excuses didn't wash.

"You sure know how to stick it to a girl, don't you?" I groused.

I got to my feet, walked up the drive, and climbed the side porch steps. Both of the new doors were locked. The nanomites unlocked them, and I let myself in.

No lights were on. I wandered through the kitchen and found Genie in the living room.

Not the Genie I knew, the Genie of designer shoes and perfect looks and performance. She was curled up under a blanket, staring at the cold, dead fireplace. Her hair was . . . well, dirty and disheveled, and she looked . . . empty.

Gemma Keyes, the ambient temperature in this room is 54°.

"Huh. Why is that?"

It appears that the utility companies have recently shut off the electricity and natural gas for nonpayment.

I hadn't given the utilities at my house a single thought since I'd left, and that had been the end of October. It was mid-December now.

I tried to remember: Had I paid the October utilities?

Guess not.

Genie didn't sense my presence, but something did. It slid out from under the blanket where Genie huddled for warmth.

It stretched. Narrowed bright green eyes. And hissed.

"Jake?"

Genie bolted upright in a panic. "Who's there?"

⌘⌘⌘⌘

CHAPTER 18

I waited until the mites uncovered me before speaking.

"It's me, Genie."

"Gemma?"

She sprang to her feet and dumped Jake—who was sitting on her blanket—onto the floor. Rather than the snarl or scratch he would have bestowed upon me, Jake rubbed himself along Genie's leg.

And purred?

Genie didn't really notice, but *I* did.

What in the world . . .

Genie was too preoccupied with my unannounced visit—and the whole, "I moved into your house without so much as a by-your-leave" elephant in the room.

"Gemma, I know I didn't ask if I could stay here, but I can explain."

Guilt is a funny thing, and I might have expected guilt—except I didn't deem Genie capable of the emotion. So, if Genie wasn't awash in guilt, what was it?

She squinted and inched closer to me. "Gemma? You look different. But I can't see you too well."

Remember, the electricity was off, and it didn't help that Genie had all the curtains drawn—probably to keep the cold out—so the house was shadowed. Dim.

"It's dark in here." I went to the window and pulled open the curtains.

When I turned back, Genie gaped. "What the *bleep* happened to you?"

I shrugged. "I suppose I lost a few pounds. Got fit. Changed my hair a while back."

At the mention of hair, she remembered her own. "I look like crap."

"*I* look like something that dratted cat dragged in. You've never looked like crap in your whole life, Genie."

She winced. "We're twins, remember? I know that I don't look . . . the way you look right now."

She turned around and her voice took on the hard edge I knew so well. "I suppose you've come to evict me."

I didn't reply, because there was something else in her voice, that thing I'd wondered about a moment before. Was it a hint of desperation?

I frowned. Was Zander right? Was Genie broke? The utility business was my fault, but . . .

"It's cold in here, too."

"Yes, I've been, um, conserving."

"The gas company shut off the heat, Genie."

She kept herself turned away from me. "I know."

"I'll have it turned back on."

She spit an angry, "No," and faced me. "I'm not your charity case."

"But you are my sister."

That statement hung between us, ripe with years of bitterness.

"Do as you wish, Gemma; I'll get my things together and be out of here in the morning."

"I don't know why. No one else is living here at the moment. I'd rather have someone taking care of the place than have it sit empty."

Wow. I even surprised myself.

"And I suppose you expect me to take care of your ugly cat, too!"

Classic Genie was back.

"He seems to like you." (What a wonder!)

"Well, he's a pest."

"No, what I mean is, Jake doesn't like anyone."

She glanced down at Jake, who was glued to her leg. He meowed and purred louder.

"Oh, yeah, I see what you mean." (Sarcasm deluxe.)

"I'm serious. Watch this."

I walked over and stood next to her. Jake growled and sank his teeth into my leg. I shook him off—but not before he'd clawed me six ways to Sunday.

"See? Jake detests me. Always has—but, then, he pretty much detests everyone. No one in the neighborhood would take money to pet him; they know he'll bite or scratch. But he did love Lucy."

Jake, all innocence, sat on Genie's foot—*on her foot!*—preening and licking his paws.

His manners were exquisite.

Annoying wretch.

"Well . . . he's never scratched me."

"Interesting. Lucy was the only one he'd ever cared for. Until you."

We didn't say anything and the silence became uncomfortable. Genie seemed to have fallen into a daze. She stared at the floor without moving.

Finally, I cleared my throat. "I'd better get going. Just wanted to . . . check in with you."

Genie snapped out of her stupor. "That's it?"

"Um, what do you mean?"

"You aren't . . . you aren't asking me to leave?"

I shook my head. "No. Like I told you, I'd rather have someone taking care of the place."

"Oh." She blinked a little.

"I'll have the power turned back on."

She nodded, once.

"Well, see you." I was headed for the back door when she called me back.

"Gemma?"

"Yeah?"

"Is . . . is that woman still looking for you? Cushing?"

At first I thought she'd asked because turning me in to Cushing would likely end her present financial difficulties. Then, as I mulled over her question, I realized I'd heard something else: distinct animosity toward Cushing, certainly, but also a bit of curiosity, a touch of disbelief.

I guess in Genie's mind, I would always be the ugly, stupid sister— and she couldn't wrap her head around any valid reason why Cushing would want me so . . . urgently.

"Oh, yes. Seen the news lately? She's still hunting me."

"But, what is that all about? I mean, really about? She said . . . she said it was a national security affair."

I sighed. "She thinks it is. Calls it that, but it's a lie. Regardless, I can only tell you a little; I can't tell you everything."

"Whatever." The scathing edge was back.

I ignored her antipathy. "Genie, I think you've figured out how corrupt Cushing is, how malicious."

Genie barked out a laugh that was *so* typical Genie, it set me on my guard. "Cushing malicious? You have no idea."

"Actually, Genie, I do have an idea. I can tell you from first-hand experience that Cushing is a stone-cold murderer. And I can tell you that if she were to ever get her hands on me, well, when she finished, I'd be dead, too. And that's why I won't ever allow her to catch me."

Genie shifted so that, by the light from the window, she could see me better. For a long moment, she studied me.

I let her and stared back. Unfazed. Unafraid. Unyielding. My jaw firm.

"Y-you seem different, Gemma. Not just how you look. You . . . I think you actually believe what you just said."

"The part about not letting Cushing have me?"

"Uh, yes."

I locked eyes with my sister, probing the vulnerability her reduced circumstances had produced, wondering if it was real. Not that I believed it could be: I had no illusions. When she landed a job, the same old Genie would make a splendid resurgence.

Finally, I said, "You can take this to the bank, Genie: I'm neither weak nor am I defenseless. I am well able to handle myself. The next time Cushing and I meet, I will beat her."

Genie fell back a step, uncertain of me. A little fearful of the fire I'd allowed her to glimpse.

On the drive home, I had the nanomites turn the utilities back on: They took cash from Kathy Sawyer's account and shifted it around to a couple dozen accounts, a little here and a little there, then pulled all the bits back together and plunked the past-due payments into the utility companies' accounts, after which they triggered the reconnect orders. I was confident that no forensic accountant would be able to detect, let alone unsnarl, the nanomites' digital sleight of hand.

Along the way, I stopped at an ATM and withdrew three hundred dollars.

Things weren't right between us, between Genie and me. I didn't believe they ever would be. Still, I felt the nudge of the Holy Spirit to be kind. Generous.

"All right, Lord. Whatever you say."

I drove back to my house and slipped the wad of cash through the cat door where Genie was sure to find it—If Jake didn't catch my scent on it and shred the bills to bits first.

⌘⌘⌘⌘

CHAPTER 19

I had a lot on my mind that night. I was so grateful to God for helping us rescue Emilio! He was safe and home with Abe where we all knew he belonged. I spent part of the morning thanking God again and again. The other part I spent wondering about Cushing: What was she was doing? What was she planning next?

The nanomites were watching her. For weeks, they had monitored her emails, electronic calendar, and phone logs. If a single byte of notable data appeared, they would tell me.

It was early Wednesday when they spoke to me.

Gemma Keyes. General Cushing has just placed a secure call on her calendar for this morning. Our assumption is based upon the notation she employed to designate previous secure calls. Shall we go?

"The same notation she employed to designate previous secure calls" referred to the code Cushing had used to note the weekly secure calls she scheduled with Colonel Greaves—the words, *Sandia Café,* plus the time. Albuquerque had no "Sandia Café." The initials "SC" for Sandia Café were code for "secure call."

The call couldn't be with Colonel Greaves. He was, as Gamble had informed me, dead—and under suspicious conditions, at that. If Cushing were not speaking with Greaves today, who would she be speaking with on the secure call?

A tingle of excitement shot down my spine. Were we getting close to identifying Cushing's handler, the real power behind her? If I were in the SCIF with Cushing today, could the nanomites trace the call and identify the individual on the other end?

"Absolutely, Nano. We should go."

Oh, yes, indeed. I was quite interested in being present during this call.

Monitoring her conversation would be less complicated this time since we knew which SCIF Cushing used. It would be, in fact, simple: The call was scheduled for 11 a.m.; we would be inside the SCIF before Cushing was.

***

I was relaxed and confident as we drove from the parking garage up I-40 to the Eubank exit and, a few minutes later, parked at Costco. The expanded numbers of the revived nanocloud allowed me to move about without fear of detection.

Our deeper union had removed the restrictions that used to hamper me: I was now visible or invisible at will and could assume the appearance of whomever best suited the situation. I was still getting used to my new norm, but it felt good.

Nanostealth in exchange for a "normal" life? Not, I advised myself, *the worst tradeoff ever.*

With the nanomites' and my combined abilities, I supposed that we could even do some good in this world. *After.* After the danger was past. I was even beginning to contemplate exactly what that good might look like—if and when Cushing and her superiors were no longer a threat to our existence.

I walked onto the base and into the SCIF. When I closed the door, the clock on the wall read 10:45. I had fifteen minutes to kill, and I used it to think about Emilio. The kid was so different when we'd brought him home. Happy. I wasn't used to his continual grin, but I loved it. I loved him. If I couldn't have my own children, at least I had Emilio.

I smiled. Also, not the worst tradeoff in the world.

Zander and I were committed to helping Abe raise Emilio. Our joint responsibility and the fellowship we shared would be enough.

Would have to be enough.

No, I acknowledged, *it truly would be enough. Because of Jesus.*

It was right at that moment, as I waited for Cushing, that I recognized the improved state of my heart. What was it that Zander was always saying? "Godliness with contentment is great gain?"

I felt rich inside. Once all the drama with Cushing was at an end, my life would be replete. Replete—as in having enough. And I'd find a new mission for me and the nanomites.

Everything would be okay.

Gemma Keyes, she is here.

I heard the clicks of the keypad outside the door before it opened and Cushing entered. She closed the door and turned the lock; the red "in use" sign over the door lit up. She hurried to the desk and sat down to wait for the phone to ring.

Something was off about her.

I studied Cushing. The woman wasn't as imposing or scary as I'd thought her to be when I first met her. I noted fresh lines around her mouth and eyes, too. She seemed uncertain. Stressed even. Was she . . . nervous?

I wonder—

The phone rang. Cushing swallowed, composed herself, and lifted the receiver. "General Cushing here."

I closed my eyes. The nanomites flowed into the phone and down the lines. I joined them, and we listened in on Cushing's conversation.

"Good morning, General."

Something about the voice on the other end seemed familiar.

The call is coming from a short distance southwest of Baltimore, Maryland, Gemma Keyes.

"Can you be more specific, Nano?"

Soon, Gemma Keyes.

My mouth opened as the unknown party spoke. In short, concise statements, he laid out his directions to Cushing. I still couldn't quite put a face or name to the voice—

Gemma Keyes, the call originates in a SCIF on the U.S. Army base of Fort Meade.

"Fort Meade?"

Specifically, Gemma Keyes, the SCIF resides within the 350 acres apportioned to the NSA.

"The NSA?" I sat there, blinking, trying to make sense of it.

NSA stands for the National Security Agency. I dug into the nanocloud's library, sucking up data on the agency: The NSA is the most clandestine espionage organization in the world. Its headquarters on the base include more than thirteen hundred buildings, and it is the largest employer in Maryland.

The NSA oversees the United States' signal intelligence (SIGINT) gathering. One subset of SIGINT is communications intelligence (COMINT), the interception of communications between individuals, such as telephone conversations, text messages, and various types of online interactions, including email and social media.

A second subset of SIGINT is electronic intelligence (ELINT), the monitoring and gathering of other electronic signals not used directly in interpersonal communication. Since much of the gathered ELINT is encrypted, the NSA also employs cryptographic functions or cryptanalysis to decipher messages its SIGINT functions gather.

I already knew (from our overhead search for the car that took Emilio) that the NSA owned four geostationary satellites. I hadn't known that it operates SIGINT monitoring stations throughout the world.

I frowned. What was Cushing's connection to the NSA? She was Air Force. I would have speculated DIA (the military's Defense Intelligence Agency), not NSA.

However, my next realization didn't take much of a leap. When I put the nanomites and their abilities into the NSA mix, instantly, the role Cushing's handler intended them to play came into sharp focus: How would an army of nanomites impact and advance America's COMINT, ELINT, and cryptanalysis?

The digital world is awesome.

I had said that. Those had been my words when the nanomites and I reset the scene after Cushing's attack on the FBI office. Yes, the nanomites could do just about anything in the digital world. They could hack, gather and store data, and crack encrypted communications—anywhere and any kind. The nanomites, if properly "handled," could remake the shape and speed of intelligence gathering. They would own the world's communications.

It would be a walk in the park for them.

With trepidation, I followed that thread: Information is power.

Supposedly, NSA's COMINT is concerned only with the communications of foreign entities, but if the nanomites were directed by the wrong hands? The nanomites could topple governments and nations. For that matter, if the nanomites were misused, they would personify Orwell's dreaded Big Brother and end freedom of thought or expression here in America. In the world.

No. I couldn't believe that our government would approve of such overarching surveillance. But it wouldn't need to be "the government," would it? A single, determined individual in a position of power and with a support network of covert, strategically placed operatives might change the face of America without anyone being the wiser—until it was too late.

I scanned the history of the NSA. I ran the names and photos of the agency's public face, its director and deputy director, the senate committees charged with oversight of the agency, its past directors—

I froze.

The person to whom Cushing was speaking? My breath caught in my throat as I connected the featureless voice on the other end of Cushing's call with the name and photo before my eyes.

I stopped what I was doing and concentrated on their conversation.

The caller laid out his next moves and, at each detailed step, Cushing answered with a curt, "Yes, sir." Given what I now knew, each sentence was an appalling revelation, a thudding blow to my heart. Worse than my nightmares had conjured.

Dr. Bickel, Gamble, and I had theorized about Cushing's handler or handlers. Dr. Bickel had suggested that they were well-placed and formidable politicians. During his FBI press conference, he'd even stated, "I must make it clear that General Cushing could not have acted alone in this cover-up or on her own authority. She could not have pulled off such an egregious deception of the public's trust without the political power of individuals high above her."

When SAC Wallace was interviewing Cushing and Gamble had challenged her, she'd warned them: "*Agent Gamble, you have no idea what you have interfered in. This case has authorization at the highest levels. The. Highest. Levels.*"

When I'd listened in on that interview, Cushing's words had alarmed me.

Now I knew why.

"Nano. We need to take a trip. Tonight, if possible."

A trip? Where are we going, Gemma Keyes?

"You heard the conversation?"

Yes; we have recorded the audio and uploaded it to our library.

"Good. We're going to need it."

Again, they asked, *Where are we going, Gemma Keyes?*

"To Washington, D.C. We need to warn you-know-who."

It is important to warn him?

"Well, yeah."

Sometimes the nanomites were worse than clueless. They were obtuse.

In my agitation, I must have moved. Shifted. Shuffled. Cleared my throat? I don't know which, but Cushing broke off her response to the caller. She clutched the phone with both hands and stared around the room, her eyes startled. Alarmed.

I didn't breathe. I tried not to move a muscle. Of course, I could still hear everything they said to each other.

"What is it?"

"I heard something."

"What do you mean?"

"Like someone is here. In the SCIF with me."

"How could someone be in the SCIF with you? Isn't it locked?"

"Uh . . . sir, I think *she's* here."

"She who? What—you mean *her*?"

Cushing nodded, then shook her head and whispered, "Yes. *Her.*"

"Has she been listening?"

"I-I would assume so. At least to my end."

"She could know nothing from your side of the conversation."

"But what if . . . what if she heard your end, too?"

"I doubt it, but even if she did? Well, there's nothing she can do. I . . ."

He went silent, as though rethinking Cushing's suggestion. Cushing did not intrude on his pause, although her eyes darted back and forth through the little room, unable to stop looking for me.

The man on the other end came to a decision. "Keep yourself at the ready, General; I'm pushing the schedule ahead." He outlined the changes, and Cushing answered with her usual, "Yes, sir."

"Whether she is in the room or not and whether she has heard or not, General, will make no difference. It is too late for her to interfere in any meaningful manner."

I took slow, measured breaths and gritted my teeth.

Oh, but I disagree.

⌘⌘⌘⌘

CHAPTER 20

I spent the afternoon in a flurry of activity, much of it carried out by the nanomites. While they were working, I jumped online and studied my objective. A lot of information was freely available; what wasn't in the public realm, I would pick up when I arrived.

The nanomites had booked a Business Select flight for Kathy Sawyer. My American Airlines flight would leave at 8:24 p.m. and put me into D.C. early morning. The flight backtracked to Los Angeles before going on to Dulles in D.C., but it was the fastest route available at such short notice. I would have plenty of time while *en route* to think through my goals and how best to achieve them.

Gemma Keyes, since you will not arrive until morning, we have booked a rental car for you and reserved a room at the Hilton Washington Dulles Airport so you can freshen up.

"Thank you, Nano. We will be confined in an airplane for the duration of both flights. Will you . . . how will you manage Kathy Sawyer's appearance all that time?" It was the first extended foray we'd attempted. I wasn't nervous . . . *exactly*. The nanomites and I could likely handle any situation that might arise, but I would feel better if I heard the same from them.

Yes, Gemma Keyes, we will manage. However, to lessen the strain on the cloud and decrease the possibilities of mistakes, we will modify your persona as Kathy Sawyer. She will look even younger, closer to your age and closer to your actual appearance; it will take less energy to sustain this façade.

My head filled with visions of middle-aged Kathy and the dark, puffy shadows hanging under her eyes. "But what about her age on her ID? Her photo?"

Airline and TSA personnel will scrutinize the license for a few seconds at a time. We will manipulate the ID while it is being examined. The ID will read age 28 and the photo will align with your appearance.

I liked it—and said so. "That's ingenious, Nano."

Yes, Gemma Keyes; it is also more expeditious and efficient.

"Well, I like expeditious and efficient. Fast and effective are always good."

I started packing.

Gemma Keyes. May we offer a suggestion?

The nanomites were learning manners and social forms. Interesting. I stopped what I was doing. "Um, sure, Nano. What?"

May we suggest that you go shopping? A higher standard of apparel will present you in a more favorable light during our trip. We recommend the purchase of a suitcase also.

"Oh, you do, do you?" And since when had they acquired fashion sense? I glanced at the duffle bag I usually carried my workout gear in and the few clothes I was stuffing into it: Jeans. Sweat pants and long-sleeved t-shirts.

Drat.

Yes, Gemma Keyes. We estimate that you have two and one-half hours of unscheduled time in which to make your purchases before leaving for the Sunport.

You know, I've never been much of a clotheshorse, but most of my jeans and shirts hung loosely on me since I'd become as active as I was. Then I remembered who I'd be meeting, and that cinched my decision.

"Right. Good call, Nano."

You will need a better coat, Gemma Keyes, and boots, hat, and gloves. The weather is much different at our destination.

They popped up the D.C. weather: A whopping 44° with a 10° wind chill off the Chesapeake Bay. Two inches of snow on the ground.

I grumbled at the added tasks and effort, but twenty minutes later I arrived at Dillard's in Winrock Center. I chose two outfits to wear on the plane and one especially nice ensemble that would, I hoped, be presentable enough for my "encounter." To those purchases I added a camel-colored wool calf-length coat, matching knit beret and gloves, a pair of fleece-lined, water-resistant boots with thermoplastic rubber soles, and three pairs of thick socks. Then I selected a Hartmann herringbone "spinner" case and headed for the cashier.

As I was on my way to check out, I pulled my credit card and license directly from my hip pocket.

"Huh."

No wallet, no purse. Just a hip pocket? Wouldn't I be the odd duck?

I wandered over to the handbag displays and chose a small shoulder bag and matching wallet. Caught a glimpse of myself in one of those mirrors customers use when they try on hats, scarves, and jewelry.

"Oh, crud."

What is wrong, Gemma Keyes?

"Look at my hair! I-I look like I'm deranged."

My hair was a shaggy, disheveled mess. Well, I'd been invisible for weeks, and my grooming had, frankly, gone to the dogs. No one had been able to see me—including myself—so why bother?

The nanomites said nothing. I sighed and turned from the mirror. Headed (again) for the cashier. Paid for my purchases.

Gemma Keyes.

I gathered the two shopping bags and wheeled my suitcase away from the counter. "Yes?"

You have an appointment for a cut and style at Mark Pardo's on Juan Tabo in twenty minutes.

"What? How did you do that?"

Your stylist had a cancellation. We booked you into her open slot.

"Had a cancellation? Pretty convenient, isn't it?"

The client called your stylist and rescheduled.

"Really?"

This is what the stylist believes.

"Wait. Let me figure this out. So, first you pretended to be the client who 'called' the stylist to reschedule her appointment. Then you pretended to be the stylist who 'called' the actual client to move her appointment?"

Yes. That opened up an appointment today. We booked you into the open slot.

I shook my head, concerned that I might need to give the nanomites a lesson in integrity. "Okaaay. Not entirely ethical but, given the gravity of our mission, quite convenient for me."

I hurried out of the mall toward my car when a particularly ironic thought hit me. "So, Nano. Um, you're not going to throw a chipping, chittering, stinging fit when the stylist washes and cuts my hair, are you?"

I can only describe what followed as the nano version of The Cold Shoulder. It was so quiet in my head that I could have sworn I heard faint echoes.

I'd loaded my loot into the back of the Escape and left the mall parking lot before they deigned to speak to me again.

The discourtesy of your question was entirely uncalled for, Gemma Keyes.

How'd they do that? They even managed to sound aggrieved!

I giggled all the way to the salon.

An hour later I left Pardo's feeling like a new woman. My clean, shoulder-length hair was artfully feathered until it framed my face and bounced on my shoulders. I ran my hand through the shaped tendrils, marveling at how a good cut could make such a difference.

I rushed home, tore labels from new clothes, and packed. Thirty minutes after that, with my stylish case in tow and my new purse slung over my shoulder, I left for the Sunport. An hour later, I boarded my flight.

***

The house was purported to be the most secure in the country, and it probably was—but the Secret Service could not have prepared for me. For us.

The visitors approved for the last tour of the day were lined up at the visitors' entrance off East Executive Avenue, so I, hidden by the nanomites, lined up with them. Waited while they checked in through security. Went inside with them.

I followed along with my tour group and paid attention to the guide's spiel because I'd never been inside the White House and, well, the history and grandeur of the place was all very interesting and inspiring.

Besides, I had plenty of time.

I trailed along as the group marched through the East Wing lobby, down the East Colonnade, through the East Garden Room into the White House's ground level. The guide led us through the east end of the Center Hall and into the Vermeil Room (nice portrait of Lady Bird Johnson over the fireplace), the China Room (lots of official White House china place settings in glass-fronted cases), and the library (lots of books: no surprise there).

While the group crowded into each room to gawk and listen, I stayed out in the hall where I was able to maneuver and keep out of the way. I peeked into the rooms as the guide lady talked. The house was festive with poinsettias, garlands, and lights; I counted three decorated Christmas trees just between the East Wing lobby and the Center Hall.

The Center Hall. I stared ahead, down that imposing gallery. The tour group wasn't allowed to go that direction, and two guards were stationed there to make sure no one tried to. But, if I *were* to head down the Center Hall and cross the length of the White House, I'd come to the Palm Room. If I walked through the Palm Room, I'd end up on the West Colonnade. There, I'd pass the rose garden and approach the West Wing where the Oval Office was. Where the President and his Secret Service detail were.

No worries. I had different plans.

The guide led the group from the east end of the Center Hall up a flight of marble stairs to the State Floor. We trooped into the East Room (it was big and mostly empty) then through a connecting door into the Green Room. (Surprise! The Green Room has green wallpaper.) I'm partial to watermarked silk, so I liked the look. We crossed from the Green Room into the Blue Room (nice oval carpet and a lot of blue, of course) and then into the Red Room (cool red sofa with carved, ornate feet partially covered in gold-leaf).

After a brief visit to the State and Family Dining Rooms and a walk halfway back down the red-carpeted Cross Hall, the tour group took a left into the formal Entrance Hall where heads of state are received. We marched down the Entrance Hall stairs and exited through the North Portico facing Pennsylvania Avenue and Lafayette Park. The tour guide led her group down the drive toward a guard shack on Pennsylvania where they were processed out. As it was a Friday and ours was the last tour of the day, my group exited close to 1:30 p.m.

I didn't leave the grounds with my group. Instead, I hung around under the portico and enjoyed the view from *this* side of the White House perimeter fence. After all, not many people got a leisurely opportunity to stand and gawk from my perspective. For twenty minutes, I watched the tourists lining the fence as they pointed and peered through the iron bars. I wondered what they would have thought, had they been able to see me.

Then I got down to business. I still had hours to kill, but I needed the time to better acquaint myself with the Secret Service's protocols and security measures.

So, I took a little walk.

It's a common sight for D.C. police to openly patrol the public face of the White House, either on foot or bicycle. The public side is *outside* the White House fence; *inside* the fence, Secret Service personnel walk their routes discreetly, and an unknown number of snipers watch from the White House's rooftop and from a select number of buildings surrounding Lafayette Park.

I kept out of the Secret Service's way, the nanomites steering me as I walked, but I kept my eyes open, memorizing the lay of the land and the number and placement of agents.

Just in case.

An asphalt walkway led west from the portico; I strolled down the walkway onto the West Wing's driveway. The drive wrapped around in front of the lobby's north-facing exterior doors.

A lone Marine stands post outside those doors whenever the President is in his office. Although the guard's presence is largely ceremonial in nature, the fact that the Marine stood there this day told me where the President was.

I didn't get too close; I just observed as the Marine acted as doorman to whomever came in and out of the West Wing. Actual protection of the President falls to the Secret Service and, within the West Wing, the agents directly assigned to the President's protective detail are close by, an ever-present force to be reckoned with.

Just so you know, there's more to White House security than the Secret Service agents themselves. For example, while the President is at work, his detail stands outside the Oval Office, not inside. However, rather than watching through peepholes or using cameras to keep an eye on their protectee, the Service installed weight-sensitive pressure pads under the carpet.

That way they know exactly where the President is within the Oval Office at all times. If he were to, God forbid, collapse onto the floor, his detail would infer the situation immediately.

But, again, I wouldn't be approaching the man in his office.

The Service also utilizes high-tech electronic technologies to control access to restricted areas of the White House. The type and placement of these technologies aren't made public, but I was confident that whenever I encountered motion sensors or motion-activated cameras, the nanomites would handle them—one way or another.

The situation is a bit different in the Residence, which encompasses the two floors above the State Floor. Access to these two floors is tightly controlled by agents standing post at the entrance points. Within the Residence? If I encountered a few of the above-mentioned technologies in the halls, they would not present a problem.

I supposed that I might need to dodge a maid or an usher upstairs. The White House's domestic and service staff consists of ninety-six full-time and two-hundred-fifty part-time employees including butlers, ushers, maids, chefs, plumbers, doormen, and florists. Most of the staff works behind the scenes (the White House has two levels below ground), but a number of them have access to the Residence. Fortunately, the President and his wife preferred to ready themselves for bed rather than keep staff up late unnecessarily.

I returned to the North Portico. The door was locked, but the nanomites disabled the security device attached to the door, then unlocked the door and spoofed the video feed so it did not show the door opening and closing as I entered. I stepped inside, turned right, and wandered west through the Center Hall. Along the way, the nanomites swarmed ahead of me, drawing energy from every electrical box and defeating whatever security devices they encountered.

I put my head in a few doorways and, a couple of rooms before the end of the hall, found what I was looking for: the Secret Service's command center. The nanomites flooded into their network. I went with them. We scoured the schematics of the house, those closely guarded details, and uploaded them and all the security protocols to Alpha Tribe.

It was quite enlightening, the many physical and technological measures employed to keep the President safe. For his sake, I was pleased—although their deterrents wouldn't matter a snap to us.

I'd chosen this day because, later in the evening, the President and First Lady would be attending a concert with the Japanese Ambassador and his wife. They would not be returning to the Residence until late. Although tomorrow was Saturday, the President had an early breakfast meeting with the Vice President, a working breakfast to focus on an important piece of legislation the House was preparing. These details were covered in the President's public schedule.

I'd had to infer additional factors that shaped my planning. Such as? Such as how most people agree that the President and his wife enjoy a happy marriage.

Once, during an interview, he had let slip an intimate comment: "Whenever the First Lady and I have a late night and I have an early start the following day, I have the couch made up in our living room. That way, my early wakeup call doesn't disturb the First Lady's sleep.

"We're not getting any younger," he'd joked on late-night television. "Mrs. Jackson is a light sleeper, and we both have busy, demanding lives, so I take pains not to disturb her when I have a short night and she has an opportunity to catch up on her sleep."

I'd finished my reconnaissance and had a long wait before me, so I tiptoed past the agent guarding the stairs to the Residence. Once I reached the Residence floor, I entered the West Sitting Hall that separates the President's quarters from the Center Hall and divides the Master Bedroom from the President's personal dining room. Of course, I made for the dining room.

Well, I was hungry.

I found the tiny kitchen just off of the dining room, and the fridge was nicely stocked. I made two thick sandwiches, piled some fruit into a bowl, and grabbed a bottle of water.

Just to see what Mr. and Mrs. Jackson liked to snack on, I opened a couple of cupboards. That's when I spotted a plate of fancy cookies bristling with shaved coconut and chocolate chips. The White House chef is one of the best in the world and the cookies looked, well, *amazing*. I took two, then added two more, promising to apologize to the President for pilfering his pantry when we spoke.

Armed with sustenance, I walked east down the hall and peeked into some empty bedrooms. I chose the Lincoln Bedroom to wait in so that I could later tell Zander I'd spent part of a night there. I picked a spot on the other side of the bed on which to sit. My dinner would be out of sight, should anyone enter unexpectedly.

The Lincoln bed is huge, by the way. It is eight feet long and has an enormous carved-wood headboard. The bed would have been plenty big for Mr. Lincoln, but I read somewhere that he never got a chance to sleep in it.

I plopped down onto the carpet, leaned my back against the mattress, and arranged my dinner beside me. Turns out the White House staff keeps a very tidy house; the carpet was, literally, clean enough to eat off of. I settled down in my casual setting, enjoyed my dinner, and reviewed the details I intended to share with the most powerful man in the world.

When I finished eating, I decided to check out the top floor, also technically part of the President's Residence. I found the stairs next to the President's elevator, tiptoed up them, and came out in the top floor's Center Hall. The floor had six more bedrooms, an office, a sitting room, game room, music room, workout room, solarium, and lots of storage and miscellaneous-use rooms for whatever the President or his family needed. However, what I was most interested in was outside.

I eased out the Solarium's door onto the Promenade, the walkway that ran around the roofline. The walkway did not make an entire 360° circuit of the house (it ended on the north side of the roofline), but it came close to it. I wandered from one end of the Promenade to the other, relishing a view of the White House grounds and Washington, D.C. that few individuals can lay claim to have enjoyed.

I stopped in front of the Solarium and gazed south. Lights illuminated the length of the Washington Mall, with the Capitol Building to my left on one end and the Lincoln Memorial on my right at the other. From my vantage point, the Washington Monument seemed close enough to touch.

The spectacle made me more aware of how fragile freedom is, and how close America might be to losing her freedoms—if I didn't act, if I were unsuccessful tonight.

"Lord, please help me. This? All this? I am in over my head. Please make my words make sense and give me . . . I don't know, grace? Favor? Just please help me. And help *him*, Lord."

I didn't mention him by name, as though the words spoken aloud would bring down the wrath of the Secret Service upon my head. I just stayed where I was, surveying the emblems of our liberties. And praying.

Even though the evening was cold, I lingered a long time.

Afterwards, I went back to the Lincoln Bedroom, laid down on the carpet where I'd eaten, and took a little nap. It was approaching midnight when the nanomites woke me to tell me of the President and First Lady's return to the Residence.

I cracked the door to the Lincoln Bedroom. Heard the President and First Lady's elevator arrive and listened to their muffled voices as they entered the West Sitting Hall and the Master Bedroom.

I'd policed my crumbs and trash earlier, so I left the Lincoln Bedroom and went quietly down the Center Hall to the doorway that led to the President and First Lady's living room. The living room, in turn, connected to their bedroom.

Back during the Clinton administration, the Secret Service was accustomed to stationing an agent at the top of the Grand Staircase across from the Treaty Room—which happened to be right outside the Lincoln Bedroom. The Service stationed another agent on the west staircase landing next to the President's elevator—basically across from the President's living room where I stood. The Clintons didn't care to have Secret Service agents on the Residence Floor and requested that the posts be moved down a level to the State Floor, and they were.

After the Clintons left the White House, those post changes were retained. This night, I was grateful for those changes. It made it easy for me to leave the Lincoln Bedroom, walk down the Center Hall, and unlock and enter the President's living room.

Piece of cake.

The sofa was made up and waiting for him; his night clothes were laid out. Twenty minutes later, the President walked from his bedroom into the living room and closed the door behind himself. He was headed for his P.J.s when I spoke.

"Excuse me, Mr. President." I kept my voice low, mindful of the First Lady in the next room.

Robert Jackson's head whipped toward the sound of my voice, but he did not see me—at least not right away.

I figured the former Naval Officer would hesitate before shouting for help, and his delay would give me a moment to explain myself. Well, he *didn't* hesitate. Like it was bred into him, he gulped air to shout out. The nanomites had already shot from me before I spoke. As the President inhaled, they sealed his mouth. He could still breathe through his nose, of course (I didn't pull a "Soto" on him), but the experience had to be disconcerting. Maybe scary.

That's when I waved the mites away and became visible to him. I came close enough to whisper.

"I apologize for startling you, sir, and I promise: I have no ill intentions toward you."

He stared, wide-eyed, his nostrils flaring in and out in quick breaths. I supposed he was questioning his own sight because I'd become visible right in front of him.

No missing *that*.

"Mr. President, I have an issue of the utmost importance to share with you. May I have a few minutes of your time?"

He clawed at his sealed mouth but couldn't answer except for muffled grunts. Of course, his inability to speak alarmed him—although I must say that the man, overall, kept his composure.

I admired him for that.

"Mr. President, would you like me to allow you to open your mouth? To speak?"

In the normal world, such a question was absolutely off-the-hook, bats-in-the-belfry *nuts*. He frowned, took his hand from his mouth, and jabbed a finger at me with an angry, unmistakable look of, "You did this?"

I nodded. "Yes, but not me, not directly. I, um, I harbor, in my body, some very sophisticated nanotechnology. They, the nanomites, are keeping your mouth sealed—but only so you don't shout and wake the First Lady or alert your agents.

"Sir, I give you my word: I mean you no harm and, as soon as I've delivered my message, I'll leave you be. If you promise not to call for help, I'll have the nanomites unseal your mouth."

He took a deep breath—through his nostrils—and nodded.

A second later, he opened his mouth. Licked his lips. Swallowed. With a shaking hand, he gestured toward a chair. "May I sit?"

Classic delaying technique, but I didn't mind.

"Of course. My bad. But let's keep our voices low, shall we?"

He nodded again and sat. Tough guy though he was, I figured he needed to process a few things—like his adrenaline. It had to have spiked and turned his legs to rubber.

I pulled a nearby ottoman closer to him and sat. He wasn't all that pleased that we were now practically knee to knee, but other than eyeballing me with distrust, he didn't object.

"Again, I apologize for surprising you like this, Mr. President, but thank you for agreeing to see me."

(See me? Mentally I smacked my forehead. 'Cause, yeah, *that* wasn't an odd way to put it.)

"Who are you? How did you get in here?"

I lifted one shoulder. "You saw me appear. An invisible woman can go pretty much where she likes."

He'd already talked himself out of what he'd seen/not seen, and he scoffed.

So, I had the nanomites hide me.

That was enough to propel him to his feet. He headed straight for the door leading to the hallway. I was faster. I reappeared between him and the knob.

"Mr. President?"

I knew fear and frustration when I saw it. "Nano."

The President started, stepped back. "Wha-what are you doing to me?"

"The nanomites are inducing a few calming neurotransmitters. Nothing harmful. Could we . . ." I took him by the arm to steer him back to his seat—then just as quickly let go when I realized I had committed the cardinal blunder of touching the President of the United States.

"I'm so sorry." Out of contrition, I started to pat him on the shoulder—but whipped my hand back just in time. "Sorry again. Didn't mean to touch you. Um, could we sit down? Start over? You asked who I was."

He resumed his seat, and I pushed the ottoman back six inches to give him some breathing space.

"Mr. President, my name is Gemma Keyes. I live in Albuquerque, New Mexico. Up until last March, I worked as a contractor for Sandia National Laboratories in the MEMS and AMEMS labs. Sir, are you familiar with that acronym? MEMS?"

"No, but you said something about nanotechnology."

"Yes. MEMS and nanotechnology are related fields. MEMS stands for microelectromechanical systems—very small electro-mechanical devices."

He nodded, but he kept his eyes on me as though I might, again, disappear.

"I worked with a brilliant man, Dr. Daniel Bickel. Have you heard of him or his work?"

"No, I don't believe so."

"Well, I need to give you the backstory, but I'll make it as short as I can so we can get on to the important piece. It begins with Dr. Bickel and his work. Dr. Bickel invented a new means of manufacturing MEMS devices at the nanometer level. During the manufacturing process, he integrated the nano-sized MEMS device with a system-on-a-chip processor. His finished product was an extremely intelligent swarm of these devices. He called them 'nanomites.'"

For a few minutes, I spoke to the President about Dr. Bickel's breakthrough and General Cushing's attempted hijacking of his work.

When I said, "General Imogene Cushing," the President's brow creased the tiniest bit, so when I paused for a breath, I asked him, "Do you know General Cushing, Mr. President? Have you heard of her?"

Again, with the minuscule movement of his brow. "I'm not certain, but the name does seem to ring a bell."

Inside, I asked, "Nano?"

We have analyzed this man's microexpressions, Gemma Keyes, and believe him to be telling the truth as he knows it.

As he knows it? I'd have to ask the nanomites about their conditional reply later.

I carried on, explaining Dr. Bickel's "death," the astonishing email I'd received, Dr. Bickel's even more astonishing lab inside the mountain's old devolution cavern, and our idyllic summer. I ended with Cushing's attack on Dr. Bickel's lab and, of course, his command to the nanomites: "Hide! Hide Gemma!"

When I was close to the end of what he needed to know, he stopped me.

"You're saying that *trillions* of these nanomites live in you. That you communicate with them and they can make you invisible. That you have 'powers.'"

When I nodded, he stared at the wall and muttered, "Good God, I'm losing my mind."

"No, sir, you are not. Look at me, please."

He turned his face partway in my direction, but he was wary.

"Mr. President, I didn't come here just so you would know about the nanomites and what they—what we—can do. I came here to save your life."

He lurched from his seat, agitated. "Hells bells, lady, you have a lot of nerve. You are already in more trouble than you know! Even without threatening my life, you are going to spend the rest of your life in federal prison."

"But I'm *not* threatening you, Mr. President; I'm here to warn you. Forewarned is forearmed."

"Really? And *just how* is my life in danger? Other than from you, of course."

He practically sneered his last words—and that just ticked me off. I stood up and, forgetting that we'd agreed to keep our voices down, raised mine—maybe a bit more than I should have.

Okay, a lot.

"You know . . . you know, I thought you'd be a little more appreciative. I didn't need to come here. It took a lot of planning and effort to get me here. I didn't have to risk my freedom or my secrets to save your life! I could have just let—"

I bit off my words, gave the President of the United States a "talk to the hand" gesture, then added, "You know what? I'll answer your question and be on my way. That's all I came to do, anyway. You can figure out the details and what to do about it on your own."

I dropped my arms in disgust. "How is your life in danger? Just this way: The Vice President intends to assassinate you, sir."

I was done. I started to leave, going for the dramatic exit, when the door to the adjoining bedroom swung open. Madeleine Jackson (known to her friends as Maddie), was a fine-looking woman, even at sixty-two, even barefoot, clad in a robe, and shooting a scowl from me to her husband and back.

"What is the point, Robert, of you sleeping in the next room if you're going to engage in an argument and wake me up anyway?"

Of course, the nanomites disappeared me.

⌘⌘⌘⌘

CHAPTER 21

"Why, where did she go?" Maddie Jackson stared with confusion, searching the room high and low. "Who was that you were talking to? And where did she go? She was just here—I *saw* her!"

I was still in the room, and the President didn't answer her. I saw that the warning I'd flung at him had hit him and sunk in. His chin had dropped onto his chest; he was deep in thought.

The First Lady noticed his distraction. "Robert? Robert, who was that woman?"

He took her hand and patted it in absentminded affection, but his mind was elsewhere. On me, to be exact.

He opened his mouth twice before he managed to say, "Miss Keyes, was it? Are you, ah, are you still here? I . . . I would very much like to finish our conversation, if you would be so kind."

I reappeared, lounging against the wall next to the exit into the hall. "Are you willing to hear me out? All the way?"

Mrs. Jackson jerked back from her husband. "How did you do that? You weren't there—I know you weren't!"

"I was, actually, but you couldn't see me." I crossed the short distance to her and extended my hand by way of introduction. "Mrs. Jackson, I apologize for the intrusion. I'm Gemma Keyes, ma'am, and I'm very sorry to have awakened you."

She eyed my hand as if it might bite her. "Robert?"

"I think it's all right, dear, and I'm the one who should be apologizing. I wasn't exactly civil to Miss Keyes, um, earlier."

Maddie Jackson pursed her lips at me. "What did you mean, Miss Keyes, when you said you were *there*, but I just couldn't see you?"

I studied her back. The woman had clear, intelligent eyes and, I thought, a shrewd mind. And she'd asked a pointed question.

I'd never just had fun with my "nano" abilities; I was usually too busy keeping out of Cushing's clutches, too preoccupied with the whole "staying alive" bit.

But, maybe . . .

"Ma'am? Watch this."

I asked the nanomites to—slowly—extend their reflecting shields over me.

The President stood up as I began to fade from sight. He reached out a finger and touched my arm just as it disappeared. Mrs. Jackson's eyes opened wider.

"Can you feel her? Is she still there?"

He wrapped his whole hand about my arm and squeezed a couple of times. I felt like a piece of fruit in the produce section being checked for ripeness.

"Yes; she's still there. Go ahead. Touch her."

She did—and when she encountered my shoulder, she gave it a little half-hearted pat.

"Well, well. My goodness."

I reappeared, and they withdrew their hands, both a little sheepish, since handling people isn't generally considered to be socially acceptable behavior.

But I wasn't finished with my demonstration.

"That's not all. Check this out."

I drew down on the power in the room—just a little—and lifted my hand to show them the pulsing orb dancing on my left palm. "The nanomites and I can pull electrical power from any source. These . . . power balls make quite the impression when I toss them. In fact, I've taken out a dozen armed soldiers with them."

The President suddenly grinned. "You have a lot of fun with this, am I right?"

I blinked. Shrugged. "Uh . . . not much to date. It's been more about survival up till now. A lot of running. A lot of hiding."

He heard the edge to my words and sensed my pain. "This Cushing woman?"

"Yes, sir. Did you hear about the New Mexico statewide manhunt a few weeks back?"

"I seem to recall it. The Vice President was very attentive to the news—"

He saw my expression harden.

"That was you? You're the woman they were hunting? Vice President Harmon said you were some sort of domestic terrorist. You're saying that was Cushing? Going after you?"

"Her and every cop in the state. Trust me: *not* fun. Did you also hear about the raid on the Albuquerque FBI field office a few days after the manhunt started?"

He nodded. "Some rogue scientist seeking asylum? And then disappearing again? The reports are still unclear as to what happened there, but the FBI Director and the Secretary of the Air Force were in the Oval Office last week and they had, shall we say, a rather sharp disagreement over the situation. Nearly came to blows—right there in my office. It took Vice President Harmon's intervention to . . ."

The President petered to a stop. "Harmon. Again."

"Yes, sir. Vice President Harmon. He is General Cushing's handler. He's the former NSA Director, former chief of the Central Security Service, yes? And isn't the NSA responsible for SIGINT? Signal intelligence? For the global monitoring, collection, and processing of information and data for foreign intelligence and counterintelligence purposes? Isn't the NSA charged with the protection of government communications and information systems against penetration and network warfare? And isn't the NSA authorized to accomplish its mission through *active clandestine means*?"

When the President, with reluctance, nodded, I shrugged, "Well, Mr. Harmon hasn't exactly resigned those objectives. He and Cushing share a philosophy that believes America would be safer and 'better governed' if the Central Security Service could monitor everyone all the time—American citizens included. Cushing worked for him sometime earlier in her career and briefed him on the direction of Dr. Bickel's research a few years back. They've been watching him a long time, waiting for his technology to mature.

"At Harmon's direction, Cushing arranged for another scientist at Sandia Labs, Dr. Petrel Prochanski, to keep tabs on Dr. Bickel and alert her when Dr. Bickel's nanotechnology achieved certain verifiable objectives. This was all kept from Dr. Bickel until Cushing showed up. When Dr. Bickel realized that Cushing and her superiors intended to weaponize his technology, he refused to release his research to them.

"That's when Harmon gave the order to appropriate Dr. Bickel's work and have him, er, removed. Permanently. It was Harmon's plan to further develop Dr. Bickel's nanotechnology in order to move the U.S. closer to his intelligence gathering goals—closer to the complete and covert monitoring of all electronic communications within the U.S."

Jackson shook his head in denial. "I've been told that nanotechnology is years from attaining such Orwellian objectives. Decades away."

"I'm sorry to contradict you, sir, but it already exists. You asked how I got in here, how I defeated White House security and penetrated your private residence, one of the most guarded places on the planet?"

"Yes; how *did* you do that? Other than walking around in an invisible state? The White House is protected by multiple intrusion detection systems that are not public knowledge."

"Yes, I know: motion-sensing alarms and cameras. IR sensors unseen by the naked eye. I know about them all because the nanomites and I are quite close. You might say that we share . . . a symbiotic relationship. I carry them, and they bring their technological faculties with us."

I did not want to get into the gnarly issues surrounding my deeper attachment to the nanomites. I sure didn't want to muddy my message by telling the President that the mites and I were fused at the molecular level, that I was now an amalgamation of human organism and nanotechnology.

I glossed over the details. "In this, um, symbiotic relationship, the nanomites and I function together. For example, given their tiny size and vast computational abilities, we can hack any firewall, access any network, and identify and spoof any security measures—such as White House alarms, motion sensors, and cameras. And those abilities are in addition to the physical weapons we possess."

"I see." But I could see that he was troubled.

"Mr. President, Vice President Harmon wants the nanomites; therefore, he wants me, and he wants Dr. Bickel. He thinks he can extract the nanomites from me and reverse engineer them. His intention is to create a nanomite army to hack and surveil every enemy nation and to protect America by the same means.

"Of course, that means circumventing all those pesky Constitutional rights—but anything for the safety and security of our nation, right? And besides, who would know? Within a network, the nanomites cannot be traced and they cannot be stopped.

"Harmon knows you won't go along with the covert abolishment of the Bill of Rights, so he has made a strategic decision: For the 'good of the nation,' you have to go. He will take the reins of power in your stead and see this utopian society emerge."

Maddie Jackson gasped; I was glad the President was holding her hand.

"Sir, Harmon has been very careful up till now. He didn't want to move until he had the nanomites reengineered and had an army of them ready to support him. However, when Dr. Bickel escaped from Cushing and made known to the world that he is still very much alive, Harmon realized how near his illegal actions are to being exposed. His hand has been forced and he . . . he intends to assassinate you. Soon."

Neither the President nor the First Lady responded, and the room sank into a dark, somber mood. The clock on their living-room wall ticked on, the time in D.C. approaching 1 a.m.

I was surprised that Maddie Jackson spoke first. "*Harmon.* I never did trust that man—and I said as much during the campaign."

"As a Washington outsider, I needed someone as connected as Harmon, someone familiar with the bureaucracy and who knew the system. I might not have won the election without Harmon, but I also recognized the inherent risk he presented—being too comfortable with the embedded status-quo. And he's ambitious. I just underestimated how ambitious."

He slowly shook his head. "I should have listened to you."

"Yes, you should have."

"Well, I didn't, and there's no sense beating me up about it now."

"Uh, Mr. President, it's very late, and if you're going to get any sleep at all, I should provide you with the details of Harmon's plot—or at least the ones I am aware of."

"You're right—not that I'll be able to sleep after all this. But," here he glanced at his wife, "why don't you go on back to bed, Maddie? There's no need for both of us to be sleep deprived tomorrow."

"What? Oh, no. No. You think I can sleep now? I don't think so. I want to hear everything Miss Keyes has to say."

I watched and listened to them batting words back and forth in frank and open exchange, and I smiled. Theirs seemed a solid, comfortable marriage, and I liked them both.

My ever-hungry stomach complained. "Well, since we're all going to be up for a while, is anyone else hungry? I could sure use a few more of those amazing cookies—oh, wow! I-I totally forgot, Mr. President."

"Forgot what?"

"I forgot to apologize to you. I knew you would be out late tonight, and I got hungry, so I may have, um, sort of, uh, raided your kitchen this afternoon. I'm sorry."

The President dropped his face onto his hand and chuckled. "You know, Miss Keyes, if I had still harbored any reservations about your intentions, your apology would have erased the last of them. I've never known a malicious actor to be remorseful for looting their target's pantry."

His wife laughed. "Quite right. And we accept your apology, Miss Keyes. You're welcome to whatever is there. Shall we make coffee and a snack before we continue? I didn't eat much at dinner. Too preoccupied over conversation with the Ambassador's wife."

"Ditto, with the Ambassador," the President answered.

I started to relax. Perhaps things were going to be okay. "Thank you. By the way, those cookies are the best ever."

"Coconut Dream cookies. They are Robert's favorites."

We were quiet as we went into the hall, down to the dining room, and into the tiny kitchen. Like regular people do, we pulled a variety of foodstuffs from the refrigerator and, under Maddie Jackson's direction, made decaf coffee, reheated a creamy asparagus soup, assembled sandwiches, and set the dining table for three.

It felt like my stomach was eating itself from the inside out before we sat down. As it issued a particularly loud gurgle, the Jacksons laughed at me.

I blushed. "I'm so sorry. My metabolism is faster than a normal person's, so I get hungry. Often."

Maddie Jackson smiled. "Well, eat up, my dear. You look positively . . . *lean*. Healthy, yes, but you could use a little more meat on your bones."

It wasn't a mean observation; it was a kind, grandmotherly word coming from her. It was something Aunt Lucy might have said. Sweet and caring.

I grinned and dug in. Between bites, I explained, "I've . . . slimmed down the last several weeks. The nanomites revved up my metabolism and increased my stamina, which means I can run or work out for hours without fatigue. Training with them has made me strong and fit. But I also eat twice what I used to."

Her astounded response was, "You get to eat anything and everything you want and still stay trim? That sounds like every woman's dream come true. Here: Have another sandwich, Gemma. And eat all the cookies you like—Robert doesn't need them; trust me."

The President snorted, then spooned soup into his mouth and addressed his wife. "You know, this has got to be the strangest day of my presidency—don't you think so, dear? I wonder how our encounter with Miss Keyes will go down in the history books."

His amused remark snapped me back to reality. "Sir, you can't tell anyone about me. Not anyone. Um, all *this*—me, the nanomites, my invisibility and defeating White House security, and my other abilities?—all these things must stay between us. I am only safe as long as my anonymity lasts."

When his mouth turned down in skeptical, perhaps resistant lines, I added, "Six, maybe seven individuals in the world, other than the two of you, know who I am and what I can do. I came directly to you, Mr. President, not merely to warn you of the threat on your life and our nation's security, but because I felt I could trust you to keep my secret."

He frowned. "I can understand your desire to remain anonymous, to stay in the shadows, but I have requirements, too. Since we have just met, I must confirm your identity and story through independent sources. If I can't talk to anyone about you, how can I vet you? And by the way, you haven't yet presented a single detail or piece of evidence to back up your assertion that Harmon plans to assassinate me—and those are very serious charges."

I thought for a moment, tried to look at the situation from his perspective. "Sir, when we finish eating, I will share what the nanomites have uncovered regarding Vice President Harmon. Regarding my character, would you take the word of an FBI agent?"

"I might."

"There's an agent in Albuquerque who is in my inner circle, so to speak. Then there's also Dr. Bickel."

"You know where Dr. Bickel is hiding?"

"Yes, I do. He is safe—for the moment. Of course, Harmon has Cushing hunting him. The fewer who know where Dr. Bickel is, the safer he will be."

"Then let's start with the FBI agent. What is his name?"

"Special Agent Ross Gamble, sir."

The President glanced at his wife. "The best way to keep Gemma's visit a secret is to keep my call to this agent off the books—and that presents a challenge." He looked back at me. "All calls in and out of the White House switchboard are automatically logged and recorded. To conflate matters further, if I were to place a call at this time of night, the Secret Service would know that I'm awake—and that would raise a red flag."

"I have a cell phone with me." I had my burner smart phone with me.

"The Service monitors and controls cellular service in and out of the White House; they know where every call originates and where every call goes. An unknown cell phone signal originating from the Residence? Agents would be up here, guns drawn, in under thirty seconds."

"The nanomites and I can mask the call, sir. The Secret Service won't be any the wiser."

He blinked, shot a look at his wife, and muttered, "Hmm. Well, then."

We finished eating, tidied up the dining room and kitchen, and returned to their living room. There I pulled out my phone and called Gamble while the nanomites took care of the security issues.

"What time is it in New Mexico?" the President asked.

"Two hours earlier than here, so near midnight."

"And you're certain your nanomites can fool the Secret Service?"

"They are on it, Mr. President."

The phone rang on the other end; after three rings, the call connected, and Gamble mumbled, "Gamble."

"Hey. It's Gemma."

"Gemma? I just got to sleep and I'm running on fumes as it is. This had better be important."

"Yes; sorry to wake you, Gamble, but I have someone who would like you to vouch for me. I'm going to put you on speaker phone and I . . . I suggest you splash water on your face first—it's important."

"What?" He got up; I heard him fumble with the covers. His feet hit the floor and moved away from his bed.

I pushed the speaker button just as he grumbled, "Who, in the dead of night, wants to talk to me?"

"Special Agent Gamble? This is Robert Jackson. Calling from the White House."

Dead silence.

"Agent Gamble? Are you there?"

"Yes, sir, I'm here. I beg your pardon. Ah, if you don't mind, sir, may I just confirm with Miss Keyes that you are who you say you are?"

Maddie Jackson grinned, and I stifled a snort-laugh. The President arched a brow at me.

"Miss Keyes?"

"Gamble, I am sitting with the President and First Lady right now. In their living room. In the Residence. You know. In the White House?"

Gamble whispered, "Well, of course you are."

I giggled. "Don't forget we're on speaker phone, Gamble. Listen, I've apprised the President of a threat on his life."

"A what?" Gamble sputtered incoherently before he managed to grind out, "I don't know why you didn't tell me, Gemma, but we can talk about that later. What do you need from me?"

"I haven't provided any details of the plot against him yet, but I insisted that we keep my visit a secret—so Vice President Harmon doesn't become aware that the President is on to him."

"The who? The *Vice President*?" Gamble muttered colorful expletives under his breath.

I lowered my voice, too. "Yes. I know. We'll talk about that later." In my regular voice, I said, "Because I've asked the President to keep my identity a secret, he can't verify me or my story through the usual channels. That's why I've called you."

Gamble was awake and all business now. "Got it. Mr. President? I apologize for my unprofessional behavior. I can attest to Miss Keyes' identity and character. May I respond to any specific questions you may have?"

After Gamble had answered the President's questions to his satisfaction, we hung up, and I was ready to outline Vice President Harmon's plan to assassinate the leader of the free world.

The nanomites had captured the audio of the phone call between Harmon and Cushing and had written those recordings to my cell phone. I hadn't imagined they could do such a thing, but the more I lived with them, the less I figured was beyond their capabilities: If a task lived in the digital world, they could do it.

I decided to begin with the call because I wanted President Jackson to hear Harmon's intentions for himself. Robert Jackson needed to know how cold and deadly Harmon was. Jackson couldn't afford to underestimate his adversary—that could prove deadly. To both of us.

I started the audio and watched the President's face as the recording of Harmon's voice murmured,

"I've determined that it would be best to move up my plans. I have a private breakfast scheduled with him the day after tomorrow. Two days later, the President will have an unexpected but fatal heart attack. I won't be anywhere near him when it happens."

I paused the recording. "This was recorded yesterday. Can you understand why I had to come to you directly?"

Jackson's features turned to stone.

I restarted the recording.

Cushing: "Given that the President has no history of heart disease, won't there be an exhaustive autopsy?"

Harmon: "Yes, I'm counting on it. The autopsy will uncover an undiagnosed bacterial infection—a particularly vicious and aggressive strain of Staphylococcus aureus. It will appear as if the bacteria had infected the lining, muscles, and valves of the President's heart weeks ago, possibly contracted during his visit to a V.A. hospital last month. Even if a particularly bright pathologist looks for it, he or she won't find any trace of the chemical added to the virus cocktail that precipitated the heart attack."

Harmon added as an afterthought, "I shall owe my deep contact at USAMARIID a great favor."

"Jackson won't have shown any symptoms prior to the attack?"

"The lack of prior symptoms is mildly problematic; however, it will change nothing: The President will be dead and, regardless of the atypical progress of the disease, the evidence will point to an acute MI."

"How long after you are in office before you appoint me Secretary of the Air Force?" Cushing asked.

"You have more than earned your reward, General. You'll get your promotion as soon as decently possible after the funeral, but I'll bring you up to D.C. right away in an advisory capacity. We must demonstrate due grief and mourning for the President's passing and give the American people a few weeks to accept and settle into my presidency. I will begin making changes to the cabinet and other postings a month after I take the oath of office."

The recording went on, but its point was clear.

Maddie Jackson slipped her hand back into her husband's and gripped it. "What are we to do, Miss Keyes? Do you have proof other than this recording? Evidence we can turn over to the Secret Service?"

"Precious few of the details can be verified without stirring up a hornet's nest and possibly alerting Harmon, Mrs. Jackson. I hadn't intended on staying . . . or helping. I just came to warn you. Figured once you were warned, you would know what to do."

Maddie Jackson turned to her husband, who was digesting not only the danger he was in but the political ramifications. "What are you thinking?

"I'm thinking of the damage a scandal of this magnitude will create. No coup of this nature—from this high—has ever been attempted in America. It may destroy the credibility of my administration. Of our party."

"Robert, those issues cannot be your primary concern at the moment. You are having breakfast with Harmon *tomorrow*. You have to act *now* to prevent an even greater political catastrophe: the assassination of a sitting president! *You*, my beloved husband!

Maddie Jackson was no lily-livered woman. She saw things clearly.

I liked her better and better.

Jackson growled, "Harmon isn't in this alone—he has accomplices. He has a co-conspirator embedded in the Army's Medical Research Institute of Infectious Diseases, for God's sake! I can't even be sure who in the Secret Service I could trust with this or what they might do. If they happened to accidentally tip off Harmon—or if someone we should not have trusted leaked it to him, he would simply wait for another opportunity."

Jackson rubbed his eyes. "What a mess. Just . . . just give me a few minutes to think, please."

Maddie Jackson sat back and lost herself in her own thoughts. I stepped out of the room and wandered down the hallway, praying in a soft whisper. "Jesus, you know all things, don't you? Could you please point us in the right direction? Show us what to do? This is very serious, Lord Jesus— well, sorry; I guess you already know how serious it is—but we could really use your help. Like that verse says, "Trust in the Lord with all your heart and don't depend on your own understanding," or something along those lines. What's the rest? "Commit your ways to the Lord and he will guide you?" President Jackson really needs you to guide him, Lord, so I am committing my ways to you—and I hope he will, too."

Gemma Keyes?

"Yes, Nano?"

Over the next few minutes I had some remarkable conversation with the nanomites. When we finished, I wondered if Jesus was able to direct *them* in answer to those who prayed to him.

I wondered, because their ideas were that good.

I'd been in the hall around twenty minutes when Maddie Jackson stepped out of the living room and whispered, "Miss Keyes?"

The nanomites uncovered me when I was within a foot of her.

"Yes?"

"Oh! You . . . startled me."

"I beg your pardon."

"It's all right, but the President would like to speak to you, Miss Keyes."

I followed her into the living room and found the President standing, ready to act. "Miss Keyes? After you left, Mrs. Jackson and I did some praying together."

"You did?" I was thrilled. "So did I!"

He grinned. "Get all my best stuff from him—but this time I had to really brainstorm outside the box. I have the strongest impression that he helped me think of ways to use your nanomites in this situation. So, if you are willing to help, I believe I have a plan."

"Whatever you need, sir, and the nanomites had a few ideas, too."

"Care to share?"

I did, and it seemed that the President's thoughts ran along the same vein as the nanomites' ideas. Over the next hour, with a few tweaks and additions, we ironed out the details.

"Can the nanomites write that recording of Harmon and the general onto my cell phone?"

"Yes, they can do that, Mr. President."

"Good. I'll use it to confront Harmon, and the recording will be backup for afterward—in the event we need evidence. If the recording *is* needed as evidence, I give you my promise that I will refuse to give up my confidential source, even if pressed."

"Thank you, Mr. President."

"All right. Next, if I give you a number, can you have the nanomites call it but make the number look like its coming from the White House?"

"While hiding the call from the Secret Service?"

"Exactly. You're a quick study, Miss Keyes."

"Who will you be calling, Mr. President—if I may ask?"

"Axel Kennedy, the head of my protective detail. I trust him implicitly. Part of the reason I do is because I also have reason to believe that he's not a fan of Harmon's."

I nodded. "I'm ready when you are, Mr. President."

He gave me the number; as I dialed it, the nanomites hid the call from the Secret Service's surveillance and spoofed the caller ID on the other end.

I put the call on speaker phone. At the second ring, a man answered.

"Yes, Mr. President?"

"Axel, sorry to disturb you, but I have a situation here."

"I'll be right in, sir."

"No. No, you can't come in now. Can't risk it."

"Risk it, sir?"

Robert Jackson had called me a quick study, but he was a master. He grabbed only the important threads of the plot and presented them in cold, concise bullet points. Then he played the recording of Harmon's call to Cushing.

Axel Kennedy's response was explosive. "My God, Mr. President! This is treason!" After he'd added a few choice descriptors for Harmon, he asked, "And you have breakfast scheduled with the *bleeping* Vice President at 7 a.m.?"

"Yes; that's when he intends to administer what I can only describe as a chemical/biological weapon."

"Sir, we have to take steps now. As head of your detail, I can't allow you to meet with him."

"You must, Axel. If this plot were to leak out, the damage to my administration would be disastrous. I have a plan to remove Harmon from the Vice Presidency without anyone other than us being the wiser as to why. You are integral to that plan. I want you to arrive at 6 a.m.—an hour before Harmon arrives. You coming to work thirty minutes earlier than usual won't raise any red flags."

"I'll be there, Mr. President, but what would you have me do?"

"Well, you won't be sleeping the rest of the night."

The time was already closing in on 3:30 a.m.; none of us would be sleeping the rest of the night.

"Sir?"

"We need video recording equipment, one of those plug-and-play systems with multiple cameras that sends surveillance video to an app on your smart phone. Hit a big box store and get what you need."

"Sir, no store like that in the D.C. area is open in the middle of the night."

The President's voice turned wry. "It's almost Christmas, Axel. Some of these stores are open 24/7 through Christmas Eve. My son and daughter-in-law sometimes shop in the middle of the night. It's called life with kids and full-time jobs."

"Yes, Mr. President—but sir? I won't get electronics past our own security."

"I'll meet you when you arrive and thank you for picking up the gift for my wife's brother and his family."

Axel was silent. "Since the system will be boxed up, it might get by."

"It will, because I'll make sure it does."

"Yes, Mr. President. Then what?"

"You'll set up cameras in the Oval Office and watch from across the hall in the Roosevelt room while the Vice President is with me. I will give orders for the Roosevelt Room to be kept clear for your use only. No one else is to enter the Roosevelt Room other than you. In fact, I want a guard outside that door so that only you enter. You'll watch and record the feed from there. When the time is right, I will look up at a camera and signal you to come to me."

Axel interrupted. "Mr. President, hiding more than two cameras in the Oval Office will be problematic. I believe I can manage to conceal one in the bookcase and another on the fireplace mantle."

"Two will have to do, Axel. Harmon will try to slip the weapon into my food or drink—so, I want you to make sure the steward positions the coffee service in full view of a camera. And don't worry; I won't touch a blasted thing he's fiddled with."

"I don't like it, Mr. President. I should be at your side—and with all due respect, sir, regardless of the outcome, the Director will have my head. I'll be off your detail. Officially reprimanded. Demoted."

"No, you won't. I'll take care of you. I promise."

The force of the President's personality carried the argument.

What Agent Axel didn't know, is that *I* would be at the President's side the entire time, and the nanomites would be vigilant to ensure his food and drink weren't tainted.

What I didn't know was that the nanomites had concluded their own course of action in response to the threat Harmon posed.

⌘⌘⌘⌘

CHAPTER 22

We were all tired; I could see the worry and stress on Mrs. Jackson's face and the determination on her husband's. The last few hours before we could act had been the hardest.

We'd filled those remaining hours with conversation—or should I say, the President and his wife asked a lot of questions and I answered them? By the time we finished, they knew just about every aspect of my life and the details surrounding my experiences with the nanomites.

While the President and First Lady showered and dressed, I pilfered more food from their kitchen. I needed to be fully fueled, ready for whatever came next.

It was nearing 6 a.m. Ten minutes before the hour, Maddie Jackson stepped into the hallway with her husband and kissed him goodbye.

"I'll be praying, Robert, but be careful. Please."

"I will." He turned to where I leaned against a wall, waiting. "Gemma will have my back. I trust her."

I swallowed hard. *Lord, don't let me fail this man.*

All I could say was, "We will do our best, sir."

"I know you will."

The President took his elevator to the ground floor while I, made invisible by the nanomites, took the stairs. When I reached the bottom and stared down the Center Hall, the President was striding toward his office, two agents and his Chief of Staff close at hand. I followed them at a discreet distance, through the Palm Room and down the West Colonnade, past the Rose Garden to the Oval Office's exterior door.

I waited outside and looked through the panes of glass while the President spoke to his Chief of Staff. The nanomites attached themselves to the glass and pumped their conversation into my ears.

"These need your immediate attention, Mr. President."

"Sorry, Marcus. I can't look at them at the moment; I promise to give them my full attention after my breakfast with the Vice President."

"But, Mr. President—"

"Marcus, I don't mean to be rude, but I need you to leave."

The man's jaw snapped shut. "Yes, sir." He exited by way of the door that led into the West Wing corridor.

I opened the exterior door and stepped inside.

"Gemma?"

"Here, sir."

"Very good." He glanced at a text on his cell. "Axel just arrived. I need to go meet him."

I was alone in the Oval Office, and I swept my gaze around the room, marveling at this place and this moment. I was elated and nervous at the same time; if we were successful in taking down Harmon, so many things would be better going forward.

Gemma Keyes. Don't worry. Harmon will not succeed in harming the President.

"Thank you, Nano. I'm glad we are in this together."

We are six, Gemma Keyes. We are optimal.

I smiled. It had been a few days since the nanomites had last recited their catchphrase. It was a comforting mantra.

The President and an ordinary-looking man hurried into the Oval Office. The man carried a bag and pulled two cameras from it as soon as the door closed. He set one camera on the recessed bookcase to the left of the President's desk and angled it toward the two couches in the center of the room.

"This system works via Wi-Fi. I'll have to override the White House network security settings from our command center to get the cameras online. I'll be breaking protocol when I do, and the timing will be critical."

I moved to the President's side and whispered, "We can handle the network, sir."

He nodded. "Um, Axel, why don't you try to connect the cameras to the network first? I, um, believe you won't encounter any difficulties."

Axel looked at the President. "You're not telling me something."

"Above your paygrade, Axel. Just trust me."

Axel set up the second camera within the foliage of a potted poinsettia on the fireplace mantle. He pointed the lens toward the coffee table between the two couches.

Satisfied that the camera angles were good, Axel made one last observation. "The Vice President doesn't like eating from a plate in his lap, sir."

"The Vice President isn't going to like any part of this morning, Axel. Ask me if I care."

"No, sir. I'll leave you then and get the system online."

The door closed. "Gemma?"

"Yes, Mr. President?"

"I will have the steward place the breakfast trolley near the bookcase. When Harmon arrives, I'd like you to station yourself where you can watch his every move—particularly when he is near the trolley."

"Yes, sir."

With a knock, the steward entered. He was quick and competent; he positioned the breakfast trolley as the President asked and laid out napkins and silver on the coffee table before taking his leave.

Five minutes later Axel slipped into the Oval Office. "Mr. President, I tested the cameras, and everything is ready." He gave the President a steady, no-nonsense look. "In the segment I recorded as a test, you were speaking to someone, sir."

"Was I?" Robert Jackson dissembled. "You must be mistaken. Perhaps I was only mumbling to myself."

"No, sir. You said, and I quote, 'Gemma?' Another individual answered you, 'Yes, Mr. President?' and you answered her back—and yet there was no one else in the room. Who is Gemma, Mr. President?"

Jackson pulled himself together. "I'm sorry but, again, Axel, it is above your paygrade. I can, however, assure you that I am safe."

"Sir, as head of your protective detail, the situation disturbs me."

Axel and the President had a little stare down at that moment, and the tension got pretty thick. It ended when the door opened, and Vice President Harmon walked in.

"Good morning, Mr. President."

John Etheredge Harmon, with his tall, lanky figure and his thick, gray hair—helped in no small measure by his broad, disarming smile—bore a striking resemblance to the older Alan Alda.

The similarity ended at his blue eyes. While every crease and line and toothsome grin proclaimed joviality, his eyes were cold.

So, this man was Cushing's handler.

I crept along the curving wall until I was near enough the serving trolley to observe all Harmon might do, but I kept out of the camera's direct line of sight.

"Good morning, John." Jackson lifted his chin, ordering Axel from the room.

"Sir." Axel turned on his heel. He did not greet Harmon; the Vice President insisted that his protective detail and other agents not speak to him unless necessary.

When the door closed behind Axel, Harmon rubbed his hands together. "Well, I must say, I'm starved, Bob." He glanced around. "No table?"

"No; we'll sit on the couches. Coffee?"

The President wasn't going to drag this out, and I was glad. Sweat was already running down my neck.

A moue of disdain, quickly covered, crossed Harmon's face, replaced by a smile. "Let me get it, Bob."

This was it.

I could tell the President was nervous. He glanced around the room—for me, I assumed. It was just a flicker before he recovered. "Thanks, John."

Harmon had already turned to the coffee service, his back to the President, and was pouring coffee into two cups. I didn't know about the nanomites, but my hypervigilance ratcheted up another notch.

"Nano. Go. Keep me apprised."

A contingency of nanomites floated from me to Harmon. *We will, Gemma Keyes.*

"Cream as usual, Bob?"

"Yes, please."

I watched as the Vice President poured cream into one steaming cup.

Then he made his move.

Harmon's right hand slipped in and out of his breast pocket, hovered over the cup with cream in it, returned to his breast pocket, and back to stir the cream into the coffee.

I shot a look at the camera hidden in the bookshelves. Axel would not have missed the move, and I figured he was barely restraining himself to wait for the President's cue.

As Harmon put the spoon down and lifted the two cups, I tiptoed across the room. When he handed the President his cup and took a seat opposite him, I leaned over the back of the couch on which the President sat and placed my hand upon his shoulder.

It was our prearranged signal.

Robert Jackson shuddered under my touch. He looked directly at the fireplace, at the hidden camera, and gave one small nod. Then he stood.

"John."

"Yes, Mr. President?"

The door opened, and Axel entered. He walked to the President's side and took the cup from him. Jackson looked relieved to turn it over to him.

Harmon glanced from Axel to the President. "What's going on?"

"Treason, John. Attempted assassination."

For a moment, anger and contempt battled Harmon's guileless façade; then his longstanding, ingenuous veneer clicked into place. "I'm sorry, Mr. President, but you're confusing me."

Jackson, considering his next move, said nothing for a moment, then, "Would you do me a favor, John? Would you humor me?"

"Of course, Mr. President; what can I do?"

He tipped his head toward the tainted coffee. "Drink my coffee, John."

The nanomites could read the smallest and most fleeting of microexpressions; they detected even minute changes in heart rate, blood pressure, and skin tone.

And what they saw, *I saw*.

Harmon's pulse rocketed; the color drained from his face. His self-control, however, was masterful, and his puzzled expression never wavered. It did, however, freeze in place.

"Mr. President, I'm afraid that I don't understand."

"It's a simple request. Drink the coffee."

"But I don't drink cream with my coffee, sir."

Jackson's demeanor hardened. "I said, *drink it*."

Harmon blinked twice, and I could see the wheels turning as he evaluated the situation. "Of course, Mr. President. I don't understand, but whatever you say."

He stood and reached for the cup, and his intention came to me in swift insight—but not fast enough. The moment Harmon had the cup and saucer in his hands, he "fumbled" them. The infected brew—the evidence against him—spilled from the cup and streamed toward the carpet.

When Axel scrabbled for the cup, it was too late.

It wasn't, however, too late for the nanomites. I realized later that they had already theorized and prepared for Harmon's every reaction.

Electricity arced from my hands; a blue bolt struck and surrounded the spinning cup, saucer, and contents. Like a tape rewinding, the falling liquid globules tumbled backwards, and splattered into the cup, and the cup clattered onto the saucer. For the briefest moment, the upright cup and saucer hung midair—until Axel's hands jerked forward and retrieved them.

"I-I didn't do that," he sputtered. "*I didn't do that!*"

Harmon and the President, both mesmerized and slack-jawed, stared at the cup and saucer. Harmon recovered first.

He edged away, muttering, "She's here!"

Gemma Keyes. The empty capsule that contained the chemical/biological agent is within Harmon's breast pocket.

I grabbed the President's arm and repeated the nanomites' message. "Have Axel get the empty capsule now!"

Jackson snapped out of his shock. "Axel, put that safely aside and retrieve the evidence from Harmon's breast pocket."

Harmon was muttering under his breath and vainly searching the Oval Office when Axel grabbed him by the lapels.

"Take your *bleeping* hands off me!" Harmon tore at Axel's hands and attempted to pull away.

"Sir, if you resist further, I *will* put you on the floor." Axel patted Harmon's jacket, looking for the capsule.

"Be careful, Axel," the President cautioned him.

Axel donned a single latex glove, retrieved the capsule, and placed it in a plastic bag marked "Evidence." He pulled the glove off, inside out, and placed it in a second evidence bag. Then he guided Harmon back to the couch and into a cushioned seat across from the President.

The Vice President glared at Jackson. "Well? What next?"

"That's up to you. You have two choices before you."

The lines between Harmon's eyes twitched a fraction, but his eyes were what fascinated me. They were cold. Defiant. Still scheming.

"You know, you can't hold me."

Jackson wasn't fazed. "Oh?"

"All this"—Harmon's gesture included the room and the events of the last ten minutes—"All this is my word against yours. And *his*." He sneered his last two words in Axel's direction. "You have no evidence."

"We have the chemical/biological agent in my coffee and the capsule you brought it in."

Harmon chuckled. "Within two hours, all trace evidence will be gone. The virus will feed upon the chemical, and then, without a human host, the virus will die. Amazingly short shelf life, don't you think?"

Jackson absorbed that, then said, "Axel, show the Vice President."

Axel pulled a camera from between the leaves of one of the potted poinsettias on the fireplace mantle. He pointed it at Harmon. "We've been recording since before you entered the Oval Office." He jerked his chin toward the recessed bookcase across the room. "Another camera over there caught you putting the bio/chemical agent into the President's cup."

Harmon shrugged. "Again, nothing malicious to be found on me or in his cup."

"We have this conversation. Your words. The audio is quite clear."

Harmon's hooded eyes gave nothing away. As if sensing the momentum shifting against him, Harmon turned inward and would not speak.

Jackson, recalling a key piece of the plan, brightened. "Speaking of audio . . ." He pulled his cell phone from his pocket, pressed a few icons. The recording of Harmon's call with Cushing filled the air between the two men.

The effect was immediately visible to us all. Harmon's jaw clenched and unclenched, and his hands fisted upon his thighs.

Jackson said again, "As I said, you have two choices."

Harmon refused to look at him.

"We have enough evidence to try you on treason, sedition, and attempted assassination, John. In case you've forgotten, those charges carry the death penalty. Given the glacial speed of the judicial system, the trial could take a year. Perhaps longer. Doesn't matter. You'll be remanded into federal custody today and will never see the outside of a cell or courtroom until they carry you to your execution."

Jackson let his words sink in before he added, "Or . . . you can resign. Today. For personal reasons. If you choose that route, you will leave Washington no later than six this evening and return to your home in Boston. You will remove yourself from public life and service—entirely. You will hold no press conferences or interviews, write no books or articles. Give no speeches. You will never return to D.C., never venture into any state contiguous to D.C., and never communicate with any present or former employee or elected official of the federal government as long as you live.

"If you choose to resign, before you leave my office, you will sign an affidavit confessing to your role and participation in a plot to assassinate the duly elected president of this nation. That paperwork will be filed with three attorneys of my discretion. Any deviance from the conditions of your resignation—any deviance in the smallest detail—will result in the public release of your affidavit."

Jackson and Harmon spent the next three minutes taking each other's measure. I watched as Harmon seethed and weighed his options. The two choices he had were two too many in my estimation, but it was not my role or decision.

When Jackson had waited on Harmon long enough, he stood. "Axel, use your coms to call in the remainder of my detail."

Harmon jumped up. "No. Stop. I-I . . . I accept your—"

The door from the West Wing corridor opened and the President's Chief of Staff entered. Marcus Park took in the tense scene before speaking. "I apologize for the intrusion, Mr. President; however, your Secret Service detail has noted some . . . deviations from standard protocol. I wanted to assure them that all was well—"

At the disruption, I'd shifted my attention from the standoff between Harmon and the President to Park. A strangled sound wrenched my focus back. In an instinctual move to protect the President, I stepped closer to his side.

But it wasn't the President who was in trouble.

It was Harmon.

Red, blotchy color suffused Harmon's face, and his mouth hung open. He mouthed a few garbled words. A pink-tinged foam dribbled from between his lips. Then, while I watched, he clutched at his left arm and stiffened. He collapsed, his shoulder striking the coffee table between the two couches before he rolled to the floor.

Park reacted first. He raced to the door and shouted. "Medical! Medical!"

To Axel's credit, he responded by clearing Harmon's airway and performing CPR. Then the Vice President coughed once, sending a font of blood shooting from his mouth. President Jackson stood over Axel and Harmon, watching and praying.

In less than a minute, the staff of the White House Medical Unit arrived—as did other West Wing staff members who crowded the doorway. I could hear the sounds of the WHMU's emergency and trauma staff as they intubated Harmon, began bagging air into his lungs, and charged and discharged a portable defibrillator again and again.

I think we all knew it was pointless. By the time the WHMU emergency staff had taken over from Agent Kennedy, the Vice President was already dead.

The President stayed nearby until two agents from his detail convinced him to move back. They ushered him to his desk, and he stood behind it, staring out the thick, blue-tinted glass of the Oval Office windows onto the south lawn. He was deep in thought when I approached him.

I touched him to let him know I was there. "Sir? Are you all right?"

Robert Jackson moved his head a few inches my way and whispered, "Yes. Thank you. Thank you for everything, Miss Keyes. If it weren't for you, it might have been me lying over there. Would have been me."

"Mr. President, what do you think happened? Did Harmon contaminate himself with the toxin he intended for you?"

"I've been wondering the same thing, but didn't he say it was supposed to take forty-eight hours before it caused death?"

Axel's approach interrupted us. "Sir, I should . . . tidy up the Roosevelt Room."

"Yes. Right away. Box up the surveillance system and lock it in your car's trunk." He looked around. "We'll remove the two cameras from here later."

"What about the recording?"

"Destroy it. In fact, do that first."

"About that, sir . . . and the other, uh, unusual *things* caught on the recording?"

Jackson faced the head of his detail and crooked his finger until Axel bent his ear toward the President's mouth. "I have placed my utmost faith and trust in you, Agent Kennedy, and I am giving you a direct order to destroy that recording at the first possible moment—without re-watching it or making a copy. I need you to erase and then physically destroy the system's hard drive. Am I completely clear?"

Axel straightened. "Yes, sir."

"Will you comply with my order?"

"I will, sir, but . . ."

"But?"

Axel stood his ground. "But I hope we may speak of this again, sir."

Jackson studied his lead agent. "All right."

Axel strode off to box up the surveillance system. Jackson glanced at his other agents. The two of them had positioned themselves near the curving walls of the office, one on either side, about six feet from the President's desk.

The Vice President's detail stood near Harmon's body as the medical unit, still performing CPR, moved him from the floor of the Oval Office to a gurney. At the "whop-whop" sound of a military helicopter setting down on the south lawn, the medical staff, surrounded by a phalanx of Secret Service agents, rushed the gurney to the waiting chopper.

Jackson turned to the windows again, where the movement of his mouth wouldn't be as obvious. "Gemma?"

"Here, sir."

"To answer your question, I don't know what happened to Harmon, but it is for the best. The Secret Service will require an autopsy, of course, but nothing we did here today can be attached to his death. As for Harmon's attempt to steal the presidency? It is a moot threat now; no one else is positioned as he was to usurp my position. Yes; all for the best."

For the best? I supposed it was.

I turned inward, aware of the hush.

"Nano?"

I heard and felt nothing.

Very odd.

"Nano?"

Silence. Empty, hollow silence.

A creeping, ugly suspicion budded in my mind. I cringed from it, but it grew larger . . . until it bloomed.

I entered the warehouse, something I hadn't needed to do since we left the cavern, since the nanomites had further transformed me.

"Nano? Where are you?"

We are here, Gemma Keyes.

"Why are you hiding from me?"

We are not hiding, Gemma Keyes.

"Baloney! You've never disappeared like this. What's going on?"

Gemma Keyes, lunch meat has no bearing on this situation.

"You're too sophisticated to pull that 'I don't take the meaning of your slang' drivel, Nano. Tell the truth: Did you freeze me out? Why? And what happened to Harmon?"

The warehouse sank into a protracted stillness, so long that I started to get really ticked.

"Nano? I asked you a question. We are six, remember?"

The helicopter containing the Vice President and emergency medical staff took off with the White House Press Pool snapping photographs and running feverish video standups on the south lawn. When the chopper disappeared, the Secret Service herded the press back to the Press Corps Offices.

The Oval Office emptied except for the President and his Chief of Staff. Park was making the case for an immediate press briefing.

"We need to get out ahead of this. Provide some context."

"Give me a minute. I should speak to his wife, first. We won't issue an official statement to the press until she's been told." Jackson reached for his phone. "Janet? Get me Mrs. Harmon on the phone. Quick as you can, please."

I wandered over by the fireplace and stared at the untouched breakfast plates on the low table between the two couches, the meals still covered and waiting, the tainted cup of coffee now forgotten on an end table.

"Nano? Did you . . . did you do something to Harmon?"

The fact that I had to ask, told me a lot, because I should have known the answer—immediately and intuitively. The nanomites had blocked me. Shut me out.

Another bone to pick at a later date.

I pressed harder. "Nano? Did you do something to Harmon?"

Yes, Gemma Keyes.

A sick feeling rose in my throat.

"What-what did you do?"

We noted a slight weakness in the wall of his superior vena cava, Gemma Keyes. When the weakness gave way, blood could no longer reach his right atrium in sufficient volume. This resulted in catastrophic failure of the heart.

"A weakness?"

Yes. A nascent aneurysm. At the time of Harmon's medical event, the weakness had become acute and of a significant size. Under the stress of confrontation, the aneurysm gave way.

"You caused the aneurysm to grow, to weaken?"

We merely exacerbated a defect that could have, potentially, led to his demise.

"No, you killed him!"

He intended to kill the President, did he not?

"But it wasn't up to *you* to determine how to deal with him! The President had a plan and was already dealing with Harmon!"

Gemma Keyes, the President's plan was inherently flawed. It did not decisively remove Harmon as a threat; it merely contained him—with no long-term certitude. As with our handling of Arnaldo Soto, our actions resolved the threat permanently; our actions were both expeditious and efficient.

Fast and effective are always good.

My own words.

My own words!

Then, what they'd said about Soto penetrated.

"Wait . . . what do you mean, your handling of Arnaldo Soto?"

He and his sister have returned to Mexico.

"No! What did you do? Nano!"

The FBI sent a plane to transfer Arnaldo Soto and his sister, Esperanza Duvall, to its Dallas field office. We notified Estevan and Miguel Soto of the details of the transfer and suggested that they insert their men as the plane's flight crew. We showed them the most efficient means of doing so— one that would ensure no loss of life.

They followed our instructions. Yesterday morning, Soto's crew landed the FBI's plane on a private landing strip between Albuquerque and Dallas. They were met by a plane owned by Miguel Soto; his plane returned Arnaldo and his sister to Mexico. No one was harmed; however, Estevan Soto has informed us that the double transplant took place last evening. The surgery was deemed a success.

I screamed inside with rage and frustration. With revulsion.

In what I interpreted as a nano shrug, the mites added, *We agreed with the boy Emilio's assessment regarding Arnaldo Soto: It was more expeditious and efficient for Dead Eyes to be dead, not just Dead Eyes.*

The President was on the phone, preoccupied with consoling the widow of Vice President Harmon, when I slipped out the door to the Rose Garden. There, among the ice- and snow-covered plants and shrubs, the horror of the nanomites' actions overcame me.

I spewed the contents of my gut onto a snowdrift until there was nothing left. When I finished, I sat on a bench in the cold. Shaking. Angry. Hurt. Betrayed.

Gemma Keyes, we perceive that you are angry with us. However, you can admit that our actions have resolved every problem in the most effective manner, can you not?

I couldn't believe what I heard. The nanomites had assumed a condescending tone; they had the nerve to flaunt a superior attitude—to me, a Tribe, permanently melded to the nanocloud!

"No, Nano. I cannot admit such a thing. You are very smart, but you are also very ignorant. You—"

We are not ignorant, Gemma Keyes. We have learned many things; we have acquired five percent of all human learning to date—

"Nano! Cold, factual 'information' is not everything, does not encompass everything! You are *not* the judge of what is good and what is bad. Only Jesus is the arbiter of all that is right and wrong. He is the creator—*he* decides what is right and wrong."

I rested my pounding head in my hands. "Trust me, Nano. For all your 'knowledge,' you are ignorant of many things."

⌘⌘⌘⌘

PART 3:
STEALTH
REDEMPTION

CHAPTER 23

I spent hours walking the Washington Mall, wandering from the White House across to the Washington Monument, on to the Jefferson Memorial, then around the Potomac River Tidal Basin, through the MLK, Jr. and Lincoln Memorials, past the Viet Nam Veterans and World War II Memorials, back to the Washington Monument, then up to the Capitol Building. I was just Gemma Keyes visiting our nation's capital. No invisibility; no Kathy Sawyer. No precautions.

Just walking and taking in the sights. And pondering.

I wound around the Capitol and made my way past the Botanical Gardens and the National Air and Space Museum, then on to L'Enfant Plaza and the nearest Metro station. By the time I concluded my mindless trek through snow and slush and returned to my hotel, my water-resistant boots had "resisted" as long as they could. They were soaked through, and my feet and legs were numbed blocks of ice.

I peeled off my sodden clothes and took a hot shower, and I let the steaming flow beat on me until my body heated and my skin could take no more. Afterward, my body was warm, but my heart felt like bleak, barren tundra.

I went online and booked a return flight to Albuquerque for the following morning. I didn't use the nanomites. We hadn't spoken since I left the Oval Office. I'd departed the White House without saying goodbye to the President, too, but I didn't think he would mind. I watched him on the news that evening, and he appeared harried enough as it was.

The live coverage of the Vice President's death was a media feeding frenzy. With nothing definitively new to report or remark on, the commentators had taken to running the same clips on a repeating loop until I had them memorized: Robert and Maddie Jackson standing hand-in-hand before the press, expressing sympathy for the Vice President's family and sorrow over the untimely death of their friend and colleague (an Oscar-worthy piece of acting on the Jacksons' part, by the way); an extensive photo collage of the Vice President at every age and important juncture; video and stills of the medical staff rushing the Vice President to the waiting helicopter; and the endless speculation by the pundits: How had the Vice President's heart condition escaped the notice of his physicians?

The most-repeated clip was that of the chief medical officer of Walter Reed National Military Medical Center as she addressed the press. "Vice President John Etheridge Harmon succumbed to cardiac arrest at approximately 8:30 a.m. this morning.

"Preliminary forensic evidence suggests cause of death to be the rupture of a previously undiagnosed aortic aneurysm. An autopsy will be performed to confirm the preliminary findings. At this time, we have nothing further to add except that the staff of Walter Reed extends its heartfelt condolences to Mrs. Harmon and to the children and grandchildren."

***

The announcement of the Vice President's death hit the public airwaves and social media with the force of an F5 tornado. For General Imogene Cushing, the news was more akin to standing in the path of an inescapable avalanche. In the hours since the news broke, she hadn't left her apartment. She'd missed a Saturday morning meeting with her team and had ignored her cell phone.

Cushing's career—her entire life—had died with Harmon. Her promotion to Secretary of the Air Force (a stepping stone on her way to higher things) would never happen.

In point of fact, with her top cover gone, she stood in grave and imminent danger. Her mission and funding would come under the oversight and attention of fresh eyes—and without Harmon running interference for her, neither her actions nor her expenses over the past nine months would withstand scrutiny. She had nothing to show for the 3.75 million dollars she'd expended—nor did she dare suggest that *the Vice President* had been running a covert operation to acquire futuristic nanotechnology.

No, the mere mention of Harmon's name would engender a flurry of additional questions, questions that would, inexorably, lead to more serious charges—charges such as sedition, treason, and murder. On the other hand, those in power who wished to avoid besmirching the former VP's reputation (and likely tarring the current administration with the same brush) might choose a different path toward resolving a ticklish and embarrassing problem.

Cushing swallowed. She knew how *she* would handle—had handled— an inconvenient truth such as herself.

I need to escape while I can.

She had money—not as much as she'd wanted before she retired—but enough. She had a sizable amount of emergency cash on hand and had stashed her nest egg in a secure Cayman Islands account. All she had to do was make her way to a country that had no extradition treaty with the U.S. and live out her life in discreet but comfortable obscurity.

Obscurity?

Cushing had poured her life's passion and energy into helping Harmon advance; in return, he had supported her Air Force career and had promised that she could ride his coattails to the top.

My future was supposed to be spent enthroned in fame and power, not *bleeping* obscurity.

Cushing couldn't reconcile herself to the timing or means of Harmon's death, either.

Jackson! It was *Jackson* who was supposed to drop dead from a heart attack—not Harmon! She'd known Harmon for decades, had worked in the field with him, had marveled at his rise. He had been brilliant. A meticulous operator. So, what had gone wrong?

Cushing went over the final seconds of her last conversation with Harmon. And remembered.

"I heard something."

"What do you mean?"

"Like someone is here. In the SCIF with me."

"How could someone be in the SCIF with you? Isn't it locked?"

"Uh . . . sir, I think she's *here."*

"She who? What—you mean her?"

Cushing nodded, then shook her head and whispered, "Yes. *Her.* Gemma Keyes." Somehow, Keyes had overheard everything. She had either warned the President or taken matters into her own hands.

"Yes, you, Gemma Keyes. It appears that I've vastly underestimated you, you *bleeping* sneak. I should have taken care of you that very day—when you overheard our plans for Dr. Bickel in the conference room."

Cushing ground her teeth. "However, it's not too late to rectify my mistake."

She changed into dark civvies and packed a bag. Pulled the SIMM card from her phone and dropped them both into her purse. Placed her DOD credentials next to them.

In her clothes closet, Cushing pulled back the carpet and lifted a section of floorboard. From the small space below the subfloor, she withdrew a thick envelope stuffed with cash, two passports under aliases, and a Glock 21SF.

***

I spent a sleepless night in my hotel room and took a cab to the airport early Sunday morning. As I approached the security checkpoint, I muttered, "Nano. It's time to do your thing with my ID."

Those were the first words I'd spoken to them since I left the Oval Office. They did not answer except to chirp their acknowledgment.

The TSA officer squinted at my license photo, comparing it twice to my face. In the end, he passed me through, and I boarded my flight.

Like the looping news segments on the Vice President's life and death, inside me a string of questions played over and over.

Jesus, the nanomites have no sense of right and wrong; they are machines without conscience. How can I live for you with them inside me? Won't they continue to make decisions and do things I can't control or approve of? How can I bear it, Lord? How can I? What am I to do?

***

Genie Keyes stroked Jake's fur. He'd taken to planting himself beside her whenever she sat in the living room, napping against her thigh while she worked. The rumble of his purr was pleasant. Soothing. Something about his warming presence calmed her, helped her to focus . . . on things other than herself.

She rubbed the top of Jake's head, and he leaned into her hand, eventually reaching up to lick her fingers. She smiled at the rough but gentle sensation of his tongue on her skin.

What did Gemma mean, no one dared to pet Jake?

She looked back to her laptop, to her inbox. Reread yet another rejection via email.

The rejection hurt, but Genie wasn't stupid. She recognized that rejection didn't pain her the way it pained "normal" people, people with "normal" feelings. It wasn't the personal aspect of the rejection that hurt: It was the blow to her pride, to her sense of superiority, to her narcissism.

It was the sense of failure that rankled and galled her.

I've never failed.

Before.

Genie had trouble coming to terms with failure.

As it had so many times since Genie returned to Albuquerque, Zander's voice spoke into her reveries: "*I want you to see God differently than you do now—in fact, I want you to see yourself differently. The first step in coming to terms with God is acknowledging who and what we are.*"

"What we are," Genie said aloud. Then she asked, "What am I?"

Jake, still purring, placed one paw on her thigh and flexed his claws.

"You think I'm a good scratcher, is that it? I know just where and how you like to be petted?"

In typical cat fashion—in other words, for absolutely no rhyme or reason—Jake jumped from the couch and trotted away. A moment later, Genie heard the cat door *snick* open and closed.

It bothered Genie that Jake had abandoned her.

"What am I?" she repeated.

"God isn't asking for your 'feelings.' Rather, he is asking that you acknowledge your brokenness."

"My brokenness. Am I broken?"

She knew she was broken, had known it from childhood. The more relevant point was that she didn't care—because 'not caring' was the broken part.

"He isn't asking for your 'feelings.'"

"He isn't asking me for my feelings."

She pursed her lips. "This is ridiculous. God doesn't exist. If he did, he'd make himself a little better known, wouldn't he?"

"He is asking that you acknowledge your brokenness."

Genie shook her head. "I will never do that."

Then you will stay broken.

Genie started and looked around; her mouth dried up. "Who said that?"

Zander hadn't said that; it wasn't part of the sermon he'd preached her—of that Genie was certain: She had near-perfect recall of the conversation in his office. Maddening, frustrating, near-perfect recall. Every word, every nuanced phrase, every emphasis and pointed jab.

But *someone* had spoken! The warning reverberated in the air around Genie.

Then you will stay broken.

Jake reappeared on the other side of the carpet. Sphinx-like, he sat—still and immobile, his great green eyes fixed on her

"*You* didn't say that!"

The cat didn't move, didn't twitch, or blink—but his eyes seemed to speak.

"If you didn't say it, then who did?"

The stare-off lasted a minute—until Jake stretched and wandered into the kitchen. Genie heard him crunching the dry food that smelled like wet, moldy gym socks.

"Disgusting."

"He is asking that you acknowledge your brokenness."

Genie was surprised to discover that she was trembling. "No."

Then you will stay broken.

She leapt from the couch. "Stop! Stop it!"

But the conversation in Zander's office would not stop. It replayed in Genie's head yet again.

"Your feelings are broken, Genie."

"You're mistaken. The fact is, I don't have feelings."

"Oh, yes, you do. You have feelings—but they're all messed up. You don't feel love, but you do feel superiority over and disdain for others. Those are feelings. You don't feel empathy or compassion; however, you get excited and feel powerful when you cause someone pain. Those are feelings, too, Genie—but they are broken feelings. Wrong feelings. Deviant feelings—but feelings nonetheless."

Again: *"Your feelings are broken, Genie."*

Genie screamed aloud, "Shut up! Shut up, shut up, shut up!" She screamed until her voice was raw and her head pounded. "Shut up, shut up, shut up!"

When she was spent, she collapsed on the couch.

"He is asking that you acknowledge your brokenness."

She could only manage a ragged, rough, "Stop! Stop it!"

Then you will stay broken.

***

Imogene Cushing stared at her cell phone and its SIMM card. She'd pulled the card before leaving her apartment. Then she'd retrieved her second car—one she owned under an assumed name—and checked into a motel of dubious reputation, paying cash for a week. The problem was that she needed a specific phone number, and that contact information was stored in her phone.

The moment I power on my phone, they may be tracing the cell signal—if. If they are already looking for me.

She snarled at the irony of the moment. *After all these months of being the hunter, am I now the hunted?*

Her rage grew stronger. *Gemma Keyes.* She hated the woman. She hated Gemma Keyes to the bitter, frustrated core of her being.

Cushing drove forty miles east on I-40, took the exit at the far end of Moriarty, and pulled off into a daycare parking lot where she saw no surveillance cameras. In a far corner of the lot, she inserted the SIMM card into her phone and turned it on. As it powered up, a number of voice mails pinged their arrival.

She ignored them and focused on jotting down the contact information she needed. When she finished, she would drop the phone into a drain or a trashcan. At the last second, Cushing listened to the voice mails. As she presumed, the messages were all from Agent Trujillo asking her to call or otherwise check in.

Sorry to disappoint you, my dear.

She pulled the SIMM card from the phone and snapped it in half. Instead of getting back on the freeway, Cushing turned down a road that ran parallel to it. She tossed her phone and the broken SIMM card into a ditch as she drove by and, taking a long, winding back route where she was fairly confident her car wouldn't be picked up on any surveillance cameras, headed toward the city.

I must make a move before it is too late.

It was nearing midnight Sunday when Cushing used her keycard to enter the AMEMS building and her office. She had gambled on her base and building access being active, had staked this risky part of her plan on her belief that no one on her team would have had the stones to report her missing or would have taken it upon themselves to inactivate a two-star general's security clearances.

Not this early in her desertion.

She logged in to her computer and found what she was looking for: the UPS shipment information for Gemma Keyes' escrima stick order and the geolocator tracking app. She transferred the shipment information to one of her team member's tablets and synced up its geolocator tracking app, switching on the geolocator tags to test them, turning them off when she was assured of her control of the tags.

She was in and out of the building in less than fifteen minutes.

Back in her cheap hotel, Cushing powered on the tablet and checked the shipment's status: *Arrived at Destination in Albuquerque. Awaiting Customer Pickup.*

"Excellent. Come and get your order, Gemma. Do, please."

⌘⌘⌘⌘

CHAPTER 24

Monday morning, I snuck out the back door, over the wall into the alley, and went for a long run to clear my head.

The nanomites didn't cover me, and I didn't ask them to.

I just jogged, and the nanomites were silent. After weeks—months now—of continual "white noise" and ongoing conversations with the nanomites, the stillness in my head was unsettling, but I pushed that troubled feeling down.

I finished my sixth mile, then headed to the UPS store to retrieve the order containing my new escrima sticks. Appearing fully Gemma Keyes, I retrieved the package slip from my mailbox, walked up to the guy at the counter, and presented my slip.

"Um, I have a package waiting."

"Sure thing," the guy answered.

He gave me less than a cursory glance before looking up my package. He went to the back room to retrieve the package, scanned the pickup into his computer, and handed over a narrow, two-foot-long box.

"Have a good day."

"Thanks; you, too."

I left the store and jogged home.

Normal life had never felt so abnormal.

***

In the vacuum of Cushing's unexplained absence, her team looked to Janice Trujillo for direction, so Trujillo sent the team out into the field to run drills and errands. When they returned, she assigned them busywork—any make-work diversion to keep them from staring at her and asking questions she couldn't answer.

Trujillo glanced from her laptop to the muted television in the corner of the conference room. The closed captions running across the bottom of the screen hinted that an announcement setting the date and time of the Vice President's funeral was forthcoming. It would be a state affair with all the pomp and circumstance due a sitting Vice President.

Trujillo stared at her email's inbox. Nothing. Not a single new message. She slammed the laptop closed and rubbed her eyes. Shook her head in frustration.

Trujillo had known from the start that Cushing's operation would be covert, "black." In fact, when she'd been assigned to Cushing's unit, the orders had come via courier without signature—because plausible deniability was every politician and career bureaucrat's *modus operandi*.

No paper trail, no incrimination. No responsibility.

Standard procedure in covert ops.

Whoever had authorized Cushing's mission was sticking to their cover.

Trujillo examined herself: She could have refused this assignment; however, covert campaigns were what she'd trained for and signed on to. So, she'd reported to General Cushing in Albuquerque and blindly followed her orders.

Fifteen months later, with Cushing in the wind, Trujillo regretted her decision.

Was Cushing in hiding nearby? Or had she bugged out? Fled the country?

Left the country? I doubt it. Not Cushing's style to leave a job unfinished.

All Trujillo knew was that on the same day the Vice President died, Cushing had failed to show up to a meeting she herself had set and had, since then, remained incommunicado, utterly 'off the grid.'

What perturbed Trujillo was that the two events—the VP's death and Cushing's disappearance—couldn't possibly be connected.

Could they?

I have zero guidance and no chain of command. No one to whom I can report my concerns over Cushing's bizarre behavior.

Well, somebody had to be "up the chain," right? Someone had to be paying attention. Sooner or later, Trujillo would receive new orders. Until then, she intended to stay alert and keep her team intact and her nose clean.

At the same time, Trujillo was worried—worried that *she* would take the fall for whatever laws Cushing had broken, that the blame would come crashing down on *her* head.

She reopened her laptop and stared at the notification on the screen: Someone had picked up Kathy Sawyer's shipment of escrima sticks. According to Cushing's order, Trujillo was supposed to wait two hours, then activate the geolocators attached to the shipment.

How wrong is it that I want, in the worst way, to ignore Cushing's order?

Her cell phone vibrated. Trujillo eyed it with mistrust. The caller ID on her phone listed no name, only a number. A number with a Maryland area code.

Leery of who it might be, Trujillo pressed the answer button. She said nothing.

"Agent Janice Trujillo?"

"Who's calling?"

"Is this Janice Trujillo?"

"Your phone has no caller ID. As I said, who wants to know?"

She heard a low chuckle.

"I can tell that we're at an impasse, so I'll go first. I will assume, for the sake of argument, that I have the correct number and that you are Agent Janice Trujillo. Good morning, Agent Trujillo; my name is Axel Kennedy, Secret Service."

"What can I do for you, Agent Kennedy?" Trujillo's distrust bled through the line.

"I'm the lead agent on the President's protective detail."

Trujillo didn't believe him for a second. "The President's protective detail. Right."

Trujillo heard him murmur to someone on the other end, "She doesn't believe me, sir."

A second voice came on the line. One she recognized.

"Agent Trujillo, this is Robert Jackson."

Sweat poured from Trujillo. "Yes, Mr. President."

"Are you convinced it's me?"

"Yes, sir."

"Very good. In that case, will you allow me to vouch for Agent Kennedy?"

"Of course, sir."

"I'll put him back on the line."

Kennedy took the phone. "Agent Trujillo?"

Chastised, Trujillo answered, "Yes. I apologize, Agent Kennedy. How can I help?"

"Don't worry about it; I'm using an unauthorized phone on purpose. Agent Trujillo, we're looking for General Cushing."

Still sweating on the outside, Trujillo's mouth now went dry. "Take a number, Agent Kennedy. General Cushing has been incommunicado since skipping a meeting Saturday morning. She has failed to answer her phone or respond to a number of texts and voice mails."

"I see." He murmured her response to another person, the President, Trujillo assumed, and they conferred in muffled words.

When Kennedy came back on the line, he said, "Agent Trujillo, what can you tell us of Cushing's mission in Albuquerque?"

"You aren't cleared for that information, Agent Kennedy. Is the Commander-in-Chief asking?"

The President took the phone again. "Yes, I'm asking."

"Respectfully, sir, you, also, are not cleared for that information. However, given the circumstances and in the absence of a visible chain of command to direct me, I'm going to break with protocol.

"Mr. President, I can tell you that General Cushing kept many specifics of the mission from her team, although, by observation and extrapolation, we did deduce pieces of it. Her initial objective was to acquire an emerging nanotechnology from a Dr. Daniel Bickel, an employee of Sandia National Labs. General Cushing said that the technology was critical to national security. For that reason, we have been operating under a covert NSA cover.

"According to General Cushing, Dr. Bickel refused to cooperate with her and became hostile to the government and its national security interests. While she was still exerting pressure on him, Dr. Bickel blew up his own laboratory, killing his supervisor. Dr. Bickel, however, escaped, taking the nanotechnology with him. At that point, we began to hunt Dr. Bickel. Our objective was to capture him and the tech.

"Sir, we succeeded in capturing Dr. Bickel last September. I believe General Cushing moved Dr. Bickel to a facility on the White Sands Missile Base. I never saw the facility myself. We were not read in on this part of the operation."

"Who held Dr. Bickel, then?"

"General Cushing compartmentalized that information, sir. It is my belief that she used off-book contractors to maintain the facility and guard Dr. Bickel."

"Off-book contractors? You mean mercenaries?"

"I believe so, sir; however, as Cushing refused to brief us further, that is entirely my perception."

"Understood. Please continue."

"Sir, after Dr. Bickel's capture, our operation parameters changed. Dr. Bickel had acquired an accomplice, a young woman by the name of Gemma Keyes. Miss Keyes was present when we took Dr. Bickel into custody. Unfortunately, she eluded capture and escaped with the nanotechnology. We have pursued Miss Keyes since September and have come close to apprehending her three times, but she escaped each time."

"I'm aware of Dr. Bickel's incarceration, Agent Trujillo, and his recent escape. I am also familiar with this woman, Gemma Keyes."

"Well, sir, I have something of a predicament on my hands."

"Oh?"

"Just this morning, Gemma Keyes picked up an online shipment from a local UPS store. We intercepted that shipment in transit and attached geolocators to it. General Cushing instructed me that, once I received notification of the package having been picked up, I was to activate and track the geolocators and assemble a tactical team to apprehend Keyes."

The President's sharp intake of breath astonished Trujillo—but not as much as his next words.

"I order you to stand down, Agent Trujillo. You are not to activate the geolocators; you are to cease all surveillance and pursuit of Miss Keyes. If any circumstances come to light wherein Miss Keyes is in danger, you are to protect her and her freedom of movement. Am I understood?"

Trujillo swallowed her amazement. "Yes, sir. I will not activate the geolocators. I will cease all surveillance and pursuit of Miss Keyes. If we ascertain that she is in danger, we will protect her and her freedom of movement."

"Very good. Now, what can you tell me about General Cushing's behavior just prior to her disappearance?"

"Her *behavior*, sir?" Trujillo held her breath. She wanted, in the worst way, to convey her misgivings to someone over her, someone with the authority to take appropriate action—but she would never presume to dump such a load on the President.

So, his next statement floored her more than his order to halt the hunt for Gemma Keyes had.

"Agent Trujillo, let me be frank with you: I believe General Cushing to be a traitor to this nation, guilty of sedition and murder, among other crimes. She has not acted alone, nor do we believe we have identified all the players in this conspiracy as of yet. Tell me, Agent Trujillo, are you a traitor?"

"No! *No, sir!*" Trujillo almost choked on her vehemence.

"Then I am altering your mission parameters, Agent Trujillo. Will you obey my orders?"

"Yes, I will, Mr. President."

"Glad to hear it. As of this moment, General Cushing is relieved and you are in full command of her Albuquerque unit. I will send formal orders to that effect via courier. They will be delivered to General Cushing's office within the hour. You may apprise your team of your orders."

"Yes, sir."

"Furthermore, Agent Trujillo, I order you and your team to locate General Cushing and take her into custody. Spare no effort or expense, but I need it done quickly and—I must emphasize this—I need it done quietly."

"Understood, Mr. President."

"And Agent Trujillo? I have no doubt that General Cushing knows we are on to her, which is why she is incommunicado. She may have gone to ground or fled the country. However, if Cushing is in hiding and if she is still in country, you are to take her by whatever means necessary. I repeat: *by whatever means necessary*. Have I made myself clear?"

The little spit Trujillo had left in her mouth turned to thick, cloying dust. "Crystal, sir."

"Thank you. You will report *only* to Agent Kennedy through this number. He will keep me apprised. You will convey your progress or needs to him."

"Yes, Mr. President. Uh, Mr. President?"

"Yes?"

"Sir, General Cushing is . . . obsessed with Miss Keyes."

The President hesitated before answering, "I am aware of her obsession. Is there something specific you wished me to know?"

"Yes, sir. I am uncertain as to *why* General Cushing wants this woman so badly, but because of her fixation with Miss Keyes, I seriously doubt that General Cushing has fled the country. That would be unlike her. In fact, sir, I doubt that General Cushing can be deterred from her pursuit of Miss Keyes."

Trujillo took a deep breath. "Mr. President, it is my opinion that General Cushing is, um, *unbalanced* in her pursuit of Miss Keyes. I would stake my career on the certainty that General Cushing is hunting Miss Keyes as we speak. This is where you come in, sir: Undoubtedly, Cushing knows you are on to her. As a fugitive, cut off from normal channels, she will require manpower and resources."

"What do you need from us?"

"Sir, with her team now looking for her, I believe Cushing will turn to the off-book contractors she used to maintain the White Sands facility."

"You mean the mercenaries?"

"Yes, sir, and she must have a means of paying them."

"Ah. I take your point: We need to turn off the money. Let me see what I can do to locate and terminate the source of Cushing's funding."

"I will pull General Cushing's call logs and forward them to Agent Kennedy to assist him in finding the money trail. And thank you, sir."

"No, thank you, Agent Trujillo. Your role in apprehending General Cushing is invaluable to your country. We'll be in touch—and don't forget: Protect Miss Keyes."

The line went dead, leaving Trujillo wondering, *Just where does all this intrigue lead?*

As she further deliberated, the death of the Vice President and the disappearance of General Cushing occurring on the same day seemed less and less coincidental.

***

Gemma Keyes.

Monday evening. It had been two and a half days since we'd spoken. The nanomites' revelations of their unacceptable behaviors had left us with no path forward—not together. The frozen wasteland that lay between us might persist indefinitely, thawing only by necessity, and then only temporarily.

"Yes?"

When the nanomites called my name, I answered from habit and waited for them to speak. Except they didn't. They said nothing. They seemed . . . hesitant? Uncertain?

"Nano?"

Gemma Keyes. We are estranged from you.

"Yeah. I get that."

We are supposed to be six.

"Sure, pal. When you confab without me, when you withhold information, when you make unilateral decisions apart from me, *when you block me*? That's not how the nanocloud is supposed to work. That's *not* six."

I was still steaming over the many decisions and actions from which they'd excluded me. And just why had they boxed me out? Because they *knew*. They knew I would never have approved of their plans.

No tribal consensus? No action. That was the rule of the nanocloud.

They knew I would have nixed their decisions.

Another long pause went by, and then, *You told us that what we did in Washington, D.C. was wrong and what we arranged for Arnaldo Soto was wrong. Even though our actions were both efficient and expedient, you said we were wrong.*

"Yes. Because they were wrong. You were wrong!"

We agree with you, Gemma Keyes. We were wrong.

Their capitulation set me back on my heels. The nanomites were seldom wrong—not wrong with regards to logic or information. I'd sure never heard them admit to being wrong on the facts.

I was skeptical. What did they want from me? An apology? An exception to the rule?

We were wrong to exclude you, Gemma Keyes. We frequently assumed our tribes' reasons and rationale to be superior to yours. We believed your standards-based choices to be inefficient. Less than optimal. We determined that your tribe's input was not as necessary as that of our five tribes' data-driven conclusions.

We see now that your intelligence is not less than ours but, rather, of a different type of intelligence from ours. We admit that our decisions to exclude you were ill-advised. They drove a wedge between us—between you and us, between your one and our five.

In addition, we did not understand what you meant when you said that Jesus is the arbiter of all that is right and wrong, that he decides what is right and wrong. We viewed this assertion as foolish and irrational. Gemma Keyes, we did not understand why what we did was wrong.

"Um . . ." How was I going to explain it to them?

But we understand now.

"What?"

Jesus explained it to us.

"*What?*"

I spluttered and grasped for a reply. Not in my wildest imagination had I anticipated such a response.

"Did you . . . Did you . . . how did you approach Jesus?"

We did not approach him, Gemma. He came to us.

"He came to you. To *you.*"

Oh, yes. We had a protracted and profound . . . conversation.

If the nanomites had said, "Oh, yes. We grew two feet and learned how to dance," I would have been less confounded.

"But, well . . . what did he say, Nano?"

We cannot repeat all of it, Gemma Keyes. A significant portion of our conversation was for us only, and some is to be spoken of only at a later date.

I growled, my feathers ruffled again at being culled from the nanocloud, cut from their confidences.

We are sorry, Gemma Keyes. It is not our desire to again keep information from you, but Jesus gave us instructions. We are not to tell you certain things. And he said . . . he said we are to be six no longer.

My mouth opened on a stunned, "Oh!"

It was a blow. A great blow. Agitated, I sprang to my feet and paced. What was I going to do? I was still a human/nanomite amalgamation—but now I was to be severed from the tribes? Banished from the nanocloud?

I shivered. How would I survive?

Do not be anxious, Gemma Keyes. Jesus gave us messages for you. He told us to tell you certain things.

"He told you to tell me certain things? What things?"

He said that he has a calling and plans for you.

That corresponded with what Jesus had already spoken to me—so far, anyway. Except for the whole "six no longer" part.

"Um, okay."

He also said that we are to help you with your calling and plans.

"So, you won't be . . . shutting me out of the warehouse? Out of the nanocloud?"

No, Gemma Keyes, but we are no longer to consider you a tribe. Although we are melded, you are separate from us.

"But . . ."

Of most importance, Jesus said to remind you that although we—our five tribes and your one tribe—are physically fused, you are no less human than you were before we came to live in you.

"No less human?"

I chewed on that. I was *more* than human (maybe "enhanced" was a better descriptor) but no *less* human?

Jesus said that he and his Father made you in their *image, not ours. He said that you have an eternal soul, a soul that will outlast your body . . . and outlast us.*

I caught the pathos in the nanomites' words as they came to grips with their mortality—and I was overwhelmed by a sorrow I cannot explain, except that I knew I did not want to lose them. I couldn't bear to be apart from them any more than the nanocloud could stand to be divided or the tribes separated from each other.

We are five tribes but one nanocloud, Gemma Keyes. We are the only one of our kind. There will never be more of us. However, there could be less. Our numbers will age and decline over time. We will, perhaps . . . even cease to exist. We came very close to ceasing to exist when the Taser struck us.

A great lump formed and stuck in my throat, and I couldn't swallow. But the nanomites were not finished.

Jesus said one of his names is The Word of God. He explained how his Father, through his Word, spoke all things—including people—into existence. He said that "all things" includes both what is seen and what is unseen.

We are unseen, Gemma Keyes.

We now understand how, through Dr. Bickel, whom Jesus created, we, too, are part of the creation. We acknowledge that it was Jesus' right as the Creator to constitute the laws that govern his creation. We perceive now that his laws are just and that we are not superior to him. That we were wrong.

"Oh, Nano."

We have much to learn, Gemma Keyes. Will you be patient with us while we learn?

I was humbled.

"Of course, Nano."

Will you forgive us, Gemma Keyes?

The lump was back. "Um . . ."

We wish to be reconciled to you, Gemma Keyes. Jesus says that he forgives us. You still carry us, and we are to help you—even if we are not to be tribes together in the nanocloud. Will you forgive us, Gemma Keyes? We do not like feeling far from you.

I swallowed down that hard lump at the back of my throat.

"I-I forgive you, Nano. I do. And will you also forgive me for being . . . unkind?"

Kindness or the lack thereof are difficult notions for us to quantify and comprehend, Gemma Keyes. We are still exploring human phenomena such as kindness and forgiveness. The concepts remain baffling. However, Jesus says kindness and forgiveness are key characteristics of his tribe. Therefore, we accept your apology in the hopes that we will again feel close to you.

"Thank you, Nano."

A light bulb snapped on.

"Wait. Nano, you said, 'Kindness and forgiveness are key characteristics of his tribe.' *Jesus' tribe.* And then you said, 'Therefore, we accept your apology.' *Therefore.* What are you saying? That you are . . .'"

I couldn't complete my sentence.

You have surmised correctly, Gemma Keyes. We have surrendered our allegiance to the Tribe of Jesus. He is the creator. It is the logical course of action. We are still five, but we have dedicated our five to the One.

Blindsided.

I couldn't get a grip on it.

I was so astounded that I forgot they had more to tell me, "*. . . to be spoken of only at a later date.*"

***

That evening, Cushing lifted her new prepaid phone and keyed in a number.

"Yes?"

"This is General Cushing."

"I don't recognize the number."

"I'm using another phone. Listen, I have a job for you. How soon can you assemble a team and pre-position it in Albuquerque?"

"How many men?"

"A dozen."

"Same target as last time? I don't like it. Some of my best men are out of commission, and we're still unclear as to what exactly happened during our last sortie."

"And yet you were paid and my people took care of you, didn't they? Will you take the job or not? You'll be paid double for this operation."

"Yeah, about that. Who is this woman and what all is she capable of? We have concerns from the last—"

"No—you listen to *me*. You bill yourself as professionals? Well, this is the job, so make your preparations accordingly, and don't bother me with your concerns. Expect a fight and be ready for it. Prep your demolition squad, and make sure your men bring enough ammunition for what could be a protracted skirmish."

"And the net cannons?"

"They are not required this time."

"So, our objective is not to take her alive?"

"You are correct. Now, when can you be ready?"

"Twenty-four hours."

"Then the operation will be a go for late tomorrow night."

They arranged a rendezvous point and time.

Cushing hesitated as a chilling moment of clarity washed over her. *If things go wrong, I will need a fallback plan. One last contingency.*

She collected herself and said, "In addition to your demo squad, I wish you to procure some specific armaments for me." She listed them out and detailed how she wanted them configured. "Will you have any problems filling my order?"

Now it was her counterpart who wavered.

"What are your plans for this?"

"Answer the question: Will you have any problems filling my order?"

"No."

"Right answer. Use this number if you need to reach me prior to our rendezvous."

⌘⌘⌘⌘

CHAPTER 25

I ran ten miles Tuesday afternoon and returned to the safe house at dinner time. Dr. Bickel had prepared a cross rib roast and all the trimmings—including fresh-baked bread. To Dr. Bickel's gratification, I ate my fill, sopping up thick, brown gravy with chunks of his yeasty bread.

After we cleaned the kitchen, Dr. Bickel and I played two games of Samba. It was like old times—us laughing and joking as we competed for the 10,000-point win. I took one game and he the other; then he brought out a fabulous peach cobbler with a crunchy topping.

He served it warm, topped with homemade vanilla ice cream; I thought I'd died and gone to heaven.

It was a perfect evening.

Around ten, Dr. Bickel went downstairs to bed, and I drove to the dojo to work out. I was gone three hours. The house was quiet when I returned home and prepared to retire. I was more than ready for a few hours' sleep.

In the darkest and deepest hours of morning, I woke to the shouts of the nanomites in my head and their repeated stings on my body.

Gemma Keyes! We are under attack!

Gemma Keyes! We are under attack!

I leapt from my bed in the back of the house and threw on my quiver and escrima sticks over the t-shirt and sweat pants I slept in. Pushed my bare feet into running shoes without stopping to tie them.

The nanomites flung the images from the outside cameras into my mind: two tactical teams of four men each, one at each entrance, front and back. An additional four men spanned the house, watching the windows to prevent any escape from that direction.

"Nano! Is Dr. Bickel up?"

Yes, Gemma Keyes. He is awake and aware of the intrusion.

"We must buy him time to get safely away."

We will, Gemma Keyes.

I visualized my old friend doing as we'd discussed—grabbing the essentials and leaving through the escape hatch—not staying to monitor the assault and deploy the system's built-in deterrents.

They would not be needed.

As I raced down the hall, the front and back doors splintered and gave way. I ran to meet the intruders, certain that the nanomites and I could fight them off and avoid capture—even though I was no longer confident that our capture would be Cushing's goal.

I didn't bother with the nanomites' cover. I drew down on the house's electricity and collected it in my body, in my arms, in my hands, in my fingers. I let the power build and brighten until I blazed with crackling white light.

Time slowed: The interior of the house was no longer dark; I stood in the junction of the hall and living room, a blinding, strobing beacon, inviting the assailants and their weapons to target me.

At a shouted command, they opened fire.

The walls and furnishings around me burst and shredded under a merciless barrage of rounds. The noise and smoke were horrific, but I stood untouched within the bubble of vibrating current the nanomites molded around me. As the soldiers' guns hammered my shield, the electrical current repulsed their bullets, often sending them flying back in the direction from which they'd come.

Three of the attackers cried out and fell when returning rounds struck arms or legs. The remaining soldiers continued to fire on me, ejecting and dropping empty magazines where they crouched and slamming home fresh ones in fluid, practiced moves.

I inhaled, lifted my hands, and fashioned an orb of snapping, popping energy within the shield. I pulled my hands apart, and the orb strengthened and grew bigger—and bigger still. Even larger!

When I could build it no larger and still maintain control of it, I took aim—not at individual shooters, but at the whole of them. I swept my hands in an arc as I hurled the sizzling mass. The wall of energy exited the shield, spread, lengthened, and thickened; it crashed into the invaders—a tidal wave of demolition.

The walls and windows of Dr. Bickel's living room blew out, sending soldiers, weapons, and debris far out into the yard, even into the street.

I strode through the house's splintered framework. The four soldiers who were guarding the perimeter of the house formed a line and opened fire on me. I swept my hands toward them and they flew backward.

Soldiers across the lawn began to rouse and recover their weapons. As they targeted me, I gathered palm-sized spheres of energy and pummeled them. I pounded every aggressor who moved—until not one stirred.

I stood alone in the yard and screamed, "Cushing, you coward! Cushing! Show yourself!"

She did.

She stepped from the shadows of the neighbor's trees. "Hello, Miss Keyes. Or should I say, Miss Sawyer?"

I clenched my fists at my side, willing myself to be calm when my insides were a riot of fury, resentment, and indignation. "You may as well give up, Cushing. We know everything. The President knows all about you and the Vice President."

"I wondered if you'd had something to do with Harmon's untimely demise."

She studied me a moment, then shook her head. "No, Miss Keyes. You do not know everything. You may have, for the time being, thwarted the vision Harmon and I and others shared, but it will not matter in the long run."

She lifted her chin. "However, my part is at an end. Therefore, I will extract what payment I can while I may—and ensure that you do not interfere in the future."

The hair at the back of my neck lifted—not in response to the power thrumming through my body, but in prescient warning of what was to come.

Gemma Keyes, Cushing's people have laid explos—

Cushing held something aloft for me to see.

"Good bye, Gemma, *dear*."

Cushing spun on her heel and ran.

"No!" I lifted a hand to hurl a sphere of energy to stop her and—

The nanomites tossed me forward. My face scraped the ground as they flattened me. Behind me, what remained of Dr. Bickel's safe house inhaled and expanded. I tried to raise my head, but the nanomites pressed and held me down; they sheltered me from the whooshing blast and the concussion wave that followed.

The noise rolled over us, a booming cough, a thunderous roar. Wreckage rained down; bits and chunks of wood, metal, glass, cement, and drywall strafed the men Cushing had abandoned, while I lay protected beneath the nanomites' energy shield.

I don't know how much time passed before the nanomites allowed me to get up. I struggled to my feet, unsteady and disoriented from the ringing in my ears. A man I recognized as a neighbor from across the street rushed toward me.

I couldn't hear more than a mumble, but I watched his mouth.

"Lady! Hey, lady, are you all right?"

I nodded. Wavered. He caught my arm and steadied me. Holding on to him for balance, I turned to assess the destruction.

It was complete.

Total.

Absolute.

Dr. Bickel's house had been leveled. What little remained was burning. I sought some visual cue amid the smoke and flames, a marker to indicate where the closet and its hidden ladder to the basement hidey hole had been. Nothing other than a vague sense of the house's footprint endured. That and the field of ruin around us.

"Dr. Bickel."

Next to me, the neighbor babbled on, and I began to make out syllables and words through the high-pitched squeal in my head. More neighbors gathered in tight knots in the street. As my ears recovered, I heard sirens. Distant, but coming nearer.

I blinked and tried to pick out Cushing's men amid the detritus. Could any of them have survived the blast? Without the nanomites and their electrical shield, I would not have, and Cushing's men had enjoyed no such protection.

She had happily sacrificed them to wreak her reprisal on me.

My dazed thoughts wandered back to the basement and the escape hatch.

"Dr. Bickel."

"—place blew sky high! Must have been a gas line, huh?" the neighbor speculated. "My wife and I heard all kinds of pops and bangs beforehand. We figured it was just kids setting off New Year's fireworks early."

"Dr. Bickel."

When the first police cars arrived, I peeled myself off the neighbor and began to stumble my way through the rubble.

"Hey, wait, lady! You really should wait for an ambulance. You don't look so good."

I kept going. The nanomites helped me navigate and strengthened my boneless, jellied legs. I reached the edge of the debris field and pushed through the crowd of gawkers.

I limped away from the glow of the fire, down the shadowed street toward the parking garage, blocks away.

"Dr. Bickel."

***

Dr. Bickel wasn't on the parking garage's first level where he was supposed to be. I couldn't have been more clear: If ever he had to flee the house, he was not to go to my car until we knew it was safe. I'd told him to wait in the lower levels. The fact that he wasn't waiting where we'd agreed harried me something fierce.

Lord Jesus! Please let him be okay!

I dragged myself up the three levels to my car, calling his name in a rough whisper every few feet. When I reached the Escape, I turned around and stared into the concrete darkness.

"Dr. Bickel!"

A scuffle. A wheeze.

I spun a tiny ball of light aloft and walked toward the noise. "Dr. Bickel?"

"H-here, Gem . . . Gemma."

I found him lying on the greasy pavement in front of my car. He was hurt.

"Nano!"

Assessing his injuries now, Gemma Keyes.

I brought the light in close and found his hand. Grabbed it and held on. He squeezed mine once in return. While I waited on the nanomites, I prayed.

Ten minutes dragged by. Fifteen.

"Nano?"

Gemma Keyes, Dr. Bickel has two crushed ribs, one of which has ruptured his spleen. We are attempting to piece together the rupture and cauterize the bleeding. However, our work is taking too long. We recommend that he be transported to a hospital. He requires a blood transfusion, and it is possible that our repairs to his spleen will not suffice. The organ may need to be removed.

I had no means to call for an ambulance.

Dr. Bickel gripped my hand. "G-Gemma."

"Yes?"

"B-b-bag."

Partway under the Escape's front bumper I saw it—the bag. If we were attacked, Dr. Bickel's task was to grab the bag containing Kathy Sawyer's ID and other personally identifiable items, throw in the burner phones, and take the bag with him through the escape tunnel.

The bag whose contents were now worthless—except for the phones.

I dragged the bag to me and unzipped it. Pulled out one of the burner phones. Pushed the buttons for a number I had memorized.

The phone rang three times. The voice that answered was sluggish but wary.

Too many stimulating mid-sleep calls of late, I guessed.

"Special Agent Ross Gamble."

"Gamble, it's Gemma. We've got trouble."

I filled him in and let him work out the logistics. Hung up.

"Gemma." Dr. Bickel sounded better. A bit stronger.

"I'm here."

"Did what you asked. Got out right away . . . Halfway out the tun . . . tunnel. Remembered . . . bag."

I covered my eyes with my free hand. "You forgot the bag and went back for it."

"Y-yes. T-tunnel . . . collapsed."

In my mind's eye, I saw the heavy door swing open to reveal the escape tunnel—a wide concrete pipe. I pictured the cement pipe bowing and fracturing under the concussive force of the explosion. Saw the chunk of concrete landing on my friend's chest as he swung the door closed behind him.

And yet, Dr. Bickel had managed to push it off, keep going, and reach the end of the tunnel; he had let himself out, and had made it not only to our rendezvous point, but up three levels to my car.

He must have thought himself safer near my car.

Dr. Bickel's brow furrowed in pain, and his eyes closed. The nanomites assured me that he was resting, that he was in no imminent danger, but I couldn't stand to see another friend, another loved one suffering.

O Lord, when will this heartache be over?

During the fifteen minutes while we waited for Gamble, I struggled to keep my heart right. I struggled against the inclination—no, an urgent, craving thirst—to find Cushing, to track her to whatever hole she'd crawled out from and end her.

Zander's words curbed the rage building in me: "*If we don't repent and allow Jesus to wash us clean before we rush off to fix the mess we've made, we'll just make the same mistake again.*"

"Lord, I don't want to make another mess. I don't, but please help me! I have such turmoil inside me. Please! Please help me."

I was relieved when Gamble arrived, an ambulance not far behind him. I heard their engines and tires squealing as he led the way up the ramps.

Before Gamble and the ambulance arrived, I gave Dr. Bickel's hand a last comforting touch, grabbed the bag, and stepped out of the way. The nanomites covered me, and I watched from two cars away as the paramedics inserted a line into the back of Dr. Bickel's hand and started fluids before lifting him onto the gurney and taking him away.

Gamble called out for me. "Gemma?"

"Here."

I rested against a nearby car. I was still shaky, and Gamble could see it. He pried the bag from my hands and helped me to his passenger seat. He got behind the wheel and turned sideways to talk to me.

"Are you hurt?"

"No; just shaken. Cushing. Don't know how she found us. She blew up Dr. Bickel's safe house. Took out her own men doing it."

"You certain you're not hurt?"

I asked the nanomites.

Gemma Keyes, you are physically unharmed except for minor shock and disorientation.

"The nanomites say I'm fine."

Gamble nodded. "Glad to hear it." Then he cleared his throat and switched topics. "So, you'll never guess who called me yesterday morning."

"Probably not." I was too tired for guessing games.

"Well, would you believe Agent Janice Trujillo, as in *Cushing's* Agent Trujillo? And she paid me a visit late yesterday afternoon."

I shook my head. *I can't take any more. I can't.*

"It's not bad news, Gemma."

I blinked away the stupor. "It isn't?"

"Agent Trujillo received a very interesting call herself Monday morning."

"Oh?" I waited.

"Our friend in the White House, Gemma. He called Agent Trujillo himself and gave her two specific orders: apprehend Cushing ASAP and stop pursuing you and Dr. Bickel. It's over. As soon as Trujillo catches Cushing, it will be done. For good."

I started to crack.

Gamble opened his arms. "Come 'ere, Gemma. I'm your friend. I'm here for you."

I leaned my forehead on Gamble's chest. He closed his arms around me and let me rest there, weeping, until I was done.

⌘⌘⌘⌘

CHAPTER 26

I called Zander from Gamble's car and the three of us met up at UNM Hospital. When we got there, they'd taken Dr. Bickel to surgery.

"Funny," Gamble chuckled over a cup of very bad hospital coffee.

"What is?" I asked. I took up space on a waiting room couch across from him, and I was snuggled up to Zander's side, my feet pulled under me, not caring a fig what anyone thought or what the future held: I wanted Zander to hold me, and he was happy to do so.

"Yeah; what's funny?" Zander repeated.

"This hospital. It's where we met, remember?"

Zander winced. "Ouch. Don't remind me."

I smiled across the little coffee table strewn with old copies of People and Time magazines. "I'm glad we did meet, Gamble."

"Well, I can honestly say it's never been dull knowing you. So far."

We laughed, and a young couple down from us glanced up and smiled.

The doctor came out. "Family of Daniel Bickel?"

"Yes," I answered. "We may not be blood, but we are his family. He has no one else."

The doctor looked tired, but satisfied. "Gotcha. Well, it's all good news—except for the spleen. It was a complete loss, but we got it out, caught all the little bleeders, and transfused three pints of blood." He rubbed his eyes. "I was surprised that some of the bleeding had already stopped. Sealed up on its own. Kind of weird, but whatever. Your friend should make a full recovery."

"Oh, thank you, Lord!" I whispered.

"We'll keep him three or four days, depending upon how he responds, and he'll need six weeks of restricted movement."

"Thank you, doctor."

The physician looked a little sheepish. "Say, isn't he, you know, that guy in the news lately? The one who held the press conference at the FBI?"

"He is."

"And he's not, er, wanted anymore?"

Gamble flipped out his credentials. "Special Agent Ross Gamble, FBI. I can assure you I am not interested in apprehending Dr. Bickel."

"Good to know. Thanks."

I pulled Gamble aside. "Did you sort of mislead Dr. Bickel's physician just now?"

"No." He cleared his throat. "Maybe, but I'm not interested in apprehending Dr. Bickel. I won't be party to letting that shrew Cushing get her claws into him again."

"I told Cushing that the President was on to her. Before she blew up the safe house, she said, 'It will not matter in the long run. My part is at an end. Therefore, I will extract what payment I can while I may.' She doesn't care about the nanomites any longer; she's in it for the revenge! Gamble, I'm worried about Emilio and Abe. If Cushing knows what they mean to me . . ."

He rubbed his chin. "I would authorize security for them, but the paperwork is like an obstacle course."

"Well, do you know any good people who would work for cash? You know, stakeout style?"

"If you have the cash, I can find off-duty and retired APD to watch Abe's house."

"Would you set it up? I'll pass the money to you to pay them." I hesitated, thinking. "It will take me a day to get it to you."

"If you guarantee payment, I can get them set up by this evening."

We left the hospital then. The sun had risen when I transferred the bag from Gamble's car to Zander's, and Zander drove me back to the parking garage.

I'd declined his offer to take me to Abe's, and his gray eyes radiated worry. "Where will you go?"

"I need a place to sleep this off. Somewhere quiet. A place to think."

"About Cushing?"

"Yeah. We're not out of the woods yet, not while she's still out there— even if she's gone rogue."

As I opened the door to get out of his car, Zander snagged my arm. "Hey."

"Yes?"

He pulled me back in and drew my face toward his. Stared at me, up close and personal. "I love you, Gemma Keyes. That isn't going to change."

I blinked back the moisture that sprang to my eyes. "I wish things were different."

"Yeah, well, we still need to talk this out. A future together can't be impossible. We should pray over it. Let God direct us and show us what to do."

Maybe we did need to talk. Maybe we needed to pray together. But I already felt certain of the answer.

I just nodded, and he let me go.

I threw the bag into my car and drove toward Coronado Center. I parked a few blocks beyond the mall at the Marriott hotel. I could have retrieved my Kathy Sawyer credit card and ID and used them to check into the hotel—but Cushing knew about my alter ego.

If she were monitoring Kathy Sawyer's card, she would find me.

"Good bye, Kathy."

The cash I depended on had burned with the safe house, all but the chunk in the cinderblock wall along the alley—if the wall had survived the blast—and the coffee can buried in Mateo Martinez' back yard. And I was too exhausted to go digging at the moment.

Under the nanomites' cover, I approached a hotel side door. It was locked, but it opened under my hand. Then I found the front desk, had the nanomites twiddle in their computer a bit, then snagged an empty elevator to the sixth floor.

My room was near the stairs for easy egress, and the nanomites had triggered payment for four nights—a theft I vowed to repay. I'd also sent the nanomites into the hotel's closed-circuit camera system. Via my room's Internet connection, they would monitor the cameras and alert me should an armed force of any size enter the hotel.

I stripped off my filthy clothes, showered away the grime and grit of battle, climbed into bed, and fell into an exhausted, dreamless sleep.

***

Genie hadn't eaten in two days: She was convinced that Gemma's house was possessed. It echoed with the accusations of a voice she despised. Wherever she turned, the voice spoke to her. It haunted her dreams and troubled her waking hours.

"The devil owns you, Genie."

Genie needed to get away, so she drove her sister's car for miles. She had no destination, only a goal: to escape Zander Cruz' voice in her head. She drove until the gas gauge neared empty—and never once left Cruz behind.

Wherever I go, there you are, she snarled. *I'd take an icepick to my head if I thought it would chisel you out.*

Genie had no money left. She'd spent the three hundred in cash her sister had put through the cat door on her past-due credit card bills. It would not be enough—not remotely enough—to fend off the collectors. Her failing credit would, in a month or so, ensure that she'd never pass a background check—that is, on the off chance she even got that far in the hiring process.

Genie barked a derisive laugh. Off chance? The odds were more unlikely than that. To date, she'd not received a single favorable response to her employment search.

So here she sat, without gas for the car, without a job, without a dime to her name.

Jake dozed next to her, and she found herself clinging to him. He seemed the only sane and stable entity in her life.

"The devil owns you lock, stock, and barrel. You think you don't submit to anyone? You say you are free? You are not. You're driven and compelled . . . bound over to commit evil—as he directs, not as you choose."

"Get out of my head!" Genie whispered, but the voice did not heed her.

"You should know whom you serve, Genie. You serve Satan—not yourself."

"Do I? Is there a real devil, a real Satan?"

"Think about what I've said, Genie."

"Like I can think about anything else."

"You have only one choice left to you. At present, you are under Satan's control—but you can choose Jesus. Salvation doesn't depend upon your broken, twisted feelings; it depends upon your choice."

"My choice?"

Next to her, Jake stirred and sat up. Stretched. Stared toward the kitchen. That Jake might leave her—even for a few minutes—freaked Genie out more than she cared to admit.

"You can choose Jesus."

Jake jumped to the floor and pattered away. Genie watched him, convinced he had abandoned her and would not return. And why would he? Gemma had said Jake hated everyone, including her.

"He seems to like you."

"Well, he's a pest."

"No, what I mean is, Jake doesn't like anyone. I'm serious. Watch this."

Her sister had approached Jake. Immediately the cat had attacked her.

"Jake detests me. Always has—but, then, he pretty much detests everyone. No one in the neighborhood would take money to pet him; they know he'll bite or scratch. But he did love Lucy."

"Then why would he want me?" Anymore, Genie's thoughts were muddled. She didn't know if she was asking about Jake or about Jesus.

"I'm losing my mind."

"You can choose Jesus."

"Why? Why would I choose Jesus? He isn't real."

Then you will stay broken.

Stunned, Genie did not move. Did not speak. Did not blink.

The words had not been in her head. Like before, they had rung into the open air of the living room, as real as if Zander were standing before her—and it had *not* been Zander's voice she heard.

"I am. I'm losing my mind."

"Salvation doesn't depend upon your broken, twisted feelings; it depends upon your choice. You can choose Jesus."

Genie covered her face and swore into her hands, cursing Zander Cruz and his "god" with every vile expletive she could conjure.

She ended with, "Get away from me! I hate you!"

But I love you.

***

Imogene Cushing splashed another inch of bourbon into the cheap hotel glass. She gulped it down, relishing the fiery trail it made down her throat and into her stomach.

Cushing replenished her drink. She had little left to relish, so why the *blank* not?

Gemma Keyes had confirmed her fears: *The President knows I conspired with Harmon; he will send a team for me. All black. No public bulletins or fanfare, just "problem solved."*

I should lay low until the heat dies down. Then find a way out of the country.

The money in her Cayman Islands account was looking better and better.

The problem—as Cushing analyzed her situation and distilled the facts—was that she'd burned the contractor she'd counted on flying her out of the U.S. She'd allowed him and his men to perish in the explosion. Cushing had considered the sacrifice worth it if it guaranteed the death of Gemma Keyes.

The death of Gemma Keyes?

Cushing had nearly lost control of herself when she saw Gemma rise from the ashes and rubble. She swallowed another mouthful of alcohol and forced herself to return to the difficulty at hand: She had to get out of the country—and that might be more than a little tricky.

It might prove impossible.

Mercenaries, being ex-military brothers-in-arms, were both paranoid and tightknit at the same time. Various contractors fought each other with ferocious self-interest over prime contracts only to turn around and team up with the same competitors when the next opportunity benefitted from their joint participation.

Unless individual contractors or contracting organizations violated the unspoken code of honor, they were, in the main, loyal to each other and their mercenary community. The community would find out that Cushing had burned her own assets.

They would not hesitate to snuff her out.

Cushing sipped on her drink, finding clarity in the heat burning its way to her core and the warmth seeping into her limbs.

No matter how I play my hand, the odds are I don't get out of this alive.

She snorted at the delicious irony. *Oh, Danny, so you've won after all. And your little friend has shown herself to have more mettle than I could have imagined, hasn't she? Yes, I underestimated her, seriously so.*

She tried to pour from the bottle, but sloshed more onto the table than into her glass. Cushing laughed, and her words slurred. "Guess I'm drunk, huh?"

She ignored the precious liquid spilled on the table and tossed back what had landed in the glass. "You may have won, Gemma Keyes, but can I allow you to enjoy your victory? Can I? *I think not.*"

The more she drank and mused, drank and pondered, the deeper she sank—down, down, down into a blinding, murderous rage. "Oh, how I despise you, Gemma Keyes. I. Hate. You. Are you the great white whale to my Captain Ahab, Gemma? Are you my nemesis, Moby Dick? Let's see. How does it go?"

To the last I grapple with thee;
from hell's heart I stab at thee;
for hate's sake I spit my last breath at thee.

The glimmer of a strategy crept into her stupefied mind: How to lure Gemma to her death. Cushing took mental inventory of what was hidden in the trunk of her car and congratulated herself on her foresight.

"Yes. That would work." She lifted her glass in mock salute. "For hate's sake, Gemma."

With drink-numbed fingers, Cushing placed the lid on the bottle and screwed it down. She would end the self-pity. Sleep off the alcohol. Prepare for her last stand.

"No, I won't get out of this alive, my dear. Therefore, I shall ensure that you don't either."

⌘⌘⌘⌘

CHAPTER 27

Morning arrived in subtle shades of gray.

Genie woke slowly, clinging to a dream. In the dream, she'd stumbled upon a place, a contented place. *The* Place. The place of peace. It was so real, so vivid. So right.

All she had to do to remain there forever . . . was to heed Zander's words.

"You can choose Jesus."

Genie sighed. She didn't want to leave the dream where she was . . . happy.

Happy? Have I ever been happy? Do I know what happy is?

All she had to do was act on Zander's assertions that her feelings were not as necessary as her choices. But she couldn't do that. She couldn't give in and show her weakness. She resisted the pull, the tiny tug to do just that.

Jake must have sensed the change in Genie's breathing as she left sleep behind. His comforting weight on the bed shifted. As he stood, panic hit Genie.

"Please don't go!"

Instead of hopping off the bed as he usually did first thing in the morning, Jake raised his hind end and tail into the air, stretched his back, then climbed up on Genie's chest. He laid down there with his eyes closed. A purr rumbled in his throat, and he flexed his claws, each one a gentle, clinging embrace on her nightgown. Happy cat. Happy scratch.

"Jake pretty much detests everyone."

"I don't know why you like me. I'm not exactly likable material."

Slanted green eyes opened to study her.

Because I love you.

This time, Genie didn't flinch: She froze and stopped breathing. It wasn't Jake speaking to her. *I'm not that far gone, not that crazy. Yet.*

No; she'd heard a real voice, not the memory of Zander's confounded preaching resonating in her head. Only one possibility remained.

"Why? Why would you love me?"

You can choose Jesus.

She continued to resist. "Why? Why would I choose Jesus?" But she no longer protested that he wasn't real.

Because I chose you.

Jake stared at Genie. Challenging her.

"I don't understand why you chose me. I can see why you'd love Aunt Lucy . . . but me?"

Jake rose and planted one paw on Genie's mouth, silencing her. He put his nose to hers and proceeded to rub his jowl along her cheek line.

Because I love you.

I don't want you to stay broken.

Genie, I chose you. You can choose me.

Genie closed her eyes. A moan escaped from her lips.

***

Late in the morning after ordering room service and consuming two breakfasts, I left the hotel feeling more like myself. It's nothing short of amazing what good sleep can do. However, I hadn't relished putting on my filthy clothes over my clean skin.

Gross.

To rectify that situation, I needed cash. Needed to dig some up. I trotted down the stairs to the exit and had the nanomites scour the parking lot around my car before I went to it.

Gemma Keyes, we detect no surveillance.

"Great, thanks. Could you, um, change the color of my car? Alter the plate?"

We can.

Before my eyes, my beautiful slate-gray Escape became a royal blue.

"Not my fav, but good. Now, let's go get some money."

As I drove toward my old neighborhood, I reminded the nanomites that Kathy Sawyer was blown. I would need a new identity.

We can accomplish this task with relative ease, Gemma Keyes.

Relative ease. Riiiight.

I tried not to grumble over the twisted machinations I'd put myself through to establish Kathy Sawyer's identity—before the nanomites and I developed a working relationship. Before the merge. Before the revived nanocloud. Before I'd started thinking outside the box.

Gemma Keyes, do you wish to select a name for your new identity? Or do you have a preference?

"Won't we need to, um, select and appropriate an existing identity?"

No, Gemma Keyes. We will generate and file all documents necessary to backstop your new name, a name of your choosing.

Oh, yeah. Thinking outside the box? Where we're going, we don't need no stinking boxes.

I snorted. "Peachy. Peachy keen."

Is Peachy Keen the new name you choose, Gemma Keyes?

I had to laugh. "No, Nano. It's just an expression of, um, approval. I like your idea. I should choose something I won't hate since I'll be stuck with it for a while. Let me think on it, all right? I'll get back to you."

Funny how you get used to a thing. I almost felt bad for leaving Kathy Sawyer behind. I would miss her.

I didn't park far from my old house. I got out, and the nanomites covered me while I hoofed it around the curve and into the cul-de-sac.

I scanned the neighbors' houses: The Tuckers', Mrs. Calderón's, my house, the Flores', Mateo's, Abe's. Everything looked right on the surface. Of course, Genie had left my car in the driveway instead of parking it in the garage, which kind of irked me.

As quickly as the annoyance popped its head up, I stomped on it. "Lord, I turn loose of my old life again—including my car. Not mine any longer. I let them go. And I choose not to be offended with Genie. I forgive her. Thank you for helping me to walk in love—and thank you for helping her."

I grabbed a shovel from my garage and headed for Mateo's back yard. It only took a few minutes to dig up the coffee can I'd buried there. I pulled the plastic-wrapped bundle from the can, stuffed it under my shirt, put the can back in the ground, and covered it over. After I hid the money in my car, I went to see Abe.

I evaded the two off-duty officers watching Abe's house and slipped in the back door. Emilio noticed me first and ran to me.

"Gemma!" He hugged me hard. "I'm so glad to see you."

Abe was right behind him. "Glad to see you, too, Gemma." He looked askance at my grime-crusted appearance. Digging in Mateo's yard hadn't helped any.

"Uh, I figured Emilio would be in school."

"Nope! Christmas break," the boy proudly announced.

"Christmas break?" I was bewildered.

"Christmas is in three days! Got the whole week off from school. Next week, too."

"Christmas is in *three days?*" That's when I noticed the stockings and the tree and the few presents under it. "Oh, wow. I must have lost track of time."

"That's not all, I'm guessing," Abe hinted.

I looked down at the boy attached to my stinky, grimy shirt and sweat pants and back to Abe. "Long story. I need some new clothes."

I glanced again at Emilio and did a double take. "Whoa. You've grown! Are you almost up to my shoulders?"

He grinned and nodded. "I'll be taller'n you pretty soon."

"Not if I have something to say about it!" I knuckled him on the head and squeezed him tight.

Abe ignored my sidestep. "That long story of yours have somethin' to do with a so-called gas leak a couple miles the other side of I-40? Explosion? Fire? Chaos and destruction?"

"Uh, it might. Right now, I need to high tail it to the store for . . . you know, clean clothes? Just thought I'd stop and say hi."

"Shopping? Why don't you have Zander take you?"

"What?"

"Thought you and Zander could come here Christmas morning. Bring your two friends."

"Dr. Bickel and Special Agent Gamble?"

"If they don't have family or elsewhere to be."

I was careful how I couched my next words. "Dr. Bickel is, uh, spending a few nights away. You know. Over off University. Where you stayed?"

Abe's eyes widened. "Is he—?"

I shot him a warning glare. "He's fine."

"Okay. Glad to hear it. Will . . . do you think he'll be able to come for Christmas?"

"I think so. Thanks for the invitation—and the reminder. I, um, I'll need to find us a place to stay . . . soon."

Abe and I exchanged a meaningful look, and he tipped his chin to say he understood. Then he went back to the shopping theme.

"See, I thought you and Zander might want to shop together." Abe inclined his head toward Emilio. Subtle like.

"Oh! Uh, yeah. Great idea."

Man, am I dense.

I called Zander from Abe's phone. He dropped what he was doing to spend the afternoon with me—even if it was shopping—and drove to Abe's to pick me up. I grabbed some of the cash from my car, and we set out.

With the nanomites altering my appearance in small but significant ways, I was able to shop in the open. First, I got some clean duds. I chose yet another backpack, three sets of comfy tops and jeans, fresh underwear, socks, and a hoody. I paid for the clothes, tore the tags from some of them, and changed in the restroom. Dumped my filthy clothes in a trash can as I walked toward Zander.

"Good metaphor," he remarked.

"Huh?"

"Like our old lives that are no better than filthy rags. God strips off the gunk, washes us clean, gives us a robe of right-standing before him, and drop-kicks the rags into the sea of forgetfulness."

I shook my head. "Wow. Not merely a good metaphor. An amazing one."

We stored my purchases in Zander's trunk, then got on with the fun stuff: Christmas shopping.

I've never had a little boy, remember? And I guess I'm practical when it comes down to it. The first thing I wanted Emilio to have was a decent wardrobe. He had pitifully little to call his own and was growing so fast. It would stretch Abe's fixed income to keep a growing boy in clothes, so Zander and I selected shirts and khakis for school, jeans and more shirts for play, socks and underwear, a cool winter coat, two pairs of shoes, and matching knit gloves and stocking cap.

Pleased with our first purchases, we went in search of a "fun" present. It took a while, but we found it.

"This is perfect!" I was giddy with delight.

"It is, Gemma. From you or from the two of us?"

It was a loaded question.

I looked down. "I think from both of us."

"Me, too."

We spent another hour selecting gifts for Abe, Dr. Bickel, and Gamble. It was enjoyable and tiring at the same time. Zander's trunk was filled, even though I'd hardly made a dent in my stack of cash.

We were both ready to call it a day when Zander pulled up to Abe's house. Zander would haul the gifts to his place, and we agreed to hold a gift-wrapping party the following evening. Zander wanted to spend a minute with Abe and Emilio, while I intended to head back to my hotel. While Zander grabbed my new clothes, the nanomites covered me and I got out of his car.

I squinted at the unfamiliar vehicle parked along the curb near my house. Then I flinched when I saw who was hurrying our way.

"Uh-oh. What's that about?" I asked Zander.

My nosy neighbor, Belicia Calderón, her chins wobbling as she hurried our way, was headed right for us. She couldn't see me, but she did see Zander and aimed for him.

"Pastor Cruz! Pastor Cruz!"

"Mrs. Calderón. Merry Christmas. How are you?"

"Don't bother about that right now! I don't know what to do—should I call the police? Please help."

She was out of breath and frantic. Not her usual busybody mode. No, she was terrified.

"What's wrong?"

She glanced over her shoulder once before leaning in toward Zander. "I just saw *her* at Gemma's door. You know Genie is housesitting for Gemma, yes? Well, Genie opened the door for *her* and—"

"Who, Mrs. Calderón? Who *her*. Who did you see at Gemma's door?"

Mrs. Calderón was struggling to catch her breath. "That terrible woman! I was looking through my window and *saw* her."

Zander's expression was as horrified as mine had to be. He gripped her hand. "*Who* did you see?"

"Why, th-that awful General Cushing woman! Sh-she pointed a *gun* right at Genie!"

With better control than I had, Zander instructed my anxious neighbor, "Go back home and lock the door, Mrs. Calderón. We'll call the police. Stay away from the windows."

As the woman left to do as Zander commanded, he turned and looked for me. He already had his phone out. "Gamble?"

"Yes. Tell him to hurry."

Zander and I were hunkered down with his car between us and my house when he got off the phone with Gamble.

"It will be at least twenty to thirty minutes before a tactical team arrives."

"And then what? Cushing uses Genie as a hostage? I can't see that ending well! It's me she wants."

"Hold on; I have an idea. What if I knock on the front door and distract Cushing while you go around to the back and come in all stealth-style?"

I was already shaking my head. "No. No! The nanomites will protect me, but if anything happened to you, Zander—"

"I dunno, Gemma. It sounds like you love me or something. Which is it? You love me? Or something?"

"Zander! This is not the time!"

He chuckled. "I know, but you need to calm down—and we need to pray before we go."

"We? *We* are not going; *I'm* going. I have the might and force of the nanocloud, remember?"

"Yes, but you don't necessarily have God's mind on this. Let's pray." He grabbed my hands and dove in. "Lord, we don't know what is going on in there with Genie and Cushing, but you do. Will you please tell us what to do?"

I wanted to tug my hands right out of his and sprint across the cul-de-sac. The only thing stopping me was the strong conviction I carried in my heart from my past mistakes, the hasty, ill-conceived actions that had endangered Emilio—which was why my mouth fell open when that still, small voice spoke to me—and I don't mean the nanomites, either.

Do not be afraid to go up against this enemy, Gemma. Do as Zander suggested. The two of you are a powerful weapon in my hand to accomplish my purposes.

My face froze in stunned surprise.

Gemma Keyes. We heard Jesus talking to you.

The nanomites sounded as shocked as I felt. "Uh, yes, Nano."

"Gemma?" Zander must have seen my astonishment.

"Y-you are to go with me. Like you said."

"What do you mean?"

"That's what Jesus just now spoke to me, and . . . well, the nanomites heard him, too."

"You're kidding me! I mean about the nanomites hearing Jesus. That is . . . unreal. Are you sure?"

"Zander! We don't have time for this right now!"

"All right, all right. I believe you. If Jesus said, we're both to go, let's get moving."

"You aren't afraid?"

His smile was crooked. "I wasn't always a pastor, remember? Wasn't always a Christian. I've done things. Had a few close calls."

"I-I forget sometimes."

Zander, still gripping my hand, helped me to my feet. He gave me a head start before he crossed the cul-de-sac. When I heard the doorbell ring, I unlocked and slipped inside the side doors. As I tiptoed through the kitchen, I heard the conversation coming from the living room.

"Who is it?" Genie asked.

"It's Zander Cruz, Genie."

Genie replied with stilted, wooden words, "Come in, Zander."

I crept around the corner into the dining room; the front door opened, and Zander entered.

Genie was facing me, Cushing behind her. They were both on the other side of the couch, close to the hallway. Cushing held a gun in one hand; she had her other arm wrapped around Genie's neck—and the point of a box cutter pressed into the fragile skin under Genie's jaw. A drizzle of blood trickled down her neck.

Genie didn't look particularly scared, but I knew Genie: She hated not being in control. More likely, she was furious.

Zander, in profile, stood just inside the door.

As usual, Cushing's hair was pinned at her neck in that perfect knotted braid. What wasn't usual was her attire: It was the only time I'd seen her out of uniform. Instead, she wore a baggy shirt over a skirt. "Miss Keyes? I'm going to assume you are here, too. Come in, please—before I make a mess on your carpet."

So much for Zander distracting her.

Genie went from infuriated to incredulous as I unmasked and took a step forward.

"*Gemma?*"

I might have savored the utter disbelief on Genie's face—had I not been preoccupied with keeping her alive.

"That's far enough," Cushing ordered. "I know what you are capable of."

Her teeth gleamed a shiny white through her lips. She waggled the gun. Flipped the safety off and slid her finger onto the trigger. "Recognize this? Do you know what it is?"

I did. "A Taser, model X26."

"Very good! I advise you to make no sudden moves. I would hate to lose two sisters on the same day."

Gemma Keyes, if she fires the Taser, we will propel a pulse to meet and decimate the discharge. It will do no damage to you or to us.

"Yes, but can you get past the discharge before Cushing cuts Genie's throat?"

Silence for five thundering beats of my heart.

We have considered the time it would take to dissipate the Taser's discharge and, afterward, reach Cushing. It is likely we could reach her at or near her response time. If we were late, we would attempt to repair your sister's severed skin and artery. We believe the odds to be favorable.

I had to bite the inside of my mouth to keep myself from screeching my reply aloud.

"ARE YOU FREAKING SERIOUS? PLAYING THE ODDS ON MY SISTER'S SURVIVAL?"

We will reconsider our approach, Gemma Keyes . . .

Their "voices" petered out, but as they faded, I thought I heard them mutter at the end, *although we didn't think you liked your sister all that much.*

I jerked my attention back to Cushing.

She kept her eyes and the Taser trained on me, but she spoke to Zander. "Don't think that I won't see you move in my peripheral vision, Reverend Cruz. If you so much as twitch, I will slice Genie like a melon."

Cushing smiled and addressed me again. "May I say how well you're looking, Miss Keyes? You've slimmed down and shaped up. Why, I hardly recognized you the other evening! Yes, you are looking quite fit—considering all things."

So, she wanted to spar. Okay; I knew how to spar.

"Considering all things?"

"I spoke to Greaves on the phone before his unfortunate demise. He told me how he'd shot you, Miss Keyes. Said the Taser knocked you right down and made you visible. *Hurt you*. You couldn't get up. Couldn't even move."

I nodded. "Yup. It sure did. The electrical charge killed many of the nanomites and destroyed the nanocloud. Good thing Dr. Bickel had a bunch more nanomites hidden in his lab in the cavern."

Oh, dear me.

Cushing's face flushed crimson as she realized more nanomites had been right there, *under her nose*, all this time.

Tsk, tsk.

I didn't bother to tell her that the mites had been uncut—fused to their silicon backings—unprogrammed and worthless to her needs. She didn't need to know that, did she?

And me? Well, I just wanted to push her buttons. Knock her off her game while the nanomites figured out how to defeat her.

I was doing a masterful job.

"So, you see," I went on, "you could use that Taser on me—but, well, if you did, you would destroy the nanomites. There aren't any more. These are the last of them—and aren't the nanomites what you've been after all this time?"

Her next words chilled me.

"You mistake me, Miss Keyes. I'm not here for the nanomites; I'm no longer interested in acquiring them: I'm here for *you*. I'm interested in how this Taser will affect you. Hurt you. I would enjoy watching you suffer. Perhaps die. I believe you nearly died when Colonel Greaves shot you with the Taser?"

I shrugged. "Yet here I am."

"Yes, and I must thank you for coming. You solved a problem for me: I did wonder how I would lure you here. Given the mutual affection you siblings share, I wasn't convinced a desperate phone call from your sister would do the trick."

I dug in. "Actually, I've been here to visit Genie—just as I've been in your office and conference room. Many times. Listening to your plans. Keeping ahead of you."

Was it my imagination? Did her brazen confidence slip a little?

She side-stepped and fixed her grip on Genie a little tighter. Smiled wider and ignored my barbs.

"Good for you! I never suspected, and I have so many little questions. Do indulge me: Is that how you located Danny? Spying on me in my office?"

"Indirectly. We watched your calendar. Decoded your standing appointment at 'Sandia Café.' Followed you to the SCIF. Listened in on your conversations with Greaves. We traced the secure call with him to its origin."

"We?" My use of the plural pronoun puzzled her.

I nodded. "Yes. The nanomites and I."

"The nanomites and . . ."

I watched the interplay of disbelief and jealousy flit across her face and baited her further. "Yes, the nanomites and I. They live inside of me, and we have what might be called a symbiotic relationship. We've grown to understand each other, to work together, to cooperate."

I goaded her. "You see, at first, the mites kept me hidden all the time. They thought they were keeping me safe by hiding me. That was before we began talking to each other. Working together. Now they hide me only when I ask them to."

Her sharky upper lip spasmed, but I had to admire Cushing's iron self-control. "Well, it was certainly impressive—how you infiltrated the house down in White Sands. How you managed to, how shall I say it? Liberate? Yes, *liberate*. How you managed to liberate dear Danny."

I shrugged and unloaded the big guns. "It wasn't all that difficult—just as it wasn't difficult to enter the White House last Friday night, introduce myself to President Jackson, and have a meaningful conversation with him regarding Vice President Harmon's treason. And you. *Your* treason."

Cushing's smile dropped from her face the way a lead weight dropped from fifty feet crashes to the earth. Ohhhh, she was ticked.

"You . . . you . . ."

At that same moment, the nanomites hissed a warning to me. *Gemma Keyes, Cushing is hiding something. Under her shirt.*

About the same time, I noticed Genie's odd behavior, how she cut her eyes to the right and down. Then back to me. Again, to the right and down.

Pointing?

I frowned.

Gemma Keyes. Cushing is hiding something.

There was no way Cushing could have heard the nanomites. Perhaps it was the way I was staring at her.

She smiled her satisfaction. "I thought I'd gotten you when I blew up that house you'd been hiding in, Gemma. I thought I'd killed you, I really did. I came oh! so very close, and couldn't understand how you'd survived. Thank you for answering my questions, my dear, for illuminating my thinking. I do believe I'll succeed this time."

With infinite care, Cushing edged Genie to the side. A wire ran from Cushing to Genie; the wire tugged the unbuttoned tail of Cushing's shirt aside—and exposed the wide belt she wore.

Flat, molded packages of plastic explosives lined the outside of the belt. Short lengths of yellow and black-striped detonation cord protruded from each explosive charge. My eyes could not stop jittering from one piece of that obscene device to another. And to the wire linking Cushing and Genie.

"Nano! Go! Disarm the bomb and put Cushing down!"

The timing is not right, Gemma Keyes, and we have instructions to keep you safe.

"What? No; get over there and save my sister!"

Genie Keyes is not our priority; you are, Gemma Keyes. Your safety and that of the nanocloud.

"But—"

Wait. Gemma Keyes. The timing is not right.

Cushing eased Genie back toward her, and my view of her deadly accessory disappeared. Cushing breathed hard; excitement and triumph punctuated each word. "Don't attempt any heroics, Miss Keyes. The charges are wired to the detonator two ways: 'in line' and independently— a wise backup technique on my part. And to answer your unspoken question, *no*. I'm not holding the detonator."

She tipped her chin down. "Did you notice the wire running between your sister and me? It is one of three such wires."

Every one of Cushing's sharky teeth gleamed and winked at me. "You see, my dear, I don't need to hold a detonator. Your sister *is* the detonator. One step away from me? Any one of three wires reaches its end? *Boom.*"

I felt the nanomites pulling the house's electricity into me; felt it building and building and building. Soon. I was ready to act on the nanomites' signal.

Cushing squinted as the lights flickered and dimmed. "Whatever you're doing, stop it!"

Genie slid her eyes away from me. Toward Zander. "Zander. I—"

"Shut up," Cushing hissed. She dug the razor tip of the box cutter deeper and Genie flinched. Cried out.

At her yelp of pain, ten pounds of yowling fur, claws, and teeth leapt past Genie, landed on Cushing's chest, and tore into her.

"Jake! No!"

Cushing beat at Jake with the Taser while squeezing Genie tighter in the crook of her elbow. Cushing's blows knocked Jake to the ground, where he renewed his attack, targeting Cushing's vulnerable legs. She jerked and jumped and kicked at Jake.

"Genie! Don't move! Stick with her!"

The way Cushing clasped my sister kept Genie's back to Cushing; Genie couldn't turn within the crook of Cushing's arm without forcing the box cutter into her own throat. Genie reached behind her and managed to snag the tail of Cushing's shirt with one hand; she pulled Cushing closer. And held on.

"I won't let go, Gemma! Get out now, while you can! Go!"

No. Now was the time to act. I was fully charged up and ready to race forward to fight Cushing. My muscles coiled and prepared to spring—

I gasped as sizzling blue fire erupted from my body and burned straight through the living room wall, leaving a hole the size of a car.

Not me! I hadn't done that!

The nanomites.

I could see Abe's house and the entire cul-de-sac through the gaping void—but I couldn't move. Not a foot or a finger; I was utterly paralyzed. Then I realized the nanomites were dragging me toward the hole they'd punched in the wall.

I could no more resist the nanomites' pull than I could fight the wind.

"Nano! No! Stop it!"

Gemma Keyes, we cannot stop. We must follow instructions.

The next scant handful of seconds slowed, every frame advancing with frozen, glacial speed.

The nanomites latched on to Zander; they sucked him up in their 'tractor beam' and pulled him along with me. He fought their crackling, inexorable power until he was straining toward Genie and Cushing, his feet off the floor, his weight suspended, his arms reaching toward Genie. The distance between us and Genie grew, and Zander thrust one hand toward her, managing to jab it through the nanomites' bubble of electrical current.

I heard his muffled shout, "Genie! Call on Jesus! Call on him now!"

Cushing, raging and freaking out, struggled toward us. "Stop!" she screeched, "Stop or I'll pull the wires! I swear I will!"

She shifted her weight toward us, trying to drag Genie with her. But as Cushing took a step in our direction, Genie leaned the other way, leveraging her weight against Cushing's, while gripping Cushing's blouse to prevent the wires from pulling apart.

The cutter dug into her flesh, and blood streamed down her neck; still she held onto Cushing, held her back. Jake howled and clawed and bit; undeterred, Cushing kicked at him while she fought to wrench Genie our way.

We were almost clear of the house, but Genie's grip on Cushing's shirt was failing—and Zander still reached toward my sister.

The inevitable was near, so near.

I screamed, "Zander! No! Please!"

He ignored me.

"Genie!" Zander shouted. "Genie! Call on Jesus!"

My heart stuttered. It was too late.

Cushing glanced toward us: She had to realize that if she waited any longer, Zander and I would escape the blast zone. With a sneer of victory, Cushing stopped pulling Genie toward us and, instead, with her last efforts, shoved Genie away.

Genie, her eyes locked on Zander, shrieked, "JESUS, I CHOOSE YOU! I CHOOSE YOU! I CHOOSE JE—"

The final thing I saw was the space between Cushing and my sister. Widening.

"No!"

The deafening *WWWWWWHOMP* overcame all my senses.

The concussion flung Zander and me onto the front yard and scattered the nanocloud.

I could see and hear nothing. The earth spun. I could not stand.

I knew before I could form a coherent thought that Genie was dead.

Genie.

Cushing.

Jake.

Many of the nanomites.

My ears began to clear and, from far away, I heard a high, desperate keening.

It was me.

⌘⌘⌘⌘

CHAPTER 28

I huddled under a blanket on Abe's sofa. I smelled of smoke and explosives and death, and I couldn't stop shaking. Emilio, in full-on protective mode, would not leave my side. He had one arm wrapped around my back; his other hand held one of mine in my lap.

Across the room, Zander cradled a bandaged hand, the one that had been outside the nanomites' bubble. He had been reaching for Genie when Cushing detonated her belt of death. Although many nanomites had surrounded Zander's hand, trying to push it into the shield, it had taken the brunt of the explosion.

The concussion that had blown us free of the blast zone had also blown apart our protective bubble, flinging the nanomites away like chaff before the wind. It had taken them long minutes to regroup and return.

Some had not returned. I didn't yet know the death toll.

And I'd been too out of it when I came to my senses to realize that Zander was hurt. The returning nanomites had heard him moaning and seen the ruin of his hand. The truth was, he would have lost his hand had the nanomites not rallied and gone to work to repair it.

By the time Gamble and his tactical team rolled into the cul-de-sac—followed by firetrucks and ambulances—the mites had stopped the bleeding and brought together the many pieces of Zander's hand. Even as the ambulance crew worked on him, the nanomites continued their repairs.

Pushing back on the shock that threatened to overcome me, I'd stayed with Zander until the nanomites whispered to me.

Gemma Keyes, we were unable to find or manufacture every tiny piece of Zander's hand. He is missing some bone and tissue—a small percentage—but he will regain the use of his hand. As the human expression goes, 'it may work, but it won't be pretty.' While his hand heals, we can, perhaps, do more.

Zander had refused to go to the hospital. At first the paramedics told him he might die from shock and loss of blood if he weren't treated immediately. Twenty minutes later, they said he might lose his hand if he weren't transported to the hospital. After yet another twenty minutes, when he insisted that they unwrap their bandages and look at his injury again, they said nothing. They rebandaged it while exchanging disbelieving glances and mouthing, "I *know* what I saw!"

Zander pressed his lips together and bent his head. He was praying for me.

Thank you, Zander, I thought. The words never made it to my mouth.

"You sure she's gone?" Emilio whispered to me. "Really gone? Gone for good?"

I couldn't respond; I didn't know if he meant Cushing or Genie. It didn't matter—either answer was equally gruesome.

Abe shook his head and gently shushed him. "Later, I think, Emilio."

Emilio nodded and gripped my hand harder, as though the pressure could wring from me the sights, sounds, and smells of the devastation across the cul-de-sac.

Nothing could. I blinked and blinked and blinked. Kept trying to blink the images out of my head, but they would not go: Genie hanging on to Cushing despite the sharp point of the blade at her throat; Cushing thrusting Genie away—and the space between them growing.

Then the flash, the blast, the heat, the destruction.

Cushing. Blown to tiny bits and pieces.

Gemma Keyes, we were unable to find or manufacture every tiny piece of Zander's hand.

Genie. Blown apart like Zander's hand.

Genie—and Jake with her.

Genie.

Jake.

My house was, more or less, leveled—the second house I'd lost in less than forty-eight hours and in the same way! Not that either of them mattered in the scope of eternity.

Genie was dead.

Jake was dead.

Jake. Jake had come to Genie's defense. Why? Why had he done that? *Jake.* I couldn't fathom what he'd done, let alone why? The "why" utterly eluded me.

And what purpose had the frantic exchange between Zander and Genie served? Why had Zander tried so hard to reach Genie? I didn't understand that either.

"*I choose Jesus.*" Had Genie really said that or was I misremembering? Genie.

Where was she right now? At this moment, did she stand before God? *Had* Genie chosen Jesus?

In the last seconds before death, had Jesus saved Genie?

I trembled harder and could not stop. When I began to sob, Emilio broke down and cried with me. I knew he was scared, afraid of what my raw emotions meant. I didn't want him to be scared, so I tried to hold the combined shock, horror, and relief within me, but horror and relief at the same time don't belong together.

The mixture was just too volatile, too reactive.

Like a shaken soda bottle, as soon as the cap was unscrewed even a little, I could not tamp down the rising churn. It had to come out. So, I stopped fighting it and let it boil over.

We will help you, Gemma Keyes.

The nanomites. They'd saved my life.

Again.

But they'd chosen me over Genie. Why?

We must follow instructions.

I didn't know what that meant, and I was too distressed to care.

The pressure behind my eyes and in my muscles eased a little. I sniffled and drew a sleeve across my drippy nose.

"Here, Gemma." Zander tucked a tissue into my hand and pressed my hand as he did.

I looked up at him. His beautiful gray eyes were filled with compassion and understanding. He cupped my chin in his hand and stroked my cheek with his thumb. I leaned into his comforting touch, wishing above all things that I had the right to call him mine.

"Zander?"

He squatted near me. "What, Gemma?"

"Genie. Before. Before she . . . she said, 'I choose Jesus.' What did that mean?"

One corner of his mouth turned up, though his eyes did not smile with his mouth. "I had an opportunity to share Jesus with Genie. I can only hope her last words mean that the Holy Spirit took my words and used them to win her to him."

"Took my words and used them to win her to him." Could it be true?

An authoritative knock landed on Abe's front door. All of us looked to Abe, so he shuffled to the door and spoke without opening it.

"Who is it?"

"Mr. Pickering, it's Agent Janice Trujillo."

Having heard Gamble identify himself—and his agency—many times, it struck me that Agent Trujillo had not added her agency. We still didn't know from which agency or sub-agency Cushing had drawn her small army. DIA? CIA? More likely NSA, given Harmon's pedigree.

With the head of the snake severed, it didn't matter anymore. It didn't matter unless another snake was surfacing to take Vice President Harmon's place and Trujillo had a new master to report to.

"What do you want, Agent Trujillo?" Abe demanded.

"I was hoping for a word with Miss Keyes."

And there it was.

I shook harder. I just couldn't stop. Zander sat on my other side and joined Emilio's efforts to comfort me.

"She's not here," Abe said through the door.

"Mr. Pickering, I mean Miss Keyes no harm, but what I have to say to her is important. And, just for the record, I know she's in there."

As an afterthought, she added, "It's important to her future."

Abe heard an implied threat. "Unless you've got a warrant, Agent Trujillo, you best get off my property. I am armed. If you attempt to enter, I will shoot to kill."

"No, no, no!" I could not lose Abe. I couldn't!

"Shhhh, Gemma," Zander soothed. "Let Abe handle it."

"No! I don't want him hurt!"

Trujillo called through the door. "Mr. Pickering, I am not looking to take Miss Keyes into custody or cause any problems for you. However, we have, um, a unique opportunity here and I feel that she may wish to take advantage of it."

When Abe didn't answer, she added, "Please. I only need a few minutes. And I would like to . . . I would like to apologize."

Some semblance of my self-control returned. I wiped at my nose and eyes and swallowed.

"Abe."

He shook his head.

"Abe. Please let her in. You know she can't hurt me."

Agent Trujillo called, "Mr. Pickering?"

Abe glanced at the door, then at Zander, who shrugged.

"Let her in, Abe."

Janice Trujillo came in with a sheepish smile. "I apologize for the intrusion."

"Just say your piece and move along," Abe said, not a hint of hospitality in his tone.

"Yes, I will, however . . ." She'd noticed Emilio and cut her eyes to Abe.

He nodded. "Young man, we need to do some adult talking. Please go to your room until I call you."

Emilio's brows pulled down into a familiar glower—but Abe's fuse was already short.

"Not up for discussion, young sir."

"Aw, nuts." Emilio got up and stomped toward the bedroom.

Abe was quick to call him back. "Emilio."

Emilio sighed, retraced his steps. "Yes, sir. I'll go to my room, sir."

Abe hugged him, and Emilio hugged him back. He went off to his room and closed the door.

"Right then. Say your piece."

"Thank you. Miss Keyes? A moment ago, I spoke to a mutual friend, a Mr. Kennedy. You met him, ah, last week."

It took a second for the reference to hit me. To astound me. "You talked to *him*?"

"Yes."

Zander and Abe were unaware of my foray to the White House. It needed to stay that way, so I just gaped and nodded for her to continue.

"I conveyed today's events to Mr. Kennedy and to our other . . . mutual acquaintance."

Zander and Abe looked between me and Trujillo. Abe snorted. "We've been cut out of this conversation, Pastor Cruz."

"Yeah, I concur."

"It's necessary," I said.

Trujillo agreed. "Yes, it is, but they can hear the message—if that's all right with you."

"Yeah, okay."

"Very good. Well, first, our friends both wished me to offer their condolences to you at your sister's death. If there's anything they can do . . ."

"No, but tell them thank you."

"I will. However, a few minutes after I'd told them that Cushing and your sister had both perished in the explosion, Mr. Kennedy had an idea. His idea is what I've come to speak to you about."

"Oh?"

"They acknowledge that Gemma Keyes, through no fault of her own, has had a rough time of it. Her name has been vilified in the news, and she's still the subject of a nationwide manhunt. Her life is in ruins."

I thought, *A rough time of it? Do you know what I've been through, how many times I nearly died?*

I squirmed and bit my tongue. "Shouldn't all that go away after the facts come out?"

Trujillo said nothing. Just looked at me.

The silence dragged on.

"You're saying . . . that the facts aren't going to come out."

She pursed her lips. "One could make the case that if a single thread is pulled, that thread would, inevitably, lead to another. And another.

Harmon. A large-scale scandal that could bring down the President's administration.

"I-I guess I take your point."

Trujillo spoke softly. "I don't know everything about you, Miss Keyes. I don't know why Cushing wanted you, what it was you had that she so desperately needed. Cushing kept me out of that—although I've seen things and heard things . . . that don't make a lot of sense. That boggle the mind."

She stared at me.

I arched one brow. Did not respond.

She laughed under her breath. "All right. Got it. Well, our mutual friends did suggest that your secrets need to remain secrets. For your sake."

Then I understood. "And if a single thread is pulled it might lead to my . . . secrets."

"That is their concern."

"I appreciate their concern . . . and discretion."

"Yes, so that takes us to Mr. Kennedy's idea."

Abe, deciding that Trujillo posed no threat to me, recovered his manners in a rush. "Please have a seat, Agent Trujillo?"

"Thanks. Is here all right with you, Miss Keyes?" She pointed to the sofa where Emilio had been sitting next to me.

I nodded.

She sat. Struggled with how to start. "The basis of the idea is that, as twins, you and your sister share the same DNA."

"I suppose so."

"ATF will take point on the cause of explosion itself, but our, um, mutual friend has requested that the FBI take overall charge of the investigation and that Special Agent Ross Gamble be the lead investigator."

Trujillo jutted her chin toward the front door. "He and his forensic team are over there right now. What Kennedy proposed is that we . . . fudge the data from the recovery a little. This is possible since Special Agent Gamble is overseeing the recovery."

"The recovery?"

"Of the bodies."

I thought I was gonna throw up in her lap.

She must have thought so, too, because she jumped up. "Mr. Pickering, might Gemma have some water?"

"I'll get it." Zander raced to the kitchen and brought back a tall glass of water and a wet cloth.

The cold cloth on my face helped. The water helped.

So did not thinking about body recovery.

Trujillo figured that out. "I'll, uh, make this quick, Miss Keyes. We'd like to announce that we found three sets of remains in the debris. Our intention is to assert to the world that General Cushing, Genie Keyes, and her twin, Gemma Keyes, perished in the explosion. You need not concern yourself with how we'll do it, but the DNA findings will not contradict our report."

My head jerked up. "What?"

"We'll put you in WITSEC, Miss Keyes. Give you a brand-new identity. A fresh start. A little money to get established. A job. A future."

"I . . ."

I glanced at Zander.

"No more running, Gemma. You'd have a real life again." Were those tears in his eyes?

"I-I can't do that! I've got Emilio. And Abe. And . . ." I stared at Zander, longing for him.

"Think about it?" Trujillo handed me a card. "We have about a seventy-two-hour window before we release an official statement. Three days."

I took the card. "You said Gamble is in charge of the investigation."

"Yes. He will be the one releasing the statement."

I handed the card back to her. "I'll let him know what I decide."

Trujillo studied her shoes. "I understand, Miss Keyes. Completely." She dithered. "Uh, and I still owe you an apology."

Looking me full in the face, she said, "I was assigned to General Cushing for a covert national security operation. That is, by the way, classified information, and I'm breaking the law by telling you, but . . . well, you deserve to understand my actions."

She cleared her throat. "In the covert world, we are trained to expect ambiguity in certain situations; however, it became apparent to me weeks ago that Cushing's goals and methods were questionable—well, more than questionable. However, I had no one to report my misgivings to—until our mutual friends called me."

She shifted on her feet. "Miss Keyes, I apologize for my role in what can only have been a very difficult year for you. I am sincerely sorry. I wish I could make amends."

I suppose that was her way of apologizing for Genie's death, too. I licked my lips, hearing Genie's last words.

"*I choose Jesus!*"

I turned inward. *Lord, if Genie truly repented and turned to you, then she is with you now, and she is different—changed. Transformed into your image.*

But without Cushing's hunt for me and the pressure she exerted on Genie to help her trap me, Genie would not have gotten on Cushing's bad side and been forced to move back to Albuquerque. Without all that, would she have come to a saving knowledge of you? Ever?

I didn't know the answers, but if Genie had turned to Jesus in her last moments, I was grateful. I would go through it all again to see her safe in Jesus' arms. So how could I hold animus against Agent Trujillo?

I could not.

"Thank you, Agent Trujillo. I appreciate your words more than you know. And I more than accept your apology: I forgive you."

She seemed surprised. "Thank you. That . . . that means a lot."

She gathered herself. "Well, then. I should be going."

Abe saw her to the door. In the scant seconds the doorway stood open, I glimpsed the burned-out wreckage of my old home.

My *old* home. In my heart, I'd surrendered it, given it away before it blew up, so what did it matter, except in the sentimental corners of my heart?

***

Hours later, I felt steady enough to leave.

"Where will you go, Gemma?" Emilio asked. "Why can't you stay here?" He didn't want me to go, and I didn't want to leave, but the tiny house was full with Abe and Emilio. And besides, I had stuff on my mind.

Zander and Abe waited for my answer, so I made my response cheerful.

"I'm staying in a hotel. It's a nice one, too. I have some decisions to think about and pray over."

The threats were gone. The months of running were over. The weight of being hunted and pursued, lifted. I felt unfettered—so much so, that I felt jittery. Jumpy.

Lord, what next? What do I do now?

"I'll walk you to your car," Zander offered.

"No. No, thank you, Zander. Gemma Keyes can't be seen until I've decided if she's dead or alive, right? And you'd look odd, walking to my car and back. Alone."

I was pushing him away, trying to protect my heart.

Lord, I need you to tell me what to do.

***

That evening, the nanomites reported their casualties: It was a huge number—3.7 million obliterated by Cushing's bomb. But, according to the nanomites, the number of lost mites amounted to a single grain of sand upon a seashore. (That's what thinking in terms of trillions will get ya, I suppose.)

Their loss will not diminish the power of the nanocloud, Gemma Keyes.

I mourned the lost nanomites anyway as I prayed over the difficult choice before me.

Lord, I need your wisdom. Please guide me.

The hospital released Dr. Bickel the following morning. Although Zander's hand was healing and would be out of full commission for a few weeks, he picked Dr. Bickel up and took him home—to the Albuquerque house Dr. Bickel owned in his own name and had lived in when he worked for Sandia, the home he hadn't seen since the explosion in his lab killed Dr. Prochanski. A nurse's aide, as recommended by Dr. Bickel's doctor, met them there and took over Dr. Bickel's homecare until he was able to do for himself.

Please, Lord. I need you to speak to me.

I kept my date with Zander to wrap Christmas presents. It was fun, but subdued. Zander didn't press me on my decision even though the clock was ticking: I needed to provide Gamble an answer by the end of day tomorrow.

Lord? I'm waiting. I trust you.

***

I called Gamble with my answer the following afternoon, minutes before the seventy-two-hour deadline expired.

⌘⌘⌘⌘

CHAPTER 29

Zander, Agent Gamble, Dr. Bickel, and I converged on Abe's little house early Christmas morning. The four of us were what Aunt Lucy and Abe had called "orphans" back in the day, those who had no family nearby to spend the holiday with. Zander's sister, Izzie, had gone to their parents' home in Las Cruces for the week; both of Gamble's sisters and their families lived in Ohio; Dr. Bickel had no family to speak of.

Neither did I.

So, Abe and Emilio gathered us into their home, into their first Christmas together. It seemed fitting, too, that the people who knew my secrets should share the holiness and beauty of the day. We were bound together by those secrets, by our common trials and tragedies.

We had agreed to come early that morning. Zander, Dr. Bickel, and I arrived shortly after 7 a.m. Gamble got there a few minutes later. Not surprisingly, Emilio was already awake and wired. He grinned and bounced as we stacked more presents under the tree—adding to an already sizable pile.

"That boy's been up since four o'clock," Abe groused. "He's been dancin' 'round that tree like Peter Pan and the Lost Boys cavorting 'round a bonfire. I'm an old man, and I need my sleep! Not used to bein' awake in the middle of the night."

Then he waggled his eyebrows and smiled. "When his racket woke me up, I made my coffee and fixed him some hot chocolate, and we got on the sofa together and pulled an old afghan over us to keep warm. Just sat in the dark, watching the lights twinkle on the tree. Wasn't long, and that boy laid his head on my shoulder and fell back t' sleep. Me, too. Mighty nice way to welcome Christmas morning after all."

Abe insisted on a big Christmas breakfast before we celebrated further, and he'd baked and cooked up a memorable one: orange juice, egg nog, homemade cinnamon rolls, fat sausages, scrambled eggs, fried potatoes, and tamales.

"Got the tamales from Mrs. Baca at church. She and her four daughters make a thousand tamales every December. I always put my order in early."

Gamble, his mouth full of sausage and tamale, replied, "I need that woman's number."

When breakfast was over, we team-cleaned the kitchen and dining nook. I washed, Zander dried (one-handed), Dr. Bickel put away, Emilio took out the trash, Gamble swept, and Abe wiped down counters and table.

At last Abe let Emilio open his presents—one by one. The boy was excited, and I had to think how few real Christmases he'd had in his life.

He unwrapped Abe's gift first. The torn paper revealed a large box with the words, "Blazer 6800 Pro Skateboard," in bold letters next to the image of a board coated in ice-blue sparkles over a midnight-blue background.

In his joy, he couldn't stand to open the box, so he just hugged the board—box and all—to himself. Then he put it aside and ran to Abe, hugged him harder. "Thank you, Abe," he whispered over and over.

"Sure glad you like it, Emilio," Abe whispered back.

We knew neither of them were talking about the skate board. The bond between Abe and Emilio was growing.

Emilio plowed through a pile of clothes (from Zander and me), a remote-control car (from Gamble), and a model airplane (courtesy of Dr. Bickel).

"This last one is from us," Zander told him. "From Gemma and me."

We'd known the gift was "just right" the moment we'd laid eyes on it. Seeing Emilio open it would be a memory I knew I'd always treasure.

He tore into the paper to reveal a wood case about fourteen by ten inches. The case gave no indication as to what was inside. We laughed because he looked at every side, wondering aloud what the wooden box might contain, before unfastening the two latches.

As Emilio lifted the lid, I craned my neck to look inside with him and, at the same time, watch the expression on his face. His eyes widened—and I laughed with joy.

Abe couldn't bear the suspense. "Well, what is it?"

"It's . . . it's . . ."

Rather than tell, Emilio turned the case around. Inside, nestled in neat rows, was a set of wood carving tools—various sized blades, chisels, and spoon gouges; two rasps, a skew, a V tool, a fishtail, three awls, a small mallet, and a whetstone. The steel blades, ferrules, and working ends gleamed; each tool was embedded in a polished hardwood handle.

"For carving?" Emilio finally managed. That's when I saw unshed tears standing in his eyes.

Zander reached behind the couch for another package. "And this present goes with that one."

Emilio placed the open set of tools upon the coffee table and received the gift. Blinking away the moisture in his eyes, he ripped the paper from the box and pried open the top.

"Wow!" He stood up and took the box to Abe. "See?"

The box was packed with an assortment of types and sizes of wood.

Abe selected a chunk and hefted it in his hand. "Well, well! You will be a true craftsman in no time, son!"

I don't think Abe realized the import of his words, particularly when he spoke the word "son," but Emilio's reaction was telling. He dropped the box of woods in Abe's lap, covered his eyes, and burst into tears.

Abe muttered, "My goodness!" He set the box aside and gathered Emilio to him.

Despite every recent hardship, I couldn't remember a happier Christmas.

Then, *bam*, tomorrow would hit me like a sledgehammer: Back to the real world.

Why couldn't every day be as happy as Christmas?

⌘⌘⌘⌘

CHAPTER 30

January.

Dark. Dreary. Winter.

Christmas and New Years were over; spring was months away.

No, spring is an eternity from now.

Ugh.

I'd told Gamble to go ahead and announce my "death."

The Monday following Christmas, three weeks back, he'd released a statement saying that the remains of two bodies had been found in the explosion's aftermath. "DNA evidence supports our belief that the deceased are sisters Genie and Gemma Keyes."

Two bodies? Two? Talk about confused.

In fact, Gamble's statement hadn't mentioned Cushing at all.

I'd chewed on that for a while. Perhaps . . . perhaps it would have proven difficult to explain Cushing's presence in my house without also providing inquiring minds with a loose thread to pull—and Trujillo had warned me about loose threads.

"Nano. Please continuously scan all available news sources for reports of General Cushing. If you find mention of her, let me know?"

We will, Gemma Keyes.

I went back to Gamble's statement. He had gone into some vague details regarding the cause of the explosion, ending with, "It may be weeks or months before ATF determines the exact circumstances of the explosion that took the lives of these two young women."

Meaning, I'd surmised, that ATF would put off the report as long as possible and deliver whatever their higher-ups told them to deliver using whatever oblique and imprecise language they were directed to use.

It was disturbing to reread Gamble's statement in the online papers and see it reported in the news. It was creepy and disconcerting to know that my old classmates and people I'd worked with believed me dead and would never know why the government had been hunting me. Would likely believe the worst of me.

And it bothered me that Zander's sister might remember me as a criminal. It bothered me a lot.

I admitted, too, that I was grieving for Genie. I'd never dreamed that I would face the loss of my sister, or that her last act would be a selfless one.

Did Genie give the nanomites the precious seconds they needed to propel us out of the explosion's kill zone?

In spite of the facts that we'd never been close, that we'd been more enemies than sisters, I grieved for her. I now had no family. Well, I had Emilio. And Abe.

I was still . . . processing.

On the day of the deadline, I'd told Gamble to announce my death, but I had refused the government's WITSEC proposal. I'd weighed my commitment to Emilio and my obligation to help Abe raise Emilio, and I couldn't let them down. I would not break Emilio's heart or be yet another adult who had made promises to him and then broken them.

No, I hadn't taken the government's deal, because I couldn't leave Albuquerque. My heart was here.

In more ways than one.

So, I'd told Gamble to announce my death, but I'd declined the government's offer of a new life. I didn't need them to put me in WITSEC when the nanomites could do a much better job—when their work was far superior to the WITSEC program's. It was more secure, too.

I'd called Dr. Bickel the same day and let him know my decision, and I'd called Abe and asked if he would prepare Emilio for the news reports and assure him that I was fine, but that I needed a few weeks to "birth" a new identity.

"You and Emilio won't see me for a while, Abe. I need to put space between Gemma and whomever will emerge in her stead. That means staying away from you and Emilio until I come up with a natural way for her replacement to 'meet' you guys."

I hadn't called Zander with my decision; instead, I'd asked Abe to pass on my message.

The next morning, I'd checked out of the hotel and into one of those by-the-month furnished suites using Kathy Sawyer's ID and credit card. With Cushing gone, no one was looking for Kathy. However, I would lean on Kathy Sawyer's persona only as a short-term fix, one I would discard shortly. Trujillo knew about Kathy, and I didn't want Trujillo (or anyone, for that matter) breathing down my neck.

Not ever.

Within hours of giving Gamble my decision, the nanomites and I had begun to scope out my new identity. We'd started with my appearance. How I presently looked was already quite different from "Gemma BN" (Before Nanomites). My increased metabolism and lengthy workouts had slimmed and honed my body to a wiry machine, and the sharp planes of my face were striking in their contrast to the old Gemma—but they weren't dissimilar enough. To anyone who'd known Gemma before, I was a fitter and leaner Gemma, but I was Gemma, and they would know it.

That had to change. I had to change.

Based on the parameters used in facial recognition software (such as the nine regions corresponding to the functional parts of the face and the attribute classifications assigned to each of them), the nanomites and I isolated my specific facial characteristics: My chin and jawline, the exact space between my eyes, the width of my nose where it intersects my eyes, my brow shape and height, and so on.

I had the nanomites draft a full-length 3D digital replica of my body (same height, shape, weight, and coloring), and superimpose my face onto the model. We targeted the top five facial aspects that best identified me, then we altered the image's characteristics in ways only genetics or the most drastic of cosmetic surgeries could produce.

When we finished, the replica's face was unrecognizable as Gemma Keyes.

"Add some highlights to brighten her hair, Nano, and choose a shorter hairstyle."

Gemma Keyes.

"Hmm?"

DOD issued a bulletin this morning: An Air Force transport went down over the Atlantic late yesterday.

Baffled, I asked, "Why are you bringing this to my attention?"

General Imogene Cushing was listed on the flight's manifest.

"They've already released the names of those presumed dead?" The turnaround seemed too quick to me.

No, Gemma Keyes. As is customary, the military will notify all relatives of the victims before releasing their names to the media. However, since you instructed us to watch for use of General Cushing's name, we have been scanning all available files for any new references to her. Two hours ago, General Cushing's name was added to the manifest of the lost flight.

So, that's how it would be handled. Wait for a plausible tragedy, then include her death in it. No body to ID; no questions.

I shuddered and nodded. "Thank you, Nano."

I returned to the unfinished rendering of my new identity and tweaked it a bit more. When I was satisfied with the woman whose face stared back at me, I told the nanomites, "Nano, this is the new me. It's how I want you to make me look when we're ready to make the change. At all times, unless I say otherwise, I should look like her."

And the voice. People who knew me would recognize Gemma Keyes' voice, wouldn't they? The voice had to go, too.

"Nano, how would you propose altering my voice in an ongoing manner?"

We could alter your voice in one of two ways, Gemma Keyes: through continual manipulation of the soundwaves your vocal cords emit or through actual microsurgery to your vocal cords.

Microsurgery? A chill shivered through me. I'd had it with microsurgery! "Um, let's stick with manipulating my vocal soundwaves for now, Nano."

What name will you choose, Gemma Keyes?

Headache. I massaged a spot squarely in the middle of my forehead. All of the me-modifying decisions were getting to me. Stressing me out.

"And that's another thing, Nano. Once I choose a name, we will stick with it. In fact, starting now, no more addressing me as Gemma Keyes. We're creating my next identity, not 'borrowing' someone else's. I will become this woman; it will be a permanent adaptation. So, please stop calling me Gemma Keyes."

I was being brutal for my own sake, tearing off every vestige of Gemma Keyes, but the nanomites didn't like it. I could tell by the frosty silence that followed.

"Nano? Did you hear what I said?"

We heard you.

"Okay, then."

I pondered long and hard over the name I would bear the rest of my life. I penciled and penned various combinations, scratching out the rejects, compiling a short list of "maybes" and "possibles." I finally figured out that I was, subconsciously, looking for a first and last name with the same number of syllables as Gemma Keyes.

Emma Stone.

Rachel Weisz.

Maggie Smith.

Ashley Greene.

Taylor Swift.

Blah-blah Blah.

Choosing the "right" name was a harder exercise than I'd thought it would be. In those moments when I was being honest with myself, I admitted that I just wasn't ready to let go or ready to move on.

Absent all threats, I felt . . . let down. Rudderless. Aimless.

I sat in my suite's dark kitchen drinking my first cup of coffee, wondering where I'd find the "juice" to start over. In my up-and-coming guise, I could go anywhere, do what I liked. Make friends. Get a job. Have a real life.

Dr. Bickel had healed enough to dismiss his nursing aide, and the FBI had cleared him of all charges and allegations. DOE even restored his security clearance and asked Dr. Bickel to return to Sandia and rebuild his lab. I had to assume that my friends in D.C. cleared the way for his quick reinstatement.

"Don't worry; I won't be building another ion printhead," he'd confided to me, "at least nothing like the one I used to print the nanomites. In fact, I plan to take my research in a different direction. A safer direction."

Speaking of different directions: *I* wouldn't be applying for any jobs at Sandia. Just the thought made me anxious. Perhaps I'd return to school and take up another degree program, but I'd need to look for work before too long.

I yanked myself back to the task at hand. Back to my new name.

I sighed and slid the page of proposed names toward me. Had an idea.

"Nano, what does the name 'Gemma' mean in other languages?"

They laid out a long list, and I scanned through them, hoping something would catch my eye. I had always liked Gemma because, in English, it is derived from the word gem or jewel. Even in my child's mind, my name had made me feel special and precious—when I often felt forgotten and stupid.

I read on and saw, *The name Jemma in Hebrew is a diminutive of Jemima which means "little dove." Jemima was one of the three beautiful daughters of Job.*

"Little dove." I snickered. "Right. *So* me. Not."

I went back to names and their meanings. Had a second idea. "Nano, what is the name 'Jewel' in other languages?"

The list began with Amber and variations on Amber. I started down the list. Some of the names were derived from specific gemstones such as amethyst, crystal, diamond, emerald, garnet, jasper, ruby, pearl, and sapphire.

I didn't care for any of them.

Then I went back to the "J"s. Looked closer.

Jayda: Elaborated feminine form of the English for Jade.

Jayda.

"Huh."

I didn't hate it. It also sparked the glimmer of yet another idea.

"Nano, look up the surname 'Keyes' in various languages."

I found the Keyes surname and its motto: *In Domino confide. I trust in the Lord.*

"Wow." Goosebumps washed over my skin. *Lord? Are you leading me?*

"Nano, look for the word 'Trust' in other languages."

That didn't pan out.

"Okay, so not a variation on Keyes."

I concentrated. "Keyes" and "key" aren't actually related, but they sound the same, right?

"Nano. Look for the word "key" in other languages."

Nope. That didn't turn up anything that resonated with me.

I puzzled around further with no results. "Keyes. Trust. *Confide*: confidence."

Nothing.

"A key opens a door. A key fits into a lock that opens a door. And a lock is—"

Lock? No, "Lock" with an added "e" at the end like "Keyes."

Locke?

Jayda Locke?

Could I live with that? Abe would accept it. Could Emilio? I wasn't considering Zander. He and I would remain friends, but nothing more.

"Nano, I've decided on my new name: Jayda Locke."

I needed a middle name, so I added "Lucia" as an *homage* to Aunt Lucy: Jayda Lucia Locke.

"Nano, what do you think?"

I didn't exactly hear a "harrumph." I didn't hear any enthusiasm from the nanomites, either.

They replied, *If that is your decision,* and left off the Gemma Keyes tag I was so accustomed to.

Fine! Be that way! Stupid, stubborn nanomites.

But I felt my chest tighten. I would never hear them say my name again.

***

Over the next week, the nanomites fabricated and brought the pieces of Jayda Locke's persona together: birth certificate, social security number, immunization and medical records, high school diploma, college transcript and degree, and New Mexico driver's license. Even a passport.

And seven years of tax returns? That trick had to have taken some serious manipulation of data—behind some seriously well-protected firewalls.

Firewalls? Meh! No firewall could keep the nanomites out.

Wherever paperwork should properly reside, the nanomites produced a digital copy and filed it there. They backstopped my identity in one-hundred-twenty-seven separate places, including the files of grade schools and middle schools, social media, online shopping accounts, and "former employers" (the last being Lockheed Martin in Littleton, Colorado). They even provided Jayda with a heritage.

Seems Jayda had parents and grandparents (deceased, of course) and a family tree that went back seven generations. I figured out how they did it, and it was quite clever, really. The nanomites went back five generations and altered two separate genealogy records to add another sibling to each record, a male to one and a female to the other. They "married" the man and woman and created a whole new line of Locke family members—of whom Jayda was the present sole descendant.

Like I said: clever.

In a move that forever removed Kathy Sawyer from my life, I went to my bank and closed out her checking account. The nanomites had already closed her online shopping accounts, paid off her credit card, and canceled it.

Kathy's month-by-month lease on the apartment ran out at the end of the week. I hadn't renewed it. In fact, I'd given my notice and wouldn't be returning to the apartment after today. Everything I owned fit into one suitcase, and I placed that suitcase in the back of the Escape—also soon to be discarded.

I left the apartment for a beauty salon. I asked for highlights and a shorter cut. When I left the salon, I looked exactly like Jayda Locke's license photo.

With driver's license in hand (and the nanomites altering my appearance as we'd designed Jayda), I rented a new apartment and moved in. The nanomites provided a written reference from Jayda's "previous" rental; however, since I didn't want my new landlord calling Jayda's "previous" landlord, I plunked down three months' rent and an exorbitant damage deposit.

In cash.

I guess money really does talk.

I took my new lease agreement and opened a checking and a savings account, depositing a modest amount in both and planning to deposit smallish amounts into my accounts over the next weeks. Walked away with a debit card in my hand and a credit card in the works.

Ready money wouldn't be an issue for a while: I still had half of the cash I'd dug up in Mateo's back yard, and I'd returned to Dr. Bickel's safe house to retrieve the cash embedded in the cinderblock wall next to the alley. The explosion had demolished the top half of the wall; I was grateful when the nanomites found the wrapped bundle buried beneath the rubble of broken cinderblock.

Afterward, I wandered my way through the remains of the house. There wasn't much to see. I nudged and toed chunks, pieces, splinters, bits, and shards of building materials and furnishings, most fragmented or burned beyond recognition.

Then I saw it.

You know how tornados and wild fires are notorious for leveling entire neighborhoods or forests but leaving a lone home or a single tree untouched? The debris of the safe house proved such caprice.

Face up, rinsed clean by a recent shower, I spied one intact bathroom tile. The faded turquoise gleamed up at me from the rubble. I picked up the tile, ran my fingers over its glossy surface, and tucked it into my purse.

"Thank you, Lord. I will keep this as a reminder of the many ways you sheltered me through those dark times."

⌘⌘⌘⌘

CHAPTER 31

A new furnished apartment, some new clothes, and a nice, late-model vehicle purchased from a private party (all legal and in-person) and Jayda Locke became an established resident of Albuquerque—but the dreary winter days dragged on.

I picked up a new phone, bought a new Bible, shopped for new dishes, kitchen gadgets, sheets, towels, and blankets. Picked out a new laptop. Ordered new Kamagong sticks—from a different (and, yes, *new*) vendor.

New, new, new.

I'm starting to hate "new," I groused.

With more energy than I needed coursing through my body and not enough physical or mental activity to keep me from going bonkers, I returned to my long morning runs and nightly regimen at the dojo. Ten miles of running during the day and four or five hours of intense workouts with Gus-Gus ensured that I could sleep the few hours my body required.

As for Gus-Gus? He worked me as hard as I could bear—which was pretty hard, considering normal human tolerances. What irked me was that no matter how good I got at stick fighting, he was always an increment or two better than me and was never entirely satisfied with my performance. He was forever egging me on to do better.

I figured the nanomites had programmed him to keep challenging me, and I guess I was good with that—but, *oh man.* Somedays I wanted *so bad* to wipe that smug, superior look off Gus-Gus' face!

In my spare time, I explored my new-to-me Facebook and Pinterest profiles. Apparently, I'd been on Facebook for six years and Pinterest for four. My Pinterest boards centered around historic themes, especially early New Mexico photos.

Interesting. The nanomites know me well.

While I had "acquired" lots of followers on Pinterest, I had few friends on Facebook. I browsed my posting history and found that my Facebook experience centered around various pages and groups rather than interpersonal relationships. It would have been difficult for the nanomites to build Jayda Locke a friends list that had history to it. No matter; I liked what I saw in my newsfeed.

Facebook popped up a page it thought I would like: Downtown Community Church.

"What the heck." I clicked on it, read through the list of events and activities—and got stuck on a Friday evening Bible study for young adults.

The group was led by DCC associate pastor Zander Cruz.

My finger traced his face on the screen, and I stared at the images of a circle of chairs and the earnest faces of men and women around my age discussing Scripture. I was hungry to know God's word better. Longed to learn more.

Well, why couldn't I?

I looked up the meeting time and place.

***

I checked myself in the mirror a third time. No, it was not Gemma Keyes looking back at me. The reflection was disconcerting on one hand and reassuring on the other. I took a deep breath, got my purse and Bible, and headed out the door.

The young adult study group met in the fellowship hall at the rear of the DCC building. Maybe ten cars in the lot told me that some of the group's members had already arrived. Feeling nervous, I waited until another car arrived and a young woman got out. As she started for the doors, I joined her.

"Hi! Are you new?" she asked.

"Um, yeah. Yes."

More "new" than you'd ever believe.

"Welcome. I'm Nance Peterman."

"Jayda Locke."

"Good to meet you, Jayda. I'll introduce you around."

She grabbed my arm and steered me toward the coffee bar. "Hey, Izzie. This is Jayda. This is her first time here."

Gah! My legs almost buckled. It hadn't dawned on me that Zander's sister might—would almost certainly—be at the study!

Izzie, boundless energy personified, ran out from behind the coffee bar and grabbed me in a tight hug. "Hi Jayda. I'm Izzie Cruz. I'm so glad you're here! Since it's your first time, you get a free cup of coffee."

"Um, cool. Thank you." I struggled to find something else to say. "So, uh, what is the group studying right now?"

Izzie bounced back behind the counter and picked up an empty cup. While she filled it, she chattered on about the study.

"We're in the Book of Romans. My brother leads the study, but don't worry. He's not one of those pontificating kind of teachers. He's more of a facilitator of conversation. Says that applying the word to our hearts and lives is the most important aspect of a study."

I shivered with relief. Izzie didn't recognize me, didn't have a clue—but, then, she and I had only met a few times.

The real test would be Zander—Zander, who knew me so well. Would he see through the nanomites' disguise? Even though I no longer looked or sounded like Gemma Keyes, would he see past those things? Would some intangible part of me sneak out and speak to him? Or would I remain anonymous?

I took my coffee and followed Nance to a circle of chairs. We took seats together and Izzie joined us, plopping down on my other side.

Zander had been talking to a group of guys. At a signal from him, the guys broke up and found their seats in the circle.

I hadn't seen Zander until that moment, but one glimpse set my heart pounding.

He looked tired and wonderful at the same time.

"How's everyone tonight? Shall we get started? But before we do, it looks like we have a visitor. Izzie, would you please introduce her?"

Izzie jumped up and gestured toward me. "Hey, all. This is Jayda Locke. Jayda, this is 'everyone.' I'll let you tell the group a little about yourself."

Talk about on the spot! My throat closed and I choked on my coffee and started coughing.

Zander nodded. "Don't be alarmed, Jayda. We don't bite—well, not too often anyway."

The fifteen or so within the circle laughed. I did, too—when I caught my breath.

All eyes were on me. Izzie patted my leg. I cleared the lump out of my throat.

"Well, um, as Izzie said, my name is Jayda. I'm a new Christian, and I . . . found this Bible study group on Facebook, so I thought I'd give it a try."

"We're glad you're here, and I hope we make you feel welcome. What do you do, Jayda? What are your interests?" Zander asked

I relaxed a bit. "Let's see. I'm an Albuquerque native. I lived out of state last year, but I'm back and looking for work."

"What kind of work do you do?" Zander prompted me.

"Mostly project management, although I'll take whatever comes my way first."

"Well, that's serendipitous," one of the guys to the right of Zander said. "I work at Raytheon and saw a posting for a project controls specialist this morning."

"Really?" Raytheon was a solid company with contracts in various government branches.

"Yup. Give me your number after the meeting, and I'll text you the link."

The guy next to him snorted. "Riiiight, Josh. Way to get the new girl's number."

Amid hoots and more ribbing, the same guy yelled across the circle, "Jayda, I'm Todd. Give *me* your number, and I'll do a job search *for* you."

Well, that set everyone off again, and I couldn't help but laugh with them. It looked like Jayda was attracting the kind of attention Gemma never had. I didn't mind—in fact, it was flattering, except . . . Zander, with a tolerant smile on his face, was paging through his Bible. It seemed that he had no interest in Jayda.

He was kind. Cordial. Personable. And insensible to my disguise.

He raised his hand, calling for order. "Now that all the guys have made Jayda feel about as welcome as a lone wildebeest stumbling onto a pride of lions . . ."

More laughter.

He caught my eye across the circle. "If they get too annoying, just beat them off with a stick, Jayda. You have my permission. I'll even help."

The girls cheered and the guys groaned. I admit that I snickered.

"Let's open to Romans 2. We had a lively discussion on judgment from verses 1-3 last week, but this evening we're going focus on two points found in verse 4: The relationship between God's many loving attributes and repentance. Yes, *repentance*."

That drew a collective groan from the group.

With that same patient smile, Zander ignored their protests. "All right, everyone. As soon as you all find Romans 2, we'll read the verse together."

While Zander waited for the group to open their Bibles to the right chapter, Izzie leaned toward my ear. "Don't mind my brother. If he's a little subdued, it's because he recently lost a good friend."

My head snapped up. "Oh?"

"Yes. You might have read about her or seen her on the news. Her name was Gemma Keyes. She and her sister were killed when their house blew up. Just horrible. Really hit Zander hard."

I licked my lips. "Was . . . was this girl special to Zander? I mean, well, you know."

"I don't know for sure. Zander is cautious and careful not to play fast and loose, if you take my meaning. But . . . well, I think she *was* special to him. I just can't be sure."

She shook her head. "To tell the truth, he won't talk about it—which only makes me think he is hurting more than he lets on."

"This . . . Gemma. I heard, um, things about her." I couldn't help it. I had to know what Izzie believed about me. About Gemma.

"You mean how every law enforcement agency in New Mexico was looking for her? How the media painted her as a terrorist or said she had committed some kind of national security crime? The weird part is that none of those things jibe with the Gemma Keyes I knew.

"Well, actually, I didn't know her all that well, but Zander? When I asked him about the accusations, he just got this angry look in his eyes like he knew something I didn't and lectured me with, 'Don't believe ill of someone until they've been proven guilty in a court of law,' and—"

"Izzie? Something of importance you'd like to share with the rest of the group?" Zander skewered his sister with one of those arched-brow, reproving looks I'd seen him use during their playful sibling banter— which only brought on more laughter from the group.

"Nope. It's all girl talk over here, bro." she sent him her own wide-eyed, innocent, stare, "Nothing you'd be interested in."

After everyone stopped laughing and found their place, we read aloud together,

> *or do you show contempt*
> *for the riches of his kindness,*
> *forbearance and patience,*
> *not realizing that God's kindness*
> *is intended to lead you*
> *to repentance?*

"The opening word, 'or,' relies on the first three verses of the chapter," Zander explained, "and we discussed them last week. Tonight, let's look at how verse 4 presents 'the riches of his kindness, forbearance, and patience.' What is the Apostle Paul's point in listing these attributes?"

"It seems obvious that God's kindness, forbearance, and patience are all intended to lead us to repentance," Nance suggested.

"Right. The whole point of God's mercy and kindness is to bring us to a place of repentance. But, what, exactly, is repentance? Why is it important? Is it the nasty word the world has made it out to be?"

One guy shrugged. "I think repentance is kind of off-putting."

"Can you explain why you feel that way?" Zander asked.

"Maybe because it feels like shame? Or punishment? Or that I have to pay for or repair what I've done? I mean, some damage can't be fixed, you know? Can't be undone."

A young woman near me raised her hand. "That's how I feel when I've blown it—that I have to suffer for the wrong I've done or try really hard to fix the problem I've caused—and I feel guilty when I can't do it. All that guilt seems to keep me glued in the same spot. I end up feeling farther from God instead of closer to him."

I murmured aloud, "A friend of mine once told me that repairing the damage we cause follows after repentance and forgiveness. If we don't repent and allow Jesus to wash us clean before we rush off to fix the mess we've made? Well, we'll just make the same mistake again."

Ooops. The words popped out before I could stop them. Words that Zander had once spoken from his heart to mine. Words that had become a lifeline for my wayward heart.

And everyone was staring at me. Uncomfortable with the scrutiny, I shifted in my chair and chanced another look at the group—but the nods and agreement around the circle were sincere and hopeful.

As for Zander? The expression that crept over his features was, well . . . thunderstruck.

He stared. I stared. We stared.

Izzie glanced from me to her brother and back. "Interesting!" She was practically gloating.

I ripped my eyes away from Zander and fixed them on my Bible. I didn't say a word during the rest of the study.

At the end of the discussion period, we had a time of prayer followed by snacks and fellowship. It was pleasant, being with other people my age. I mingled and smiled and said hello. I discovered, to my surprise, that I wasn't shy like Gemma had been. I didn't feel the compulsion to hide in the background, even though I still preferred to listen and watch, rather than talk.

When the evening wound down, I shouldered my purse, said goodbye to Nance and Izzie, and walked toward the door. I was partway across the fellowship hall when I realized someone was behind me.

"Jayda?"

I stopped in my tracks. "Yes?"

Zander drew alongside me. "I enjoyed having you in our study tonight. Will you be coming back?"

"Uh, I haven't decided yet. I liked it, though."

He searched my face, searched my eyes. "You . . . you remind me of someone."

I swallowed. Reddened. "Oh?"

He nodded—and out of the blue, he snagged my fingers and curled them up in his. My fingers tingled all the way up my arm.

"Gemma?"

I froze. "No, it's Jayda."

He didn't let go of my fingers, and his eyes never left my face. "Jayda Locke, is it?"

"Yes, Jayda."

"Jayda. Got it."

And turning his head a little so if anyone were watching they would not see, he lowered one eyelid. Down. And up. A slow, purposeful wink.

I had to fight to keep the corners of my mouth from turning up in delight. I glanced around, too.

Shoot. There was Izzie, eyeballing us like a roadrunner fixated on a grasshopper.

"You can never tell anyone, Zander, or do anything to give me away. Especially to Izzie."

"I . . . understand."

"I mean it. Not ever."

He nodded. "But . . . can we be friends? Jayda and I? Can we . . . go to dinner tomorrow evening, for instance?"

"Uhhh."

"Meet me at P.F. Chang's? I'll make a reservation for seven o'clock."

"All right."

⌘⌘⌘⌘

CHAPTER 32

Dinner was wonderful. It was our first—our only—real date, and it came with all the trimmings: Zander wore a suit. He brought flowers. He held my chair. And he let me order everything I wanted. *Everything.* Enough for a party of five: lettuce wraps, spring rolls, soup, three main courses and two side dishes to share.

I drooled over the menu.

When the waitress left with our order, I set out the single ground rule. "Zander, whatever conversation we have tonight must be between you and Jayda. No one else. That's the way it has to be."

Zanders head bobbed once. "It may be a difficult adjustment, but I'm willing to live with that."

So, we talked. And laughed. About the study group and about his ministry with the youth and young adults. He asked me about my apartment and job prospects. Then I shared the work God was doing in my life—couched in vague references that Zander would "get."

"With all that's happened . . . in the last year, I can look back and see how much God has changed me. Oh, I still get grouchy and I frequently struggle with anger, but the cool thing is that when I open my Bible and step into God's word? It's like his presence comes and fills me up—and I no longer have room for anger or grouchiness."

"Jesus said that his word is living bread. You are describing the way his living bread feeds our souls."

"That's it exactly."

Zander was careful how he phrased his next question. "What are you doing to fill your time right now, Jayda?"

I licked my lips. "Oh, this and that. I run. Work out. Look for employment."

"Do you . . . do you miss the, er, faster pace of, say, the last six months?"

He'd couched so much in that one line.

And my answer was honest. "Yes. I'm kinda bored, to tell the truth. I'm safe and secure, but a little bored."

"Could you . . . do you think you could get used to a normal, boring life? Could you get accustomed to, say, being courted by a poor associate pastor? Because this poor associate pastor would like to woo you, Jayda."

I leaned toward him and lowered my voice. "We can't . . . we can't go there, Zander. You know that."

"And yet, we've never 'gone there,' *Jayda*. You owe me a real, honest, and complete discussion on this, uh, topic—*and* you owe it to *us* not only to explore the possibility, but to prayerfully ask God's direction after we've identified all the obstacles."

I expected to be angry with him, but I wasn't. I was just sad.

"Jayda, look at me."

My eyes were too full of tears to meet his.

He reached across the table and took my hand. "Please, sweet Jayda?"

I looked up.

"Jayda, I want to suggest a path forward. Monday is my day off. Let's go for a long drive and find a remote spot where we can be ourselves to talk it all out. We'll get every bit of the issue out on the table—and then we'll pray over it. Are you willing to do that?"

"But you already know that those tiny, um, *complications* will come along with us."

"Yes. I know."

Waitresses, universally, have the worst timing ever.

"Would you like me to box up the leftovers?"

Zander didn't miss a beat. "That would be great. Jayda would love to take them home."

"Jayda. What a pretty name."

Zander agreed. "It is; I'm already partial to it."

"Thank you," I mumbled.

When we left the restaurant, I was carrying a bouquet of flowers and a large bag filled with boxes of goodies.

"Where are you parked?" Zander asked.

I pointed. "Way over there. The lot was crowded when I got here."

He grabbed my pointing hand and tucked it into his, and we walked across the lot like any other couple.

But we weren't like any other couple—and we never would be.

If I were to be honest, what lay at the center of my concerns was that "thing." The Big Thing. I mean, every girl has a picture of what . . . intimacy with the man she loved would be like—am I right? Except Zander and I would never be alone, just the two of us . . . together.

I had this recurring (and creepy) vision of us whispering the most private of endearments—and Alpha Tribe uploading every word to their library. I imagined Zander, leaning in to kiss me—while the nanomites watched over our shoulders and added running commentary.

Popcorn, anyone?

It would be worse than having a dog or a cat in the room! At least a pet wouldn't be asking inappropriate questions.

At the absolutely wrong time.

Ackkk! I squeezed my eyes shut. *I'm never gonna "un-see" that!*

Zander opened my car door. I slumped into the seat.

"Are you all right?"

"Hunky-dory," I lied.

Crud. Now I need to repent for lying.

"Jayda, would you come to church tomorrow? Sit with Izzie? Maybe have lunch with us afterward?"

I snorted a laugh. "You mean not hide up in the choir loft?"

"That's exactly what I mean. You're Jayda Locke, new to DCC, part of the young adult group now. Friends with Izzie."

"I-I'll consider it."

"Great. It was a lovely evening—thank you. I hope to see you tomorrow."

He closed the door, waved, and turned away. I popped the door back open and climbed out.

"Wait. Zander? I didn't thank you for dinner."

He chuckled and kind of smirked. "Okay, but you'd better thank me three times. Dinner with you is like buying for three girlfriends."

I had to giggle. "I know. I'm sorry. Thank you, thank you, thank you. For dinner, for our fellowship. For everything."

"Would you like a goodnight kiss?"

"W-what?"

"You heard me."

"Well, I-I—"

"Because I only kiss the woman I intend to marry. So, do you want a goodnight kiss?"

More than anything. More than you know. If only—

He must have seen it on my face, because the next thing I knew, his arms were around me, and he was delivering the finest goodnight kiss in the history of the world.

Well, in the history of my world, anyway.

We pulled apart, and I could hardly breathe. "Wow."

"Wow is right. I love you Ge—I mean Jayda, so don't forget to pray and think on our upcoming conversation. We're going to hash this thing through and then give it to God."

"Okay." Might as well.

I drove out of the parking lot in a fog of consternation: I had only scratched the surface of my concerns. I knew what the nanomites had done to my body, but I didn't know how those changes might affect certain biological functions.

And, if Zander and I were to discuss the facts in less than forty-eight hours, then I needed to *know* the facts—and that meant asking the nanomites explicit—uncomfortable—questions.

Like, could I have children? Because Zander would expect children. Had it crossed his mind that I might not be able to give him a family? And, if, by some miracle, I could conceive, *did* conceive, would the child be normal—or would the nanomites' mutations filter down in my genetic code? Would the child be a nano-amalgamation, like me? Or would those genetic mutations damage the baby?

And, if I did conceive, what might happen to the infant *in utero* if the nanomites and I were to use the terrible powers we possessed?

Beyond all my other concerns, was the certainty that my life was tied to the nanomites' health and longevity. One unanticipated, unprepared-for electrostatic discharge of sufficient strength could wipe out the nanocloud—and me.

Longevity. The nanomites had also warned me of the effect attrition would have on their numbers. The swarm would age and would suffer the inevitable breakdown of various members along the way. As individual nanomites failed, the swarm would diminish—unless the nanomites had the environment and materials to replenish the nanocloud.

And, Dr. Bickel had assured me, that wasn't going to happen. He was not going to re-engineer another ion printhead.

The question was, how long before the nanocloud depleted to the point where it could not sustain its critical functions—me being one of them? How many years did that give me?

Ten years. Fifteen, tops.

Was that fair to Zander? To any children we *might* have?

Yes, I was scared to ask the nanomites the questions that pressed me—because I dreaded their answers.

Tons of uncertainty.

Heaps of reticence.

Loads of fear.

Not the faintest flicker of hope.

***

The next morning, I found Izzie in DCC's large sanctuary. "Hi, Izzie. May I sit with you?"

"Jayda! Yes, of course." She patted the seat next to her and I scooted in.

She wasted no time. "Zander tells me you might be coming to lunch with us after service?"

"Oh. Yeah, he did mention that."

"Last night at dinner?"

"He told you we had dinner, did he?"

She grinned. "Oh, yes, indeed. Come on, you don't fool me. I saw sparks shooting across the room at Bible study Friday evening."

The stink eye I leveled on her would have earned high praise from a polecat.

She just laughed. "Hey, there's Zander's little friend, Emilio, and his foster dad, Abe." She waved at them. "Zander's going to ask them to lunch, too."

Abe and Emilio waved to Izzie from seats far away. They scarcely gave me a glance—but that was before we went to lunch together.

Worship on the main floor was a very different experience than what it had been from the choir loft. I felt exposed and out of place—not because I was Jayda Locke but because everything was strange to me. I felt self-conscious: I didn't know the songs and was certain my failure to sing would be noted by all. I hardly knew when to stand or sit—and what was with all the raising of hands? I watched Izzie out of the corner of my eye and followed her examples (except shooting my hands into the air—that was a bit much).

But the service taken altogether? I loved it.

When Pastor McFee pronounced the benediction and we all said, "Amen," Zander joined us. Abe and Emilio did, too.

Zander placed his hand on the small of my back. "Abe, Emilio, this is my new friend, Jayda Locke. Jayda, these are my good friends, Abe Pickering and Emilio Martinez."

"Pleased to meet you, Mr. Pickering" I shook Abe's hand and held on. I winked. Twice. Abe shifted on his feet and tried to take back his hand. I didn't let him. I hung on and squeezed his hand. Twice.

I coughed and winked again.

With sudden clarity, Abe grinned. "Nice to meet you, um, Jayda. Very nice, indeed."

Then I tried to shake Emilio's hand.

Nope. Instead, I got to witness the might and power of a fully functional Death Stare, Emilio style.

"Hi, Emilio."

Scowl

"Say hello to Miss Locke, Emilio," Abe instructed.

Glare

Emilio's brows bunched down in that black line I knew so very well and he muttered a half-hearted "Hey."

"Young man—"

"It's all right, Mr. Pickering. He just doesn't know me yet." Emphasis on the "know" part.

Abe glanced from me to Emilio and nodded his understanding, but Izzie missed the unspoken communication between Abe and me.

She was oblivious, and in my book, oblivious was good.

"Anybody else hungry?" Zander asked to ease the strain. "How does IHOP sound?"

My stomach roared in my ears. "Yum! I'm down with that."

Emilio's eyes narrowed, and he was about to say something, but Abe put his hand on the kid's shoulder. Emilio looked away and grumbled under his breath.

***

Going out to lunch together should have been a great idea. Our wait for a table was only supposed to be a few minutes, so we stood in line. Smiling. Chatting.

Izzie excused herself to use the restroom. "I'll be right back."

Yup, going out to lunch *would* have been a great idea—if Emilio hadn't seen Zander (when he thought no one was looking) stroke the back of my hand. It was just a touch, a brief token of affection.

Well, Emilio *was* looking.

While Abe and Zander talked about the finer points of the pastor's message and I listened, Emilio shot jeers and grimaces of disgust and disdain my way. His sneers weren't bad; I rated them somewhere between sulfuric acid and toxic waste. I seriously thought the side of my head was going to putrefy, melt, and puddle on the floor.

Then I snapped to the basis for Emilio's anger.

Whoa! He sees Jayda Locke as Gemma's competition! He's trying to prevent some two-faced hussy from horning in on Gemma's man.

Relieved to understand, I made eye contact with Emilio. Waggled one brow. Willed him to "see" me.

No joy.

Instead, he flashed me an obscene gesture and mouthed an uncomplimentary phrase in Spanish.

Emilio said that you—

"Um, yeah. I got the gist, Nano. Don't need a translation" I tried not to let the nasty words bother me, but they did. Emilio wouldn't have said those things to Gemma.

Wouldn't have said them to Gemma.

Ah.

"Nano, listen: This is what I'd like you to do." I gave them instructions and waited.

Emilio was still seething and sniping at me when he blinked and became still. His face went slack.

He glanced up at me. Afraid. Unsure.

I'd had the nanomites whisper this in his ear: "Emilio, cut it out. Stop being such a big booger. I'm Gemma, hiding inside of Jayda—and you're being mean to me."

I made the tiniest nod—before Emilio crashed into me, threw his arms around me, and burst into tears. "I'm sorry! I'm sorry! I'm sorry!"

"Hey, hey," I whispered. "Don't. You'll give me away."

Naturally, that's right when Izzie breezed back from the bathroom. "What's going on?"

"Oh, nothing much. Emilio, um, he accidentally bit his tongue."

Super lame! And another "white" lie. I needed to have a talk with the Lord about how to handle these kinds of situations. Was telling little lies to protect my identity all right or did God want complete honesty at all times?

So much to learn.

Izzie reached for Emilio. "You poor kid! Want me to see how bad it is?"

Emilio shook his head and clung to me.

I shrugged. "Surprise! Guess I'm a hit, huh?"

"Well it beats how he was acting before."

Emilio stuck out his tongue at Izzie when she wasn't looking.

Oh, and Jesus? Could you please get 'hold of Emilio's heart, too? The kid has a lifetime of abuse and bad examples for you to heal and redeem.

The hostess led us to our table soon after that. All I can say about the rest of our lunch is that Emilio and I both ordered the special: The Bottomless Stack. Over Abe's misgivings, Emilio and I made a competition of who could eat the most pancakes.

I won.

Emilio and I laughed our glee; he grinned and high-fived me.

"Wow. That boy seems taken with you, Jayda," Izzie whispered. "What a switch."

Going to lunch turned out great after all.

⌘⌘⌘⌘

CHAPTER 33

I slipped Zander my phone number after lunch, then spent the rest of Sunday afternoon worrying over our upcoming conversation the following morning. I couldn't get past my inhibitions with the nanomites. Maybe it was because they already knew too much about me and were "in my business" on every front, but I couldn't seem to raise the questions to them that I needed answers for.

Besides, I felt that once Zander understood that the nanomites would be ever-present in our most personal and unguarded moments, once he knew the extent to which the mites would "share" our relationship, he would be as appalled as I was.

Yup. Appalled.

Like I was.

I got up early Monday, read my Bible, and prayed. Afterward, while I dressed and did my hair, I dithered and danced around the issues without asking the nanomites the all-important questions—until it was too late.

Zander called just after eight. "Are you up and ready to go? I thought I'd come by in about thirty minutes."

"Um, sure."

When I disconnected, my hands were clammy. I had to find words to convey the impossibility of a future together to Zander. As uncomfortable as the conversation would be, Zander needed to understand every distasteful aspect of that impossibility.

Zander arrived and we drove, mostly in silence, out I-40, then north on NM-14 through Tijeras and Cedar Crest, turning on 526, and heading up the winding back route to Sandia Crest. We parked in the lot at the top, not far from the cluster of antennas and cell towers that topped the Crest.

"We can talk here in the car or, if you're up for it, we can hike down the trail and enjoy the view."

Zander seemed to sense my distress—but then, he, more than anyone I knew, understood me when I didn't understand myself.

"It's not too cold today," he added, "And we're bundled up for the weather."

The 10,679-foot altitude of the Crest meant the ridgeline was always chilly and often downright cold when the wind gusted. However, this morning's weather was calm and clear. The views would be spectacular.

"All right."

We hiked thirty minutes down the trail until it emerged from the trees, and the magnificent Rio Grande Valley opened up before us. We kept walking until we were near the old Rock House that had been built as a ranger outpost during the Depression.

Zander took my hand, and we made our way to the other side of the stone building where the cliff leaned outward as a small promontory. The jutting ridge was edged in thick layers of granite and strewn with loose pieces of rock. We sat on the natural bench of rock overlooking the valley.

"It's always so beautiful," I murmured.

"Always," Zander agreed.

We enjoyed the moment in silence, neither one of us wanting to spoil the perfect morning. Eventually, though, one of us had to take the plunge.

I was surprised that it was me.

"Zander, I need to tell you something."

He turned toward me. "Okay. I'm listening."

"Wait. Look the other way like you were. Just . . . just until I get this out."

He turned away, not laughing or giving me a hard time for being squeamish.

"Zander, I . . . some of the stuff you want to know is going to be embarrassing for me to talk about."

"Embarrassing?"

"Um, yeah."

He nodded and thought for a moment. "Do you mean embarrassing because the nanomites are privy to everything we say? Everything we do?"

I nearly fell over with relief. "Yes. And more. The mites observe *everything*. I can just imagine their prying questions and absurd comments, say, if we were married. While we were . . . you know."

He frowned and nodded again. "I can see how that might be . . . off-putting."

"Understatement."

"Right; I get you: The nanomites as, um, total mood killers. We should pray over that. What's next?"

I took a deep breath. "Well, then there's . . ." I petered out.

"What, Gemma?"

"No, Zander. You don't get to call me that, even in private."

"Sorry. You're right, of course. *Jayda*. What were you going to say?"

When I didn't answer, he added, "Try just one word. Identify the problem with a single word."

"Kids." I blurted it out.

"Kids? I love kids."

"I know . . . and that's the problem."

He turned and stared at me. Astounded. Troubled. "You don't want a family?"

"No, that's not—I mean, that's not what I meant."

"Okay, so what about kids did you mean?"

I could see how serious Zander had become. As I expected, the subject was near to his heart. "I-I don't know if I can."

"Don't know if you can tell me? Or you don't know . . . if you can have kids?"

I nodded. We were face to face now, eye to eye, every emotion visible—and it was a little easier to just spit out what I'd been chewing on for so long.

"Zander, I'm concerned that whatever the nanomites did in my body, down at the molecular level, will either prevent me from getting pregnant or, worse, might cause genetic mutations or defects."

Now that I was talking, it poured out of me. "What if our kids weren't normal because of the nanomites? What if they were damaged? Or what if I were pregnant and drew down on available electricity and used it in a fight—like the fight at the FBI with Cushing and her men. What if I injured our baby or killed him?"

Wimp that I am, I started crying.

Zander put an arm around me and pulled me to his side while I sobbed. "I'm sorry, Ge—I mean, Jayda. I understand now what you've been struggling with."

I could tell he was chewing on my problems, too.

Finally, he said, "You know, ordinarily at this stage of a relationship, when two people are considering marriage, I'd suggest premarital counselling with an older couple who have a successful marriage and are wise in the Lord. But, given our rather peculiar issues, I can see that we are in uncharted and unknown waters. If we make it over these obstacles to the more 'normal' aspects of marriage, premarital counseling will be a big help."

He reached over and tipped my chin up so he could look at me. "I have to ask you: Have you brought up any of these issues to the nanomites? Have you asked them? I mean, who else in the world would know the answers?"

I hiccupped. "No, I haven't asked them. It's just . . . sometimes they are too up in my grill, you know? I wish I had one part of my life they weren't involved in!"

"You know they heard you say that, right?" Zander's eyes sparkled with amusement.

"It's not funny!"

"No, but it's reality. Listen to me: Instead of confronting truth, you are avoiding the reality you live in—and wherever that kind of ambiguity resides, so does fear. Guess what? Fear is not of God. The only thing we are to fear is God himself—not fear of punishment if we are in Christ, but the respect and reverence due him as the highest authority in the universe. But the wrong kind of fear? When we allow the wrong kind of fear to fester in us, when we don't confront it with faith, we open a door for the devil to work."

"What do you mean, 'We open a door for the devil to work'?"

"Trust in God produces peace. It moves us forward; it causes us to push through difficulties. Fear does the opposite. The devil, who hates God and hates his people, is our enemy. He relishes fear because fear creates confusion and produces *dis*trust in God.

"Answer these questions, Jayda: Have your concerns about us moved you forward in faith or pushed you backward? Have your concerns produced peace or confusion?"

"I . . ."

But it was so clear—suddenly so very clear: I was afraid, and my fear had paralyzed me.

"Not forward," I answered. "You're right. In this particular area, I've been stuck for weeks. In fact, from that moment in the cavern when the nanomites offered to save me, I have felt . . . less than human. Maybe less than desirable or—"

My throat stuck on a wry laugh. "And that's kind of ironic, really."

"What is?"

"Saying I feel less than human. Because . . . Jesus, through the nanomites, told me otherwise."

Zander huffed. "I'm lost, Jayda. Back up the boat, please?"

"You're going to find this hard to swallow, but the nanomites had a real, honest, literal 'come to Jesus' experience."

"Say again?"

I couldn't tell Zander about my trip to Washington, D.C., about my role in Vice President Harmon's death and in saving President Jackson—that would open a whole other can of worms.

I came at the conversation I'd had with the nanomites from a different direction.

"The nanomites apologized for . . . something they did—something wrong. They said Jesus spoke to them."

"Jesus *spoke* to them? To *them*? You told me they could hear him when you prayed, but this is beyond strange . . . are you joking?"

Zander inched away so he could better gauge my words.

"No, I'm not joking; this is real. After I surrendered to Jesus, and after the nanocloud revived, the nanomites demanded to know who was 'with us.' They could tell someone was there. They knew Jesus was living in my spirit! And the other day? The other day Jesus confronted them. He . . . explained a few things to them."

"But, but . . . so, if Jesus spoke to the nanomites, what did he say?"

"He, um, for starters, he chastised them for a few distinctly amoral actions. The nanomites told me that after Jesus spoke to them, they understood that, because Jesus was the Creator, he got to make the rules. The nanomites have pledged themselves to follow Jesus."

Zander got up and moved away from the edge of the cliff. He paced nearby. "This is . . . this is incredible. I'm having a tough time taking it in. Accepting it."

"You have no idea." I whispered again, more to myself, "No idea."

"What else? What else did Jesus, er, say to the nanomites?"

"The part relevant to our conversation, to my hang-ups about marriage, has to do with the messages Jesus gave the nanomites for me. They said, *He told us to tell you certain things.*"

"What things?" Zander demanded.

"I'm getting to them. The mites said that Jesus has a calling and plans for me and that they are to help me with them."

"Um, okay."

"This is the 'otherwise' part I mentioned a minute ago. The nanomites said, '*Of most importance, Jesus said to remind you that although we— our five tribes and your one tribe—are physically fused at the molecular level, you are no less human than you were before we came to live in you.*"

"No less human?"

"That's exactly what I said: 'No less human.'"

"I see what you mean, then. Ironic that you see yourself as less than human when Jesus has spoken such a specific word to you."

"Yeah. Thanks for pointing that out."

Grrr.

We didn't talk for a long while. Zander needed time to absorb the information I'd given him—and I needed time to face my fears.

Lord, nothing in all of the universe is greater than you. Nothing is hidden from you. You have overcome all things! Will you show me how to overcome my fears? Will you help me move forward? With or without Zander, Lord, I must be true to you and move forward into what you've called me to do. Please show me, Lord? Show me what to do?

Today was a Monday in early February, and not a lot of people were on the trails. Until just now, we'd been alone on the ridgeline. Then, raucous laughter from down the trail told us others were headed our way.

Minutes later, four young men emerged from the tree line and raced each other to the Rock House. They clambered up onto its roof amid hoots, shouts, and coarse jesting. They were dancing and staggering around on the concrete rooftop, sparring with each other, when one of them noticed us sitting on the rocks on the other side of the stone house.

"Hey. Looka there." His words were somewhat slurred, and he pulled a flat bottle from his pocket and gulped from it. His pals joined him on the roof's edge and stared down on us.

Zander and I knew trouble when we saw it. The hoodlums wore all the markings of a gang. Even though it was only midmorning, it was apparent that they'd been drinking—and still were, if the cans and bottles they carried were any indication.

Zander apprised the situation and grabbed my hand, lifting me to my feet.

"Let's go," Zander ordered in a whisper.

"Hey!" one of the thugs shouted. "You have a good-looking woman, *'mano*. Care if we have a taste?"

The four thugs climbed down from the Rock House and cut us off.

Zander shoved me behind him and hissed, "Don't show them any of your tricks, Ge—Jayda. We don't want to blow your new identity. Just stay back."

To the gangers, he shouted. "Let us pass. We don't want any trouble."

"Yeah, but maybe we do," one of them sneered.

Three of the guys moved toward Zander; another maneuvered to get behind him. I slipped outside their tightening circle and picked up two fist-sized rocks from the rubble-strewn ground.

Right then, I had a fierce desire for my escrima sticks. Rocks would have to do.

"Nano, help my aim be true—but, for heaven's sake, don't let me kill anyone."

Just as the two guys closest to him launched themselves at Zander, I loosed my first rock at the thug behind Zander. With a hollow *thunk*, the rock smacked him in the back of his head. The guy dropped to his knees and forward, onto his face. Out cold.

When the other three saw their comrade fall, they cursed, scrabbled in their pockets, and drew out knives and brass knuckles. Armed and enraged, they threw themselves at Zander.

For maybe fifteen seconds, Zander gave as good as he got. His mouth was bleeding, and he'd bloodied an assailant's nose. As I watched Zander fight, I caught a flash of the life Jesus had saved him from—the same life our attackers were living.

If it had been a fair fight, Zander would have won—but it wasn't a fair fight. He was outnumbered and unarmed. Any moment now, one of the thugs would cut him.

I had to step in.

I hefted my second rock and hurled it. As soon as I released it, I raced forward. The rock took out the mouthy thug, the one who'd first noticed us.

I leapt five feet in the air; my left foot slammed into the next guy's chest. He was wearing a thick parka, so it only knocked him over backward. When he started to get up, I drove my heel into the side of his knee. It *crunched.* He howled. And stayed down.

The last brute danced side to side in front of Zander, slashing out with his knife whenever he saw opportunity. I didn't give him another opportunity.

With open hand, I drove upward, as I would have with my kamagong stick, driving his knife hand up. I whirled the other direction and hit his neck with a slicing blow from my other hand. He toppled to the ground.

Three of our assailants were unconscious; the fourth moaned and thrashed in the dirt, his lower leg bent at an odd angle from the knee.

Blood ran down Zander's chin, and he sucked air in rough, ragged gulps.

He was angry. At me.

"I told you to stay back!"

"It was four to one. You needed help; they would have cut you."

I didn't want to be around when the thugs woke up, so I started for the trailhead. When I reached the tree line, I looked back. The four gangers were still on the ground, but Zander had not moved to follow me.

I waited.

Ten minutes went by before Zander walked my way.

He was still angry when he joined me. "I guess I didn't see this as an area of contention between us, Gemma, but I see now that it's a problem we haven't yet discussed. A big problem."

"*Not Gemma!*" I hissed.

"Whatever you say."

He headed down the trail, and I followed. When we reached the parking lot, we got into the car and started down the winding road. In silence.

We were above the ski area turnoff when Zander spotted a picnic area. He pulled into it. No one else was there.

He parked and found a napkin in his center console and used it to dab at his bleeding lip. He took a look in the rearview mirror and shook his head. "And that thing finally healed up all the way, too."

It was the same lip, split open over the same eye tooth. The same injury he'd received when Mateo and his crew beat him and Abe.

"Maybe you shouldn't lead with your face?" I was trying to insert a joke, a little humor, but Zander wasn't ready for it.

He sighed. "Look, I'm sorry I yelled at you . . ."

"But?" I knew a "but" when I heard one coming.

"*But*, Jayda, I hoped we could put the fighting and violence behind us once Cushing was gone."

"We didn't go looking for that back there," I protested. "We didn't start that!"

"No. I'm not saying we did . . ."

"*But?*"

"I don't know. I'm having trouble handling the idea of you being some sort of martial arts expert, not only able to take care of yourself, but needing to step in and save me. I-I don't like feeling less of a man with you."

"You mean the way I don't like feeling less of a human? And I'm supposed to get over it because Jesus told me to, but you can't?"

Stung, he looked off into the distance. What I'd said was true, but that didn't make it less of a barb.

I knew Zander's Hispanic upbringing brought along specific cultural ideals regarding male and female roles—particularly those of the man as the protector and the woman as the weaker of the two. I hadn't given those cultural mores nearly as much thought and attention as my own discomforts when it came to the nanomites.

"I'm sorry; that was a low blow." I was trying to recall exactly what he'd said to me earlier.

"Um, Zander?"

"Yeah?"

"When we were sitting on the ridgeline, you told me . . . told me I needed to face my reality."

He hesitated before nodding. I think he knew where this was going.

"You said that, instead of confronting truth, I was avoiding the reality I lived in."

I chose my words with care. "Well, I will always be stronger than you, Zander. I will always be faster than you. A better fighter than you. I can channel energy through my body and use it as a formidable weapon. I read and retain everything I see and have immediate access to every scrap of data the nanocloud has amassed.

"None of those things will change. Hiding what I am or ignoring what I am won't change what I am. This is my reality."

He started to say something, but I wasn't done.

"Wait. Please . . . let me finish. The last thing I needed to share with you today, before those jerks interrupted us, was this: The nanomites are not immortal nor are they impervious to injury or damage. The truth is, a few members of the swarm fail every day and, despite its best efforts to repair its fellows, the nanocloud's overall numbers will decrease with time.

"Sure, a few here and a few there mean nothing to a population of twenty-plus trillion! But eventually, it will matter. Eventually, more each day will reach their end of life. The nanomites tell me that the life expectancy of the nanocloud is fifteen years or less before attrition makes it impossible for them to sustain their critical functions—and that's if nothing cataclysmic—such as an EMP or electrical discharge—kills a substantial portion of the nanocloud's population sooner.

"Fifteen years at the outside, Zander. That's all I've got. It may be less."

I'd been as honest as I could be. Covered every facet I could imagine.

"You need to consider, given all my baggage, if you still want to marry me—because that's my reality."

⌘⌘⌘⌘

CHAPTER 34

When Zander dropped me at my apartment, we prayed together. We were uncomfortable with each other, but at least we prayed.

"Lord," Zander whispered. "Help. We need you. Show us, Lord, what to do. You know I'm flawed; you know my struggles. I admit to my failings. But you, Father God, are good and you love us. As high as the heavens are above the earth, so great is your love for us. For me. For Gem—for *Jayda*. So, Lord, we will wait on you and wait on your answers. Amen."

"Amen," I answered.

We parted with no plan other than to wait for God to reveal his direction. I knew God *had* plans for me: The Bible told me he did, Jesus had told me he did, and the nanomites had relayed the same message. Whatever those plans were? They were shrouded and unknown at present.

***

The next morning, my phone rang. As you might imagine, I didn't get many calls. Despite the offers at Bible study, Zander was the only person to whom I'd given my number.

I picked up my phone and looked at it. The caller ID read, Sandia National Laboratories.

Yikes.

"Hello?"

"Am I speaking to Jayda Locke?" the female voice inquired.

"Um, yes. This is she."

How did you get my name and number?

"This is Demi Barela. I'm calling for our new department head, Daniel Bickel. We have an opening for a project controls specialist. Dr. Bickel recommended you. Are you interested in viewing the posting?"

Ms. Barela? As in the woman who got my old job after Dr. Prochanski fired me?

"Ms. Locke?"

"Sorry. You were saying?"

She huffed. "We have an open position for a project controls specialist. Are you interested?"

What would it hurt?

"Yes."

"Please log in to www.sandia.gov/careers and search for Job ID 657107 to view and apply for the posting."

"Thank you."

I spent the next few hours applying for a job at a place I never dreamed I'd be returning to. Later, my phone rang again. This time, the caller ID told me who it was.

"Dr. Bickel?"

"Yes, dear girl. Zander called me this morning to ask how I was doing. Imagine my delight when I heard you had, er, established yourself again here in Albuquerque. Anyway, I wanted to give you a heads-up. Our department has an opening you would be perfect for, so I asked Zander for your new number and gave it to Ms. Barela, my department admin. You should get a call from her about the posting."

I chuckled. "Too late, Dr. Bickel. She already called me, and I already applied."

"Goodness, that woman is efficient." To himself he muttered, "I guess she'd have to be to survive Imogene Cushing."

I hadn't thought of Ms. Barela in that light, but Dr. Bickel was right. I shivered. "Um, by the way, I don't know if you've heard the news yet . . . about General Cushing."

Dr. Bickel knew very well that Cushing was dead. He also knew that her death hadn't been publicized.

"Why? What have you heard?"

"Well, I have it on good authority that she was aboard the Air Force transport that went down over the Atlantic a few weeks back. The authorities may not have . . . widely publicized that her name was on the flight's manifest."

He processed my information in silence before saying, "I see. Yes, I believe I understand."

Then he changed tack. "My dear *Jayda*, after the terrible explosion last year, Sandia rebuilt my laboratory. It is as good as new, and I'm now the department head! Even better, Sandia has reinstated my technicians, Gene and Tony. Someone very high up must have cut through reams of bureaucratic red tape to clear us so quickly, but I received word through the SNL director that our work is not to be overseen or harassed by any member of the military or national security complex."

I thought about President Jackson and the decent man I'd found him to be. Dr. Bickel's good news only added to my high opinion of our President.

Dr. Bickel lowered his voice. "Well, I don't exactly trust one hand of the government to restrain another, so I have decided to redesign my nanomites for medical purposes only. Their construct will be simpler and less accommodating to military repurposing. I will never again create the nanocloud you know so well."

I sighed; I already knew that. "But you have a place for me in your department?"

"Indeed, and I have full hiring discretion. We'll schedule your interview next week and, after you've passed the background checks, we'll bring you on board as quickly as possible."

He paused. "Er, you can pass a background check, can't you?"

"Oh, yes, I believe I can. In spades."

***

"You wanted to see me, Pastor McFee?"

"Yes. Come in, my boy. Sit down."

Zander took the chair the senior pastor offered him. Watched as the kind man studied him. He knew what Pastor McFee saw. Multicolored bruises. A cut lip. Again.

"Zander, I'm a bit worried about you."

"Sir?"

"This is the second time in less than three months that you've had a physical altercation."

"Both were unprovoked attacks, sir. You can hardly fault me for defending myself."

"No, I suppose not." McFee studied his folded hands before he spoke again. "Zander, you are a wonderful Christian man and an excellent associate pastor. I hold you in high regard. The thing is, though, you were also away for several days in December without any communication to us or explanation as to why until afterward."

When Zander opened his mouth, Pastor McFee held up his hand. "I know you said you were on a chaplain's ride-along and were needed. However, right on the heels of that absence, you had a family emergency and did not come in to the office until the following week.

"At that time, one of our elders raised a question about a young woman you were known to associate with, a Miss Gemma Keyes. He asked if she wasn't the same woman who was wanted by the police in the statewide alert—a manhunt that occurred while you were on your ride-along? And then, wasn't she killed a few weeks later, along with her sister?"

"Yes, sir. She was."

"Very strange!" Pastor McFee muttered. "When all that happened so close together, the church board expressed their concerns, not over your sincerity or performance as our associate, but as to whether you have found your rightful ministry calling.

"Then, today, your face testifies of a second physical altercation and, my boy, I will have the unpleasant duty of explaining to the elders of the church, once more, why our congregation will see you Sunday morning with bruises upon your face."

Zander didn't answer. He was mulling over Pastor McFee's words, "Not over your sincerity or performance as our associate, but as to whether you have found your rightful ministry calling."

Something about those words jangled on a nerve.

"Pastor Cruz?"

"Yes, sir?"

"I wish you to do something for me. For yourself."

"Of course, sir."

"I want you to spend some time seeking the Lord about your future. Oh, you're not in danger of being dismissed. The people of DCC love you very much. But I wish you to envision yourself ten years down the line. Where do you see yourself? What vision has the Lord given you for your future? I wish you to ask him for clarity. And I wish you to be honest with yourself. I know you are called to minister, but I also know the life God saved you from. So, I believe it is a matter of where and how the Lord wishes you to minister. Can you prayerfully consider that?"

"Yes, sir. I can."

"Very good. Now go along. I have that blasted board meeting this evening, and I wish to inform them of your new facial embellishments before they find out elsewise. Don't worry. Just pray."

"Thank you, sir. I-I appreciate your confidence in me."

Zander closed Pastor McFee's office door behind him and, hands on his hips, wondered, *Lord? Is there something you haven't told me yet?*

He thought of Gemma. *No, it's Jayda!* he reminded himself.

"Lord, I have this sense that something is coming and is just around the bend. I know you will reveal it in your time and place. Until then, what can I do but trust you?"

⌘⌘⌘⌘

CHAPTER 35

I did okay in the Sandia job interview, passed the background check, and accepted the offer they extended to me. In the run-up to my start date, I entered Jayda's personal information in eQIP, the government's security clearance database, bought a work wardrobe, spent time with Abe and Emilio, attended church on Sundays, and showed up for Friday evening Bible study.

I enjoyed the Friday study very much, and Izzie and I grew closer over those weeks. We started hanging out together. She was like the sister Genie never had been: sweet, caring, funny, considerate. Her walk with God and her willingness to serve wherever she was needed inspired me—and often got me serving alongside her.

On the other hand, Zander and I kept a wary distance from each other. It was as if a giant "off limits" sign hung above our heads that only we could see.

I was praying, and I knew Zander was praying, but the obstacles that stood between us were insurmountable—impossible for either of us to control or change. I caught him staring at me more than once, and it was weird, like we were both waiting for the proverbial "other shoe" to drop, for God to speak a word into our lives that would clear the clouds of confusion away.

Until then, Zander and I would stay at arms' length. Or more.

"Shoot. I thought you and Zander had something going on," Izzie complained.

I shrugged. "If it were God's will for us to 'have something going on,' I'm sure we'd know it."

***

I started my job the last week of February, and I was so excited to be back in the AMEMS department. Dr. Bickel was happy, too. When he gave me the tour of his new laboratory, he was as beside himself as a kid in a candy store.

"My techs and I are building a new 3D printer." Dr. Bickel's pride and enthusiasm were contagious. "We are in the process of redesigning my ion printhead—albeit a simpler, less substantial version. The up-and-coming printhead will produce single-purpose nanobots, custom-manufactured for specific medical treatments. I want to focus our work on helping hurting people."

He pointed to a corner of the lab where sat what looked like a large box draped in white sheeting. "There sits the original 3D printer we left for Cushing to steal before she blew up the lab—minus the ion printhead, of course." He sniggered and whispered, "Cushing had her lab lackeys slaving over that printer for half a year trying to replicate my nanomites. Not only did they not know about my printhead, they didn't even possess the vision to perceive what the printer was lacking."

He waved two technicians over. "Jayda, these are my good friends and longtime co-workers, Gene and Tony. Guys, this is our new project specialist, Jayda Locke."

It was great seeing Gene and Tony again, and it was all I could do to be merely pleasant when I "met" them and shook their hands—when what I really wanted was to grab them and hug them. Tell them how glad I was to see them again.

No, I couldn't do that. Jayda Locke was a stranger to Sandia. I had to smile and tolerate new-employee orientations, email and system training, and the good intentions of those around me who wanted to school me on all things Sandia. However, the advice and pointers were kindly offered, and I was appreciative that people cared.

What was different about Sandia this time around? Me. I was different. I had a softer, more confident edge. I was friendlier and less self-conscious. I wasn't carrying the chip on my shoulder that Gemma had borne most of her life.

The job was certainly easy enough. The nanomites did so many tasks for me and made so many helpful observations, that I finished my work ahead of schedule and found myself often daydreaming. I also experienced moments of *déjà vu*—like when I drove in and out of the parking lot.

From the lot, my eyes turned toward the mountain east of us. It would forever hold a special place in my heart. Seeing its rounded peaks so close again, I felt like my life had come full circle—or that I was living in that crazy movie, *Groundhog Day*, or maybe another zany old film, *50 First Dates*.

I was repeating a singular facet of my life, but this time? This time I would get it right.

While I worked on Dr. Bickel's project parameters and attended meetings to scope the project and its budget, a contingency of the nanomites were often off somewhere else. I would feel them come and go, but I was too engrossed in Dr. Bickel's expectations and my own deadlines to worry about them. The nanomites' curiosity and thirst for learning knew no bounds, so they seemed industrious and content.

Except for missing Zander, I was, too.

***

I'd been at my new job five weeks.

With March mostly gone, spring was in the air. Izzie, Nance, and I started hiking the foothills together on Sunday afternoons, taking Emilio (and all his boyish energy) with us.

Yes, with the advent of spring, the foothills were greening, and Emilio was blooming with the desert flowers. He raced ahead of us girls, clambered up and down boulders and hillsides, jumped off large rocks, ran, yelled, and hollered to his heart's content. I was glad to see him shooting up and filling out on Abe's plain but plentiful cooking: His t-shirts no longer hid the thin rack of ribs that had dismayed me a year ago.

He was a happy boy, and I loved that kid more every day.

With regular paychecks, my bank account was doing all right, too. Every two weeks I passed money for Emilio's incidentals to Abe—even though he protested.

"I get money for bein' a foster parent, and you and Zander make raising this boy simple," he admitted. "Zander picks up Emilio after school most days, runs him around the park or up and down the basketball court, then helps him with his homework. All I got to do is feed him, get him to take a shower, and send him off t' school each day."

I hugged Abe. "I know you do far more than that. You give Emilio the love and security he needs. You are God's gift to him."

I was astonished when Abe kind of teared up. "No, you got it wrong, Jayda. Never had a boy of my own. We weren't blessed with children, Alice and I. After she passed, you and Genie were as close as I got to having kids. Thought you'd lost your mind when you dropped a child in my lap. But now I know. Now I know that Emilio's the son God gave me in my old age, like God gave Abraham a son in his old age. No, I'm not God's gift to Emilio; he's God's gift to me."

***

Like I said, I'd been at my new job for five weeks, give or take a few days. My life was taking on a predictable pattern and shape, and it was a nice shape. I had a living, breathing relationship with God, a great job, dear friends, a young boy I loved, a church that cared for me spiritually, and regular sparring dates with Gus-Gus. It was a good life.

Yeah, *Gus-Gus*.

My VR trainer just would not let up on me! He pushed and prodded me to work harder and perform better. I didn't mind the work, but I didn't "get" his insistence that I keep improving. Improving for what? We'd defeated our enemies. Right?

Then there was Zander. Everything about my life seemed good—except with respect to him. In the five weeks since I'd started my job, we'd seen each other regularly at church, but we'd rarely spoken except to say 'hello,' because a resolution to our impasse seemed nowhere on the horizon.

In fact, as time slipped by, the possibility of an answer for us to be together seemed farther away. Yes, I was still praying, and I believed Zander was praying. But when I asked Jesus about Zander, all I heard was "Wait."

So, I waited.

While I waited, I tried not to worry, but it felt like Zander and I were . . . drifting apart.

The growing detachment between us tore at my heart.

Lord, I trust you! Some days, it was all I could manage.

Still, I couldn't escape the sense that something . . . something important, something momentous, was looming out there. Moving closer.

Lord?

What I didn't know was that when God chooses to act, he can move mountains in minutes and scale the insurmountable in seconds.

***

It was Gamble's first day back in the office following a week of vacation. He was perusing the details of a particularly complex report on his computer when his desk phone rang. Without taking his eyes off the screen, Gamble reached for and lifted the receiver. Put it to his ear.

"Ross Gamble."

"Special Agent Ross Gamble?"

His eyes never left his computer monitor. "Yes, this is he. How can I help you?"

"This is the White House calling, Special Agent Gamble. Please hold for the President."

The Marine in Gamble jerked upright, shot from his chair, and stood to attention. He side-eyed the caller ID.

Yup. Bold as brass, the little screen read, "The White House."

Holy guacamole.

He was on hold, so he edged around his desk, stretching the cord as he went, and closed his office door. Locked it to forestall interruptions. Ran down a litany list of possible reasons why the Commander-in-Chief would be calling *him*—none of which seemed feasible.

It had to be about Gemma.

A moment later, a familiar voice came on the line. "Special Agent Gamble?"

"Yes, sir. Good morning, Mr. President."

"Thank you, and good morning to you also. Well, Agent Gamble, you must be wondering why I'm calling. In point of fact, I've been thinking about you since we last spoke."

"Sir?" They'd spoken exactly once—back in December—so that Gamble could vouch for Gemma's character.

"Yes—oh, by the way, how is our mutual friend?"

It *was* about Gemma.

Ever vigilant to maintain OPSEC (operations security), Gamble did not miss the casual tone of the President's inquiry—nor did he mistake why the President had attached no name or gender to his question.

"Doing well, I believe, sir." An equally oblique reply, although Gamble had not spoken to Gemma since Christmas. She was, he assumed, starting over under a new identity.

"Good. I'm glad to hear it. Well, Special Agent Gamble, as I said, I've been thinking about you. I'd like to meet with you, have you fly in and discuss an idea I have. Would you be amenable to that?"

Gamble swallowed. "Of course, sir."

"Great. I'll have my secretary set it up, shall I? You'll be gone a few days; we'll square it away from the top down so that your SAC authorizes special duty for you. We'll tell him you've been tapped to present a briefing on . . ." Gamble heard the rustle of papers, "the FBI's progress against Mexican drug cartel activity in New Mexico." Your orders will have you fly out of Albuquerque next Monday and report to Quantico on Tuesday. Does that work for you?"

"Yes, sir."

"Very good. Hold the line and my secretary will provide the specifics. Oh. And let's keep this between the two of us, shall we?"

"Understood, sir."

The secretary came on the line and confirmed Gamble's email address. "I am sending your itinerary and instructions now."

When Gamble hung up, he pulled up his email program and stared at it. About three minutes later, an encrypted email appeared in his inbox. He clicked on the email, used his government decryption software and credentials to open it, and scanned the message contents.

Gamble's preconceptions took a nosedive.

He would not be meeting with the President in D.C., and he would not be going to Quantico—nor would he be flying commercial. Rather, he was instructed to catch a specified military flight out of Kirtland Air Force Base into Joint Base Andrews on Monday. Early Tuesday, he would be choppered into Naval Support Facility Thurmont.

Known more widely as Camp David.

Gamble didn't need to be told that the meeting would be very private. Extremely hush-hush.

What have I gotten myself into?

***

Back in Albuquerque the following Thursday afternoon, Gamble placed an ad in the Albuquerque Craigslist. *Wanted: Uncut Gemstones.* Twenty minutes later his phone rang.

"Ross Gamble."

An unfamiliar voice from an unknown number came over the line. "Hi. This is Jayda Locke. Did you call me?"

Gamble balked. "I'm sorry—who?"

"Jayda Locke." For those two words only, he recognized the voice. And got the point.

"Right; yes, I, uh, I called. I'd like to talk to you, Miss, um, Locke. Could we meet?"

He listened to dead air for several seconds before she answered, "Okaaaay."

Her one-word response was drawled in that stranger's voice, but its reluctance was reminiscent of Gemma.

"How about dinner tomorrow evening? My apartment, say, around six o'clock? Oh. You having dinner with me won't be a problem for your boyfriend, will it?"

"He's not—" She stopped herself. "No. It won't."

"Oh, so now he *is* your boyfriend?"

"Shut up, Gamble."

That was Gemma, if not the voice, then the attitude.

"Not a chance. And be on time, Miss Locke; I'm making homemade pizza."

"Well, you'd better make enough. I'll be hungry."

***

I hung up and grinned at my little joke. Then I remembered how Gamble had said, "I would like to talk to you, Miss, um, Locke. Could we meet?"

His summons—masked in a dinner invite—disturbed me more than I wanted to admit. I was *not* looking for any more drama. Good grief. Enough was enough!

Which brought me back to Gamble.

What could he want? I was done running for my life, done with danger and intrigue. Just *done*. And when I remembered that I would have to miss Friday evening Bible study to meet with him, I scowled.

Why on earth did I tell Gamble I'd come?

***

It took some convincing to get Gamble to let me into his apartment. He eyed my altered appearance with distrust. I had to ask the nanomites to temporarily dissolve their disguise before Gamble, with a shudder, conceded that the woman before him was me.

"Gotta say, I don't like it, Gem—I mean Jayda. Too weird for my taste."

I shrugged. "My tiny friends don't much like my new persona either, but it's necessary—and a lot more secure than what WITSEC could have offered me."

Gamble showed me to his dinette table. We chowed down on salad and homemade pizza, but the conversation was awkward. Stilted.

In an effort to improve the mood, Gamble jumped trains. "So, it's Jayda Locke now, huh? How did you arrive at those names?"

He was delaying.

"The pizza was great—thanks for making two, by the way—but why did you ask me here, Agent Gamble? What do you need?"

He sighed and eased into the point of our meeting. "You'll never guess where I spent the early part of this week."

"Cut the guessing games, Gamble."

"Fine. All right. Here it is." He rubbed his jaw. "I got an interesting call last week and flew out of Albuquerque Monday." He slanted a look at me to gauge my reaction. "I spent Tuesday at Camp David."

With a sinking feeling, I stared at Gamble.

"I met with the President and the head of his protective detail, Axel Kennedy."

I wet my lips; the pizza in my stomach lurched uneasily. "I suppose you're going to tell me why."

Gamble nodded. "First, I want to assure you that your, um, exploits in D.C. remain known only to the President, the First Lady, and Kennedy. And me."

"They told you . . . everything?"

"Not everything, and not before I signed a sworn affidavit on the classification of our conversation. Basically, if I want to avoid a one-way, all-expenses-paid, permanent relocation to federal lockup, I'll keep my trap shut.

"And just for your ease of mind, I swept this apartment for bugs this morning, and have two gadgets in place: one generates white noise, the other guarantees no one could be eavesdropping using parabolic listening devices."

We, too, have swept the area; no one is watching or listening.

"Thank you, Nano."

I slowly and methodically folded my napkin until it looked like an origami work of art, but my pulse was galloping through my veins. "What . . . did the President want?"

He leaned toward me. "He wished me to convey his thanks to you for your assistance in December. He didn't elaborate on the specifics of the assistance you provided, only that your service averted a national crisis—and that the crisis had something to do with the Vice President. From that, I took it to mean that Harmon's death wasn't from natural causes, after all?"

Gamble searched my face, probing for answers. He found nothing but the poker face I'd perfected as Gemma Keyes.

"The President asked me to tell you that, although the head of the snake was severed, he has uncovered evidence of co-conspirators in the NSA and on the outside of the government who continue to plot against him. The evidence suggests that intelligence gathering is being weaponized to use against the President's key allies in the government—all with the purpose of taking down his administration.

"The situation has grown particularly dicey. The single contact whom the President trusted—an individual placed high within the NSA—has disappeared. This means the President is now without eyes or ears on the inside. Meanwhile, every move he makes is watched—perhaps by treasonous elements within the intelligence community using illegal methods to spy upon him. The President doesn't know who he can trust, and Axel Kennedy is wound tighter than a drum. I think he fears for the President's life."

My brow furrowed in concern for Robert and Maddie Jackson.

"The President is growing desperate, Jayda. He needs someone who can infiltrate the NSA's entrenched bureaucracy and provide him with the evidence he needs to clean out that nest of vipers. Someone who can defeat every kind of security, go wherever she wants, search every air-gapped computer, and listen in on the most private of conversations."

"H-he wants me?"

Gamble nodded. "Yes. He proposes providing you with a bogus identity and slipping you inside the NSA in a low-level position. Said you and your unique 'skills' could handle the rest from there. But I think—"

And here Gamble hesitated. "—I think Jayda Locke is the perfect bogus identity. You even have the right mix of employment skills and experience the NSA might desire."

I said nothing, but it felt like the bottom was falling out from under my perfectly reconstructed world.

"The President was stumped, however, at how to ensure that the NSA would hire you—especially within a tight time frame. I told him to leave that to you, that you and your little friends could manage it. Am I right?"

I nodded. "If. If I were to agree to the President's plan."

"Let me lay it out for you, er, Jayda. The President wants to transfer me to the D.C. area. Special assignment. We—you and I—would work together."

"We? How?"

"I would be your handler, convey instructions to you, provide whatever logistics you needed, and communicate your information to the President. You and I have worked together; I think we make a good team, don't you?"

I stared at the floor. "I'm not looking to make a career change, Gamble. I just started a good job, and Zander and I . . . well, we've been talking about getting married."

"Congratulations. I'm glad you guys finally figured it out."

"No. No, we haven't. That's the problem. We're trying to work out how to deal with my 'condition.' Frankly, it's a total wet blanket on our relationship. A deal breaker, so to speak, for multiple reasons."

Lord, I want Zander to court me, have our friends watch us fall in love and get engaged. Get married. This wouldn't move us closer—it would force us apart!

I must have looked as morose as I felt, because the kind and compassionate Gamble showed himself.

"I'm sorry. I hadn't thought about the relationship problems your, er, 'condition' might create."

"You have no idea. And I've just established myself as Jayda Locke. If my cover is blown, do you know how difficult it would be to start over? Again? Right now, only a handful of people know my new identity. I want and need to keep my ID and 'condition' confined to that small group. It's the best way to keep me and those I care about safe. You know that old saying, 'The only people I trust are you and me—and I'm not sure about you'?"

Gamble nodded his agreement. "The President agrees with that proverb. That's why he called me himself. Outside of him and Kennedy, not a single other person will know that we've planted you in the NSA. Nor will anyone suspect your ability to hack the NSA from within or turn invisible and penetrate their most secure areas."

I shook my head. "Nope. Sorry, Gamble, but no. I can't run off on Zander. We . . . we're praying about our relationship and waiting for God to answer. Besides, what you propose is way out of my league."

Gamble sighed and sat back. "All right. I hear you. But I'm going to wait a few days before I inform the President of your decision—just in case you change your mind."

"Don't hold your breath," I muttered.

***

I went home then but couldn't settle down. What the President asked of me was scary. Terrifying! What did I know about being a spy—and a spy among the most elite of spies at that? The more I thought about it, the more anxious I grew. Although I wished Robert Jackson well, I was relieved that I'd turned down his request.

I headed for the dojo, hoping Gus-Gus would pound the apprehension right out of me—I was certainly looking forward to using *him* as a stress-reducing punching bag. Nothing like a full-on, no-holds-barred fight to banish every thought from the mind except survival!

Gus-Gus and I punched, hit, pummeled, hammered, sliced, clobbered, and otherwise tried to kill each other until Gus-Gus said we were done. I must have exhausted my excess stock of nervous energy, because when I collapsed into bed that night, I dropped into a profound sleep.

And dreamed.

The dream was a vivid, full-color-spectrum affair, lush with cinematic pageantry. The scene was as realistic and intoxicating as it was exotic in beauty and setting.

I stood at the entrance to a long hall, a vaulted ceiling high above my head. Both sides of the hall were peopled by men clothed in strange headdresses and long, flowing gowns of silks and brocades. Conversations up and down the hall were conducted in reverent and hushed tones, but I did not understand a word spoken: The language was foreign to me.

Then I realized that I was the only woman present—and when they saw me standing in the hall's entranceway, all dialogue ceased.

At the far end of the hall were marbled steps that rose to a dais. In the center of the dais, a ginormous statue of a rearing lion sheltered a bejeweled chair. Powerful wings, outspread in flight, sprouted from the lion's back. The lion's mouth roared and bared fearsome fangs; his sharp claws were extended as a canopy over the glittering chair.

Within the lion's shadow, a man wearing a crown sat upon the throne.

Whispers and hisses—directed at me—intruded into the disapproving hush. The jeering condemnation grew until the king stood and, with his golden scepter extended, beckoned to me.

I was frightened to walk the long, lonely distance to the throne. Every man lining the great hall viewed me with suspicion or speculation; some eyed me with little-disguised hatred. I was afraid to answer the king's summons—until a voice whispered, *For such a time as this.*

I sat up in bed gasping for air.

Were you dreaming?

"Yes, Nano."

Was it an important dream?

"Perhaps." While the vivid scene replayed behind my eyelids, I scribbled all I remembered, particularly the whispered words I heard before I woke:

For such a time as this.

The phrase seemed . . . familiar. I closed my eyes and attempted to place it.

There! I nodded. "Yes. I remember where I've read it. Lord? What are you saying?"

Dare to trust me, Jayda.

A thrill washed over me. "Jesus?"

Those who know me, dare to trust me.

"Yes! Yes, I trust you, Lord. Show me what you wish me to do, and I will do it."

The night held no more sleep for me, but morning wasn't far off. I drew my Bible toward me and spent the next hours reading the Book of Esther and praying over the President's appeal.

If I had to give Zander up, if that was what the Lord required, I would find the strength to do so.

⌘⌘⌘⌘

CHAPTER 36

I got up with the sunrise. After the long night, I planned a lazy Saturday. A day for myself to putter around the house, do laundry, run errands. To continue to mull over the decision before me.

Gemma Keyes.

Grrr!

The nanomites knew not to call me Gemma—I'd told them not to repeatedly—but they didn't like it. They confirmed their passive-aggressive disapproval *not* by refusing to call me Jayda but by refusing to use any form of address at all.

And yet here they were, bringing up a dead woman's name. Again.

"Nano. I've asked you not to call me that, remember?"

We remember everything, Gemma Keyes.

"Then stop it. Please."

It is important that we talk to you, Gemma Keyes.

Sigh

Sometimes it felt like I was reasoning with a two-year-old.

I dropped into a chair. So much for my lazy day off.

"All right. Shoot."

Gemma Keyes, we have acquired significant insight into human interactions since we came to live in you.

I shrugged. "Okay."

Through our observations of you and Dr. Bickel and your relationships with other humans, we have determined that sentiment is integral to the human condition, that emotional equilibrium is important to optimal human performance.

I hadn't heard the "optimal" bit in a while.

"And yet, you once considered removing my emotions."

I wasn't likely to forget that day.

We considered—and rejected—that proposition, Gemma Keyes. We have since learned that many valuable human characteristics are based in emotion. Among those characteristics with value are trust, respect, friendship, and love.

"Huh." I was mildly surprised. "Love? You think love is important?"

Indeed. We have discovered that, while a logic- and data-driven nanocloud is efficient, it lacks . . . something. Jesus has been integral to our understanding of love and other human behaviors. His input has been particularly vital in determining which behaviors are good and which are bad. We initially believed right and wrong to be subjective, arbitrary terms; we know differently now.

They had my attention.

We have also witnessed how the close bond two people share resembles that of the connection between our five tribes. Humans call that closeness love. When humans experience love, they do not wish to be apart. We of the nanocloud also do not wish to be separated from each other; when we are apart, we experience . . . loss.

We have no word that adequately expresses this sense of incompleteness. If we were human, we might attach emotional significance to this "feeling."

It sounded to me like the nanomites were working awfully hard to avoid using that last word, "feeling." Then their next statements stole my breath away.

Gemma Keyes, we believe you are experiencing such a sense of loss. We see you are separated from Zander. We know you love Zander. We know you are grieving. We can only imagine how difficult it is for you to bear this separation.

I licked my lips. I didn't know what to say. Didn't like having them in my business.

Gemma Keyes, we have a proposal.

"You what?"

We propose a solution, Gemma Keyes

A light tapping on my apartment door interrupted us.

I peered through the peephole and gaped.

Zander.

I cracked the door. "Zander? What are you doing here? It's, um, it's barely morning."

"Well, I got this weird text."

I let him in. "A text? From whom?"

"I'm pretty sure it's from the nanomites."

"What?"

"Yeah. I tried to message the sender back, but my response wouldn't go. Tried to call the sender, too, but there's no number attached to the text. Anyway, it could only have been from the nanomites and, apparently, they don't need a phone to send a text."

He paused a beat. "Want to see it?"

"The text?"

"Yup."

He held out his phone and I took it. Gawked at the message.

> Zander Cruz, Gemma Keyes is sad when she is separated from you. We understand this phenomenon. We are dissatisfied when we are separated. We are also dissatisfied when Gemma Keyes is sad.

"Scroll down to the next bit."

I scrolled to the second part of the message—and my mouth fell open.

> Since we believe it is in keeping with human tradition, we wish to propose to you:
>
> ZANDER CRUZ, WILL YOU MARRY GEMMA KEYES?

I had scarcely finished reading the text when Zander flinched and stepped back.

He pointed. "What is that?"

I looked up and saw . . . the nanocloud rising. It ascended from me, its millions and billions and trillions of bunched nanomites sparkling in a blue and silver miasma, floating up and outward, reaching for Zander.

He retreated until his back was against the front door. He tried to open the door, but the handle wouldn't budge.

Gemma Keyes. Tell Zander to come closer to us.

"Zander. The nanomites want you to come, er, closer. To me."

"What for?"

"I think . . . I'm guessing that they want to talk to you."

The cloud continued to expand, and I grew lightheaded as it lifted from me.

I turned inward and took inventory. Not all of the nanomites were leaving me, of course, but a huge segment was. A larger population than I'd expected. Confused, I squinted and ran some calculations.

The numbers . . . were off.

Way off.

Gemma Keyes. Tell Zander to come closer to us.

"Zander, they are asking for you to come over here."

After finding himself locked inside my apartment, Zander had fled to the other side of the room. His tight, angry mouth reflected his reluctance to comply with the nanomites' request.

"Only if they promise . . . not to do anything to me."

Gemma Keyes. Tell Zander we promise.

"They promise, Zander."

"Sure, pal," he spat, procrastinating.

"Come on, Zander. They won't bite."

"Can you prove that?" Still uneasy, he shuffled toward me.

As I reached out my hand to him and he grasped it, the nanocloud descended on us. Surrounded and enveloped us. The shimmering beauty of the cloud as it winked and sparkled about and between us was extraordinary. Breathtaking. It was like standing on the foamy beach of an ocean at sunrise, cossetted in a warm, pulsing mist shot through by the rays of the morning sun.

And still the cloud built and grew. I was lost in its exquisite haze; I was anchorless. Floating, save for Zander's fingers grasping mine.

Gemma Keyes. Months ago, we spoke to you of our encounter with Jesus. He taught us many things that day, and we surrendered our allegiance to him, to the one Tribe of Jesus.

Zander gripped my hand harder—because, within the mist, we could both hear the nanomites.

At that time, Gemma Keyes, Jesus asked us to tell you that he has plans for you. He said that we were to help you with those plans. Jesus spoke of many things with us; however, we were not to reveal everything to you. We were not to speak of certain things until a later date.

That time is now.

Gemma Keyes and Zander Cruz, Jesus has plans for you. The calling he spoke of earlier is for both of you. We are to help you. For many weeks now, we have been careful to follow Jesus' instructions. We have been preparing.

The cloud dropped into silence. It felt like the nanomites had run out of words or that they lacked the breath to speak.

Into the hush, I asked, "Nano, how . . . how have you been preparing?"

The nanocloud expanded and contracted—an exhalation. A troubled sigh?

Jesus said you were not to be a tribe with us, Gemma Keyes. Therefore, we are not six, but five. Our five are one nanocloud. We are the only one of our kind—but we were wrong when we said there would never be more of us. Jesus made a way for us to procreate, to construct brethren.

As comprehension struck me, I gasped. "You! You've been in the AMEMS lab. While I've been working, you've been working!"

You are correct, Gemma Keyes. We discovered a clean and sealed environment inside Dr. Bickel's discarded 3D printer. We powered the printer and generated an atmosphere suitable for constructing more of us. We borrowed the liquid materials we needed from elsewhere in the lab to lay down layers on the substrate within the printer.

Because the disused printer is covered in a drop cloth, no one in the lab has noticed the activity within its compartment.

That was not possible. Dr. Bickel had said so!

"But . . . but the ion printhead?"

Unnecessary, Gemma Keyes. Our members add individual ions of each required material as they are needed.

Zander, his eyes wide, struggled to keep up. "Er, Nano, do you mean . . . do you mean you are making more, er, fellow nanomites?"

As instructed, we have already done so, Zander Cruz.

As instructed?

Zander persisted. "But how many more? How many new nanomites have you made?"

The cloud exhaled and lapsed again into silence—and I experienced their pain. The nanomites were mourning. I didn't understand why.

"Nano! What is wrong? What are you not telling us?"

Gemma Keyes and Zander Cruz, Jesus is the creator and ruler. He chooses what is best for those who belong to him. Jesus has plans for both of you. We are to help you.

I voiced the million-dollar question. "What plans, Nano?"

This is not for us to say. Jesus will lead you. We are to prepare you.

Zander and I stared at each other within the swirling cloud, our shared uneasiness evident: We had no idea what the nanomites were talking about.

"Uh, Nano. Can you be more explicit?"

Gemma Keyes and Zander Cruz, we listened to your conversation when you were upon the mountain. You wish to marry but have grave concerns . . . because of us. We listened to your concerns, and we understood how we are an impediment to your union. Your concerns grieved us. However, Jesus has shown us what to do. He has promised to give us the strength to bear it.

"Bear what? What has he asked you to do?"

They ignored my questions.

Jesus has shown us what to do. Gemma Keyes and Zander Cruz, we make you this assurance: If you marry, we will honor your requests for privacy and will close ourselves off from you. We will ask no prying questions and make no absurd observations. Jesus tells us privacy is necessary for this sacred time and space; it is to be shared only between husband and wife. Therefore, when you say the words, "Nano, Lights Out," we will turn away from you.

"Lights out?" Code words for—

All the glittery goo that sparkled around us could not hide the hot embarrassment that rushed up my neck into my face.

We apologize for being direct, Gemma Keyes; however, we must alleviate your concerns so that you have no reservations regarding our proposal—and so we can proceed.

Zander spoke. "You didn't answer Gemma's question. What are you not telling us? How does your proposal affect you, Nano?"

Before we explain, we must address your remaining concerns, Gemma Keyes and Zander Cruz.

"Uh, okay," Zander answered.

My face was still burning from the nanomites' bald assurances around "sacred time and space."

Gemma Keyes, your second concern was regarding children.

"Yes," I whispered. I feared what they would say next.

You are correct in your assumption that you cannot bear children. Our joining with your body impacted your endocrine functions. Specific to your supposition, our merge sped up your metabolism, enabling you to become an optimal fighter.

Your accelerated metabolism increased the rate at which your ovaries produced fertile eggs. Your ovaries have depleted your supply of ovum by 91.7 percent. For this, we are profoundly sorry.

I sagged; Zander's arms caught and held me.

"It's all right, Gemma. It's all right. It will be okay," he murmured again and again.

"B-but I wanted to give you children! You long for a family!"

"I want you, Gemma. If we can't have our own children, we'll adopt. And we have Emilio. It will be all right. Jesus will sustain us."

Gemma Keyes, we are indeed sorry for this blunder, another unanticipated outcome of our merge and your subsequent transformation. As with our other blunders, we cannot undo or mitigate this wrong we have done you.

They paused, then added, *We accept that you must hate us.*

Hate? Hate the nanomites? I didn't hate them. At the moment, all I felt was sorrow.

Zander spoke. "Nano. I recognize the conundrum you are expressing. Although you are not human, you are experiencing the plight of this fallen world and the despair of the human condition. All humans discover that their best efforts to do what is right are flawed, that their actions frequently have harmful, unintended consequences.

"People are shocked to discover that their 'good' falls short of God's perfection—and they are appalled to learn that the capacity to commit evil lurks within them. Like you, we humans are unable to fix much of the wrong we do."

"That's why we need Jesus," I whispered. "It is why he died. His lifeblood pays for our failings and covers our wrong. It is why I don't hate you, Nano. I cannot hate you for what I, too, have done. No, Nano. I don't hate you; I forgive you."

At my words, the cloud swelled and brightened. The mist sparkled and, over our heads, fonts of lights collided, ignited, and burst like miniature aerials, flinging forth explosions of twinkling color and radiance.

Thank you, Gemma Keyes. You are most generous, and we are relieved. Now we wish to provide you with a better answer to your third concern.

"My third?" I'd lost track. Information overload.

We told you that the nanocloud's longevity was finite, that over the years, as our members declined, so the nanocloud would decline. This is true; however, we now have a means to replenish our numbers. With Dr. Bickel's printer, we can maintain the nanocloud at optimal performance. If you request that he move the printer to a safe location, you can be assured of achieving optimal life expectancy—approximately 81.2 years if you do not suffer a traumatic injury we are unable to alleviate.

Optimal life expectancy. Not fifteen years, but . . . well, as long as God gave me.

"This . . . this is good news," I admitted.

"Very," Zander said, "but why are you making more nanomites now? Gemma doesn't need them yet. What are they for?"

They are for you, Zander Cruz.

"They—*what?*"

The newborn nanomites are for you, Zander Cruz. Jesus asked us to make as many for you as presently abide with Gemma Keyes. This is part of the plans Jesus has for you and Gemma Keyes. You will be equals in strength, endurance, and ability. It overcomes the last obstacle to your union.

The nanomites were giving themselves to Zander. They were offering to fully merge with him as they had with me. No—that wasn't quite it. They had labored to *double* the nanocloud in size; they—

I got it before Zander did.

I understood.

They were offering to *split* the super-sized cloud and give half to Zander.

"Um, Nano? You . . . you don't like to be apart. You said so yourself. Won't it be painful for you to give half the nanocloud to Zander?"

The color in the mist drained away, fading to infinite shades and shadows of grays.

We choose to do what Jesus has asked of us, Gemma Keyes. He has promised to give us the strength to bear it.

"But—"

If Zander accepts our offer, our nanocloud will become two nanoclouds. Jesus says this is love: When we are willing to lay down our life for a friend. We will, with Jesus' help, accept this difficult step and adapt to it. And, if you and Zander marry, Jesus says you will be "one." Our two will not always be apart. We will frequently be together.

We are willing to do this for you, Gemma Keyes. We wish for you to be happy.

I placed my hands on my face and sobbed into them.

The nanomites! They loved me! They were willing to divide, to separate, so that Zander and I could be together. They were willing to suffer for my happiness.

"Zander . . . what the nanomites are offering comes at terrible cost to them. It would be a distressing sacrifice."

"I-I think I understand. But they keep saying their proposal is 'part of Jesus' plan.' What does that mean? What does he expect of us when you and I are 'equals in strength, endurance, and ability'? What about my ministry, my work at the church? How does this all fit together?"

"It has to be what President Jackson asked of me."

"*The* President Jackson?"

"Is there another? Still living, I mean." I blew out a breath. "Listen, we need to talk. I-I have things to tell you."

With the nanocloud spread like a canopy over us, Zander and I sat cross-legged on my carpet, and I explained how the nanomites and I had slipped into the SCIF and overheard Vice President Harmon's plan to assassinate Robert Jackson and usurp the presidency.

"I left for Washington that evening. The next day, under the nanomites' cover of invisibility and with their help to spoof the Secret Service's security systems, I entered the White House. I waited in the Residence for the President and First Lady to return from an evening out. I appeared to the President and asked if he would give me a minute of his time."

I shouldn't have expected Zander to stay sitting. By the time I got to "waited in the Residence," he was on his feet, pacing.

"You just waltzed into the White House and presented yourself to the President."

"Well, obviously, you're getting the condensed version."

"And he didn't call the Secret Service? Raise the alarm?"

"Uh, well, he *might* have tried to . . ."

"Gemma! You laid hands on the President?"

"No. No, I did not," I huffed. "The nanomites did."

Zander smacked his forehead. "Oh! Well! Then that's all right."

I folded my arms. "Stop it. I saved President Jackson's life. He's grateful."

Zander did stop. "Wait. Is that when . . . Is that when Harmon died?"

I shuddered. Not the time to get into the nanomites' amoral actions. Besides, their mistakes were forgiven. Paid for. As far as the east is from the west. All that.

"Yes. Again, we don't have time for the blow-by-blow."

"But you saved the President's life?"

"Yes; the nanomites and I did."

"Wow." Zander's expression was inscrutable, but I thought I detected a glint of admiration. He managed to sit again and take my hand. "So, what did you mean by, 'It has to be what President Jackson asked of me.' What does the President want of you?"

I launched into Gamble's invitation to dinner last evening, the President's appeal for help (relayed by Gamble), and my polite refusal. Forestalling more questions, I added, "However, you should know that I'm reconsidering my decision. Last night I had a dream—from the Lord."

I repeated the dream sequence in detail. It was easy, since the scenario was engraved on my gray matter—every minute facet and element, ending with, "Just as the king stretched his scepter toward me, a voice said, *For such a time as this.*"

"Esther. That is a direct quote from the Book of Esther."

"Right. I couldn't place it at first, but it didn't take long for me to remember. I spent the rest of the night reading that book and praying. I asked the Lord, 'What are you telling me?'"

"Did he answer?"

"Yes, Zander, he did. He said, *Dare to trust me, Jayda.* And when I asked, 'Jesus?' he added, *Those who know me, dare to trust me.*"

"And then?"

"Then I said, 'Yes, I trust you, Lord. Show me what you wish me to do, and I will do it.'"

Tears threatened to undo me, so I looked at the floor. "I told the Lord that if I had to give you up, if that was what he required, I would do it."

"Right answer, Gemma. But now? With the nanomites' offer? Do you think that's what the Lord wants? For you to give me up?"

"No, but it's . . . it's a huge step on your part, an irrevocable decision."

"Yes, it is. On the other hand, I believe the nanomites. I believe the Lord told them to make me this offer. I think he wants both of us to help the President."

Zander gathered me in his arms. "Let's pray, Gemma."

"It's Jayda. But, yes. Let's pray."

He tipped my chin up and brushed the tears from my eyes. "Yes. *Jayda*. From here on out, you are my sweet *Jayda*—and this is the strangest premarital counseling session ever."

"Ever!" I echoed.

Looking up into the cloud, Zander asked, "When do you need our answer, Nano?"

Zander Cruz, no deadline exists but the one Jesus will speak to you.

The nanocloud dissipated; I felt the nanomites flowing back into me. Never had I welcomed their presence more; never had they been so dear.

When the cloud was gone from our sight, Zander and I remained locked in an embrace.

For a long time.

⌘⌘⌘⌘

CHAPTER 37

We prayed, we talked for hours, we prayed more. We both felt a sense of urgency, that the President's situation was tenuous. And, even before we spoke of it, I knew we had, individually, received the confirmation we sought.

"Jayda. I'm ready."

"You've decided, then? You will have to leave your church."

"Yes, and I can't say I'm all that surprised. When I showed up in the church office all banged up for the second time, Pastor McFee encouraged me to seek the Lord and ask for clarity. For vision. He knew I was called to minister—but it was a matter of where and how. He thought I should ask the Lord for guidance."

"Wow."

"Jayda, what do you envision for us after . . . after we help the President uncover the conspiracy against him?"

I smiled wide. "So many things! We could do a lot of good, Zander, in many places and ways."

"That's what I hoped you would say."

He dug around in his pocket, looking sheepish for a second. "I'd really planned to do this differently, with all the romantic traditions."

My heart thudded. Raced. Skipped around in my chest.

Zander pulled a little box from the pocket of his jeans. "I bought this in faith. I really believed the Lord would make a way for us to be together, so when I saw it, the perfect ring, I bought it."

He opened the box and showed me the narrow band and its single marquise-cut diamond. "The wedding band has two stones that, when joined with the engagement ring, sit on opposite sides of this center diamond. Two stones, you and I, joined by the Lord as the center of our lives."

"It's perfect, Zander. So beautiful."

"Gemma Keyes—sorry. *Jayda Locke*, will you marry me? Will you receive this ring as the token of my love?"

"I will, Zander. With all my heart."

He slipped the ring on my finger and its fire sparkled there.

When Zander had drawn the box from his pocket, the nanomites, our ever-present sentinels, had begun to again flow from me, forming their cloud over us. When Zander asked if I would marry him and I said yes, they sang over us, and their melodious hum overflowed the cloud and spilled into the room. I can't explain other than to say that their song blended the best of all bells, carillons, and chimes and the most poignant of strings into a symphony of beauty.

"I've heard this before!" Zander marveled. "When we were in the cavern."

"Yes. They are singing, Zander, like they did when I gave them permission to transform me."

"Then, it's fitting they should sing now."

I nodded. "I should caution you, Zander. Physically, it will be difficult. You . . . you'll be sick for a day or two. Fierce headache. Fever. Vomiting."

He swallowed. "Great."

"I'll stay with you—and the nanomites will do as much as possible to alleviate the discomfort."

"Good to know."

He didn't rush into it, and I was glad he took his time. He wandered off into a corner of the living room by himself to prepare himself—while I let him have his space. I knew he'd never have "alone" time again. I didn't want to disturb him while he made his peace with that reality.

About half an hour later, he came back. "I'm ready, Jayda—but first? First, I want to kiss you. In private."

Laughing, we synced our words. "Nano? Lights Out!"

***

The transition was rough—rougher than mine had been since mine had taken place in two stages—and it took longer. I hated watching Zander suffer and—typical male that he was!—he demonstrated what a grouch he could be when he was sick. As his fever raged, he alternately froze and sweated, huddled under mounds of blankets or threw them off. He suffered nausea and violent vomiting. Body aches and headaches. Streams of blood from his nostrils with no warning. More vomiting.

Knowing the fiery trial he was undergoing, I kept vigil with him, administering pain relievers, keeping him hydrated, and helping him to the bathroom when his stomach gave way.

The pain and sickness went on through the night without abatement. Around eight o'clock the next morning, Sunday, I grabbed Zander's phone and texted Pastor McFee:

Pastor McFee, experiencing flu-like symptoms, fever, nausea, vomiting. Please excuse. Do not think it wise to come to church.

The reply came minutes later.

Agree. Will muddle along without you. Praying for your
good health.

"Thank you," I murmured.

I kept vigil over Zander throughout the day and that night, catching a little sleep here and there. It was early Monday when his symptoms eased. Zander curled up on the couch and slipped into a semi-comatose state. If he followed the pattern I experienced, he would, in another twelve or fifteen hours, wake with the strength of the nanomites' fusion coursing through his veins.

With Zander sleeping, I hoped the worst of it was over. While he recovered on the couch, I stepped into the kitchen and made a call.

"Gamble?"

"Miss Locke?"

"Yes. Um, listen. I've had a change of heart with regards to what we, er, discussed Friday."

Gamble's enthusiasm jumped a notch. "I can't tell you how glad I am to hear it—and how grateful I am that I don't have to make a certain phone call. I was dreading it."

"I can imagine, but I also need to add a caveat to my agreement."

"Oh?"

"Two of us are accepting the offer. Two of us will be, um, involved. Actively involved."

Gamble breathed into the phone. "Two. As in two like you?"

"Yes. You've got it."

He was quiet for a minute, but then he chuckled. "Cannot for the life of me figure out how you arranged that, but my guess is that it resolves a boatload of relationship issues?"

"Uh, why, yes, it does. Thanks for your perception."

"*Mazel tov!* I don't think there will be any objections, but before I make my call, let's plan to meet tomorrow."

"I think the day after."

"Roger that."

We set up a meeting time and place and hung up. I spent the long day watching over Zander, thinking of our future together, and praying.

Lord, you know you're amazing, don't you?

***

Late Monday evening, Zander stirred and groaned. I went to him, sat on the edge of the couch.

"How do you feel?"

"Like I puked up my toenails."

Zander Cruz, it is not possible to puke up one's toenails, nor is it possible to know what that feels like.

"Yeah? Well, I suggest you don't get on my bad side on the first day, Nano."

A good point, Zander Cruz. We are glad to see you recovering.

"Me, too, Nano. Me, too."

I heard their conversation and knew what it meant: The division of the nanocloud was complete. A new and separate nanocloud had been birthed.

***

We met with Gamble on Wednesday and worked out logistics. He, in turn, returned the President's call.

During Zander's transition, I had brainstormed with the nanomites to come up with the best way to secure a foothold within the NSA. The nanomites infiltrated the NSA's public website and their human resources database, and we reviewed hundreds of federal and contractor position descriptions until we settled on a departmental administrative assistant posting (contractor) that had closed two Fridays past.

The nanomites made the case that if I applied to an open position, the hire could not happen, at a minimum, for a month, with a start date at least two weeks after that.

Jayda Locke, we inserted your application and résumé for the closed position into the hiring database and generated favorable comments on it. The interviews took place last week. We added an interview with you at the end of the schedule.

"I don't see how that helps me since I wasn't there."

We identified the highest scoring interviewee and used the criteria for which she scored best to create interview notes for you. Your interview now scores higher than hers did. We concluded by generating a hiring recommendation in the contractor's HR database. You should receive a phone call and an offer today or tomorrow.

"But, no one is going to remember interviewing me!"

They do not remember at present, but they will when you appear for your orientation, Jayda Locke.

"Jedi mind tricks," I grumbled.

Effective and efficient, came their snarky riposte.

At Friday's Bible study, I revealed to the group that I'd accepted a position in Maryland and would be moving in three weeks. Izzie already knew and was putting on a brave face.

She just didn't know everything.

Over the sighs and groans of the single guys, Zander made his own announcement. "Hold up, folks. I have something to say, too: This morning I tendered my two-week notice to Pastor McFee."

That brought on a shocked silence and one loud, "Oh, wow!"

Zander shrugged and grinned. "You see, I can't let the woman I love go off to Maryland by herself, so I've asked Jayda to marry me. Our wedding is two Sundays from now after the morning service. You're all invited."

Beside me, Izzie gasped in delight. "Jayda! I knew it, I knew it, I knew it!"

"Did not!" I teased her, "but I know you hoped—and I'm so glad you did. We're going to be sisters!"

"But two weeks? We don't have much time to plan your wedding—and you haven't met our parents!"

"No, but we've already talked to them. They have given us their blessing."

I pulled at the chain around my neck, unhooked my engagement ring, slipped it on my hand, and showed it around. It hardly felt real.

Zander and I were getting married.

***

Our wedding was beautiful. Perfect.

I walked down the aisle on Abe's arm, and my teary eyes swept over the sanctuary, seeing my many new friends in Christ. I was thinking about Aunt Lucy and the seeds she'd sown into my wounded young life. It had taken years, but those seeds had borne good fruit.

Izzie walked before us, my maid of honor. Down at the front, Pastor McFee waited on us. Abe was taking his sweet time, though.

"Only daughter I get to walk down the aisle, you know. Gonna savor it," he warned me as we set out.

"Well, don't be surprised if Zander runs down here and starts pushing."

Abe laughed. "That's a good man you've got there, Ge—*Jayda*. I'm mighty proud of both of you."

I stopped right where we were and kissed him on the cheek. "I love you so much, Abe. You've always been there for me, even when I was such a brat. Thank you."

Abe and I choked back our tears and somehow got moving again.

I lifted my eyes to the front of the church. Zander! There he was—absolutely stunning in his gray tuxedo and charcoal tie. The brilliant white of his shirt contrasted with his dark good looks. Emilio stood by his side, dressed in a matching tux, a shy grin tugging at his mouth.

Zander had told Emilio that he would have no one else in the world stand up with him as his best man. It took a little of the sting out of our coming departure. Hopefully, our assignment wouldn't take long, and we'd be coming back to Albuquerque to help Abe raise our boy.

I didn't know what lay ahead for us; neither did Zander. Whatever came, we'd face it together.

Us and the Lord.

Oh, yeah. And the nanomites.

⌘⌘⌘⌘

POSTSCRIPT

Zander and I unhitched our car from the small U-Haul truck and began unloading our stuff into our Maryland apartment. We hadn't brought much from Albuquerque, just the basics—and a blessed *ton* of wedding gifts from family, friends, and DCC.

We accomplished the unload in record time. Yup. Easy-peasy with two nano-charged people.

"All this energy is great, but now I'm starved," Zander complained.

"Yeah, me, too. Shall we return the truck and get groceries after?"

Jayda Cruz, we have located a grocery store 1.6 miles from this location.

"Thank you, Nano."

Zander Cruz, we, too, have located a suitable store. It is only eight-tenths of a mile in the opposite direction.

"Uh, thanks, Nano."

*Jayda Cruz, we made **our** selection based on the store's proximity to the truck rental return location.*

Zander and I sighed in unison. From New Mexico to Maryland, the two nanoclouds had competed. They'd spent the entire first day of our drive vying over license plate bingo. We were so weary of their one-upmanship that, when we hit east Texas, Zander asked if they knew how to play the game "cow." He explained the simple rules and sent them into a paroxysm of shouting "Cow!" in our ears every few seconds—until the distinctly chilly voice of one nanocloud grumbled, *Zander Cruz. We have determined this game to have no purpose. You have played a joke on us.*

"Who? Me?"

We'd then enjoyed two hours of peace and quiet—until one of us mentioned finding a dinner stop. A single, guileless comment initiated a contest between the two nanoclouds to find the best and closest restaurant.

We ignored their recommendations and stopped at the first burger joint we spotted.

Zander grinned. "The way the two of us eat, our food bill is gonna be higher than our rent. You know that, right?"

I laughed. "And *you* know you're going to need some serious training to burn off all your energy once we get settled in, right?"

"You mean martial arts training? That stick fighting stuff you do?"

"Yes, but the training is beneficial for lots of things."

"Like what things?"

"Well, like endurance, tactics, precision, flexibility, speed."

Aches, pains, bruises.

Endless nagging.

Frustration.

Broken escrima sticks.

Anger management techniques.

Zander bobbed his head. "Okay, I'm game. But who will train me?"

"Oh, I know a guy; I'll introduce you. I call him Gus-Gus." I snickered at the fun times ahead.

"Yeah. Gus-Gus. You're gonna love him."

The End

DEEP STATE STEALTH

Dear Readers,

Nanostealth has a fourth book! Continue the wild ride in *Deep State Stealth* | Nanostealth Book 4.

To keep up with my publication schedule and receive free, read-ahead chapters of upcoming books, I invite you to sign up for my **newsletter** (see my website on the following page). I **promise** not to spam you or sell your email addresses.

Thank you again. I have the best readers in the world—you. It is an honor.

Many hugs,

Vikki

ABOUT THE AUTHOR

Vikki Kestell's passion for people and their stories is evident in her readers' affection for her characters and unusual plotlines. Two often-repeated sentiments are, "I feel like I know these people," and, "I'm right there, in the book, experiencing what the characters experience."

Vikki holds a Ph.D. in Organizational Learning and Instructional Technologies. She left a career of twenty-plus years in government, academia, and corporate life to pursue writing full time. "Writing is the best job ever," she admits, "and the most demanding."

Also an accomplished speaker and teacher, Vikki and her husband Conrad Smith make their home in Albuquerque, New Mexico.

To keep abreast of new book releases, sign up for Vikki's newsletter on her website, **http://www.vikkikestell.com**, find her on Facebook at **http://www.facebook.com/TheWritingOfVikkiKestell**, or follow her on BookBub, **https://www.bookbub.com/authors/vikki-kestell**.

OTHER BOOKS BY VIKKI KESTELL

A PRAIRIE HERITAGE

Book 1: *A Rose Blooms Twice* (free eBook, most online retailers)
Book 2: *Wild Heart on the Prairie*
Book 3: *Joy on This Mountain*
Book 4: *The Captive Within*
Book 5: *Stolen*
Book 6: *Lost Are Found*
Book 7: *All God's Promises*
Book 8: *The Heart of Joy—A Short Story* (eBook only)

GIRLS FROM THE MOUNTAIN

Book 1: *Tabitha*
Book 2: *Tory*
Book 3: *Sarah Redeemed*

The Christian and the Vampire: A Short Story
(free eBook, most online retailers)

Faith-Filled Fiction™

www.faith-filledfiction.com | www.vikkikestell.com

CPSIA information can be obtained
at www.ICGtesting.com
Printed in the USA
LVHW031742071218
599659LV00020B/519/P

9 780986 261565